A teenage girl talks of her encounter with an old house and how it effects its inhabitants in "1342 Lindley Road"....

A family curse repeats itself in "A Proper Burial"...

The celebrated supporters of a newly-elected president show their love for him in a peculiar way in "Notifications"....

And, in the title story, a man grieving with the loss of his wife is pulled into the mystery of a teenage girl's murder.

These are just a few of the tales, in all of their dark and brooding glory, that could only come from...

DARK AVENUES

DARK AVENUES

BRIAN J. SMITH

The author has allowed the following stories to be reprinted here for the first time.

"1342 Lindley Road", *"Rightful Place"*, *"In Laudamus Jack"*, *"Big Brother"*, *"3rd Day Of The 3rd Week Of Every Month"*, *"A Different Kind Of Therapy"*, *"A Proper Burial"* and *"Odio"* have been written for this collection.
"Me And My Gang" published in Metahuman Press' The Dead Walk Again in Oct. 2011
"Dark Avenues" published as a Kindle book in July 2012
"Uncle Bubby" featured in Vol. 2 No. 1 of Heater Magazine on February 2014
"Dice" featured on The Wi-Files e-zine on July 2016
"Big Daddy" featured in Deadlights Magazine Vol. 1 on January 2017
"Apartment 13" featured on the November issue of The Horror Zine, then reprinted for The Horror Zine Anthology 2017
"Notifications" was featured in Dark Helix Press' Trump: Utopia or Dystopia
"Stiff Breeze" was featured on Becca Besser's Halloween Blitz October 2019

Some of the stories featured in this collection have been previously published but have been given a complete polish for creativity's sake. There are also a few unpublished pieces in here as well because I didn't want to publish a book full of reprints. I hope you enjoy reading them as much as I did writing them.

Thank you for reading my book and I hope this isn't the last journey we have together. I would also like to thank Don Noble for creating this awesome cover for my book as well.

B.J.S

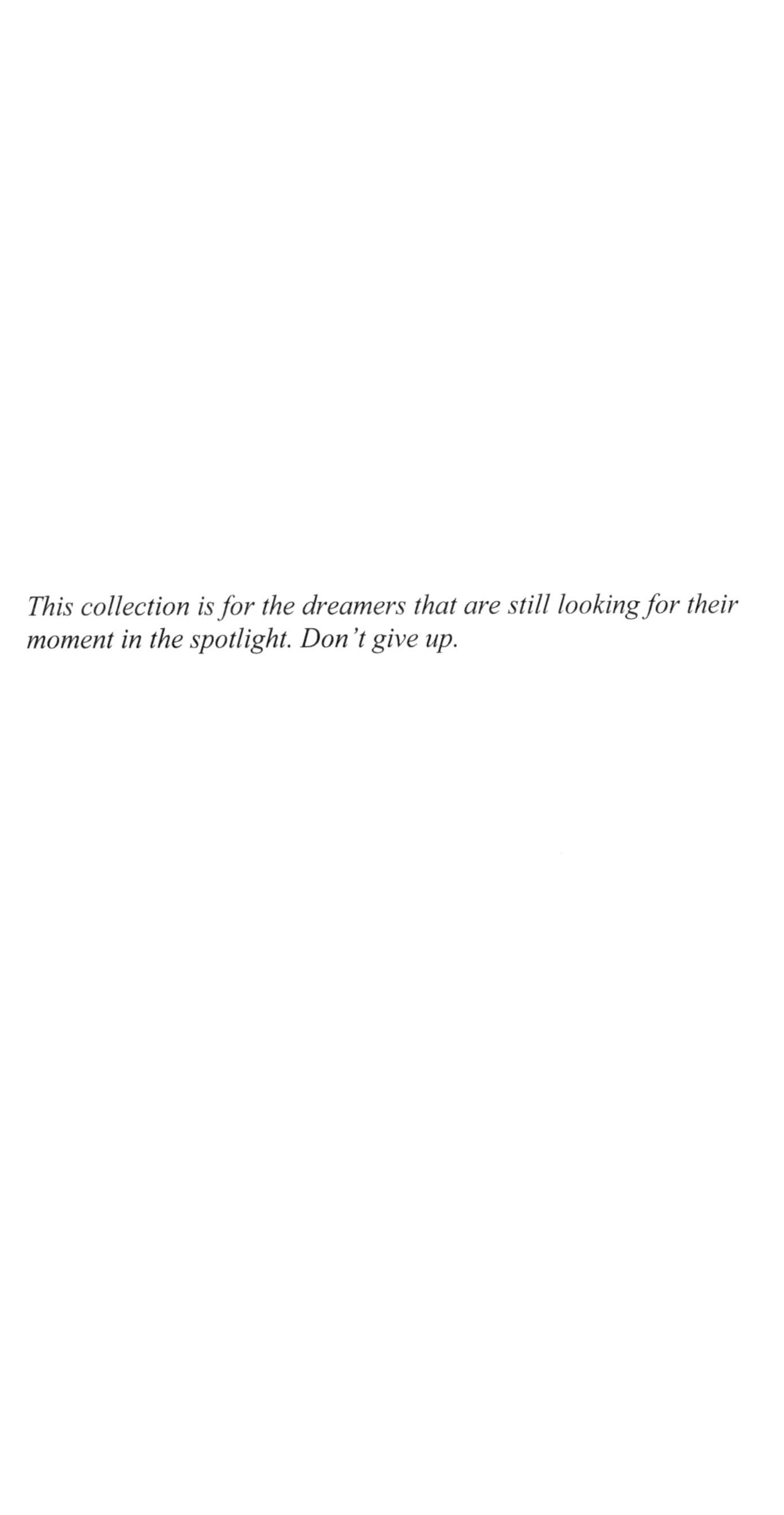

This collection is for the dreamers that are still looking for their moment in the spotlight. Don't give up.

Contents

INTRODUCTION

So here we are.

It's a cool night; the sky is that cool shade of blue that it gets before it gets dark. We're walking hand-in-hand through this dark quiet neighborhood made up of neat little houses we see at all hours of the day and night; some of the windows are still lit up with the phantom glow of a television or a lamp. You don't know who lives there and neither do I, but we both know someone does.

Relax, though. I didn't drag you here to bore you but to entertain you. Whether you laugh, cry or lock the doors at night, I'll know I've done my job.

I'm pounding all of this out on a gloomy December morning when most people like me are begging for snow which I believe is a good time to nestle up with a good book and forget about everything.

I've been writing stories since I was thirteen and had no intention of slowing down. I wasn't the popular kid; I didn't go out for Chess Club because I was (to quote a famous actress) " the geeky Stephen King kid".

As a child, I watched a lot of horror movies and t.v. shows ranging from Freddy and Jason to my personal favorite, *Kingdom Of The Spiders*. You can't have one without the other but I'm sure other people have their own preferred tastes.

My love of horror started from a dream I once had when I was five. I still remember it today.

I was standing on a lush green meadow beside of a tall leafy oak tree in a red shirt, jeans and sneakers and the sky was clear and the sun was warm. At the end of the meadow, my family was sitting on a light-blue picnic blanket spread out under the shade of another leafy oak tree waving for me to come over. I ran toward them through a patch of wildflowers when something crawled across my arm and looked down to find a monarch butterfly sitting on the back of my right hand. When I raised my hand up to my face, it opened its mouth to reveal two rows of sharp jagged little teeth and then reared its head back to take a chunk out of my flesh when I did what any person would've done and opened my eyes.

It was like some piranha-hybrid; a *pirafly* or maybe be a *butternha*. Either way they sound like something the folks at The SyFy Channel would produce by the end of the week. I wrote it in a flash fiction piece a long time ago and only one person has read it and enjoyed it; it was my sixth grade teacher and it gave him nightmares.

I don't know what anyone else would've thought about that, but I took it as a sign. I was meant to write horror.

Ever since then, I've been fascinated by horror fiction and how far we can go with it. In my opinion, there is no box because we're too busy thinking outside of it.

After that, I wrote stories for extra credit for my sixth-grade teacher. I used my stories as a tool for my boredom but over the years they became my one and only confidant; it was cheaper than a psychiatrist that's for sure.

It wasn't until after I purchased a paperback copy of Dean Koontz's Phantoms from a yard sale at fifty cents that I began to take my writing more seriously. I'd read it from front to back twice in a month, then read it again the next month and then again for the next five months. Not only was a good book but it gave me the same inspiration that the writers before me had felt when they were reading their favorites.

At the beginning of high school, I would sit during homeroom, never said a word to anyone and wrote short stories in notebooks. I had a very small clique of friends that I spoke to and that was it; I'd had my share of girlfriends (it was only two but then who didn't) but I didn't go to any of my school proms or any dances because I couldn't dance to save myself from a bullet (and I still can't).

Eventually, I fed myself on every horror and mystery writer I could get my hands on. If I wanted to write it, I had to read it.

After high school, I spent hours upon hours writing and rewriting and rewriting. Between the ages of nineteen and twenty-five, I'd dealt with mountains of rejection so I did what any other writer would do. I shook it off and kept going, pounding out more and more short stories, reading more and more novels and short story collections in hopes of getting an idea of what to do.

I my first story on *Drabblecast* as an audio file when I was 26. It was like Christmas morning; everyone showered me with praise. It was then that I finally realized that it wasn't just about the money; that it was never about the money but about entertaining people and painting a picture about a world we only know exist in our heads—and our nightmares.

Since then, I've contributed to many e-zines, magazines and anthologies on either "for-the-love" status (which was good if you wanted to make a name) or paperback and electronic copies. My mother thought I should've got something more for pouring my blood, sweat and tears into my work but she was proud of me, nonetheless. It wasn't like we were broke because most of the stories I'd wrote were during a period of my time when I worked five days a week (sometimes six during the summer or not at all during the winter) at a local eatery in the next town over.

Now, at the age thirty-six, I've managed to publish three Kindle books (one of which are included in this very collection) and even a few pieces of flash fiction in several popular e-zines and anthologies. I thought it was time to release a collection because I'd always loved short story collections whether they be single-author or multi-author platforms.

The name of this collection is from a line in the title story: *Everyone has a dark avenue of their own.*

There are plenty of tales here for you to enjoy

A group of co-workers assimilate during the zombie apocalypse.

A strange journal drives its readers to eviscerate themselves.

A western tale, a crime noir and a...

I don't want to spoil anything so I'll just stop here. From here on in, it's just you and me.

If you should feel something slithering along the back of your neck, don't be afraid to look over your shoulder...

Or should you?

Brian J. Smith
10/15/2019

1342 LINDLEY ROAD

*****

This story has been in my possession for a year and when I finished it the first time, I wanted to burn it because I thought it was just poorly written. I'd written two ghost stories in the past (one of which is featured in this collection as the title story) and I was on the verge of doing another.

When I sat down to rewrite this, I turned it into a haunted house story instead, only with a little twist. This type of house has no origin of evil; it wasn't built on cursed land or anything.

It was another type of evil altogether.

*****

1

I was thirteen when I discovered the truth about 1342 Lindley Road. The place had always been there but I never paid much attention to it because I was young and dumb and had better things to do.

Now that I'm no longer around it, I still don't like to think about it as much as I used to but then the nightmares returned.

They made it hard for me to sleep; my therapist encouraged me to write this because there isn't any other way for me to shake it off.

Like any other house, this place had its share of ups and downs, cries of sadness and moments of joy. This was the start of something both lovely and fierce but in the end they all eventually picked up and took off, never be seen or heard from again; the only traces of their presence were marked by the imprints of their furniture branded into the carpet. Memories were made, love fluctuated, children grew by the inches marked into the doorways by felt tip pens and parents aged over time whilst shaking their heads about how much this generation had changed compared to theirs.

The summer of two-thousand-thirteen was the best summer a girl like me could've ever asked for. My mother Larissa had taken me to the movies three times a month and my father Kyle and I would walk the trails around Lake Campbell until sundown and then take the shortcut back home depending upon the weather. I still had a month of summer vacation left before I had to drag my ass back to school and we all know how much of a toothache that was going to be.

We lived in a two-story brick-on-clapboard house with a shingled-green roof and a cobblestone patio with a steel mesh-topped patio table with metal-cushioned chairs, a firepit and one of those large propane grills that look like those hibernation chambers you see in sci-fi movies. The back yard wasn't much to boast about so we'd have to play badminton and toss Frisbees around the patch of grass sitting across the street from the front of our house.

The day I became familiar with said house was the day when my Aunt Ruth and Uncle Bruce came down for the annual cookout with my favorite (and only) cousin Jared in tow. After we ate, we asked Dad if we could ride our bikes around until Ruth and Bruce were ready to leave; he said yes, of course. We hopped on our bikes (I had a spare one here because my parents had bought me a new one last year before summer began) and followed the gravel road hugging the right side of our house and back around while our parents sat around the table discussing things that we didn't care to hear or weren't even supposed to know about.

The gravel road veered upward and led us to the top of a gently-rising slope that took us to the top of Lindley Road. Once we got there, we grinned from ear to ear and flew down the hill with our legs stuck out from the side of our bikes.

The wind whipped at our clothes and blew wayward strands of curly blonde hair across my face; we knew we were acting a bit childish for our age but we didn't care. Back before cell phones could do everything but microwave our lunch, it was the little things in life that meant so much to us.

Jared and I had so much in common it was almost uncanny. We had the same taste in video games, TV shows and music but food was where we drew the line; he liked hamburgers and I preferred chicken. Mom always reminded me that Jared and I had been no different than the relationship she once had with her cousin Sandra, who was currently living in Oregon.

That night, a bright pink horizon sent bottle-gas blue flames of dusk flaring across the sky; the treetops loomed above us like strange cryptic steeples. Waves of pine sap filled my nostrils and rode on the same cool breeze that ruffled our clothes and skin. Once we reached the bottom of the hill, we had to push our bikes to the top and then go again; the windows from the downhill stretch of cozy houses and double-wides occupied by old retirees and middle-aged bachelors sitting on modest lawns were sparsely lit from the mixed backwash of lamp light and television screens.

After we did it three more times, we called it a night.

When we reached the top, our chests rising and falling with each breath, Jared glanced over at The Larson Place with a probing look on his face. It was a squat-green clapboard house that sat low to the ground so that the lawn could hide its façade as if it had some kind of facial deformity. A turkey-necked street lamp was fixed to the edge of the roof on the left side of the house and stared down at the end of the driveway which then dropped down at an angle toward a thick wall of dark-green pines.

"Do you know who lives there?"

"No." I shook my head.

"Aren't you the least bit curious?"

"Not rea–"

"Well do you or don't you?" He chuffed.

"I don't know."

"I guess there's only one way to find out." He said, his eyes beaming with excitement.

He glanced back at the house, his face creased by a wide baleful grin.

"They'll kill us." I whispered.

I glanced back down the road toward my house; a tiny radiant orange light beamed across the front lawn. I couldn't hear what they were saying but all I could hear were the crickets chirping from inside the forest and the wind whispering softly amongst the trees. A loud metallic crash rang out in my right ear and startled me so that I tightened my grip on my handlebars and felt my skin prickle with fear.

He'd lowered his bike onto the shoulder of the road that merged with the front lawn and disappeared behind the lone pine tree standing between the far left corner of the front lawn and the edge of the driveway. I scanned my surroundings, set my bike down beside of his and went after him, my face flushed with both shame and excitement. The thin wall of trees standing along the left edge of the driveway shrouded our parents from seeing us which, now that I think about it, was both good and bad in a way.

For the first time in my life, I wished that our parents would've called out for us but they didn't. I'd have done it myself but I don't think I'd have forgiven myself if he stopped talking to me because I'd snitched on him; he *was* my only cousin.

A thin sheen of sweat coated my forehead and dampened my hair and the nape of my neck. It might've been an ordinary house to a newcomer's eye but there was something about it that soured on my stomach. Something glowed in the corner of my right eye, but then died before I could get a better look at it; if it'd been a passing motorist or the owner of the house then there was nothing we could say or do to talk our way out of it.

I cursed under my breath, stepped over and onto the driveway. I found him standing on the left side of the house, peering into a large window facing the end of the driveway. The glass was dotted with wayward spots of white paint and streaked with grime along the corners; flakes of white paint sprinkled the windowsill.

We saw a bare empty bedroom with outdated lime-green carpet and a small set of stairs that led past a curtain of colorful plastic beads and into the next room. Carpets of sour light poured through the windows, pooled across the floor and streaked the oak-paneled walls with cryptic shadows. The owners must've valued the tacky seventies interior enough to keep it there for sentimental purposes.

Jared pressed his face up against the glass, cupped his hands around his eyes like a pair of makeshift binoculars and squinted for a better look. I peered over the top of his head and found a crude symbol drawn across the wall beside of the doorway in what looked to be purple paint; it depicted a wide pathway leading toward a door sitting on the edge of a distant horizon.

It wasn't just the weird placement of the symbol that heightened my anxiety; it looked fresh as if it'd been drawn just a few seconds ago. Why had they kept it there if they knew it would jeopardize the market value?

"Damn." He hissed, spreading faint white clouds of steam across the glass. "These fucking beads are blocking my view."

I'd heard him curse like that plenty of times in the past but never in front of our parents. He eased away from the window, walked to the middle of the driveway and peered across the darkened porch. A second carpet of light burst across the back yard, sending strobes of light rippling across the grass but it too disappeared before I could get a good look.

I took two steps away from the window and met up with him. I knew I should've taken the opportunity to get him away from here when it presented itself but I gave into peer pressure and my own stupid childish curiosity as well.

"I'll try the front door." He whispered. "Cover me."

Just then, the goose-necked porch light gave a low hum and flickered to life. A large patch of sodium-purple light spread across the driveway and showered me like a spotlight on a police helicopter. I flinched, pressing my white-knuckled fists tightly against my thighs, and crushed a fallen twig under my right foot.

"Calm down, Mollie." Jared whispered.

He stepped under the front porch awning, his pear-shaped body shrouded by a mixture of half-light and half-shadow, and approached the front door. Tiny flakes of red paint sprinkled the film of plastic-green felt covering the front stoop as he looked back at me and raised his hand toward the doorknob.

"We need to get the hell away from here." I whispered. "If our parents catch us, we're in serious friggin trouble."

"Would you just chill out?" He said, then chuffed. "If the door is locked, then–"

The front door creaked open on scarred brass hinges and cut him off in mid-sentence; thin pockets of white smoke floated across the threshold, spun in the cool summer breeze and drifted up toward his face. Jared cocked his head toward the open doorway, his face sullen and guilt-ridden, and sucked deep pockets of sheer fog into his lungs. His body grew tense, but he stood his ground, his eyes riveted onto what was behind the door.

Fear rooted my feet to the ground and seized my lungs inside of its thick powerful grip, robbing me of the will to breathe. An icy chill snaked along the contours of my spine, prickling my skin and raising the hairs on the back of my neck. My cheeks grew hot as my heart pounded, blood throbbing against my ears.

Sweat beads cascading down my face had secreted inside of my pits and glued the back and sides of my tee-shirt to my ribs. The breeze picked up, sending an odd smell drifting past my nose. It wasn't the familiar scent of pine sap and wood smoke but the sickly-sweet smell of licorice.

From where I was standing, I prayed for a carpet of light to flood across the front porch followed by a crabby old man spouting obscenities at us while we scampered away like roaches. If that was what got us away from here, then so be it. If my parents were informed of this little incident, I would take my punishment and be done with it.

Everything I wanted to see was inside of that house, observed by the frozen hypnotic gleam flickering in Jared's eyes. Whatever was going on in there, I wasn't invited. The smell increased in both flavor and intensity, sparkling off my tongue like I'd downed a whole packet of Pop Rocks.

Something slipped out from behind the open door but I couldn't see what it was at first. I squinted into the semi-darkness flooding the driveway until I saw what lay beyond and felt my chest tighten. My eyes swelling with fear, I suppressed a wave of nausea rising toward my throat and forced it back down into the pit of my stomach.

A thick human arm hugged by a loose-fitting white shirt sleeve emerged from the swirling black folds of the doorway and extended across the front stoop. Its thick calloused fingers had a light-green tint and its neatly-trimmed nails were coated with slick pools of obsidian liquid. The wrist spun to the left, then to the right and slowly dragged its knuckles down both sides of Jared's face, spreading large purple blemishes across his cheeks.

The cool summer breeze carried the soft chorus of eerie whispers from inside of the house and filled my ears with incubus murmurs. As a wide pleasing grin spread evenly across Jared's face, tugging at the corners of his mouth, an alarm rang in the back of my head. A hot lucid tear protruded from the corner of my right eye, slid down the contour of my cheek and dripped off of my chin.

I shook the fear off my bones, brushed my tongue across my dry cracked lips and sprinted toward the front porch. My body switching to panic mode, I threw my hands up in front of me, slammed the front door shut with a loud hollow thud. I clutched a handful of Jared's left sleeve in my right fist, dragged him away from the front of the house and back up the driveway, his feet teetering out from behind him.

We hopped onto our bikes and sped away. We were halfway down the hill, my ears filled with the soft hum of bike tread on hot pavement when he glanced back at the house with a heavy morose look on his face. My body racing on fear and adrenaline, my hands shook so bad I gripped the handlebars of my bike until they hurt and the color bled from my knuckles.

"What did you see?" I asked.

When I repeated myself, he shook his head and grinned.

By the time we reached my house, neither one of us spoke a word. Pinprick stars riddled the night sky; a sickly-white moon sat high in the east, glowing behind a roiling cloud cover. We arrived back at my house and found Aunt Ruth standing beside of the road, her mouth hanging open as if she were about to call our names but then decided not to when she saw us coming.

After we put our bikes away, I gave him a hug and a kiss on the forehead. It was unusual not because he was cousin but because he was always shy about that sort of thing; we'd always make a little hide and seek game out of it. This time, however, he hadn't protested at all.

When Ruth and Bruce made the short trek from the front of the house to the driveway in front of the garage, she noticed it, too.

She crouched in front of him, her knees pressing into the cold cobblestone porch and grazed her left hand across his cheek. My spine tingled with fear as my mind reverted back to the same phantom hand that grazed Jared's cheek in the same soft, tender fashion.

I hid my reaction so my parents wouldn't notice and put on my best fake smile. Mom slipped an arm across the small of my back, waved at Bruce as he caught up with Jared and Ruth, and leaned against my left shoulder.

"Are you okay?"

"I think I ate too much." He mumbled in a sulking voice.

Bruce added. "You're still going to school next week."

Ruth raked her left hand through Jared's hair, planted a soft kiss on the crown of his forehead and corralled him into the back seat. As they drove past the front of the house, Jared clipped on his seatbelt and peered at me with a brooding look on his face.

We waved at them as they started their long trek back to Columbus. Before their headlights were swallowed by the newly-risen darkness, I noticed the blemishes on Jared's right cheek had disappeared.

2

WHEN I woke up the next morning, Mom and Dad were sitting at the kitchen table eating breakfast and giggling about something I wasn't supposed to hear.

The living room and the kitchen were adjoined, separated by an L-shaped couch; an antique wooden coffee table sat between the couch and a stone-hearth fireplace and a flat-screen television sat in the far right corner. The kitchen consisted of a sleek wooden table with matching chairs, stainless steel appliances, wooden cupboards with matching knobs and a single rectangular window above the sink draped in a thin pink curtain. Sunlight poured through the windows, laying bright patches of light across the floors while grasping at the furniture and walls with bright golden fingers.

Around the bottom of the stairs and to the left, a set of sliding wooden doors led into Dad's Man Cave where he liked to watch all of his college football games; he worked at a father and son lumber company that most people compared to one of the big wigs although he wasn't The Father or The Son. When they saw me coming, they shushed each other and grinned like a couple of teenagers. In one of Dad's tee-shirts and soft pink cotton shorts, Mom stepped up next to the stove and dropped a pat of butter into a cast-iron skillet; Dad took a sip from his mug, his plaid pajamas and a blue tee-shirt pulled tight over his tall masculine frame.

"Did you have fun with your cousin last night?"

I nodded, feigning a smile. I glanced down at the folded newspaper sitting on the table beside of his right arm and swallowed until my throat clicked.

A sense of anxiety washed over me. If they'd asked me again, I'd have caved in. They didn't so I didn't have to worry about it.

Between sips of orange juice, I told them everything that happened last night. I replaced the haunted house part with a lie about how we accidentally drove across the edge of Mister McCombs' lawn and almost knocked one of his prized lawn ornaments into the street. Dad reminded me that I wasn't allowed to bother Mr. McCombs because he was a stubborn old asshole and I giggled because he cursed; Mom peered at him from over her left shoulder and sighed in awe.

"Don't listen to your father, Mollie." Mom slapped him playfully across the arm.

Dad chuckled, raked a hand through his thick dark hair and then took another sip from his mug. Mom placed a stack of pancakes, two eggs and three strips of bacon on my plate and set it down in front of me. I ate my breakfast while they scanned the comics section in the morning paper and ignored their playful whispers.

When I used the last drop of OJ to wash down the last bite of food, they continued to stare at me.

"Do I have something on my forehead?"

I set my glass on top of my plate.

"Not really." Dad snickered. "But you've got this weird thing in the middle of your face I might want to cut off. It's right there between your mouth and your eyes."

Mom and I sighed, mouths agape.

"You look beautiful, Hun."

"Damn right she does." Mom walked over and kissed me on the forehead. "She gets that from her mother."

Dad peered up from the top of his newspaper. "We're serious, honey." He asked. "Are you okay?"

"I'm good. Why do you ask?"

"We heard you talking in your sleep last night."

"You did?"

I stiffened a little and felt my body grow tense. Mom slid her chair over to my side of the table, her spindly little shadow blotting out the light coming in through the kitchen window. The quiet confused stare on my face increased their unwavering curiosity and intensified their gaze.

"You were saying 'Get away, Jared. Get away now'." Mom said. "We were so worried about you we stood outside of your bedroom door until you went back to sleep."

After he took another sip, Dad said, "If there's something bothering you, don't ever be afraid to tell us.

"What am I supposed to tell you?"

"We're not accusing you or anybody." Dad explained. "If he did something to you last night, we're not going to be ang–"

"Oh that." I snickered. "I had a dream about the new story I'm writing."

"Oh ok." Mom said, pursing her lips and shrugging her shoulders. "We were just concerned, honey. We just want you to know that we'll always be here for you if you ever need to talk."

"I'm fine, really."

I patted Mom's hand in return and took my plate to the sink, hoping they'd shrug it off. After Mom gave me another kiss on my forehead and raked her hand through my hair, I went back upstairs. When I shut the door behind me, I snuck a glance through the window behind my bed and saw the house sitting there in all of its dark and dilapidated glory.

The place could've used a new roof and the windows were still as dark and empty as they'd been last night. Personally, I'd rather see it sitting in a pile of shit and twigs rather than looking all cocky and smug.

I closed my bedroom curtains, dug my journal out from into my secret hiding place (underneath the mattress inside the little hole inside of my box spring) and thought about what to write. As much as I wanted to talk about what happened last night because it would make it easier for me to shrug off the guilt, I couldn't bring myself to do it. I was halfway through today's entry when I had to use the bathroom.

I was halfway to the bathroom when I heard a chorus of whispers coming from my parents' bedroom. I caught a few snippets of their conversation but what I'd heard told me that they refused to shake off the conversation we had this morning.

"–afraid of what she–"

"–doesn't need to be–"

"–when she's ready."

Did they think he sexually abused me? The cold harsh reality of their lie made me feel so uncomfortable that the very thought of it sickened me to the core. I knew that if I told them the truth I would risk crucifying myself and–if they had their way–every summer for the rest of my life.

I snuck into the bathroom, did my business and got back into my room before they realized that I'd overheard them. Dad stopped by to tell me that he was going to work and that he'd see me later. I gave him a soft kiss on the cheek; he told me he loved me and lugged his big metal lunch box down stairs and out the front door.

When I shut my bedroom door, the curtains behind my bed were open again. If the window had been opened, which it wasn't, then the breeze would've parted the curtains; they were left open as if someone had done it from the inside of my bedroom.

Mom, Dad and I had made an agreement years ago that we wouldn't go into each other's bedroom unless it was an emergency or if we'd given the other permission. We weren't sticklers in that sense but we respected each other's privacy.

I was buttoning my shorts when I heard a knock on my bedroom door. Mom opened the door, wearing a short-sleeved pink tee, dark green capris and white deck shoes; her long red hair was fashioned into a small bun along the back of her head.

"We're going into town, honey." She said in a cheery voice. "Go ahead and finished getting dressed."

"Okay." I nodded.

She waited for me to slip on my sandals and then followed me down stairs. We locked up the house and jumped into her yellow Mazda and headed into town. It was summer and our little picturesque town showed no signs of slowing down; dogs barked from fenced-in yards or trotted along sidewalks with their owners in tow, children played and giggled with a sense of reckless abandon.

We parked on the right side of The Mall On Winifred Avenue and picked up a few things from Bath and Body. We browsed a few more shops and Mom bought us some new tops, and one more for me for school until she could come back and get my actual school clothes for the year. After we that, we grabbed some Mexican at Las Jose's and then did a little grocery shopping.

On the way home, we were too busy singing along to one of our favorite songs on the radio when I caught that sinister eyesore from the corner of my eye. I caught the same licorice scent I smelled last night drifting under my nose again and held my breath so I wouldn't have to. This time, there was something different about it, something that I couldn't put my finger on until Mom spoke up.

"They must be fixing that place up finally." She said, then nodded toward the house.

As much as I didn't want to look, I had no choice. If I didn't, she'd have known something was up. I peered through the window and gripped the door handle in my pale clammy hand.

The driveway looked a little smoother and darker than it looked last night as if someone had covered it with a fresh coat of tar. I thought I saw something moving across the front window but it was just a piece of my hair falling onto the top of my shoulder.

"Are you okay, honey?"

The concerned look on Mom's face was accentuated by the shafts of sunlight coating the front windshield. I peered down at my feet, licked my lips and then back up at her.

"I'm fine." I said. "That house gives me the creeps."

"Why does it give you the creeps?"

"Do you know anything about it?"

"Yeah." She said, then nodded. "I don't have the time to tell you about it, really. That house has been here long before I met your father."

"There has to be a reason why you and Dad don't want me to go near it." I said, then raised my right shoulder in a half shrug. "I just wanted to know why you wouldn't want me to go near it in the first place."

She brushed a strand of my hair away from my sweaty forehead and tucked it behind my left ear. I considered telling the truth, but I couldn't take the risk.

"Did you go near it?" She exclaimed.

"I see it outside of my bedroom window every day I wake up and every night before I go to bed. There's just something about it that scares the beejezus out of me."

She parked the car, killed the engine and turned around in her seat to face me.

"Don't ever worry about that house, honey. I'm sure it won't be up for long and it seems like the new neighbors are going to make it look perfect and then if not–"

She unfastened her seat belt and climbed out.

"Then what?"

"They'll just mow it down and put up a department store."

When we reached the back of the car, she opened the trunk. When I reached down to gather a few bags, she snatched my left hand by the wrist and held it.

"If your father and I ever catch you near that place," She said. "you won't sit down for a week."

I nodded and helped her lug the groceries inside. We were putting everything away when the phone rang. Having thought about the house and my mother's severe promise, the sound was so sudden I nearly dropped the gallon of milk onto the floor.

After she put the ice cream in the freezer, Mom picked it up on the third ring. I was about to go upstairs and try on some of my new tops when she snapped her fingers. She used the crown of her shoulder to keep the phone pressed against her ear and raised her hand in a protesting gesture.

"Hold on and I'll ask her." She said, then cupped her hand over the mouthpiece. "Did Jared look sick to you last night before they left?"

"No." I said in a curious tone. "Why?"

"Jared is running a fever of a hundred. Did he act funny to you at all?"

"Not until we got back here."

"Oh ok."

She brushed me off, carried the phone into the living room and sat down. A few minutes later, a daytime talk show blared from inside the living room.

I stretched across on my bed and picked up where I left off in my favorite Jane Austen novel. The cool summer breeze coming through my bedroom window across from the foot of my bed caressed my legs and prickled my skin.

A few minutes later, I began to grow lethargic. I flinched and, my eyelids growing heavy and limp, tugged back on my book to keep it from hitting me in the face. I finished the chapter I was reading, tucked my finger between the last page of that chapter and the next one and rolled onto my side.

I blinked and found myself standing in the corner of a wide unfurnished room with brown carpet and oak-paneled walls. There was a kitchen to my left, complete with an L-shaped Formica countertop, a tall white fridge with a metallic handle and a gas stove. The living room, which was where I realized I'd been standing in, connected to a small foyer that branched off toward the other rooms in the house.

A large picture window looked out over the back yard, exposing a wall of shaggy-green pines and gnarled oaks dappled in moonlight and shadow. The one behind me stared out onto a rough-hewn concrete porch dwarfed by cryptic shadows from an overhead shingled roof.

I snatched a few quick breaths to shake the uneasiness off of my bones and sighed, drawing that sickly-sweet smell of licorice back into my lungs. I tried to squeeze my fists together but only managed to squeeze my left hand instead. I looked down and a saw tall plastic red cup in my right fist filled almost to the brim with a clear odd-smelling liquid; a freshly-picked daisy was fastened to the right side of the cup, its shadow eclipsing the light from touching the surface of the liquid.

I raised the glass toward my face and inhaled. I pulled my head away from the rim of the cup and winced through my teeth, wishing I could take that back. I wanted to set it down somewhere, anywhere but I stood there instead.

People wandered around the room, joining tightly-knit groups of their peers in mid-conversation or welcoming new faces with gleeful smiles; a few of them stood by themselves, bobbing their heads to the music and nodding ceremoniously at passerby. Men wore tie-dye shirts, headbands, small round colored shades and frayed bell bottoms while women varied between bell-bottoms with thinly-veiled shirts and tie-dyed dresses with plunging necklines exposing sloping pale breasts.

They flashed peace signs, bright-cheery smiles, flirtatious glances and hushed conversations that always ended in either an overdone peal of laughter or an expression of mute belief. A halo of tiny rainbow-colored spotlights spun around the room, along the walls and across their faces. "White Room" by Cream spewed from an oak-paneled record player cabinet sitting in the far left corner of the room.

A tall bald man in the traditional tie-dye tee and blue jean bell-bottoms watched a wafer-thin brunette sashay across the living room. She wore a pair of bell bottoms and a pink rib vest that exposed her slender pale stomach and the curves of her white flapjack bosom. A reflective sheen of romantic hunger flickered in their eyes as if they were the only ones in the room.

"You're looking ripe tonight, Iris."

"So are you, Ethan." She said, her face creased by a seductive grin.

She sashayed across out of the room, her apple-bottom ass swaying like it would if she had a tail, and stepped through a door at the end of the hallway. He went back to chatting with a pair of redheads standing in the doorway between the living room and the kitchen; the tallest one wearing the knee-high polka-dotted wrap dress laughed at something he said; her partner-in-crime wore a bleached-white rib vest that emphasized the curves of her pale flapjack bosom.

On the far right corner, a tall heavyset man in a long dark-brown blouse and frayed denims bobbed his head to the music between taking sips from a stout green beer bottle. A colorful beaded necklace hung loosely from around his fat pale neck and the bright green headband fastened above his brows looked tight enough to squeeze the circulation out of his head.

I didn't know where I was until I gazed across the room and saw the same curtain of colorful plastic beads draped across the same doorway Jared and I had been struggling to see through. My heart thudded as a fresh pocket of sweat secreted inside of my pits and trickled down my temples; my skin tingled with fear.

A loud clanging sound blared across the room, cutting me off. Iris glided across the room, banging an old tambourine against her left hand; the cute blonde standing beside of me blotted his hands on his jeans, his chest rising and falling with each rapid breath. She raised the needle from the record, ending the song in mid-chorus only for the crowd to replace it with an occasional whisper or a loud sip.

She banged the tambourine again and gave a loud hum behind overlapped pink lips. A tall rugged-looking man in a breezy-white blouse and high-waisted blue flares stepped through the curtains of colorful plastic beads without using his hands. He scanned the room with deep-set gray eyes topped by sparse white brows; he had a gaunt tan face with a broad nose, plump lips and cleft chin.

"Evening, Father."

A joyful expression softened his features, squeezing his eyes into tiny dark slits. He inhaled, sucking the smells of the room deep into his lungs and exhaled through evenly pursed lips that creased his face in a wide pleasing grin. He tented his fingers, pressed his hand against his lips and threw his hands in the air, his eyes shining with eccentric delight.

"It's so great to see all of you here tonight." He said in a soft nasally voice. "It's not just any night but a special night."

A third redhead began dancing across the room, her body shifting in graceful but twisted gestures. Her blue kaftan dress billowing out behind her, her eyes were closed as if she were listening to music only she could hear.

Whispers filled the room as every face in the crowd followed him toward the far left corner of the room. Their eyes beamed with a ravenous mix of joy and admiration; the elation etching deep lines across their faces intensified my uneasiness. They closed their hands into tiny white-knuckled fists, raised them at shoulder level and opened their palms.

Iris sauntered next to Ethan, her face creased by a wide jovial smile. When their hands touched, their pinkies intertwined.

"Our long and exhausting journey as brought you to the end." Father said, strolling across the back window. "I know because I've been there and back and when I go back again we will go together because I feel that you are worthy, aren't you?"

"We Are!" They said in unison.

"Do you believe that you are ready to take what is yours? Do you trust me to guide you on this journey to a whole new world filled with the same promise and pleasure that I believe you deserve out of the kindness of my heart?"

The arrogant quality in his voice increased my nervousness.

"Please take us with you." Someone in the crowd exhaled. "We love you, Father."

He closed his eyes and sighed. Beads of sweat peppered his forehead and cleaved lucid concentric paths down his cheeks.

A third redhead pressed her hand softly against her chest and said in a pleasing tone, "I feel your love, Father. I'm ready to take your hand and walk side by side with you."

Father opened his eyes and walked across the room, parting the crowd like The Red Sea. When he approached his apostle, the faces in the crowd were fermented with a mix of envy for the ones whom he'd brushed past and jealousy for the others who'd never been this close to him. He seized her hands and, scanning her from head to toe, appraised the network of bright blue veins streaking across the tops of her large pale breasts.

He eased his right hand away from hers, held it high above his head and shook his fingers. His chest rising and falling, he sucked a pocket of air deep into his lungs. Tears brimmed in his eyes as he danced back and forth on the balls of his feet.

"We're ready, Father." Iris added.

At the sound of Iris' voice, everyone raised their glasses and took one long swig. They dropped their cups onto the floor and sighed loudly like actors in a soda commercial after the first sip; the chubby blonde guy standing beside of me slipped something from the right front pocket of his jeans but the lights were so dim I couldn't get a clear glimpse of what it could've been. Their faces twisted in masks of eccentric lunacy, they eagerly awaited his next move; their eyes blazed with something more sinister than hope.

A mix of fear and confusion pressed down on me like a wet blanket, wrapping me up in its suffocating folds and snatching my breath. An alarm rang in the back of my head, urging me to leave now right now and never look back but I couldn't; my stomach churned as my chest tightened with fear.

He cupped Julie's face in both hands, his face creased with a wide pleasing grin. Everyone mumbled under their breath, their lips moving in a rhythmic cadence that sent a wave of gooseflesh across my skin. He lowered his lips three inches away from her left ear and spun her head around until her neck gave a loud brittle snap.

He grinned and stared down with horrid fascination at the pool of hot brownish yellow liquid oozing out from the bottom of her dress, his eyes burning with maniacal pride.

When he dropped her onto the floor like a sack of unwanted mail, he raised his arms high over his head and backed up into the crowd. An electric silence crackled inside the room, raising the hairs along the back of my neck.

The cute blonde guy raised his right hand, opened the pair of stubby metallic jaws of the pilers he'd slipped out of his pocket, squeezed its jagged metallic jaws onto the top right front tooth and tore it from the prison of his bright pink gums; a trail of tears, snot and blood slid down his face and dripped onto the floor. His body quivering with each gut-wrenching sob, he moved onto the next tooth, then the next and then the next. Iris and Ethan slid thin razor blades from between their teeth, knelt onto the floor; she tore her dress open and exhaled as he etched a large gaping wound across the tops of her pale sagging breasts. The taller redhead knelt down, burying her fingers inside of her friend's dripping wet crotch while the once dancing ginger etched strange symbols across her back, sending rivers of blood oozing down to the floor; the shorter redhead writhed and winced with the rhythm of the sexual electricity tearing through her. The others followed suite, conducting their own act of self-mutilation: making passionate love and digging their teeth into each other's flesh until the skin broke filling their mouths with the sweet coppery nectar of blood; a heavyset man in a dark-blue tie-dye shirt and bell bottoms sobbed and began to smash his right hand repeatedly with a ball-

peen hammer his joyous laughter failing to overpower the sound of wet pulverized flesh.

My stomach churned; something rose up my esophagus and tickled the back of my throat with a sour bitterness I couldn't suppress. The cup fell from my hand, struck the floor, kicking up a small geyser of clear liquid high above the brim before it fell onto its side and spilled along the floor.

Loud cries of pain and pleasure rippled across the house in an abnormal sonata. The mixed stench of patchouli, sweat and blood spread across the room like a death cloud and stung my nostrils. A streak of nausea rose from deep in the pit of my stomach toward the back of my throat and prickled across the middle of my tongue.

Father stood in the back of the room staring at his reflection in the large picture window facing the back yard, his face creased by a thin wicked grin. He pressed his hands together, mumbled under his breath, cocked his head toward the window and grinned at me, his cold gray eyes baring down on me li–

I blinked and sat up. My book flew off my chest, bounced off the edge of my bed and, its pages flapping uncontrollably, hit my bedroom floor with a soft thud. I took a couple of deep breaths, my hands curled into clammy white fists, and sighed until the anxiety dissipated from my bones.

Outside, the sun disappeared behind the trees, spreading a bruised purple tint across the sky. My curtains billowed in the breeze, their convex shadows weaving across the floor.

There was no question about where I was, but there were other questions that were left unanswered.

Who were all of those people?

Why were they calling him Father?

I raked a hand through my hair, threw my legs over and sat on the edge of my bed. Twenty minutes past three; it sure felt like I'd been asleep for much longer.

"Did you hear your mother?" Dad bellowed from the bottom of the stairs.

"What?" I asked, then lied. "I was listening to my music and I couldn't hear her."

"She wants you to come and help her with dinner."

"Okay." I said. "I'll be down in a little bit."

I knelt down, collected my book from the pink and white braided rug spread out across the floor beside of my bed, set it on top of my bedside table and ran down stairs.

3

I'D kept myself busy for the next two days and did whatever I could to avoid thinking about that god awful place again.

On the first day, I finished the book I'd been reading, started another one (*Watership Down* by Richard Adams) scrawled a fresh entry into my journal and watched a couple of movies with Mom and Dad until it was time for bed. On the second, Mom and I camped out in the living room under a makeshift tent made of couch cushions and soft fluffy blankets, binge-watched our favorite shows and stuffed our faces with junk food until it hurt.

On the third day, I was contemplating the perfect word to add to today's entry when Mom called me down stairs. I put the cap on my pen, stuck it inside of my diary, stuffed it back inside of my secret hiding place and ran down stairs.

When I arrived inside the living room, Aunt Ruth was sitting on the edge of the couch in a pink-tee shirt, denim shorts and sandals. She greeted me with a wide joyful smile and waved me over for her one of her patent Aunt Ruth hugs–which came with a soft kiss on the crown of my forehead–and bragged about how pretty I was.

Jared was sitting next to her, cradling a bright blue bookbag tightly against his chest. He wore a white Mickey Mouse tee shirt, denim jeans and white sneakers with blue stripes. He didn't seem too eager to say hello when I exchanged pleasantries with Aunt Ruth, which left me feeling confused if anything.

"Aren't you going to say hello to your cousin." Ruth asked, nudging Jared's shoulder.

He mumbled something under his breath and shot up from the couch, his boyish features creased by a wide happy grin. He leaped over the coffee table, his stick-figure shadow floating in mid-air, and ignored the loud uncomfortable gasps uttering from our mothers' lips. I caught him in my arms, nuzzled my face against the thick tuft of coarse brown hair and hugged him tightly.

"Jared's going to stay the weekend." Mom said, carrying two cups of hot tea into the living room. "Isn't that great?"

Ruth nodded, grinning from ear to ear.

"Can we go upstairs and watch a movie?"

"Sure."

"If you misbehave," Ruth said, wagging her finger in Jared's direction. "you're gonna be in trouble. The rules at our house are the same as they are here, understand? You are to do whatever your Aunt Larissa and your Uncle Kyle tell you to do, got it?"

Jared nodded.

We hurried up the stairs, our feet pounding like a herd of angry buffalo and into the rec room between my parents' bedroom and the bathroom. Large colorful posters depicting colorful landscapes dotted the room's egg-shell white walls; a large closet was located on the right side of the room, stocked with a few tall plastic totes (a few of them were labeled MOLLIE'S WINTER CLOTHES and HALLOWEEN DECORATIONS) A flat-screen television sat in the far right corner across from a pair of overstuffed bean-bag chairs; a DVD player and two game consoles sat on the top shelf above a bottom shelf holding a mixed stack of DVDs and video games.

After I put the first disc of the entire fifth season of our favorite show, he gave me another tight hug. We sat down on our favorite bean bag chairs (he liked the blue one whereas I preferred the yellow one), pressed our bare feet against the bright blue carpet and waited for the disc to load. Although we'd seen them hundreds of times, we still laughed until it hurt. We were halfway through the second disc when Aunt Ruth dropped by.

"I'm gonna head back home, okay honey." She said, kneeling down to meet Jared's gaze. "I'll miss you baby but I hope you have fun while you're here."

When she began smoothing out the wrinkles in his tee-shirt, he gave a protest through his teeth that sounded like a whisper.

"I'll be fine, Mom."

"I know." She said in a morose whine. "Just have fun, honey."

She exited the room and stopped halfway down the stair case. She peered at him through the balustrades in the second floor railing and flashed a wide pleasing grin.

"Remember to text your father before you go to bed tonight."

"Father knows where I'll be if he needs me."

After Aunt Ruth finished her descent down the staircase, Jared hurried back into the rec room and sat down. I caught a slight trace of something odd in his voice, in the way that he'd spoke to Ruth just now. It was a tone I'd never heard him speak in but I knew there was a reason for it.

Was he going through puberty?

I hoped not. Just the thought of Jared going through it made me feel very uncomfortable.

Ten minutes later, Mom called for me. She handed me a brown wicker tray with two plates of food and two glasses of blueberry Kool-Aid; she was nice enough to give us a snack cake to go with our PB&J and potato chips.

"Do you remember the rules?"

"Sure do."

She returned to the couch as I carried the tray upstairs. When I carried the tray into the rec room, intending to put on my best French waiter impression, his chair was empty. Had he gone to the bathroom without telling me?

I didn't know if I should've waited for him to come back or not. I set the tray on the floor between our bean-bag chairs and went out to find him. I strode out into the hallway and saw the bathroom door standing wide open so he couldn't be in there.

I headed back toward the staircase, thinking he'd decided to do something else when I noticed my bedroom door was half open. Mute-gray sunlight framed the doorway and seeped out from the bottom, spreading a thin ghostly veil across the floor.

I skulked toward my bedroom, ignoring the roar of applause blaring across the living room. My heart thumping with fear, I prayed that he would leap out from somewhere and scared me but he didn't. I eased my bedroom door open with the tip of my right shoe, my skin prickling with excitement and tiptoed across the threshold.

Now it was my chance to scare him and finally get some payback for all of the times he'd done it to me. Instead, I stood inside the doorway, my right hand hanging loosely off the top of the scarred brass doorknob and gazed across my bedroom.

Jared stood on the right side of my bed, gazing out the window at the ominous eyesore sitting off in the distance like a clump of black clay. The front windows facing the driveway were no longer streaked with cobwebs and grime; they looked as if someone polished them to a clear protective sheen that reflected the sun. I wondered what other parts of the house would be in line for an impromptu makeover.

"Our lunch is waiting for us in–"

I tried to call his name but the sight of the house paralyzed me with fear. I wanted to run over as fast I could and shut the curtains so neither one of us could see it again but I couldn't bring myself to.

His shoulders were stooped over so that his arms dangled down by his sides. His mouth was drew back into a wide devilish grin that failed to expose the gum line The strong odor of licorice wafted around my bedroom, churned my gut and stung the back of my throat.

His eyes flickered with an insane euphoria that amplified my uneasiness. I followed his gaze, craned my head toward the open window and felt my eyes widen with shock. Fear seized my throat, squeezing a low pneumatic gasp from my lips.

"Father" stood half in and half out from under the front porch awning and waved his palms at us in an eerie, cordial gesture. He was bookended by the dancing redhead and Iris, their shoulder-length hair billowing around their heads like flames of red and black fire. Their thin lipless mouths tugged back into wide baleful grins that etched jagged cracks across their overcast faces and spilled thin plumes of soft gray ash into the breeze.

Jared mumbled under his breath, his gaze still frozen and strangely-bright. I drew my breath back, my palms slick and perked my ear hesitantly toward his face to hear what he was saying. His words traced the contours of my spine with frigid fingertips and sent a carpet of goosebumps trailing across my skin.

"The key to salvation is family."

The ladies moved their hands away from his crotch and up across his flat muscular chest before moving back down. When their grins widened, their upper lip slid open exposing a jagged row of gnarled black teeth.

They arched their necks, craned their heads toward the sky and glared up with lifeless black eyes. Twin streams of small black cockroaches spewed out from their lips, scuttled across their face and down their chins. A booming laugh rose in the distance, softly at first before finally rising toward a loud hearty bellow that shook the trees and buzzed inside of my ears.

The nest broke formation and shrouded their supernatural forms from head to toe. Their slick black bodies glistening under the sour gray light, they buckled and collapsed onto the porch in a large shimmering black puddle and retreated into the pocket of darkness under the front porch awning. Cold fear tingling down my body from scalp to toe jam, I clamped my hand across my mouth to muffle the scream rising toward my throat and backed away from the open window. My spine struck the doorknob, sending small ripples of pain down my back and calves and made me wince in pain.

"Oh God, Mollie." Jared said, snapping out of his trance. "Are you okay?"

"I'm fine."

"Why did you come in here?"

The insane flicker in his eyes died; an intense quizzical look etched across his face and tugged at the corners of his eyes. I sat on the foot of my bed, my hand pressed against my chest and took a few moments to collect myself.

"Are you hurt?"

"I'm fine." I said. "Why did you come in here?"

"My father called me."

"Your dad is in Columbus." I sighed.

"No, he's not." He snorted. "He's over there, silly."

He jerked his right thumb over his shoulder, motioning toward the sinister eyesore. The warm pleasing scent of pine sap floated through my bedroom now, replacing the noxious stench of licorice. I tucked a strand of hair behind my left ear, gazed down at my bedroom floor and felt my labored breathing remind me that what I'd just saw would never go away no matter how hard I tried.

"I don't even know who that is."

"You'll know soon enough." He smirked.

"I doubt that."

He stared at me, his face puckered with confusion. He bent down, inching our faces a little too close and patted my knee.

"I don't know about you," He said, parading into the hallway. "but I'm starving."

After he left the room, I took a few more deep breaths to finish composing myself, ambled over and slid the window shut, spun the locks into place and drew the curtains shut on my way out.

4

"TIME to get up, kids!"

Dad's booming voice swelled across the house amongst the sound of hurried footsteps and roused me out of a deep sleep. I sat up, rubbed the cobwebs from my eyes with the back of my hand, threw my covers aside and leaped out of bed. When I opened my door to see what all of the commotion was about, my parents were racing up the stairs with bright cherry smiles on their faces.

He waited for Jared to appear. "Get dressed because I'm taking everybody out for breakfast."

"Cool." Jared cheered, pumping his fist at the air.

Dad had set him up inside of the rec room with an air mattress we'd kept in the garage. He tried to talk Dad into letting him sleep on my bedroom floor, but he refused to give in. My father had his reason for not letting us sleep in the same room together but then I realized that Jared had his own reason for sleeping in here as well and it wasn't anything close to what my parents had thought four days ago.

We hopped into Dad's red Subaru Forrester, rolled our windows down for a taste of that sweet country air and fastened our seat belts. When he backed out of the garage, Dad took a right and followed the road hugging the right side of the house toward a steep incline flanked by tall pines and heavy-shaded oaks.

The satisfied look on Jared's face sunk into one of anger and confusion. Mom glanced at me in the reflection of her side mirror and winked, her russet-brown hair glinting in the bright morning sun.

"Isn't this the long way into town?"

"It's a good day for a nice drive in the country." Dad said, perching his arm on the car door. "Don't you think so, Mollie?"

"It sure is."

When Mom and I nodded in agreement, Jared slumped back in his seat and laced his arms across his chest. He sighed and squinted at me.

"I just wanted to see my father."

"You'll get to see him tomorrow afternoon."

His face cleaved by a pencil-thin smirk, his eyes went wide and lit up with realization. He glanced down at the floorboard behind Dad's seat and then at the back of Dad's head, his mind grasped in some sort of deep dreadful thinking. I extended my hand in a reasoning manner when he slapped it away and cupped his hands over his ears.

"Why would you say that, Mollie?"

"I didn't say–"

"What the hell is going on back there?" Dad asked, glancing at us from the overhead mirror.

"I don't know." I shrugged, my cheeks flushing. "I was just telling him that–"

"She told me that my father lived somewhere else."

"I didn't say that at all." My voice pinched with anger.

"I don't care who said what to whom," Dad said angrily. "I'm not afraid to turn this car around if you're going to misbehave ."

No matter how many times I tried to explain myself, my words came out garbled and intersected by quick clueless breaths. Mom spun around in her seat, fired a disgusted look at me from over her right shoulder and turned back around. As much as I wanted to tell them, I couldn't find the right words to begin with.

My cheeks flushed with shame. All I wanted to do was shrink back in my seat until it swallowed me up in a stitched leather embrace and remind me that all of it was just a really bad dream. I knew there was no other way to avoid my parents' scornful gaze so I swallowed my pride and did what was right.

"I'm sorry, Jared."

He accepted my apology and sat back, arms folded across his chest in a smug and cocky demeanor. He knew I wouldn't say anything to them about what happened two nights ago without risking my own neck, which was why he was acting like this.

We rode the rest of the way in silence. Although I've never considered myself to be much of a city girl to begin with, I felt better once we got into the city. Mom and I spat baby talk at a white chihuahua with black spots and a thin red collar sitting in the back of a maroon Buick; we tried to talk Dad into letting us have a dog a few years ago but we couldn't because he was allergic.

Mattie's Country Barn was one of many local establishments in town that sat on a gently-rising slope overlooking the highway running east-to-west in and out of Columbus. It was housed inside of a one-level red-brick building ringed by large flowerbeds with a slanted gray roof and a cheap white picket fence rooted along the front of the building. We'd come here every other Sunday (and not *just* because Dad liked the free coffee they offered on that particular day from nine a.m. to two p.m.) to have breakfast and spend some quality time.

Dad eased his car into the first available slot and killed the engine. He peered up at me from the rearview mirror, mouthed an "I love you" and followed it with a smile. I returned both the greeting and the smile, smoothed out the wrinkles in my shorts, and closed my door behind me.

Once we were inside, a heavyset brunette woman in a white shirt and brown khakis escorted us into a large dining area with knotty-pine tables and soft blue carpet; gilded picture frames were speckled across the scratchy white wallpaper, displaying colorful photos of nature in all of his splendor. Shafts of early-morning sunlight filtered through the light-blue curtains framing the big picture windows. We took the four sided table in the far right corner beside of the second window in the middle of the room and sat on opposite ends: Mom and I sat on the inside against the wall; Dad and Jared sat along the aisle.

The mingled aromas of coffee, syrup and breakfast food was a much pleasant smell compared to the lingering odor of licorice I'd been smelling for the past seventy-two hours. After the waitress brought our drinks, I stared out of the big picture window overlooking the tar-streaked stretch of highway below. The shopping mall sat across the street, its glass and stucco façade glinting under the mid-morning sun; there were only a few cars in the parking lot that I could see.

"Earth to Mollie."

Something jerked at my right sleeve, snapping me out of my trance. Mom slipped her right hand away from my sleeve, folded both hands together and rested them gently on the tabletop, her horn-rimmed specs glinting in the sunlight. Jared and Dad were huddled together, scanning and pointing at their menus to decide what they were getting; if Jared got something Dad wanted then he'd offer him a bite of it so he would know what it tastes like.

"Are you okay?" She asked, ignoring the display of manliness on her right.

"I'm fine."

"Are you sure?"

I nodded, still shaking off some of the uneasiness from a little while ago. She slid her chair closer, leaned over the edge of the table and took my hand, her face pleated with concern. I thought I saw something out of the corner of my eye slowly brush across the middle of the table but I wasn't for sure what it could've been.

After the waitress, a middle-aged brunette with doe-brown eyes took our order, Jared asked, "Can I be excused?"

"Sure." Dad nodded.

I cocked my head away from the table, peered over my left shoulder and watched him stride away from the table. He buried his left fist into the left front pocket of his shorts, drew the right corner of his lip into a half smile and hurried off. I thought about following him so that I could corner him about what he'd said on the way here but I didn't want to risk it.

"Is everything okay?" Dad asked, then took a sip of coffee and set the mug down. "You've been acting weird lately."

"I'm fine."

I took a drink of my chocolate milk to coat the anxiety roiling in my gut. I knew I couldn't say anything to convince them otherwise.

"I just didn't get much sleep last night." I lied. "I kept tossing and turning. I'll be good until my regular bedtime."

I nodded.

They shared an optimistic glance, then gazed back at me.

"You can't go telling your cousin the truth about his mother." Dad said, his voice firm and solemn. "If he was to find out that your Aunt Ruth had an affair while she was married to your uncle, he would lose his mind."

"I didn't say–"

Mom swiped her hand across the air and said, "Even if you didn't, you shouldn't say anything like that at all, honey. At least for Jared's sake."

It wasn't too long after that when the waitress brought our food. We waited until Jared came back before we started eating. We talked in between bites and watched the place fill up with more customers; waitresses hovered from to one table to the other, taking orders and offering refills.

Dad finished before the rest of us and nursed his coffee and signaled the waitress for the check. Once we were finished, I groaned in protest and rubbed my belly. We gathered our dishes together and waited for the waitress to collect them.

After she left, he turned to us and asked, "Did you get enough to eat?"

"Yeah." I groaned, rubbing my belly. "I feel like a big ol' stuffed pig."

A chorus of laughter burst from our table, catching the attention of a few nearby customers when something caught the corner of my left eye. I glanced over at a tall bald man in a pin-striped blue shirt and red tie carrying a dark green bucket dotted with globs of white paint across the other side of the front counter. He gave the bucket to a young skinny man with dark hair wearing a dark-blue apron under street clothes; tattoos snaked up his arms and disappeared beneath his shirt sleeves while a tiny diamond earring glinted from his left earlobe.

Something snapped beside of my head, drawing my attention away from him.

"Do you want to go to the mall?" Mom asked.

"Yeah."

"What were you looking at?" Dad asked.

"She was looking at that boy." Jared motioned toward the busser by jabbing his left thumb over his left shoulder.

"Were you checking him out?" Mom groaned, grinning from ear to ear.

"No, I wasn't."

It was a good kind of embarrassment, this time.

"Yes, you were." His voice had a slight inflection. "You want to kiss him and hug him and make little–"

"No, I don't."

I gave his shoulder a playful slap and, grinning behind flushed cheeks, shook my head. Dad gathered the check, led us away from the table and up to the front of the restaurant where a pair of cash registers sat on top of a horseshoe shaped countertop. Mom took my hand and leaned in close enough to drown me in a cloud of her favorite perfume.

"We'll look around the inside of a few places and get you some new tops."

I nodded.

"We'll go the arcade barn on the other side of the mall." Dad said, nudging Jared's left shoulder with his elbow.

"Yeah." Jared exalted, pumping his fist in celebration.

A young bubbly-blonde cashier in a button-down white blouse and black slacks (the name LORI was stamped across her nametag in perfect black script) stood behind an L-shaped wooden counter stocked with baked goods and pre-packed sugary sweets. Dad gave a frustrated sigh, his shoulders hunched, and reached into his front pocket. He slapped a thin stack of dollar bills into my hand, pursed his lips in humiliation and nodded toward the table we'd been sitting at an hour and a half ago.

"I forgot to leave a tip." Dad said. "Could you go back and set that on the table?"

Mom took Jared's hand and guided him through the crowd of people waiting to be seated and went outside to wait for us.

I slipped a ten dollar bill onto the table when I noticed a crumpled packet of blueberry jelly sitting on the corner of Jared's plate. He hadn't ordered anything that would warrant him having to use blueberry jelly since all he had were three hotcakes, two pieces of sausage and a pile of hash browns. If he didn't need it, what had he used it for?

I met up with Dad, glanced at something out of the corner of my left eye and saw the manager and the busser standing inside of the MEN'S bathroom. The manager was leaning against the door to hold it open as the busser knelt onto the floor, scrubbing at the wall between the two porcelain urinals. I craned my head past the front counter and, staring beyond the crowd of other customers paying their checks at the other side of the counter, squinted for a closer look.

The last time I'd saw it, it was scrawled across the wall that night when licorice and fear became my bedfellows. It wasn't just the symbol itself that scared me but the very reality of its presence. Instead of purple paint, the symbol was drawn in globs of blueberry jelly that resembled a child's finger painting; everything from the pathway to the door and the horizon looked just as it'd done the day I first saw it.

5

I was standing inside of a spacious bedroom with white walls striped with bright pink wallpaper and the same brown carpet I'd seen in the first dream. A pair of twin beds sat against the right side of the room under an arched window framed by elongated blue drapes; dust motes danced in the shafts of sunlight pooling across the floor.

A tall antique wooden dresser stood on the far left, topped by an array of bright ceramic knickknacks and beauty products. A small brass lamp laid on its side in the middle of the room with a shattered light bulb jutting up from the ribbed golden cap like a thin sliver of bone.

In the far left corner of the room, a wooden closet door had been flung open with such force that it was left hanging down by a single twisted hinge. A set of footsteps drummed across the other end of the hall, followed by a loud wheezing sound like something you'd hear when sitting on a leather seat.

I crossed the room on slow hesitant steps and ambled out into the hallway. The noxious mix of licorice and cherry-flavored lollipops filled the house and stung my nostrils. A large picture frame hanging on the wall beside of the bathroom doorway showed a heavyset brunette in a red sweater and black capris kneeling down beside of two young girls both with long chestnut brown hair

35

wearing light purple dresses and white sneakers in front of a faux grassy background.

Their names were pasted across the front of the photo in colorful adhesive letters that you could peel off at any time and stick them elsewhere. The girl on the left was named Abbi and the pear-shaped girl was named Daisy; the mother's name was Maureen.

A strangled cry echoed across the house. I peered into the living room and saw the curtain of colorful plastic beads draped across the open doorway and felt my heart sink toward my feet. I pressed my clammy-white fists against my thighs and dug my fingernails against the middle of my palms until it hurt.

I held my breath, peered around the corner and into the living room. Maureen was sitting on the edge of an overstuffed blue couch facing a large boxy black television sitting in the far left corner of the room next to the big picture window overlooking the back yard. Shafts of dull gray sunlight painted odd shadows across the same oak paneled walls that bottled the cries of its victims and the same brown carpet that absorbed more blood than an operating room.

Her long black hair was ruffled and stuck up from the top of her head as if she touched the wrong wire. She wore a long-sleeved green tee shirt and tight black stirrups; sporadic patterns of dirt and mud clung to her bare feet like a bad case of psoriasis.

She swiped her hand across the coffee table, sending an array of items spilling onto the floor. She rose up from her seat, walked around to the right side of the coffee table, pressed her foot down hard onto the television remote. It cracked, sending a bright red button rolling across the room and out of sight, filling the house with the sound of shattered plastic.

She walked across the room and stopped in front of a large wooden table with matching chairs sitting in front of the other big picture window overlooking the front porch. The corners of her mouth sagged into a deflated frown bracketed by deeply creased dimples; her puffy swollen eyes were telltale signs of both long contemplation and insomnia.

The last time I'd seen that particular spot empty was back at the party when Todd removed his teeth with a pair of pliers. Abbi sat on the left side of the table wearing a pair of plaid shorts and a pink tee-shirt with her back facing the hallway; Daisy sat on the facing the hallway, a thin curtain of brown hair shrouding one half of her pale cherub face.

She'd twisted their arms behind their backs and cinched their wrists together with thick bands of braided white rope. The colorful silk ties wound around their mouths muffled their agonizing cries but did very little for their gut-wrenching sobs. Hot lucid tears and snail trails of viscous green snot slid down their faces, stained their makeshift gags and reflected off of their cheeks like cheap glittery makeup.

"Now girls." Maureen said in a soft pleading tone. "You need to be on your best behavior today. When I remove your gags, you have to scream a little louder because if the house can't hear you then it doesn't count."

Her phrase resonated inside my ears and vibrated against my skull. I didn't want to believe that she would actually say that to her own children but I was old enough to realize that dreams didn't really have to make sense and neither did the dialogue. They were what they were and that was that.

The girls jerked on their restraints, their bodies wriggling like worms seeking underground shelter. Their muffled screams were greatly emphasized by the pained expressions etched across their faces. She snuck over to Daisy's chair and raked her hands through her long brown hair in slow and steady brushstrokes.

Maureen inched her head toward Daisy's face, pressed her nose against the back of her left cheek and, dragging her face down the sloping curvature of her neck, sniffed the scent of fear wafting off of her skin. The girl flinched and jerked back, her wide horror-struck eyes glistening with tears. She cupped her left hand around the back of her head, her right hand underneath her chin and held it still before planting a soft kiss onto the crown of her forehead.

"Don't fight it, Abbi." She spoke in a hushed tone. "The more you fight it, the harder it gets for us to cross."

Abbi and Daisy stopped sniveling long enough to cast long puzzled glances across the table at each other. They weren't just scared, but confused as well; this was a side of their mother they never wanted to see. She was supposed to be a role model, a symbol of courage and strength, not the guru of their nightmares.

"I'm sorry, honey." She whispered into her ear. "Since your sister ran from me, I'm gonna have to kill you first."

They groaned from behind their gags and wrenched at their restraints again, tossing thick tufts of long brown hair across one side of their face. Maureen tore Daisy's gag off of her face and sauntered into the kitchen, her body rigid as if the weight of their misery would've never played a role in weighing her down.

"Pppplease." Abbi pleaded, her lips wet and quivering. "Ddddon't do this. Wwwweeee love you, Mmmmmommy. Ddddaddy loves—"

"If your father had one ounce of love for me," She added. "then he wouldn't have traded me for some cheap whore. This house reminded me a long time ago that we have to stick together. We are all we've got and this house is a part of our family, too."

When she reemerged from the kitchen, Maureen carried a thin silver tray across the room and placed it in the middle of the table between them. She stared down at the three red plastic cups sitting in the middle of the tray and sighed with motherly admiration. Her eyes beamed with an eerie incandescent glow that sent cold shivers trailing down my spine; the right corner of her lip curved into a toothy lopsided grin.

"Wwwwe'll do anything yyyyyou want, Mom." Abbi pleaded once more. "Wwwwwhatever it is just pppplease don't do this, Mommy. We love you."

Daisy's voice became clear as she nodded, her eyes wide and hopeful. She prayed that someone had heard all of the ruckus from earlier ago and called the authorities; anytime now she would hear the sound of police sirens closing in on them.

"Please, Mommy." Abbi begged. "Don't do this please do please ple—"

A loud panicked cry rattled inside of her throat, cutting her off in mid-sentence. The cups had been filled to the brim with red punch; a black X was scrawled across one side of the cup in what looked to be the quick scrawl from a black magic marker.

Although my body was numb with fear, my cheeks flushed. Maureen bowed her head, clasped her hands together and closed her eyes. She cocked her head to the right and perked her left ear toward the ceiling; a sadistic grin spread across her face, hugging the corners of her thick red mouth with faint tiny wrinkles.

I gazed into the kitchen and felt a tremor of terror pounding through me. A tall glass pitcher with the colorful décor of a smiling blue flower rested on the countertop next to a neon-yellow box, the words RAT-B-GONE stamped in bold black font. The handle of a long wooden spoon jutted out from the left side of a double-sided sink.

Fear tightened my chest and squeeze a pneumatic wheeze from between my lips. My blood ran cold as I bit down on my bottom lip to keep from screaming. I forced the sour aftertaste back down my throat and felt my stomach churn with disgust.

"Don't worry, girls." She said with a tinge of elation in her voice. "Momma's gonna hold your hand so you're not alone. Wouldn't it be great if we could all go together?"

She opened her eyes, snatched the tall red plastic cup from the right side of the tray and approached Daisy's side of the table. Daisy jerked her head back and forth a few times, hoping to knock the cup from her mother's hand but her efforts proved fruitless. I screamed and took a step toward the living room but I could go no further.

Abbi let off a loud panicked scream and watched helplessly as Maureen caught Daisy's head in her hand, tipped it back, poured the poisoned punch down her forcibly pursed lips. When Daisy's throat flexed like it would if she were drinking, I knew it was too late. Once the cup was empty, Maureen tossed it across the living room and, watching it fly across the room, gave a playful giggle.

She clapped her hands and backed away from the table, her face twisted with the same mad pleasure beaming in her eyes. Daisy jostled and spewed a chorus of loud choking sounds that tore at the fabric of my sanity; the pained expression on her face was borne from the realization that her mother had killed her and become less of the strong feminine role model she was meant to be. She coughed as twin rivers of blood gushed out of her mouth, spurted from her nostrils in sporadic bursts and splashed down the front of her nightgown.

Her body clenched, pinching her face together. She snatched a breath, lurched forward in her seat and heaved a river of hot yellow vomit across the table. As she twitched, her eyes rolled inside of their sockets and her head slumped forward, shrouding her face in a curtain of long brown hair.

"One down," Maureen cheered with motherly approval. "one more to go."

When she grabbed the other cup from the tray, Abbi gave a terrified cry that–

I blinked and sat straight up in my bed. I was back inside of my bedroom, my chest rising and falling against the gentle rush of the wind tossing my curtains around like rag dolls. I brushed a strand of hair from my clammy forehead, tossed my covers aside and felt the cool summer air caressing my bare legs.

Thin shafts of moonlight painted odd black shadows across my windowsill before reaching toward the corners of my bedroom. The tree branches outside of my bedroom window stirred lazily in the breeze, tossing more wind than caution. I heard a loud creaking sound from outside my bedroom, a low whine that scraped at the dark suffocating silence.

My bedroom door eased opened, spreading a carpet of light across my doorway. I held my breath as a tall shadow dissected the light, its elongated arm perched on the edge of my doorknob. I leaped back into bed, quickly threw the covers back across my legs and held them until my knuckles turned white.

When I saw the bright-yellow Pokémon tee-shirt and matching yellow pants, I let out a great breath. The fear dissipating from my bones, I sat up in bed and loosened my grip but not too much.

"What are you doing up at this time of the night?" Jared whispered, skulking into my bedroom.

"I could hear you in the hallway as I was coming out of the bathroom." He jabbed his thumb over his shoulder. "Did you have a bad dream?"

He rubbed his eyes with the back of his hand and gazed out the moonlit window, his lips pursed with wonder. I tugged the covers tighter against my stomach and tucked my left foot under my right knee.

No matter how long I stared at him, all I could see was him swiping his jelly-coated fingers across the bathroom wall at Mattie's Country barn uttering a sly evil laugh. I didn't mention the symbol to anyone for the rest of the day because we were having so much fun that I didn't want to ruin it. If I did, my parents would've realized I'd either been trying to hog all of their attention or that I'd lost more than a few hours of sleep.

We'd had so much fun we'd lost track of time. After Mom and I got back from the clothing stores, Dad and Jared greeted us with milkshakes that we'd drank on the way home; we ended up not taking the shortcut back home and therefore passed 1342 Lindley Drive or at least that's what I saw on the mailbox before I closed my eyes and lowered my head between my knees so I wouldn't have to look at it. Later that night, Mom and I stayed home while Dad and Jared went back into town and picked up a couple of pizzas and some movies.

The last time I saw him was around ten-thirty when Dad carried his sleeping body upstairs with me in tow. Now, he looked all giddy and inquisitive.

"What did he say?"

"What did who say?"

"What did Father say?"

I knew what he was talking about but I wasn't in the mood.

"How did you know?"

"Know what?"

"How did you know I saw him?"

The giddiness in his face sunk to an uncomfortable silence.

"Are you having the same dream?"

"What are you talking about?"

"Listen to me, Jared." I said, taking his hand. "Are you seeing people going crazy in your dream or what? How are you communicating with him?"

"I've been communicating with him ever since the door opened." He said, shrugging his left shoulder. "I saw everything you've been seeing, Mollie. He wants you to join, too."

"I don't care what he wants."

Jerking his hand away from my grasp, he said, "Don't say that about my father."

"Your father is all the way in–"

"No he's not." He hissed, sliding off the edge of my bed. "He's right over there. When are you ever going to understand that?"

He nodded at the window behind me. I was angry that my attempts to shake this off had been for nothing. The more I tried to forget about it, the more it tugged at me like a child seeking attention.

"Did he mention The Crossing?" He said, resting his hands in his lap.

"What?"

"I heard you say, 'I don't want to cross. I don't want to go'. I assumed you were talking to Father."

I'd never talked in my sleep before the events leading up to this, so why now? All I knew was that I was fed up with it; the word "Father", that godawful house and all these damn dreams I was having.

I tossed the covers aside, threw my legs over the side and climbed out of bed. I stood in front of him, braced his shoulders with both hands and crouched down to meet his gaze.

"Listen to me, Jared." I whispered. "He's not your father. I don't know who he is but he's not your father. He's just a figment of your–"

"You're lying." He hissed. "He told me him he wants me to follow him through the door again. He said the stars will align again tomorrow night and then we can be together."

"He wants to kill you, Jared. He doesn't care about anyone but himself."

He tried to wriggle out of my grasp but I refused to let him go.

"He doesn't care about you like I do. If you'd only se–"

"You're hurting me, Mollie."

I tried to calm him down as best as I could but our voices grew louder and more intense. He squealed and kicked his feet.

"I'm not hurting you, Jared."

"Yes, you are."

"He's not your father, Jared. He's not yo–"

Footsteps paraded toward my bedroom, quick and unrelenting in their pursuit. A cold chill traced the contours of my spine and pinned my feet to the floor. Before I could open my mouth to tell him to quiet down, Mom and Dad came bursting into my bedroom with a mix of disgust and grogginess etched across their faces.

Mom hurried across the room, leaned over my bed and pulled Jared from my grasp. Dad flipped on my desk lamp, drowning the far left corner of my room in a carpet of golden ambient light and jabbed his finger in my face until the sight of lowered me onto the edge of my bed.

"What the hell is going on in here?"

"He was tal–"

Raising his head from Mom's right shoulder, Jared whined, "She said bad things about my father that isn't true."

"I didn't say anything like that." I pleaded, raking my hand through my hair.

"Yes, you did."

Crocodile tears streaming down his face, he buried his face against the front of Mom's nightgown. She cradled him and patted the middle of his back.

"I don't care who said it." Dad said in a resounding voice. "We're gonna stop all of this foolishness and go back to bed."

There was so much I wanted to say but I couldn't speak through the ball of anger bunched up inside of my throat. Tears brimming in my eyes, I laced my arms across my chest and stared down at the floor.

As he corralled Mom and Jared out of my bedroom, Dad killed the light switch and plunged my room back into a tangle of moonlight and shadows. He stood outside of my room, his lethargic face sunk with disappointment, stared down at the floor and back up at me.

"We'll deal with this in the morning."

My face blushed at the sight of my father's disapproving look, but I was sure there would be more to come. After he shut the door, I slid back under the covers and laid down.

He was playing my parents for a couple of saps and they were buying everything he was selling just like the people who "Father" had brainwashed into believing what he'd told them. If Jared had seen what I saw in my dream, maybe he'd understand why I'd said all of those things.

I wasn't so sure if I could consider him my cousin anymore because this wasn't the same Jared who always made me laugh and smile when the rest of the world didn't. This was a doppelganger who adored a delusional star-gazing sociopath who drove all of those people into committing suicide.

Eventually, I cried myself to sleep.

6

AT least my parents allowed me to eat breakfast before they decided to interrogate me the next morning.

Instead of a piping hot breakfast, they downgraded me to a bowl of Boo-Berry and a glass of orange juice. The bags under Mom's eyes told me that Jared had strung her along throughout a good part of the night.

I kept my arms laced across my chest and gazed down at their reflection in the tabletop. All of the anger and guilt pressed me inside of its heavy wet folds, strangling my throat and sucking the air out of lungs; I would've watched paint dry–or anything along those lines–if I could avoid their penetrating gaze. An uncomfortable silence permeated around the house save for the tick of the grandfather clock standing in the far left corner of the living room and the occasional shift and sip.

Dad set his cup back onto the table and slammed his fist hard onto the surface. Mom and I flinched; a small river of coffee sloshed around inside of his cup and spilled onto the table. He didn't bother to clean it up and he wasn't about to ask Mom to do it either.

"What were you thinking?" Mom sighed. "How could you say something like so spiteful like that to him?"

"We told you all of that in secrecy," He said, then shrugged his shoulders. "but I guess we can't trust you to keep a secret. Can we?"

Two days after she married Bruce Fields, Ruth called my mother and told her she had an affair with an old boyfriend she met back in college. It stirred a lot of speculation about whether or not Bruce was actually Jared's father but we were sure that he would've loved him no matter what. I was told to keep quiet about it since I'd mistakenly walked into the living room while Mom was on the phone talking to her about it.

After she was done talking to Aunt Ruth, they sat me down and told me and ever since then I hadn't said anything.

"How would you feel if someone had said that about us?"

I wrapped my arms around my stomach and hugged myself. I sucked a cloud of air deep into my lungs and then back out to slow down the river of anxiety flooding through my veins.

I licked my lips and sighed. Mom dabbed at her eyes with a crumpled ball of tissue, her face and eyes red from both crying. I couldn't stand to see them mad at me any longer.

"I didn't mean to say that to him but I had my reasons."

"There's no reason for you to act like this just to get our attention. We love each an–"

"What the fuck are you trying to say?"

"Watch your language." Dad said through clenched teeth. "You're already skating on thin ice, little lady."

I bit down on my bottom lip and sighed.

"I've never done anything like this to vie for your attention before." I said, giving my left shoulder a slight shrug. "Why would I do it now? Of all the times that Jared has spent the night here, why would I do it now?"

Mom frowned, her face creased with confusion.

"I don't know who the hell that is upstairs but that's not my cousin."

"How could you say that?"

"I'm telling you the truth." I said, then realized what I said. "I'm not saying that Jared isn't my cousin but he hasn't been acting like it since we went over there."

"Where did you go?"

Dad rose up out of his chair and planted his hands firmly against the edge of the table, his jaw tightened with anger. He sighed deeply and, his mouth set in a hard line, waited.

"We were riding our bikes and we stopped at the to–"

A loud terrifying scream burst from somewhere upstairs, tearing at the thick cloud of awkwardness filling the house. We flinched, bracing the arms of our chairs and glanced up at the ceiling. I leapt out of my chair and ran upstairs, ignoring my parents' protests; his screams grated against my nerves like the sound of nails gliding down a blackboard.

I was halfway up when I realized where it was coming from.

"Let's go together, Father." A familiar voice bellowed behind my bedroom door. "Take me ha-ahh take my hand so we can cross toge-ahh!"

As I cleared the top step, my heart thudding with shock, a thick haze of licorice stung my nostrils. I braced myself and rammed my shoulder against my door; it flew open with a splintery wooden crack. The knob struck, sending a pair of picture frames sliding down the wall and onto the floor.

When Dad and I stepped inside first, we filled the doorway, blocking Mom's view. We gasped, our faces twisted by both terror and surprise.

Jared sat Indian-style in the middle of my blood-soaked bed and bellowed a loud cry, one that spoke of pain and pleasure. He held his left foot in his left hand, his hair stuck to the reflective sheen of sweat glinting off of his brows. His deep-set brown eyes, now wide with horror, beamed with the same zealous release I'd seen on the faces of the ghosts that haunted my dreams.

He grunted, tugging at his foot. He raised his fist, wielding a bloody toenail pinched between the blocky jagged teeth of a rusty old pair of pliers and laughed at the ceiling. When I heard the soft squish of loose flesh, my heart skipped a beat and a fresh carpet of gooseflesh tickled my arms.

Laughing, he stretched his arm over the left side of my bed and dropped the freshly-plucked toenail onto a small pile of other toenails stacked on the floor; the first four toes on his left foot resembled tiny mushrooms of bright pink flesh. Mom's eyes widened with horror as she snatched her breath and clamped her hand across her mouth to stifle the next.

"We're almost there, Father." Jared said in a booming voice.

Dad hurried across the room toward the other side of my bed and screamed Jared's first and last name in a strict authoritative voice. Mom pulled me back into the hallway, screams of fear still erupting from our mouths in a continuous string of sporadic alien dialogue.

When Jared clamped the pilers onto the big toe on his right foot, Dad knelt onto the bed beside of him, wrenched the pilers from his grip and pinned him onto the bed; the pilers made a drunken descent toward the floor and slid over beside of my dresser on the right side of the room. Jared thrashed to free himself from Dad's grasp and snapped his teeth at the air between their faces. A deep animalistic growl issuing from deep inside of his throat, he nipped and missed Dad's left cheek by three inches.

Dad drew his hand back and slapped Jared across the face, the sound whipping across the house like a gunshot in an empty parking lot. Mom leaned her head against my chest and watched through wet blurry eyes as Jared flung back onto the bed in an unconscious stupor. Dad released his grip from Jared's wrists and backed away from the bed, his face creased under a mask of fear and confusion. His chest heaving, he raked a hand through his sweaty dark hair and shuffled past us out of the room. He stopped in the middle of the hallway and, pivoting on his heels, spun back around to face us.

A large red smear was painted along the bottoms of his knees. His lips quivering, he jabbed his finger at me.

"Stay here with your mother." He said to me, then to Mom. "Call Ruth and Bruce and tell them to meet me at the hospital."

Her cheeks blotchy and wet, Mom ran back downstairs and into the kitchen. I stood beside of the railing, my heart thudding and peered at my cousin lying motionless across the middle of my blood-soaked bed. In the glare of the light pouring through my bedroom window, his skin had taken on an inner glow I hadn't seen since the night of his birth when Ruth called me into her hospital room and Mom had situated me just so rightly inside one of the brown leather chairs sitting beside of her hospital bed and set him gently in my arms and beamed at how cute we'd looked sitting there (Mom had said we reminded her of a knickknack her grandmother used to own) and now I'd have given anything to have that same little boy back.

A few moments later, Dad waited for Mom at the head of the stairs and whispered in her ear. They snuck furtive little glances at me between words, then looked away from me when they realized I might've been listening. She nodded and kissed him on the cheek, her eyes red and glistening.

A minute later, he carried Jared's body out of my bedroom and took the stairs two at a time without even looking at me. After he backed out of the garage and headed down the road, Mom sauntered into my room, came out with a stack of clothes and pointed to the bathroom. I was afraid to speak because the tension had risen to a level of stress that even Homeland Security didn't have a color for.

When I was finished, I found her bunching my blood-soaked bed linens into a ball and setting it inside of my bedroom doorway. She wiped a river of tears from her cheeks with the back of her left hand, emptied my pillow cases and tossed them into a pile in front of my dresser.

I stood on my tiptoes for a second, peered over her left shoulder and into the room. The pile of toenails Jared collected were gone; I didn't know whether she dumped them into a trashcan or kept them back just in case.

Her quiet but diligent demeanor told me I shouldn't bother her but I didn't anyway.

"Do you want–"

"Go downstairs, Mollie." She hissed. "I don't want to hear one more word out of you until your father gets home."

Mom's words stung me deeply. I couldn't stand to see her like this but I understood why she was angry and maybe because she was still trying to wrap her mind around the fact that her little nephew had just plucked out his toenails one by one. I did as she asked and sat there in silence, listening to the parade of soft footsteps drumming along the ceiling.

The longer I sat there, the more she continued to ignore me. The silence that my parents deemed worthy of me to face had stretched on for what seemed like days when it was only a few hours; I could tell them that I'd learned my lesson but I knew it wouldn't be enough. This was a side of my parents I never knew existed and, for as long as I lived, I would never visit it again.

When she came back down, I buried my face in my hands and sobbed. She sat down beside of me and brushed strands of hair away from my weeping face as I confessed.

7

"WHY didn't you tell us the truth?"

The pained expression on her face only heightened the intensity of my guilt. When it was all said and done, the whole prospect of being grounded didn't seem so bad.

"I kept wondering why you'd asked about that place." She sighed. "I thought you were going to use it for one of those stories you wrote inside of your journals."

"I tried to keep him away from that place but he wouldn't listen." I pleaded.

"I know you did."

We were sitting at the kitchen table, sipping hot cocoa from tiny ceramic mugs that looked like plump orange pumpkins. In a way, I felt relieved now that I'd said everything.

"We've told you time and time again not to go near that place and you did it anyway." She shook her head. "What if you'd gotten hurt? What if someone had come out of the house and raped you or killed you or God knows what?"

She took another sip from her mug and swiped a skim of chocolate from her lips with her tongue. Tiny wrinkles of confusion were etched across her face as if she were at odds with her emotions; she didn't know whether to feel mad at me for going near it or feel glad that the truth had finally come out.

"But we weren't."

"That's not the fucking point, Mollie. We asked you to follow one simple rule and this is what we get."

A few seconds of silence floated by before she asked, "Did you go inside?"

"I told you I didn't."

"I just want to make sure you're not lying to me about that, too."

I sighed and rolled my eyes. There was no sense in rubbing salt on an open wound.

"I don't know what he saw but he hasn't been the same since."

"In what way?"

When I told her about my nightmares, she slumped back into her seat, leaned over the edge of the table and clamped her hand across her mouth; fear carved tiny creases across her face. She reached across the table to retrieve her mug, her forefinger hooking toward the handle but then decided not to. She rested her left hand on the edge of the table and, her cheeks flushing, swiped her right hand across her tear-soaked eyes.

"There was no reason for you to hide this from us, Mollie."

"I thought that if he saw that it was empty," I shrugged. "he would just walk away but he wouldn't listen. I tried to get him away from the house but he wouldn't listen to me."

"It's a little too late for that now, don't you think?"

An hour later, Dad's car pulled into the garage. Mom rose out of her seat like she'd just seen The Second Coming; the hairs along the back of my neck went stiff. When he stomped into the house, his footsteps matching the rhythm of my beating heart, the angry look on his face sent tears of cold sweat sliding down my back.

When he entered the kitchen and saw me sitting at the table, he tossed his car keys on the table hard enough to make me flinch. He shrugged out of his dark-blue flannel button-down, tossed it over the back of his chair, fell down into the chair at the head of the table and slumped down into his chair at the head of the table.

Mom leaned back against the kitchen countertop and dabbed at her tear-soaked eyes with a ball of spent tissue. She tossed the tissue into the kitchen trash can, poured Dad a fresh cup of coffee and set it down in front of him. Although he hadn't yelled at me, every move he made made me feel even more uncomfortable.

"There anything you'd like to add?"

After he took his first sip, I repeated everything to him that I'd said to Mom between sips of hot chocolate. I was halfway through when he cocked his head toward the floor, closed his eyes and rubbed the bridge of his nose between his thumb and forefinger. He perched his right arm on the edge of the table, bunched his hand into a clammy white-knuckled fist, pressed it against his mouth and took two deep breaths.

When I was finished, he clamped his hand over his mouth and sighed. He gazed at me, his eyes burning with mix of betrayal and grief, and rose out of his chair. He slid his hand down the front of his chin, glanced down at the table, sat in the chair beside of me and sighed.

I said in a dismal voice. "I want to call Aunt Ruth and Uncle Bruce and apologize."

"There's nothing you can do for them, right now." He hissed, brushing the subject off the table with a dismissive wave. "If it hadn't been for your Uncle Bruce, your aunt would've taken my head clean off my shoulders."

"What did the doctors say?"

"They had to sedate him because he tried to eat his fingers."

"Oh God." Mom said, pressing her left hand against her chest.

He made me recant the moment when the front door opened. He took a long swig of his coffee and whether it was because he was thirsty or because it kept him from slapping me, I wasn't about to find out.

"What did you see when the front door opened?"

"I didn't see anything from where I was standing." I repeated. "Jared was the only one who looked inside the house the entire time. All I could smell was something that smelled like licorice."

He and Mom shared an awkward glance and sat back down. I swept my eyes across the table at them, my mind buzzing with curiosity. There was that uneasy feeling you get when someone was hiding the truth and it was becoming too much for them to bear.

He took Mom's hand, squeezed it a few times and stared deep into her eyes. She squeezed it back, nodded and sighed.

"Are you sure about this?" She asked.

"She might as well learn now."

She stood up from her chair, poured him a refill and returned to her seat. She placed her arms across the edge of the table and clasped her hands together.

"Jared wasn't the only person that house has claimed." Mom said, then choked back a sob and said. "There's something strange about that house but yet no one can quite put their finger on it."

"Does anyone know who built it?"

"No." Dad said. "but I don't think it would change anything."

They let that sink in for a moment. I swallowed so hard my throat clicked. He tapped something into his cell phone, cupped it in his left hand and then took another sip.

He set cup back onto the table, slid his cell phone across the table and nodded. I picked it up and then wished that I hadn't. My eyes widened with fear and disbelief as I stared down at my father's cell phone and saw the picture of the man who haunted my dreams.

"Are you okay, honey?"

I nodded and slid the cell phone back across the table.

"That's the man from my dreams."

"Dreams?"

Mom told him about the two dreams. He sighed, killed the picture and tucked his cell phone back into his front pocket.

"His name is Noah Larson. He and his wife arrived in Salter Creek during the seventies when everyone was all peace and love and not war and flower power shit." He said in a sardonic voice. "He opened a new-age massage parlor in the mall while she sold vegetables at a kiosk next to that gas station beside of Wendy's."

"Kisor's?"

"Yeah." He said, then sighed. "They were having a swinger's party one night when the house possessed them, too."

"Swingers?"

They glanced at each other and grinned. Mom took a sip of her hot cocoa and set the mug back down on the table. After they told me what that meant, I took a giant swig from my mug, hoping it was hot enough to burn that image out of my head.

"That's gross."

He licked his lips and gazed down at his feet. Mom rubbed her fingertips across the knuckles of his left hand in a calm, reassuring manner.

"They found sixteen bodies inside of that house including Larson himself. They'd consumed enough absinthe and psychotropic drugs to kill an elephant before they killed each other. The sheriff found this crude symbol scrawled on the wall in the far left corner of the room of—"

"An oval painting of a pathway leading toward a door sitting on the edge of a horizon."

His brows furrowed, he asked, "How did you know?"

I reminded him that I saw the symbol painted on one of the walls inside of the house and then told them about the one that Jared had left behind back at Mattie's Country Barn. He shook his head, sighed, glanced up at the ceiling and then back down to me.

"When your tenth birthday came around," He said. "A woman named Maureen Butler moved in with her two little girls Ab—".

"Abbi and Daisy."

They opened their mouths as if they were about to ask me something, but changed their minds.

"It wasn't too long before the house drove her crazy."

"She wasn't a swinger, too. Was she?"

"No." Dad said, then chuckled. "She tied her kids to the kitchen table and—"

I waved my hands to protest him from further explanation. I felt foolish because here I was the whole time thinking that it was Larson who'd possessed Jared and killed all of those people.

"Why didn't they just tear it down?"

"After the Butler incident," Dad shrugged his left shoulder. The city condemned it when the landlord failed to keep up on much needed repairs. As the years went on, the place became an eyesore to the neighborhood but no one really bothered it."

"Somethings are born evil, Mollie." Mom stated. "They don't have to be created by evil; they just exist to do evil things. That house reads your mind and coerces you to do strange things to others in return for giving you what you want."

A loud chime exploded from Dad's front pocket, cutting through the cloud of silence permeating between us. We flinched; Mom and I clutched the edge of the table while Dad cursed under his breath and went digging through his pocket. Two curse words later, he answered it on the third ring.

Mom took my hand, tears brimming in her eyes. We waited for a thumbs-up or a nod that could tell us what the doctors were able to do for Jared.

He pressed the phone to his ear and nodded. He clamped his left hand over his left ear so he could hear better because cell phone reception in this area wasn't as good as it would've been had we lived in the city. We tried to watch his facial features to determine what she'd been telling him but his face didn't budge.

"Okay, man." He spoke in a slow syrupy voice. "Let us know if you need anything."

He killed the call, slid his hand down his face and sighed. He glanced back at his cell phone and then back at us.

"He started to come out of it and asked his mother for something to drink. When she came back into the room, his window was open and she heard a commotion coming from outside of the building." He sighed, his eyes glistening in the sour gray sunlight. "Jared had jumped out the window and fell eight stories onto the hood of a parked car."

Mom gave a heart-wrenching whine, her face dulled by a mix of shock and horror. Her eyes brimming with tears, she buried her face in both hands, slid out of her chair and onto the floor. Dad sprang out of his chair, crouched down beside of her and hugged her trembling body; her sobs were a song I didn't care to hear anymore but yet felt I was responsible for.

I clamped my hand across my mouth, slid out of my seat and ran upstairs as fast as I could. I dove face first onto my bed and sobbed until it hurt; my fingers shook as hot lucid tears trailed down my burning cheeks. A barrage of memories came flooding back to me in a wave of still images, each one just as perfect as the one before it: the day he carried me home after I fell out of the tree and broke my ankle; the time we found that old refrigerator last winter and went sledding down the hill toward Lake Michelle; the time he punched Rudy Castro (a little creep who lived at the bottom of the hill) in the nose for lifting my dress up and over my head during his sister Lori's twelfth birthday party.

I couldn't blame Aunt Ruth and Uncle Bruce if they never wanted to talk to me ever again. I should've said something when I had the chance but I didn't know all of this was my fault.

I raised my head up from my pillow and peered through my bedroom window, my hand bunched into tiny pale fists. Through the film of gauzy white tears clouding my vision, I gazed at the gothic eyesore sitting on the hill in all of its dark and desolate grandeur with more hatred than I could ever have for anything or anyone.

There was only one thing left for me to do, whether my parents liked it or not. If not for me, then for someone else.

8

LATER that night, I waited for Mom and Dad to be asleep because they'd have kill me if they knew what I was doing. If they caught me, I wouldn't be able to talk myself out of it.

It was now or never. Now that the house had taken Jared, who knew what else it was capable of doing to the next person and the one after that and so on.

When I knew the coast was clear, I slid out of bed, slipped into a white tee-shirt, jeans and a bright red hoodie. I snuck down stairs, holding my breath the entire time, and opened the sliding glass doors. I breathed a sigh of relief, stepped out onto the patio and shut the doors behind me.

The cool summer air caressed my face and hair. A veil of odd moonlit shadows partially obscured my parents' bedroom window before cascading across the roof. My gut churned with an amalgam of fear; my nerves were a spring-loaded trap waiting to be unleashed by the tinniest sounds or any sudden movement.

A slow procession of roiling black clouds drifted past the milky-white moon in a failed attempt to conceal it. Skeletal tree branches overhead weaved in the licorice-tainted breeze, scraping at the roof like the fingers of the dead clawing for their freedom.

I crept over to Dad's tool shed and jerked back on the flimsy metal door just hard enough not to scrape the bottom of it across the grass. The various smells of paint, rust and other chemicals tainted the air and stung my nostrils.

I thumbed the button on the pen-sized flashlight I found in the tool drawer in the kitchen and swept the inside with a cone of harsh white light. I found the red plastic gas can sitting under his work bench between a couple of brown plastic crates packed with other manly junk.

I didn't know how much I'd need to get the job done but I didn't care. I shut the door just as carefully as I did when I opened it and then crept back toward the front of the house to retrieve the box of matches Dad used to light the propane grill. I considered dousing the outside of the house then lighting it up so that the flames could eat their way through but there was only one way to get at something as evil as 1342 Lindley Drive.

Go for the throat or don't go at all.

With my head bowed and my shoulders hunched, I hurried up the hill away from my house. My fist clenching the handle of the gas can, I saw the ramshackle succubus sitting under the moon-lit sky like a ravenous predator huddling in the shadows to consume fresh, ignorant prey.

I peered through the wall of trees shrouding the driveway and saw halos of brightly colored lights flickering across the front window in soft luminescence. A song about incense and peppermints blared from somewhere inside of the house; faint black shadows floated across the windows as if they were projected across the screen of a movie theater, their shapes animated by the raucous mix of laughter and loud conversations.

A late-night fiasco at two in the morning. I was surprised that no one else had come by to see what all the noise was about but then if I had the chance to ignore this place then so would I.

The more I looked at it the more it made me wonder why someone would even bother to let it remain here in the first place. It reminded me of all of those televangelists my grandma used to watch on television on Sunday mornings; the ones who preached His word, gave examples on how it defined current events or personal situations and then coerce you into buying a bottle of special water, a new "New Testament" or a piece of magical cloth that can cure all of your ails; the ones who welcome you with open arms when you're "contributing" to their million dollar homes and mega-churches but yet lock their doors when your city is hit by a natural disaster.

The difference between this house and them was as plain as the nose on my face. It didn't seek a higher power through God and it didn't deliver His message through any fancy products either. Instead, it sought a higher power by telling people what they wanted to hear because it made them feel good about themselves; when you give someone enough attention they'll want it more and more because it'll ease the pain they felt when others never gave it to them. In return for the joy it brought them, they sign the contract and sell their souls to prolong the sense of happiness they hadn't felt in such a long time.

My mind flicked back to what Maureen Butler had said to her daughters in my last dream. It resonated in my head.

"The more you fight it, the harder it'll be for us to cross."
Cross?

The last time I heard a woman say that word she didn't live to tell about it. What connection did the house have with this so called "Crossing"? Was it the doorway to Heaven or Hell?

For as long as I can remember, people who committed suicide had gone to Hell. I think Hell is more than just little devils with pitchforks, towers of fire and days of prolonged misery.

Hell is trying not to throat punch the first person you see when you get to work on Monday; a traffic jam on the expressway during rush hour; a flat tire on a lonely stretch of road with no cell phone service. A parent who never comes home after they said they were just "going down the road for a little bit".

It'll always be whatever we want to make it. It's what we do to overcome it that determines who we really are.

I reached the mouth of the driveway when the nauseating stench of licorice wafted across my face. I winced and slid the front of my tee-shirt up and over my nose to shield myself from that ghastly smell. I knelt, spun the cap off of the can and carried it toward the front door; my chest rose and fell with each breath I took to calm the fire in my nerves.

I cursed under my breath for not grabbing one of Dad's old work towels from his shed and scanned the neighborhood for any witnesses. Nothing. I sighed and ambled across the driveway toward the covered front porch.

When I rammed my left shoulder against the front door, it flung it open with a loud splintery crack; the hinges gave off a series of slow piercing creaks that made my skin prickle with fear. The lights that once glowed in the window died, plunging the house into a dark and eerie state of silence that sent cold chills creeping down my spine; the stench of licorice mingled with the thick fetid odors of mold, urine and mildew. Something brewed inside of this bottomless gloom, biding its time until the next person came along to feed its insatiable hunger.

A deep chill tunneled through my body and settled into my bones. My breath blew across my face in thick white tendrils that dissipated in thin air. I brushed my fears aside, took a slow hesitant step across the doorway and stepped inside.

Large white cobwebs clung to the corners of the ceiling and danced in the cool air spewing in through the open door; a line of black gunk and dust gathered along the wainscoting along the bottom of the floor. The carpet of moonlight and shadow pouring through the kitchen windows exposed a gold-on-white linoleum floor and a yellowed Formica countertop strewed with thin jagged cracks and caked with dirt.

Odd black shadows lengthened across the living room floor and grasped the walls like desperate hands. I gazed across the house and spotted a thick wall of darkness clogging the main hallway that no sane man would venture toward.

I raised the gas can with both hands, my fingers shaking with anxiety when a burbling female voice rang in my left ear.

"We're so happy you could finally join us."

The door swung shut loud enough to vibrate the windows and drench me in a patch of semi-darkness. A chill traced the contours of my spine and sent a fresh streak of gooseflesh across my skin. I snatched a quick breath, filling my lungs with the stale musty air permeating through the house.

I lurched back, arms flailing drunkenly out from my sides and backed up against the edge of the kitchen countertop. I sighed amongst the current of pain that traced my hips, streaking down my thighs and calves.

Iris emerged from the pocket of darkness beside the front door and floated across the kitchen on skeletal gray feet that never touched the floor, her milky-white eyes surrounded by ancient-gray sockets; deep gashes etched along her throat and shoulders exposed a network of flesh, blood and sinew surrounded by large crusts of dried blood. A wide devilish grin spread across her face, exposing two rows of rotten black teeth; her skin cracked, spilling plumes of gray ash down the front of her tattered clothes.

I tightened my fist around the handle of the gas can and slid away from the countertop when a cold sensation skated across the back of my neck. I spun around on the balls of my feet and saw Abbi and Daisy standing behind me, their lithe pale forms floating above the floor like a bedsheet in the breeze.

"Jared was right." Abbi said through crooked black teeth. "You're way prettier than he said you were."

"We could always use another sister." Daisy said in a syrupy warped voice.

A gust of wind blew across the kitchen as an unseen force collided with my back and knocked off my feet. My back arched from the impact, the gas can jarred loose from my grasp and tumbled across the room, spewing a stream of gasoline across the floor. I flew across the room, my body lighter than air, and face-planted on the floor with a loud bone-jarring thud.

I winced at the rivers of pain streaming across my entire upper body and rolled onto my left hip. I blinked the stars out of my eyes, planted my hands firmly against my calves and sat up. The shadows lengthening through the house congealed into a horde of faceless white shadows that rose up from the floor, followed by a chorus of soft whispers that echoed off the walls.

They'd worn the same clothes they were wearing the last time I saw them. Ethan, the cute blonde guy and the heavyset man who were eviscerating each other at the party and Maureen and her two little girls.

Fear pinned me to the floor; my heart thudded. An alarm rang in the back of my head, urging me to run but my brain refused to register. Something crackled and popped; "White Room" by Cream burst from somewhere inside of the house. A seventh shadow floated across the room, wearing the same red tee-shirt and denim shorts he'd worn the night his curiosity got the better of him and landed next to Ethan.

"Come on, Mollie." Jared replied in a smooth velvety tone. "It's not as bad as you might think. Once you get over here, there are all kinds of fun things to do."

I swallowed the sour aftertaste burning the back of my throat and said, "You're not my cousin. My cousin died today."

"There's no need to fight it." said a deep masculine tone that might've brought the angriest of Vikings to tears.

In his breezy white blouse and dark-blue flares, Noah Larson floated across the living room, his nickel-plated eyes glinting. Maureen Butler floated beside of me, her long dark hair fluttering from the back of her head; the same wicked grin she wore when she pushed her little girl towards death spread across her face.

They weren't the source of the house's impenetrable evil, but their presence reminded me of what it was capable of; it used them to draw everyone into its evil grasp, including me.

He knelt down beside of Jared and raked his hand through his hair with fatherly love. The others floated above me in a swirling white halo like hungry vultures appraising my fear before the initial feeding.

"Some people just don't understand, Jared."

Jared shook his head. His shoulders slumped, he stared down at the floor as tears brimmed in his eyes.

"I was hoping she would." He pleaded. "I was really hoping she would finally come around to our level."

"She came here to destroy us."

Jared glanced at Larson then back to me. His milky-white eyes glistened with tears as his face wilted with sadness; it wasn't supposed to end like this.

Nothing like this at all.

"I really wanted to make her a part of the family."

"I know." Larson said to Jared, then said to me. "You've really disappointed everybody, Mollie. All we want is what is best for you and this is how you repay us."

"We love you, Mollie." The horde of phantoms softly wailed.

"I don't know what to do with you." Larson said in a sulking tone. "We've tried to welcome you into our circle and yet you refuse to join us."

"I guess," Maureen hissed. "we'll have to kill her. Won't we?"

A large wet hand reached out from the darkness and brushed across the back of my right hand. I flinched and scrambled back toward the big picture window facing the covered front porch. I glanced down at the puddle of gasoline pooling across the middle of the living room toward the far left corner of the house.

I groped my pockets, trying to remember which pocket I'd put them in but forgetting which one *exactly*. I snatched the box of matches out of my right pocket and slid the box open when I heard a protesting grimace in my left ear. Maureen bared her crooked black teeth in a wide angry grin, swooped down from the ceiling and slapped them out of my hand.

Before I could reach out to retrieve them, she seized my wrist in her right hand and stretched my arm high over my head like a piece of taffy. Her bitter cold grip pressing against my skin, I snatched a quick breath to combat the pain throbbing against my shoulder; a bone-deep paralysis locked me into place. She lowered her head, inching her face toward mine and inhaled until the pleasing scent of my misery filled her lungs.

I slipped my left hand into my pocket, withdrew a small red Bic and flicked my thumb across the wheel. A spark, followed by another then another. The phantoms broke from their flight path and swooped down from the ceiling to envelope me in a tidal wave of supernatural anger.

When something jabbed against my left rib, I dropped the lighter onto the floor. She tugged on my arm, spreading another river of pain down my entire upper body and laughed. I raked my thumb across the tip of the match I secretly retrieved from the floor and tossed it into the puddle of gasoline spread out across the floor behind them.

A carpet of bright-orange fire streaked across the living room and broke off into two separate paths, dragging a tail of light blue flame behind it. The first one struck the wall in the far right corner whilst the second struck the far left, spreading a blind-white flash that drew everyone's attention. The ghostly stick figures stopped in mid-flight, glanced at the wall of bright-orange flames and intense white heat rising through the house.

I jerked my wrist from Maureen's powerful grip and sat down hard enough to jar my teeth but not my senses. The phantoms scattered like a flock of birds in both flight and fight, their ghostly facades distorted by fear. I clamped my hand across my nose and mouth to block the thick tendrils of smoke permeating through the house; streaks of black smoke streaked the picture window facing the backyard and the sliding glass doors; a gaping maw of red-orange flame engulfed the curtain of colorful plastic beads draped across the bedroom doorway.

The oak paneled walls bubbled and popped; the sliding glass doors burst and sent a mist of jagged glass bursting through the living room. Through the haze of smoke drifting across my face, I watched the flames reduce the haunted symbol painted across the bedroom wall into a miasma of large brown blisters that popped and dissipated.

Iris hissed and floated toward the kitchen with Ethan trailing behind her until a gaping maw of flame rose up from beneath and swallowed them whole reducing them to nothing but bits of tiny black ash.

The two redheads, Daisy and Abbi danced around the house, their ghostly pale forms consumed by the flames within seconds and reduced them to ashes. The song playing in the back began to sound warbled as if the record player itself had caught fire as well.

When something plopped down in front of me like a sack of wet garbage, I jerked my hand back and clenched my fists together.

Jared crawled toward me on his stomach, his coarse brown hair and lower body ingested by a cocoon of bright orange flame. His eyes glinted with a mix of sadness, his chin bubbled and peeled away to reveal soft pockets of stringy red flesh and sinewy muscle that spilled out onto the floor and sizzled like bacon on a hot griddle. The look on his face said enough; it said he wished that he'd listened to me when I said we should've left this place behind and never looked back and now because we didn't we were the ones responsible for ringing the dinner bell.

As he fell to the floor in a fiery hulk of nothingness, Larson floated above the living room and watched in horror as his world burned down around him. His face twisted with anger, his stone-gray eyes flickered in the firelight.

"I would've given you everything you always wanted if you'd just–"

I heard the sound of shattered glass, threw my arms up and over my face and covered my head with both hands Pebbles of broken glass burst across the house, tumbled onto the floor and scratched the knuckles of my left hand.

Something thudded against the floor, luring my arms away from my face. A red brick flew across the living room, rolled across the floor, punched through Larson's ghostly form and struck the big picture window facing the backyard. When the glass burst, spewing onto the lawn, two cyclones of wind spewed into the house, stirring my hair and spreading the flames through the pocket of darkness swirling inside of the main foyer.

Something clutched the crown of my left shoulder and tried to lift me up from the floor. I slapped it away, spun around on my hands and knees and gazed through the broken window.

"Get the hell out of here." Dad said, hissing through tightly-clenched teeth.

I took his right hand, leaped over the windowsill and landed onto the porch. Tendrils of heat caressing the back of my neck, the cool summer breeze struck me hard across the face; the air seeped into my lungs and rebooted them like an old computer.

Larson floated toward me as a giant tongue of flame burst through the open window, snatched him in its bright orange grasp and jerked him back, plunging him into the fiery depths of the very Hell the house was borne from. We ran, our lungs gasping for air and fell onto the front lawn across the street.

I bent over and coughed until it hurt. We heard a cacophony of doors opening and closing as the neighbors rushed out of their homes, their sleepy-eyed gazes shifting from us to the burning house and back.

Sirens rose in the distance, crying like a pack of traumatized children.

"What the hell were you thinking?" He scowled, his face dripping with sweat.

"I didn't have a choice."

He coughed, blotted his hands against his jeans and chuckled. The sweet smell of pine-sap overriding the noxious stench of licorice seeped into my lungs with each breath I took, sealing the house's inevitable fate.

"You could've waited for me." He panted.

He slipped an arm around my shoulders when a loud splintery crash exploded from behind us. The roof had collapsed and tore apart, spewing devil tails of dust and towers of bright-orange fire toward the heavens as if it were lighting the way home for all of the innocent souls trapped inside.

DICE

When I was thirteen, I was first introduced to splatterpunk when my brother J.R. and I listened to Edward Bryant's story "While She Was Out" on audio. If you haven't read it, or heard it, you should; it's a fantastic story.

I was twenty-three when I delved into another visceral horror novel-Off Season by Jack Ketchum. When I was finished, I had to read more Ketchum and I did. Then I read Edward Lee and this story was born.

THE chains hung down from giant metal rings embedded into the ceiling and secured the hooks planted into her back, pulling the skin taught. Her feet dangling above the floor, the overhead light threw odd shadows across the wall; rivers of blood trickled down her back, buttocks and legs and dripped off onto the thick double carpet of blue plastic tarpaulin laid out across the floor. She sobbed, strands of long blonde hair clinging to her sweaty forehead and tried not to move for fear the hooks would pull away and rip her apart; a river of snot hung down from her right nostrils and clung to the corner of her thick bubble-gum pink lips.

Amidst all the pain streaking through her body, she thought how it all came to this point. She was sipping drinks and grinding up on any Tom, Dick and Harry that walked up to her on the dance floor at The Slippery Noose (or was it The Silvery Noose?). She couldn't remember because she hadn't taken a second glance at the sign over the bar's entrance when she first got there; she couldn't even see it when she and her date left long before Last Call.

By the way, who was that guy who to–

"Don't be afraid, Whitney."

She glanced upward in the direction from the voice had come and found a broad-shouldered man leaning back against the right side entryway of an open closet, his arms laced across his chest and his right foot braced onto the wall behind him. He shook his head, pushed himself away from the wall and moseyed across the room; the overhead light iced cryptic light patterns across the front of his apron which crinkled with each step he took. The straps from the goggles on his face hugged the sides of his egg-shaped head.

"Do you know what these are?" He said, sliding the back of his hand across her cheeks.

Something rattled inside of his fist rattled like broken teeth.

"I'll understand if you don't want to talk." He said. "I'd do the same thing if I were in your shoes."

"Why-ar-yu-doi-is?" She sobbed, her pleas warbled and distorted. "I love you, Anthony. I love you, baby. You know that, don't you?"

"Shhh!" He pressed a finger to his lips. "No, you don't. And neither did the others."

Others?, she thought as a chill traced her spine.

He rolled the dice inside of his left fist, held his hand up to his ears to listen to their sweet melodious rattle as if he could hear the ocean and lowered his hand back down by his side. He paced the room back and forth in slow unhurried steps like a teacher waiting for an answer. She heard the dice click inside of his fist and felt her body tingle with a mix of curiosity and fear.

"These are the keys to your fate." He knelt in front of her and set the dice in her right hand. "If you roll an odd number, you live. If you roll snake eyes, then you die."

She avoided the break-neck torrent of blood rushing toward her head and rolled the dice; her heart pounded as a noose of cold fear squeezed her throat. He retreated to a thin metal lever jutting out of the wall beside the closet door and felt a wide smile cut across the front of his fleshy oval face.

When the dice settled, she pumped at the air with her fists and screamed, "Seven! I rolled a seven."

He looked at her with sad basset-hound brown eyes. There were rules and then there were *his* rules. This was one of those times when the latter overrode the former.

"You have to let me go." She pleaded. "You said I could live if I rolled a—"

Without another word, Anthony flipped the switch and jerked the hooks out of Whitney's back, spraying blood across the room as chunks of soft pulpy flesh and frayed strips of skin clung to their curved metal tips. He sighed, watching with glee as her body plopped onto the floor–just like all of the others.

*****

"OKAY, Anthony." Dr. Robin Hammond said. "What do you see?"

"I'm walking toward third period class. Everyone is smiling at me as they pass me in the hallway and some of them are whispering to their friends while they're standing by their lockers. I stop by and kiss my girlfriend on the cheek while she takes her book out of her locker."

"Who is your girlfriend?"

"Amber Dunn. She's so beautiful she makes your heart skip a beat and she has long brown hair down to her shoulders and she's wearing a purple and white cheerleading uniform." He said and gave a small gasp. "Something squeezes my hips and then I feel air around my legs and when she looks back at me she points and starts laughing and pointing at my crotch."

"What happens next?"

"Everyone starts pointing and laughing. I look down and see my pants have been pulled down around my ankles and my dick's drooping down like a wind sock. Amber's still pointing and laughing when Scott Richards walks up and pushes me down onto the floor and then she kisses him on the lips but I'm pleading for her to stop but I'm sobbing and they're all pointing and laughing and pointing and laughing."

Anthony's left leg spasmed and jerked itself away from the couch in a spasmodic fit, kicking the glass of water he'd placed on the edge of table five minutes ago. It wobbled like a drunken dancer and tipped onto its side; a fresh puddle of water and jagged shards of broken glass spread across the floor. He sat up from the overstuffed orange couch sitting off to the left side of the room under thin white window blinds edged by the sun and flinched at the sound of shattered glass.

When the door flew open, Dr. Hammond's secretary Sydney walked into the room, her shrunken pale face twisted with disgust. She wore a light blue blouse, brown leather Doc Martens and a tight black skirt with fishnet stockings. Her fire-engine red hair was twisted into a wide fat bun fastened to the back of her head by a thin black stick.

"Be careful, Doc." She said, as the doctor knelt down to pick up the pieces. "You'll cut yourself."

"It's okay, Sydney."

"I'm so sorry, Doctor." Anthony pleaded. "I didn't—"

"You need to watch what you're doing."

"It's not his fault, Sydney." The good doctor replied in a soft tone. "Anthony's anger just got the better of him."

Sydney gathered the debris and stormed out of the room, shutting the door behind her. After Dr. Hammond sat down behind his desk, Anthony slumped back onto the couch, sweating profusely behind flushed-red cheeks. The dull gray sunlight poured through the V-shaped slit of the bright blue curtains; behind the thin black-iron railing sitting behind a pair of sliding glass doors, tall shaggy pines rose in the distance like gangly-green teeth ready to gnash at the sky.

"It seems like we're making progress."

Sighing as if he'd heard a bad joke, Anthony said, "You call that making progress? I could've hurt someone."

"From what you've shown me on the chart I asked you to make, the dreams are not as persistent as usual."

"Persistent?" He asked, confused.

"You're not having the dream as much as you did when you first came to see me."

"The pills are doing great."

"I thought so." The doctor said, brushing his hand across the air. "This is why I'm going to lower your dosage."

"Do you think that's okay?"

"Eventually I won't have to give them to you anymore." He said. "In due time, you'll be able to mingle in public just like everyone else."

"Let's not get ahead of ourselves, Doc."

Hammond scribbled something across a prescription pad, tore it off and handed it over. He led Anthony out of the office, wished him a nice day and waved him over to Sydney's desk to make his next appointment. After he slipped his prescription in his right pocket, he approached her desk.

"What?" She said, rolling her eyes.

"I need to make my next appointment."

She placed the headset on her desk beside of her monitor and tapped her fingers across the keyboard.

"I have the tenth of next month."

"I can't do that day I have to—"

"Okay, the tenth it is."

She clicked the mouse a few more times, scribbled across an appointment card and slid it over to him. Anthony took the card, slipped it into the same pocket as the prescription and flashed an angry confused stare at her; she ignored it and slipped the headset back onto to her bright curly-red hair and went back to talking. He shook off the heat from her gaze, thumbed the square white button with the black DOWN arrow and waited for the elevator to arrive.

Before the day that would stain him forever, Anthony could lure a woman like a paper clip to a magnet. Sydney, however, was immune to his cute boyish charms but he was always looking for a challenge. He tried his best to avoid her at any and all costs because he didn't want to cause any trouble between himself and Dr. Hammond.

After that terrible day in seventh grade, he became as compatible with a woman as the left shoe on the right foot. Internet dating was out of the question because then he could leave a breadcrumb behind that a blind man could find especially when someone had stumbled onto the missing women; speed-dating was non-negotiable because of the witnesses who could identify him. When he met Whitney last night, she was as easy as drunk girls got; he was less worried about getting into her pants and more about not killing her until he got her back to the house.

The events that unfolded at Logan Middle School fifteen years ago had left an indelible mark behind both mentally and physically. His brain projected the incident every second he felt Cupid's arrow flying toward him, filling him with an undying sense of betrayal he expected to see coming at any moment. The killing was his way out of ever committing to an honest relationship; at least he wouldn't be too bored.

Now that he was back inside of that corner of his brain that he loved to go into when no one was looking, he considered adding some music to his murders.

Why not? Would he go creepy fifties music like the stuff that Stephen King always put in his books or would he go with classic rock?

Whatever he planned to do, he hoped it wasn't that crap they were passing around like herpes and calling it "pop music". Half of the time, you couldn't understand a damn thing they were saying. He'd gotten a taste of that painful sounding shit two months ago before he met Whitney and just thinking about it now made his brain ache.

He shut himself down–if only for a little bit–and boarded the elevator. As the doors closed, Sydney leaned across the top of her desk and gave him the finger. He'd consider putting her on his list one day, then showing her a good place where she could stick that fucking thing.

He was halfway across the lobby when he stopped to gather a glob of hand sanitizer from the dispenser beside of the front doors and saw an old couple chatting with a middle-aged brunette in a dark blue business suit; the brunette and the old woman were seated on the edge of the couch sitting against the right side of the lobby. The brunette craned her head down to meet the woman's gaze as she massaged her hand smoothly across the back of the old woman's left shoulder. The old woman's husband sat in the chair beside of the couch, cradling her right hand in both of his and gave a sympathetic nod every time the brunette spoke.

"These things happen, Eleanor." The old man said kindly.

"He's always came home every night at ten o'clock." She stated, gripping a ball of tissue in her right fist. "The only thing I regret is letting him get that tattoo of his mother's name on his chest."

He rubbed the sanitizer into his palms, shook his head in amazement and exited the hospital through automatic sliding doors. He paced across the sidewalk bordering the front of the building, stepped down onto the pavement, walked between two cars and stopped to dig a speck of dried blood out of his fingernail. When he flicked it across the parking lot, an angry voice stopped him dead in his tracks.

"What the hell is your problem?"

His cheeks grew hot when a tall cherub-faced brunette pointed at the tiny black speck on the front of her strapless pink dress that he'd flicked off of his fingers not two second ago. The air grew thick, pressing down on him and all he wanted to do was run as far away from her as he possibly could. Instead, he fell back onto the pavement and stared up at her pale robust build molded nicely under her dress.

He took a napkin from his coat pocket–he always kept a supply of those on hand–and wiped the speck of blood from her dress. When he opened his mouth to apologize, he stopped in mid-sentence and felt his brows creasing with confusion. She sighed and scowled, her thin-fingered hand clutching the top of her brown leather purse; a network of bright blue veins streaked the tops of her swollen pale breasts like the lines on a road map.

He saw neither a Betty Boop lookalike but something else entirely different. The blue sky morphed into a plaster-white ceiling; the parking lot shifted into a rank of gunmetal-gray lockers and bright Formica floors; the vehicles in the lot became the students of Logan Middle School who enjoyed his mental demise at the hands of the upper echelon.

He stared down at the front of his jeans and saw that they were still in place, but the sound of their laughter gnawed at the marrow of his bones and tore at the threads of his soul. Something pushed on the top of his shoulder and snapped him out of his trance.

He scanned the parking lot and began the breathing exercises that Dr. Hammond had taught him. The nightmare faded, and the real world shifted back into its proper place; the laughter was replaced by the sounds of afternoon traffic and the odd tree shadows bleeding across the curbs.

Although the vision had ended, he felt himself slide back into that other part of his brain. It scrubbed the bright red blotches away from his cheeks and filled him with a malicious nirvana he hadn't felt since he left the elevator.

"Are you okay?"

"I'm sorry." He mumbled, checking his clothes for any rips or tears. "I don't usually act like this around a beautiful woman."

"What?" She blushed, pressing a hand against her chest. "You think I'm beautiful. My boyfriend tells me I look like a pig."

" Why would he say such a thing? He doesn't know what he's talking about."

A smile crawled up the right side of her mouth, spreading bright red dimples across her cheeks.

"Would it be okay if I asked you out?"

"I don't even know your name."

"My name's Anthony."

"Trisha. You know like the country singer." She extended her hand for him to shake. "I'm a tax—"

"I like country music, too." He flashed his best but fake smile.

They exchanged phone numbers and set a date for tonight at seven-thirty.

*****

THE date had gone off without a hitch. They chose a fancy Italian restaurant located on the north end of town nestled amongst a chain of shopping malls and other fancy restaurants. He chose a booth in the back for privacy and ordered the chicken parmesan while she chose the fettuccine Alfredo with stuffed crabs; he'd eaten until he was comfortably full and watched her eat like she hadn't ate in weeks.

He waited until she left to use the bathroom before dropping the pill into her Diet Coke. He slipped the empty pill packet into

71

his pocket just in time for her to slide back into the booth and smooth out the wrinkles in her dress; instead of the bright pink number she'd worn that day she chose a tight magenta-red dress with ruffled sleeves and a V-shaped slit that accentuated her breasts.

"Do you want to go back to my place for some coffee?"

"That sounds like a good idea to me."

He flashed a wink and she blushed from one cheek to the other. After she finished the stuffed crabs, her eyes became heavy-lidded and droopy. He flagged down the waitress to get her food to go and, amongst a field of glances from the other diners, carried her out to his car. He drove away from the heart of the city, tossed her food into a nearby dumpster and drove away with her face resting against the window, pressing her nose up into a wide piggish snout.

"Come one, come all." He mumbled jokingly under his breath. "See Trisha The Amazing Snoring Pig in her own habitat and awe in the wonders of her giant smelly ass."

It didn't take him long to get her back to his house but getting her in was a different story altogether. Instead of escorting her through the threshold like a newly-married couple, he dragged her into the house by her arms and shut the door before anyone saw him. He stripped off her clothes and shoes, tossed them into a black garbage bag and chucked it into the closet where he would remember to bury her along with it.

He considered using the hooks on her as he'd done with Whitney, but he was afraid she'd rip them out of the ceiling. He set her up inside of his latest contraption, leaned against the wall beside of the doorway and held the dice in his right fist.

When she opened her eyes, the mixed torrent of hot lucid tears, snail trails of snot and flop sweat glistened off of her big doughy face. She scanned the room until she finally saw him, her eyes shone with terror and brimming with tears. The straps of his latest contraption pressed against her body like a wrap dress with the sides slashed open, pockets of thick white flesh sagging over the side; a pins-and-needles sensation tingled across her arms.

"I damn near pulled a muscle getting your fat ass in here." He said. "Your boyfriend was right about you. You do look like a pig in that dress, but I was thinking more along the lines of a giant zit."

She closed her eyes and mumbled, her head flinching from each sob; a line of saliva and snot cascaded down the front of the rag stuffed into her mouth. She jerked her head around and fought to free herself from the straps but she eventually gave up and accepted her fate. He paced across the room, braced her shoulders in both hands and braced her shoulders in both hands.

"It'll only hurt if you fight it. This is what I call The Peeler. The straps hold you in an upright position and when I press a button you will start to spin and then the blades on both sides will slowly begin peeling you like an onion."

A sound of applause echoed in his ears like a television audience; they were praising him for a job well done. All of the hard work and years of preparation had now lead to this.

"If you roll an odd number and you get to live but if you— don't—you."

His awareness suddenly dulled down to a light-headedness.

A white light snapped across his vision; his eyelids grew heavy and listless. The room tilted to one side as his knees trembled uncontrollably until his body sunk to the floor. He rolled over and onto his back in time to gaze up and see her gnaw at the top of her wrist until she pinched something between her teeth and slid it out of the skin. She stuck the foreign object into the lock and picked at it until it snapped apart with a metallic clang.

She flung the straps away from her body, her skin still pale and sagging, and stepped out of the trap. The light glowing in the corner of the room traced the contours of her body as she stood over him, hands bunched up at her side.

"Sleep aids are for amateurs." She whispered and kicked him in the side of the head.

*****

WHEN he opened his eyes, he found himself inside of an old barn. Thick shafts of moonlight poured through the cracks in the walls, streaking the hay-strewn floor in bright bands of sickly-white neon.

The mingled odors of sweet-smelling oils, wood smoke and skunk piss stung his nostrils and stung the back of his throat. His arms had been pulled up high and over his head so that his feet dangled three inches above the floor. His head lolled around on his limp flaccid neck, dragging his chin back and forth across the middle of his chest.

The drug began to wear off and his eyes became more clear. The rope that bound his hands together dug a network of intersected lines into his skin.

"It'll only hurt if you fight it." A familiar voice bellowed from across the room.

Something clicked, filling the room with an explosion of harsh amber light.

Trisha sauntered toward him in nothing but a clear-plastic apron and a pair of goggles. A bright mischievous smile spread across her round pale face and her hips jutted out from the sides of the apron. He glanced down at the neatly shaven tuft of dark pubic hair between her thighs and failed to keep his cock from twitching. She approached an old dark-green blanket (the words PROPERTY OF U.S. ARMY stamped across the side in big block yellow letters) draped across a scarred wooden table and tossed it aside.

He felt his heart skip a beat when he glanced down at an array of knives, saws, a comb, a can of oil, two scalpels, a pair of shears, wire cutters, a small pair of scissors, tweezers, three different kinds of needles and a claw hammer.

"I've got to admit." She said, shifting her gaze from the needle to him. "You were much easier than the others."

"Others? What the fuck do you—"

She spun around on her heels, walked back to where she'd come from and flipped a switch on the wall. A string of recessed lights bursts open like frantic eyes, pouring discs of brass colored light onto the floor. He scanned the room, his mouth and skin quivering with fear, and stopped at the opposite side of the room.

A rank of floor-to-ceiling glass containers stood along the left-side wall with six motionless wax figures nestled inside. Some were cute, and some wouldn't have bagged a woman to stop a bullet. She'd placed them in a neat order amongst several different poses. The first one, a chiseled dark-haired freak, was dressed in a dark-red football uniform minus the helmet. The one after that wore a golfer's outfit but the last one had caught his attention: a medium-built man with pale skin and the name MELODY tattooed on his chest.

Chilled realization seeped into his bones, prickled his skin and raised the hairs along the back of his neck. They weren't wax figures at all; there was nothing waxy about them at all even if you were to count the golfer who'd obviously drowned his hair in too much hair gel. They were...were...

Actual men. From where he was standing, their ages had to be somewhere between mid-twenties to late thirties.

He then remembered she wasn't going toward the mental health facility that day but that she was running away from it because of whom she'd realized was in the waiting room. They would've remembered seeing her and put the kibosh on whatever this was; he wished they had.

The only thing I regret is letting him get that tattoo of his mother's name on his chest

"Look, Trisha." He pleaded. "I was just playing a—"

She pressed a finger to her lips, cutting him off.

"Do you know how long it takes to be a good taxidermist? A beginner like me must endure a lot of time and patience to make a person look more life-like. Sometimes you have to–"

"I thought you were a country singer." He said in a mewling voice.

"I'm a taxidermist." She said, then shrugged him off and continued. "Sometimes you have to freeze the specimen before removing the skin so it can be tanned and preserved for a later time. Then of course, there's removing all the organs like the liver, the kidneys and such."

She walked back, snatched a bright red bandana from the far right corner of the table, stuffed it between his lips; the knuckle of her middle finger on her left hand grazed the top row of teeth. She raised the scalpel, held it under the light and smiled when it winked back at her; it was like seeing an old friend. He felt his eyes bulge inside of their sockets and pulled on his restraints, tears streaming down his face.

"I'm going to start with your legs and then go up from there." She said, kneeling in front of him. "It's okay if you don't want to talk. I'd do the same if I were in your shoes.

WHEN YOU MARRY THE DAUGHTER

My mother and I went to a consignment store and I saw this strange painting of a tall skinny figure walking toward a dark dilapidated barn sitting at the end of a snow-covered meadow. I didn't know the metaphor behind it but it was a wicked fucking painting and I wished I'd bought it.

But I didn't.

The image still stayed with me though.

MY wife Laura kept bitching at me about the damn shed again today.

I told her I fixed the damn thing yesterday so there was no way it had to be done again. She says the walls are rattling and the roof was in bad shape. I love her to death but after seven years of marriage she can still push all the right buttons.

When she stepped in front of the television, she blocked my view of a breaking news report. The state police were still searching for the three college students who'd went missing while hiking through the woods along Lake Michelle last week. Laura and I never got the chance to be a parent but I couldn't imagine either one of us not going a little crazy over something like that.

"Get the fuck away from me."

"Not until you fix that fucking shed."

I can't stand that fucking shed; I hear noises coming out of there day and night and no matter how hard I try I can't ignore them. They've roused me out of a deep sleep a few times and once I'm up its hard for me to go back. For all I know it's the damn cats getting in the trash cans again. I'm not a chicken shit or a lazy person like Laura and her family like to think I am as but I know when I've done something and when I haven't.

I put in my nine-to-five just like everyone else. Don't I deserve to drink a beer and watch a football game?

I rolled my eyes and sighed, knowing that she would never shut up about it. I threw my hands in the air, leapt off the couch and slipped on my good camel-colored Carhartt jacket. I went to the garage to grab a hammer, a box of roofing nails, a half a box of shingles, my good aluminum ladder and closed the door on my way out.

When I stepped out and peered across the yard, the shed was veiled by the fallen snow. I peered through the curtain of whiteness beyond, rolled my eyes again and cursed under my breath. She was right, like all wives usually are.

My footsteps murmuring against the snow, I made my way toward the shed. I was halfway across the yard when I felt something roll under my right foot. My heart skipped a beat as I flung my arms out from my sides to steady myself; the supplies fell from my grasp and fell into the snow with a soft whispery thud.

My hammer went one way, the box of shingles the other and the box of roofing nails fell down by my feet. The ladder was nearly swallowed by the snow but the abnormal imprint it left behind told me it hadn't gone anywhere special.

I glanced down at my feet and cursed at the mess I'd made. I could still feel whatever it was under my foot so I knelt down to investigate. I brushed the snow away, the harsh cold air scratching my cheeks, and shifted my foot to the side.

I flinched, my body shaking with a mix of fear and shock, and looked away. I took a few deep breaths until I could gather the courage to look back down and plucked the severed finger from the jade-white snow. The stench of rotten flesh was overpowering;

the skin had been peeled back and the soft pink flesh underneath had been gnawed down to the bone.

I cringed, its very presence giving me a case of the heebie-jeebies, and tossed it into the thick green forest standing behind the shed like a backdrop in a feature film. I shook my head, winced through my teeth, blotted my hands across my thighs and retrieved my supplies.

When I reached the shed, I sighed and took note of all of the damage. The two slats on the right side flapped at half-mast like the flags above City Hall; a few shingles had been blown away, leaving a hole in the roof big enough for the wind to whistle through. A cold sense of dread twisted my stomach, churning my innards and made my throat feel raw and ragged; beads of sweat cascaded down my forehead, dampened the back of my head and neck and trailed down my cheeks only to freeze midway.

I took a hesitant step toward the right side of the shed and set to work. It took me more than ten minutes to nail the slats back into the place and replace the shingles on the roof when I heard a loud wet sound. I perked my ears to the wind and heard it again only this time it was coming from inside of the shed.

I slid down off the roof, dismounted the ladder and set all of my supplies off to one side. I dug my keyring out of my left pocket, unlatched the privacy lock and flung the door open. The wind rushed through the open doorway and sent spirals of snow whirling into the shed; it spun thick coppery demons around my face and stung my nostrils.

I stepped through the doorway, avoiding the long yellow extension cord that we'd run from the house. A series of low humming sounds came from the massive baseboard heaters hanging from the far right corners of the shed; bright red coils beamed like branding irons, spreading odd shadows across the hay-strewn floor.

"Well, well." A familiar but mocking voice replied. "It's about time your lazy ass came out here and did something."

"Good afternoon, Evelyn."

There are times when I can't even look at her. Her black hair fell across her massive pale shoulders like an opera curtain during intermission; her penetrating blue eyes pinned my feet to the ground.

After she ate the old couple next door, we decided to put her in the shed for safekeeping. She'd gone from a hundred and ninety pound bag of bones to a thousand pound slab of pale fat; her bruised purple skin was streaked with bright blue veins. Her fingernails were the color of the flesh she loved to consume; two teeth in the far right corner of her mouth went missing last week so Laura and I filed them down until they were sharp, jagged and just right.

The bodies of the three missing hikers hung upside down from the roof, their ankles cinched to a network of wooden rafters by thick bands of braided white rope; blood cascaded from the gaping red bite marks dotting their corpses and splattered across the hay-strewn floor. Her eyes still boring down on me, she plucked the left leg from a skinny ginger-haired woman like she were snapping the drumstick from a Christmas turkey. She gave a loud purring sound and sunk her sharp canine incisors deep into her pale waxy flesh and grounded the slick virginal (at least I thought) meat between her lips; a river of juice slid down across her mouth and dribbled off the tip of her chin.

"Can you shut the fucking door." She said between bites. "I'm freezing out here."

"You may want to be careful about where you spit your food out at."

"What the fuck are you–"

He told her about the severed finger he found in the yard. She nodded in agreement.

"Unless you wanted to watch," She said, still holding the dead girl's thick bloody leg in her right hand. "you might as well shut the fucking door."

They're right, you know.

When you marry the daughter, you marry her mother, too.

"Sorry." I said and did as she asked.

APARTMENT 13

A woman I once dated had a friendly upstairs neighbor who was always nice enough to greet us whenever we came back to her apartment. One day, when we realized he wasn't sitting out there, we found out through a family member that he died of cancer.

I wrote this story three weeks after his death as a reminder. Jeani Rector, editor of The Horror Zine was nice enough to pick it up for the November 2017 issue and include it in the anthology that soon followed.

THE smell wasn't just a nuisance but a reminder of what he kept putting off. He didn't know what to make of it but all he could think of was the smell of rotten eggs.

Rob Cross sat on the overstuffed couch, hissed through his teeth and gave a low grumbling sound. The pit of his stomach churned and a sharp bitter aftertaste collected in the back of his throat. An old college football game was playing across the flat screen, filling the apartment with the mixed chorus of cheers and jeers after a game-changing touchdown.

Earlier this morning, Linda had been quick to remind him about it after breakfast and their usual round of morning sex. She was standing in front of her polished-oak dresser, slipping a tiny blue earring into her left earlobe when she said something that diverted his attention away from a blue jay perched on a tree branch.

"What did you say, honey?" He'd asked.

She'd rolled her eyes and sighed. She buttoned the top two buttons on her floral-print scrub shirt and frowned at him in the reflection of the mirror above her dresser.

"I asked you to go upstairs and ask Mr. Flowers about that god-awful smell."

"Why don't we just call the landlord and—"

"I don't want to make a scene, honey. If he says it's nothing then we'll call the landlord."

"I'll do it." He'd said, climbing out of bed.

In the mirror above her dresser, she said, "Will you do it for me? Please?"

"I said I would, didn't I?"

"You said the very same thing last week and we were late for dinner with Tiffany and Mike."

"They're not even my friends." He'd said, plucking a pile of clothes from his dresser.

"Sorry I asked," She sighed, her lip twisted with anger. "I forgot how busy your schedule can get."

Her sarcasm stung him deeply. He bit down on his bottom lip to keep from saying something he'd regret later, carried his clothes into the bathroom and jumped in the shower. She didn't even leave him a "good morning" or even a "goodbye love you"; it was this-that-and out the door Pat.

He didn't ask to fall from a twenty-foot ladder and bounce his knee off the side of the company truck and be out of work for the past four months. If he had his way, he'd have been dressed and out the door so he wouldn't have to hear about it. He loathed being downgraded from "handyman" to "house husband" because it'd attributed to her anger when she realized she would be the primary breadwinner until he was fully rehabilitated.

They'd struggled over the years, especially when they were just a couple of fresh young faces working minimum wage just to make ends meet and when they thought things were getting worse they never gave up; ever since he got hurt it felt to him like Linda had a holier-than-thou attitude because she'd still had a job.

He hoped that wasn't the case. Beyond all the seething anger pumping through him, he still loved her with all of his heart because beneath that all of that arrogance was the woman he still loved.

How long as it been since we've had a date night?, he wondered. A bottle of red wine, a home cooked meal and a good movie is just what they needed to rekindle their marriage.

The noxious stench dragged him back down to its level and diverted his attention. He'd sniffed his fair share of chemicals in the past but none came close to smelling like this. He'd rather stick his head in a bucket of fresh tar than smell this godawful stench again; had he ever smelled like this after a job, he'd have to burn his clothes before he walked through the front door.

The microwave dinged, snapping him out of his reverie but he didn't feel hungry anymore. He inhaled the aroma of chicken flavored rice, snapped the lid back in place and slid the container back into the fridge. He grabbed two bottles of beer from the top shelf, plugged his cell phone in (fucking thing was never fully charged) and shut the front door on his way out.

Cliff View Apartments was an open H-shaped red-brick building with screened-in patios and a playground on the far end of the property. Neatly manicured hedges were rooted into tiny gravel beds spread out below each window; front porch additions varied from bird feeders to wind chimes and black-iron patio tables with matching chairs or both.

The carports out front were reserved for each tenant according to the number on their apartment; they lived in Apartment 14, so they parked in the spot marked as such.

"Good afternoon, Rob."

He stopped beside of the staircase and groaned at the sound of Carol Ebner's voice trailing after him. His shoulders slumped to hide the flustered look on his face, he turned and greeted her with his best fake smile. He raked a hand through his short dark hair, clapped his hands together and set them firmly against his crotch.

Her bedhead gray hair sticking up from her head in Medusa-like curls, she gave a kind and gentle smile and made her way over to him. She wore a bright blue jacket over a long floral-print dress, ankle-hugging socks and black shoes; the wheels of her walker whined as she skulked toward him.

"Hello, Carol."

"How are you doing?"

"I'm great thanks for asking." He nodded. "I haven't seen Gus in a few days so I thought I'd go up there and check on him."

"Thank God someone is." She said, then breathed a sigh of relief. "I've called him a hundred times about that god awful smell and he still hasn't called me back about it."

At least someone will get in trouble for, as Linda put it, make a scene.

"So you've talked to Gus since then?"

He hoped that she had so she could tell him it was nothing and he could go back inside and appease Linda's curiosity.

"I saw him about a week before the smell occurred. He came home from one of his night fishing trips and I was standing out here talking to the mailman. He had something cradled in his arm like a football but he had a blanket draped over it and he looked like he was in a rush. I asked him if he was okay and he said 'I'm fine. Mother just needs to be fed'."

Her words etched deep creases of confusion across Rob's forehead. Carol could spread gossip like a virus; a crazy unorthodox virus that made no sense whatsoever. Although they were pretending to be friendly, he and Linda had done their best to keep their distance so as to not get infected.

"Was that all he told you?"

She nodded. "I heard him arguing with someone last night at about ten o'clock. He kept saying something like 'I don't want to do it anymore please don't make me'."

"Do you think he was in some sort of danger?"

"I hope not." She said, "I would've called the cops by now but I didn't want to make a big stink about it. No pun intended."

They traded a few more pleasantries and went their separate ways.

He waited for her to wheel herself back into her apartment before he headed upstairs; the smell grew more intense the closer he got to Gus' front door. Something kicked up a loud racket from overhead that compressed his lungs with fear and he snatched a quick breath and clutched the twisted black-iron railing in a fierce white-knuckled grip. A blue jay burst from the roof like a pop-up ad and gave a loud squawk, stopping him just inches from the door.

He sighed, his body and his lungs relaxing as he scanned the promenade and watched the bird's shadow soar across the sidewalk like a floating crucifix. He shook off the smell riding on the sharp October breeze and walked up to Apartment 13. He pressed the bell with his free hand and waited for a response before he decided to knock.

"Are you okay, Gus?" He knocked. "It's Rob from—"

On the fifth knock, the door opened with a loud arthritic groan. He scanned the kitchen and waited for Gus to greet him before he stepped inside and set the beer bottles on the kitchen counter.

An overstuffed couch sat on the left across from a forty-two inch flat screen television (which displayed a news report showing policemen and doctors in lab coats combing the forest along a vast gray lake, the words SIGHTING AT LAKE MICHELLE stamped along the bottom of the screen). As with all the other apartments, the stainless-steel appliances were new and the countertop dropped off onto a small breakfast nook with two chairs. A horde of flies hovered above the nest of dishes cluttered inside the two-sided sink, buzzing softly in his ears.

Pebbles of broken glass were scattered across the middle of the living room between the couch and the television, glinting under a large patch of mute-gray sunlight. The breeze whistling through a fist-sized hole in the glass doors and sent the light-blue drapes into an hypnotic dance. His stomach knotted with fear, Rob toyed with the off-chance that he'd stumbled into a home invasion.

It still didn't explain the smell. He slid the collar of his tee-shirt up and over his mouth and nose to ward off the stench.

"Are you okay, man?"

He cursed under his breath, shut the door and marched down the hallway. When he reached the end of the corridor and peered into Gus' bedroom, he saw thin shafts of mute-gray sunlight pouring through the blinds; dust motes danced in the air as the smell began to thicken.

"Linda and I wanted—"

His heart lurching, he stopped in his tracks and clutched the doorway with hands like suction cups.

Gus was lying face up in bed in a white shirt and blue striped boxers, his body rigid and motionless. His eyes were closed but his lids gave involuntary twitches as if in a state of REM, his fingers twisting with the rise and fall of his chest. A series of deep breaths escaped his lips in tiny child-like snores that whistled through his nostrils; in the soft sunlight, his soft tan skin faded to a sickly-white pallor.

Something moved from under the front of Gus' tee shirt, poking through the fabric. When he approached the bed, Rob noticed a large pink tube protruding from the middle of Gus' stomach like a trachea; it drooped over the side of the bed and stretched toward the pocket of darkness on the far-left corner of the room. He squinted beyond the tube and, his heart thudding, felt his face and eyes widen under a mixture of fear and surprise.

The tube was connected to a giant vulva-pink egg hanging from a tiny pink thread embedded into the ceiling. It pulsated in rhythm with the tube as if it were lapping at whatever it was taking from him; a trellis of red and blue veins crept up the side of the cocoon before stopping at the crown.

Rob backed away from the bed and, lips quivering with fear, tripped over his right ankle. He gave a childish yelp as he sunk toward the floor and struck the carpet ass-first; the impact jarred his bones and bounced the back of his head off the floor like a basketball. Stars bursting across his vision, the sound of torn fabric rippled across the room.

He scowled at the dull ache growing in the back of his skull when something hugged his right foot; the pain sat him up and spread rivers of pressure up and down his leg. A long pink tube jutted from the bottom of the cocoon, stretched under the bed and began pulling him across the room.

There was no explanation for this; he waited for someone to come barraging out from behind a movie camera and tell him the truth behind all of this but all he could feel was pain, fear and the lingering tightness in his muscles. His brain conjured a snippet of conversation from earlier today, something that would (or could) make light of all this.

"...something cradled in his arm like a football but he had a blanket draped over it."

Then he remembered the news story and the men in the sharp white lab coats combing the lake for obviously whatever this was. And whatever it was, it wasn't human.

How could he have brought it here in the first place?

Couldn't he have just left it in the lake with all the other garbage?

Rob pulled his foot back, bending his knee and filled his ears with the sound of slow-tearing cartilage. He felt the tube sliding away from his ankle and waited for it to give away before kicking it across the room; his knee gave an ear-splitting tear, filling him with the undying need to scream. He rolled onto his stomach and crawled toward the bathroom when he felt something wrap around his left thigh and stop him in his tracks.

He hissed and yanked his left foot back but the tube held, pulling him farther and farther away. Before he could kick it away, the first tube made a second encore and wrapped around his right ankle.

If he could just reach the bathroom door, he could use it for leverage and free himself. He pulled his arms out from underneath him and slammed his body against the floor; air burst from his lungs as shockwaves of pain jarred his bones. He rolled onto his side and braced the doorway with both hands.

His fingers pressing into the wood, his stomach and sphincter clenched as he pulled himself into the bathroom. The same rotten egg smell coming from Gus' bedroom now seeped into Rob's clothes as he felt something burrow into his skin like a corded camera during a colonoscopy. His palms grew sweaty as his fingers began to slide off from the doorway one digit at a time.

He felt something (a third tube, obviously) cold and slimy slither across the contours of his spine and lash across the back of his head. He tried to shake off the pain and, reaching for the doorknob now glinting in the sunlight pouring through the bathroom window, gave a loud strangled cry as the darkness consumed him.

*****

"HE'S so hot." Linda Cross said, cell phone pressed against her ear. "He's a got a job with the state department and everything. He makes more money than the lump of shit I'm with now."

It was seven o'clock and she wanted nothing more than to kick off her purple scrubs and relax. The once soft gray sky now had the gas blue glow of dusk with a bright pink horizon; tree shadows bled across the promenade.

"Wasn't I right about him?"

The voice on the other end belonged to Linda's best friend and co-worker Tiffany Grant. They'd worked the emergency staff at Becker Memorial for five years; now they were about to become in-laws.

"He's that and much more." She whispered, her eyes darted around for witnesses. "After lunch we went to that motel on—"

When her fist slightly tapped the door, it creaked opened. She gritted her teeth, mumbled under her breath and slammed her fist against the side of her purse.

"What's going on?" Tiffany asked.

"He left the goddamn door unlocked. I swear sometimes I think his head is so far up his ass that all he sees is brown." She said and stepped inside. "I'll talk to you later."

"Take it easy, babe."

"You, too."

She killed the call and set her purse on the countertop next to Rob's I-Phone and called his name. After three tries, it dawned her that if he wasn't here, there was only one place he could still be. She slipped her cell phone into her pocket, noted the time on the oven and headed out and upstairs to Apartment 13.

NOTIFICATIONS

I'm not one to dabble in politics because that's my brother's job. At times, I just feel like it's one area that'll cause me more stress than I need or can afford.

When Donald Trump was elected, I was one of many who thought America didn't exactly have their "thinking caps" on. When I was a part of what I call "the social media trifecta"– Facebook, Twitter and Instagram–I couldn't believe the praise he was getting from everyone.

I still see it today and it amazes me that they'll go to great lengths to stick with him. I wrote this story because I can, because I want to and because if they're willing to do that then why should they stop there. Why not cut off a finger or maybe even a toe?

MY phone sits on the coffee table in front of me but it hasn't gone off yet. I'm waiting for my next notification but instead it just sits there like the space age piece of junk it was before I took it out of the box. I can't wait to get my next notification so I know what to do next.

As the song goes, waiting is the hardest part. I posted my last one ten minutes ago so why haven't I heard from anyone. Maybe they're just too busy to respond to it, running here and there doing this and doing that, living their own lives and—

Bullshit.

If they've got time to post their own shit then they've got time to respond to mine. They're just jealous that my selfies look better than theirs. They can try all they want to but my selfies will always be better than theirs; always.

Better luck next time, fuck tards.

Here's another one of me in the kitchen you can carry around in your pocket. It's a nice kitchen, huh? Oak cupboards, tiled countertop with nice stainless steel appliances; the place itself is in one of those red-brick apartment buildings that overlooks the city.

What the hell?

Oh, goodie!

I got one. I finally got one.

Actually, I got seven but it's not about my kitchen. It is about the tree standing in the back of the building at the edge of the hill; it stands before a pinkish blue sunset, its gnarled shadow stretching across the grass. It would make a good screen saver, that's for sure.

Hold on a minute.

AHHH!

AHHH!

There I'm back. I had to rip a branch from that tree and whip myself for seven minutes then upload my evidence. Long red scratches crease down my back like a one night stand; I even got deep enough to draw some blood.

It's how the app works.

You download the app, upload a selfie or a picture and then you base your next move on the amount of likes hence the tree branch and the number. It's no longer about self-pride and narcissism anymore; they don't care if you smile unless you were going to knock your own teeth out. It has always been like this since we elected our new President. If you didn't follow the rules, there was a stiff penalty.

I don't want to think about that but I'm sure it's bad. It gives me the creeps just thinking about it.

Oh well.

Coffee's done.

*****

I step out onto my front porch to grab the morning paper when something caught the corner of my eye. I scan the cluster of one and two story stucco and clapboard bungalows sitting on neatly-trimmed lawns when my neighbor Danny waves at me from across the street. I pick up the paper, wave back at him and then parade across my lawn.

"Hey, Danny."

"How are you doing, Trevor?"

"I'm waiting for my next notification." I say. "I got my first one this morning. It was a good one."

"The tree?"

I slip my left arm out of my sleeve and slide the side of the robe down to show him my back. He gives me a satisfying grin and a small round of applause; he is a tall portly-built man with a halo of brown hair around his big egg-shaped head and narrow blue eyes bracketed by a faint pocket of wrinkles. When I slip my robe back on, we shake hands like a couple of war buddies.

"President Trump would be proud of you, Trev." He says. "Really proud."

"I hope so. How's Melanie doing?"

"She's good." He nods. "She put the picture of that new bracelet I bought her last week and her phone has been blowing up all morning."

"Where did you get that?"

"Zeke's Diamonds and More." He says, flashing a proud smile. "She was grinding a paring knife into her right hand when I came out here to see where that little bastard stuck my paper this week."

"Cool."

"Hello, Trev."

I peer over my shoulder and see Melanie Landers slowly padding across the street; she is three inches taller than Danny and she has the silkiest mane of blonde hair I've ever seen. She cradles her right hand inside of a dirty dishcloth, her olive tan skin fading to a ghostly pallor. Cryptic blood stains spread across the fabric, and drip onto the front of her cotton-pink nightgown; the bigger stain resembling a poorly-painted strawberry.

"Hello, beautiful."

"I saw what you did to your back." She mumbles. "Good job with the branch."

"Thanks." I blush.

"Have you heard back from Tina?"

My throat locks up at the sound of that name. I hadn't thought about Tina since she chose to go to Mexico with everyone else who were displeased with the election.

"Not yet, Mel."

"I miss her so much." She murmurs. "She always made the best tuna noodle casserole."

"She sure did."

Melanie teeters toward the ground but not before Danny catches in his arms and cradles her tightly against him. Her cracked pale lips tremble as she stares down at the towel wrapped around her still bleeding hand.

"Let's get you inside and get you all bandaged up." He says, then nods to me. "I'll see you later, Trevor."

"Take it easy, guys."

I get back inside the house and put my still throbbing back to the door. It hurts but that is normal; I wince and accept the pain as much as the rest of the country. I carry the paper to the kitchen table and read the front page headline between bites of hickory-smoked bacon and scrambled eggs with toast.

MAN BURNS DOWN BUS KILLING TWENTY PASSENGERS blooms across the headline in big black font. According to the headline, the driver was taking a load of people to the border when he uploaded a picture of the bus and received over twenty likes. He had then parked the bus along the road, locked the doors on his way out and soaked the bus in gasoline before setting it on fire; he'd cut his throat before the law arrived to save anyone.

Serves them right.

Patriotism requires sacrifice; if you don't sacrifice anything for your country then you're not a patriot. I finish reading the article when it suddenly hits me from out of nowhere.

Where is *my* big sacrifice?

Those slashes on my back are just crumbs compared to what I've been seeing these days. Where's *my* fiery bus full of screaming people? Isn't *my* right hand good enough for me to cut into?

I'll have to up my game.

After breakfast of course.

*****

THERE we go.

A selfie of my left hand and another of my right foot. There is a mole on my left hand between my first finger and thumb but I don't know where it came from. I've had it since I was a kid but it isn't like I don't have plans for it; I've got *big* fucking plans for it.

I finish my work for the day (I'm a stay-at-home accountant for a number of local businesses) and flip on the television to watch the news. Glory be praised, our new President is standing tall and proud in front of a podium topped with microphones; rapid-fire camera flashes whip across the room and toss his shadow across the wall behind him for a split second before disappearing. His hair lays over his big head like a failed comb over but he looks like a dream in a charcoal-colored suit.

"I'm proud of the way things are going right now." He says in a deep monotone voice. "This country elected me to be their Leader and my people will continue to lead America in the right direction for years to come. I love the outpouring of responses to my new app. Keep them coming, America. Good day."

When he was asked about the bus driver, he shrugs and walks away amidst a barrage of more questions and camera flashes. I mute the television and let out a girlish shriek. I thumb down the volume, race into my bedroom to retrieve my cell and enter my pass code; my face glows in the glare of my phone.

No way; no fucking way.

Seven for my left hand and eight for my right foot; a woman I've known since high school compliments on my pinky toes. I thank her and like two of her recent uploads in return. I set my phone on the table, eat a quick lunch, gather my tool bag from the bottom of my closet and set it on the floor beside of the couch and slip off my right sock.

Before I can begin, my high school chum submits a pic of her own. She stands in front of her bathroom sink, a fist-sized hole in the big mirror with pieces of jagged glass jutting out from between her fingers like it were part of a glove she was looking for. Tears of blood cascade down her hand between her fingers and drip onto the floor.

She titles the pic: DO YOU LIKE?

I LOVE IT I respond.

I'll start with this one and then–

AHHH! OH MY GOD!

With my grandfather's pliers, the little nail on my right pinky toe slides away with ease. It always hurts the first time but that comes natural; sacrifice requires pain and without one you can't have the other. There's no need for me to scream anymore because it doesn't hurt so much.

I upload the evidence and wipe the blood from my toes. I perch my feet on the edge of the coffee table and lean back against the couch. My foot is still throbbing but otherwise I feel great and—

*****

THAT was a close one.

I don't know how long I was out but all I could think about is my wife Tina. She'd been walking toward a bus loaded with passengers when she'd turned and gave me a disgusted look; tears brimmed in her eyes as she stepped aboard. She'd made her way across the aisle, found a seat next to a window and pressed her hand against the glass as if she were visiting me in prison.

Maybe she thought the country had already turned into a prison or that it would if given enough time. As the bus gave a pneumatic wheeze, she flashed a sad glossy look and mumbled an "I love you" before the bus rode off into the night.

I'd woke up before I felt sorry for her. I hadn't thought about my poor "misguided" wife and I was okay about that.

I still miss all of the little things we used to do but I love my country and no one is going to tell me who I can and can't vote for. I do miss her and I wish she was here with me. Who knows what kind of damage we could've done together?

I reach over for my glass of sweet tea when I hear a car door outside. I push myself off the couch, hobble over to the kitchen sink and part the curtains with my right hand.

A trio of patrol cars sits idling outside of Danny's home, puffs of thin white smoke spewing from their tailpipes and dissipating above the curb; their roof lights sweep a bright patriotic halo across the faces of the nearby houses. Four police officers in crisp blue uniforms with shiny black-leather belts stands in front of them, waving their hands at him like drunk air-traffic controllers. Danny clasps his hands together and, his face crumpling with sadness, kneels onto the ground spouting a string of startled pleas; Melanie slowly extends her hand when one of the officers snatches it out of the air and pins it to the hood of his cruiser.

The same hand she supposedly hacked off this morning. How could she lie about something like that?

I grab my sweater off the back of the couch and hurry toward the front door as quick as one person can on one bad foot. When I step out of my house, their screams echo across the once quiet suburb; it does not take long for me to realize that I'm not the only one standing out on my front porch. One of the officers pin Danny to the big oak tree standing beside the mouth of the driveway by sticking his nightstick against the base of his throat.

"Don't do it officer, please." He pleads. "It was my idea take mine ins–"

"Sir." A tall bald bearded officer says. "Don't interfere or we'll have to restrain you."

"She knows the rules." The officer in charge says, holding her arm down on top of the hood. "She disguised her evidence and failed to comply with The President's orders. That's considered treason in The United States. She has to face a penalty, Mister Landers."

"Don't do it please. I'll pay whatever—"

Melanie tries to slip free of her captors but it was too late. The officer slips a stainless steel meat cleaver from his hip pocket, taps the right side of her hand and brings the blade down with such force it sounds like a boot being pulled from the muck. She cringes and gives a loud painful howl as her severed hand and a carpet of blood slide down across the hood; the officers release her into the custody of Danny and hop back into their cars.

"You fuckin' assholes!" He bellows.

While the cruisers speed away, she kneels onto the edge of the driveway and vomits on the asphalt. I wrap my arms around my chest, shielding my body from the cold January wind and watch my other neighbors retreat back inside. He stares at my house as if he wants to burn it down and helps her inside; from where I'm standing I hear her scream something at him and then a door slams shut.

I don't feel any compassion for them. They had not only betrayed their country but they betrayed me, too. They got what they deserve; if you don't follow the rules you have to pay the price. They need to consider themselves lucky those officers didn't shoot them in the head.

I go back inside and lock the front door behind me when my phone gives off a tiny chime. I race back inside to check it when the phone goes off again and again and again.

It's about my left hand.

Six notifications.

I stare down at my open tool bag sitting open on the floor beside the coffee table and remove a tiny claw hammer; no matter how many times I wrap and unwrap my hand around the handle, it feels like it belongs there. I tap the blunt end against the first finger of my left hand, set the hammer down and take another sip of sweet tea before I pick up the hammer again.

AHHH!

AHHH!

God Bless America.

RIGHTFUL PLACE

I know where I want to be when I die.
Who I want to be there in my last moments.
Do you?
That question alone was the inspiration for this story.

WHEN we stepped out of the trees and onto the sand, Nora and I drew the mingled odors of mud and rotting algae deep into our lungs. She licked her lips and tucked a long strand of blood-red hair behind her right ear, her pale freckled face creasing with joy.

"It looks as beautiful as ever." She said, her voice tinged with wonder.

I spun her around, planting my dark-blue sneakers into the soft brown sand, and slid my right arm around her waist. The sun warm on the back of our necks, I laid a soft kiss onto the crown of her forehead and peered deep into her almond-shaped green eyes; my lips tingled long after the kiss was done.

"Nothing in this world will ever be as beautiful as you."

She scoffed, rolled her eyes and waved me off. My daily compliments were just one of the many things she'd grown to tolerate during our seven-year marriage along with the fact that I couldn't sleep at night without the ceiling fan on at high speed. Tree shadows rippled across the faint, jagged line between the forest and the shoreline and spread out beneath our feet.

She extended her hand, her face still beaming in the warm golden sunlight, and sighed. I reached over for it, my eternal soul hungry for her touch, when she jerked it back. She raised her right leg, sending a thick curtain of hair falling across one side of her face and scratched at the inside of her thigh.

When she realized what she was doing, she lowered her leg back onto the shore and glanced up at me with a sheepish expression on her face. She slid her hand away from her leg and, her cheeks flushing with shame, swept the strand of hair away from her face. We glanced awkwardly at each other and did our best to forget about what she'd just done.

"It was the wind." She said, shrugging her left shoulder.

"Your underwear was rubbing up against your thigh, too."

"Yeah." She nodded.

I snatched her hand out of the air, brought it to my lips and kissed the knuckle on the third finger; her skin felt warm and tender on my dry, cracked lips. A single tear protruded from the corner of her left eye and slid down her cheek.

"Don't worry, baby." I whispered.

She nodded, her lips set in a crinkled red line. I wiped the tear from her cheek and slid my thumb down and across her mouth, coating her lips with the sweet taste of salt. She kissed the pad of my thumb, waited me for slide it down her chin and drew her lips back into her patent pearly-white smile I fell in love with so many years ago.

"I'm not," She mumbled. "because I'm here with you. That's all that matters, right?"

"Yeah." I nodded. "Forever and always."

"Forever and always."

We padded away from the tree line and across the shore, feeling the soft brown sand sinking beneath our feet. The aforementioned smells of mud and rotting algae were joined by the thick coppery odor of blood and the acidic tang of wood smoke. Pinpricks of sunlight bounced off the lake's mirrored blue surface; a carpet of light spread across the west side of the lake.

A pontoon boat with a large blood stain along the left aft floated past us, its frail green awning fluttering in the mid-afternoon breeze.

Orange-and-white buoys floated along the distance, bobbing with the rhythm of the water. One and two-story houses were sprinkled along the gently-sloping hills sitting on the other side of the lake, backed by large wooden decks of atypical size. The murky-brown water lapping at the shore stirred the veins of seaweed clinging to the sand; the only three cars in the parking lot on the far-left side sat blistered and cracked, their bumpers glinting under the harsh summer sun.

We marched across the shore, our lungs filled with the freshwater smells of the lake. On the far-right side, about a hundred feet away, a long-legged blonde lay cradled inside of a cheap bright-yellow volleyball net; large red stains were spread across the front of her crop-cut white tee-shirt, exposing her slim tan stomach.

I shook my head in disgust. There was no since in grieving over the things you can't change. What's done is done.

"What are you looking at?" Michelle asked, peering over my shoulder.

I braced her hips with both hands and spun her around so that her back was facing the dead blonde. She gave a startled gasp and pressed her hands onto my shoulders as if she were about to push me away. The V-shaped neckline of her shirt slid down, revealing the map of bright blue veins streaking across the tops of her perfect-white breasts.

"Is this it?"

I gazed across the water at the rank of buoys still floating in the distance and backed up about ten feet to the right. I hoped she wouldn't see the dead blonde behind her because the other dead bodies we'd seen along the way did nothing but sicken her. I caressed her bottom lip with my thumb and gazed deep into those green eyes I fell in love with so many years ago; they're the kind that could make a man's heart skip a beat.

"This is the perfect spot."

She feigned a smile and tucked a strand of fire-engine red hair behind her right ear. Behind her, the thin white-plastic supports holding the volleyball net jostled in the wind like weak supports.

My wristwatch said it was four-thirty. The sun wasn't supposed to go down for a few more hours but we still had plenty of things to do before tomorrow morning.

"I'm so tired, baby."

"I'll start the fire after you go to sleep."

"What about—"

"It's fine, baby." I reassured her. "We have plenty of time."

After we spread the blanket across the shore facing the third buoy on the right, we kicked off our sandals and stacked them on the left and right corners to keep it from being blown away. When I laid down and motioned for her to join me, she scanned me like I were a car she wanted when she was a teenager.

"Come on, honey."

She licked her cracked-white lips and stretched out beside of me. She curled herself inside the crick of my left arm, rested her hand on my shoulder and drew cryptic shapes across the front of my tee-shirt. Her skin felt warm, her hair fragrant with the smell of smoke and strawberries.

Most people thought that everything ended after the virus broke out but not us. All it did was make the world quiet and turn one street after the other into a junkyard hospital, a litter of disbanded cars and bloated gray bodies covered in jagged red cracks. In a time when the future looked as bright as the screen of an I-Pod, it'd become nothing more than fossils of a world that once was and never would be.

We'd combed too many broken cities in too many broken days. We'd fought with every fiber of our being to hold back tears whilst inhaling the stench of motor oil, decaying flesh and hot sticky blood just to get here.

She fell asleep ten minutes later. I slid away from her and rolled her onto her left hip. I sat with my knees drawn up against my chest, wondering what she was dreaming about now that everyone was dead.

I waited until the sky had that bottle-gas blue glow of dusk before I started the fire. The houses on the other side of the lake looked as black and lifeless as everything else but still managed to be magical in their own little way. The flames danced in the darkness, throwing pools of incandescent orange light across the mirrored black surface of the water.

The flames reminded me of a time in my life I'll never forget for as long as I live.

At least it'll keep me company.

*****

I'd never been so nervous before in my life; I didn't think high school graduation was this bad.

I stood at the bottom of the hill below the parking lot and waited. We'd scheduled a picnic on two separate occasions, but with me working it was always hard for me to keep my promises. She respected that, never once held it against me whenever we argued, and I loved her even more because of that.

I felt the apprehension squeezing the back of my neck. My stomach twisted into tight coils of nervousness that churned the three-course breakfast my mother rammed down my stomach. A film of sweat broke out across my forehead, slid down my temples and cheeks and dampened the back of my head.

Michelle collected the picnic basket from the back of my truck and shuffled down the hill in her wicker-brown open-toed sandals. She wore a pair of blue-jean cutoffs that accentuated the little dimples on her ass; her dark-brown areolas strained against the front of her gauzy-white tee shirt. Her bright red hair fell from a part in the top of her head, cascaded down the crowns of her shoulders and billowed in the breeze.

I haven't stopped smiling since we first met, and I don't I want to. There wasn't anything I could give her in return for all the joy and happiness she'd given me. She was the kind of woman who helped you wipe away the foolishness of your past like the steam after a hot shower and still love the person she saw in the mirror; today, as with all days, her bright affectionate smile nearly brought tears to my eyes.

When she finally caught up to me, I caught a whiff of her vanilla-scented perfume and felt my heart stutter inside of my chest. Her eyes sparkling like a church mosaic, she stepped out of the shade, her white skin beaming under the sun.

"Whatcha thinking about, cutie pie?"

"I'm thinking about how beautiful you are."

"Are you hungry?"

"I'm starving."

She winked, flashed her patent pearly-white smile and then jabbed me in the belly with her right fist. I grunted, wrapped my arms around my stomach and doubled over just enough to let her know I was going along with the joke. She giggled and ran across the shore, her tee-shirt fluttering in the breeze like a flag in a lazy current.

"Then you better come and get me, sexy man." She screamed, her voice trailing out behind her.

I pawed at my right pocket and felt a slight jab in the middle of my hand. I didn't want to tell her the truth about why I'd been working overtime at my father's lumber yard for the past six months. The picnic had been planned for days but my next move would last a lifetime.

The lake was located three miles northwest outside of Lancaster along Kenneth Road. A mixed stand of shaggy pines and leafy oaks ran parallel along a wide lip of soft-brown sand that could tell just as much stories as the walls of a person's house. When people weren't swimming here during the summer months, this had been a haven for bonfires and unplanned pregnancies.

I pivoted on my heels and ran after her. She got halfway across the shore, giggling like a schoolgirl as the contents shuffled softly around the inside of her picnic basket. I wrapped my arms around her waist, spun her in the air and set her back down.

I held her against me, the wind rising around us and slid the back of my hand down her right cheek. She purred, resting her head against my right shoulder and branched her left arm around my hip.

"I love you."

"I love you more." I brushed a strand of hair from her forehead.

"I don't think so."

"Oh, really?"

"Yeah." She nodded, caressing my beard. "I'll always love you more."

"We'll call it a draw."

We kissed, our tongues swabbing inside the juicy-red caverns of our mouths and knelt onto the sand. My body flooding with both panic and desire, I slid my hands up her stomach and cupped her breasts; my thumbs slid across her stubby-brown nipples. When we broke the kiss, I slipped my arms back around her and gazed deeply in her eyes.

"I can't begin to tell you what this year has meant to me." I said, cupping her chin inside my thumb and forefinger. *"I never knew happiness until I saw you. I've never been able to wear my heart on my sleeve so I could show you how much you make it beat and how much you make it glow. I never knew what real love was until I first laid eyes on you because no one else in this world will ever make me as happy-"*

She pressed her finger against my mouth, cutting me off in mid-sentence. The wind caressed the back of my neck and traced the contours of my spine, rooting my knees to the sand.

"All you have to do is keep loving me like you are now." She said, sliding the back of her right hand against my cheek. *"That's all you have to-"*

She clamped her hands around my face and sighed. I slid my hand out of my right pocket, opened the small red-felt box with my free hand and held the ring out for her to see. A thin gold band with a double-sided diamond mashed together to resemble her favorite symbol: the infinity sign.

There wasn't a day that hadn't gone by where she wasn't drawing that symbol. In the film of fog that covered my passenger window during a rainstorm two months ago when my truck broke down out on Red Possum Road; in the stacks of notebooks she kept inside of the cardboard box sitting under her desk in the far-left corner of her bedroom; on a few neatly painted canvases hanging on the walls of my little apartment above my parents' garage.

Her face lit up and her eyes sparkled in the afternoon sunlight. She gave a strangled cry and clamped her hand over her mouth to stifle a second. Tears ran down her beet-red cheeks and dripped off the edges of her jawlines.

A spring of bright red hair fell across her forehead above her right eye. She slipped her trembling hands away from her face and pressed them against her chest in a mock prayer.

"Will you make me the-"

When she nodded, craned her head to the sky and shrieked a resounding *"YES!"*, a renewed energy burst through my body like the first shot of caffeine. As she stared down at me, her face creased by a wide delightful smile, I jerked my head back, pumped my free hand at the air and wrapped her in my arms. After I

******

Something snapped, stirring me out of a deep sleep. I sat up, my skin prickling with fear, and scanned the lake with wide panic-stricken eyes. My body stiffening, I gasped and clutched the blanket in two bony-white fists.

When I glanced back to my right, I saw the posts that supported the volleyball net lying shattered across the sand. The net wrapped around the dead blonde's body as if she were drunkenly posing for a shot in an issue of Sports Illustrated. Her arms were lying across the sand in a mock surrender and her legs were bent at the knees; her tiny pale hands were curled at the knuckles, burying her nails deep into her palms.

I yawned, worked the edge of my hands against my eyes until they were clear and then stretched until my limbs hurt. I winced at the film of cotton coating my tongue, rolled onto my stomach and pushed myself up on my feet. I scanned the forest we'd come out of nine hours ago and inhaled the rich scent of pine sap deep into my lungs.

The wind sighed through the trees like a frustrated child. A bird shrieked and flew across my line of sight, its crucifix shadow floating across the surface of the lake.

Michelle was still asleep, the corner of her mouth glistening under a fresh coat of saliva sliding out from between her lips. I skulked away from the blanket and padded across shore. Limp arms of glistening green seaweed clung to a few sporadic patches of sand, soaking it under their grasp; a sunfish flopped crazily along the shoreline, its gray-yellow scales glinting under the diminishing sunlight.

I slid the collar of my tee-shirt up and across my nose and knelt down beside the dead girl's body. My heart twitched under a mix of dread and disgust. I couldn't stand to see her lying here, baking under the sun's once harsh-white hundred-degree heat, smelling like something that'd just...well died.

I bet her friends didn't even help her.

I bet she couldn't even call her parents to tell them that she loved them because they'd probably died long before she did.

So young and yet so dead.

I tucked her hands together and rested them gently against her inner thigh and then wrapped the rest of the net around her entire body. I buried my heels into the sand, pressed my hands against her waist to roll her into the water when something shifted inside the net. I jerked back and squeezed my fists together, pushing my fingernails deep into the middle of my palms until my knuckles turned white.

I rolled the dead girl onto her back and began to pat her down. When I reached the waistband of her shorts, a pale thin-fingered hand rose up through the net and snatched my wrist out of the air. An icy chill sliced across my hand and coiled around my arm, prickling my skin with cold unbiased fear.

I snatched a quick breath, beads of sweat cascading down my temples and cheeks, and tried to jerk my wrist free. Something shifted in the corner of my right eye, drawing my attention away from its unearthly grasp. The blonde woman was sitting straight up, her lips drawn up into a lopsided grin exposing two rows of jagged black teeth; her eyes had a milky-white pallor and her skin was teeming with tiny red cracks.

Her face creased by eerie fascination, she gave a hearty chuckle and tipped her head back. Her grin spread wider now, exposing rotting gums to go with her still-rotting teeth.

"It's still suicide, baby." She said in a slow gravelly voice.

I wasn't sure what she'd said so I waited for her to repeat it again.

When she did, I said, "No it isn't."

"What the fuck was I thinking? I couldn't serve food at The Quaker Benefit back home in Chauncey so then why the fuck am I playing volleyball?" She said, staring down at herself.

I didn't have an answer to that and I never would.

She leaned back on her right elbow, planting her hip into the sand and bent her left leg before sliding it up against her inner thigh. She brought her left hand up to her mouth, curled her palm together into a half-fist and bit down on the middle of her pinky. The hungry erotic expression on her face was pure evidence that in all of this confusion, under all these extreme temperatures, my mind had taken the train to Crazy Town; it was probably the goddamn conductor.

"Don't you want a slice?" She said, baring that same black grin. "Just for old time's sake."

I ignored her demonic pleas for necrophilia, dug my heels deep into the sand and rolled her across the water's edge and into the lake, kicking peals of sand out from behind me. I lost my footing, cursed under my breath, held my arms up and across my face and fell onto the sand.

"I would've been the best thing you ever had." She growled. "The best thing you ever–"

I stood, brushed the sand off of my shorts and watched her body float across the lake, her tightly-wound cocoon cleaving a V-shaped tail across the water's murky brown surface. Three minutes later, she sank out of sight, spreading a reflective scatter of tiny crystalline bubbles in her wake. An ear one minute, her hair the next and then nothing.

Nothing more than a casualty of a biochemical whoopsie-daisy created by Uncle Sam.

I walked back to the blanket and stared out at the same spot where the girl had sunk and fought back against the ball of sadness swirling inside of my chest. A fresh set of tears obscured my vision and my cheeks grew hot. I heard a soft groaning sound from behind me and quickly swiped the back of my hand across my eyes to wipe the tears away before Michelle could see.

"Take a picture it'll last longer."

She looked up at me from the blanket, drew a sly smile across the corner of her lips and cocked an eyebrow at me. She yawned, pushed herself up and crawled toward me like a frisky feline, her apple-bottom ass emphasized by the blood-orange sun. We kissed each other with lips as dry and cracked as an old sidewalk and gazed deeply into each other's eyes.

"Are you hungry?"

"The last time you asked me that you poked me in the gut and took off."

"I don't think I'll be going anywhere this time."

She brushed a strand of hair from her face and leaned in for another kiss. I broke the kiss, cupped her left cheek in an L that I'd fashioned out of my right hand and brushed my thumb across the tip of her chin; her skin felt cool and waxy in the sunlight.

"I couldn't pass up the chance for one last kiss."

"It's not your last." I reminded her. "We'll have plenty more where we're going."

My watch beeped. We stood up, shed our clothes save for our underpants and placed them in a pile in the middle of the blanket. We glanced awkwardly at each other and scanned the tiny red blotches spreading across our skin.

At first, they'd started along her inner thigh and spread down across her knees. In the time I'd take for us to reach Kenneth Lake, they'd crawled up my arms and across my chest.

"How do you want to do it?"

"Just like we said we would." I nodded. "Did you have another idea?"

"Not really."

"I'm always open to–"

Needles of pain jabbed deep into the pit of my stomach and doubled me over. I cradled my gut in both arms and, my throat and lungs burning, spewed a tiny puddle of blood onto the sand. Through the film of hot tears blurring my vision, I raised my hand, fingers spaced evenly apart and motioned for her to stay away.

When I was finished, I wiped the tears from my eyes with the back of my hand and brushed a mound of sand over the puddle. She'd been wiping her own tears away by the time I'd finished composing myself.

I sat back down on the blanket, the fire in my throat losing its sharpness, and gazed up at my soon-to-be dead wife. She sat next to me Indian-style, slipped her right arm around the back of my neck and placed her hand on my right shoulder. When she rested her head on my left shoulder, I slipped my left arm across her lower back and cradled her left hip.

I caught a whiff of her strawberry perfume and felt my skin prickle with joy. It filled my nostrils, reminding me of all the "stops" we'd made along the metaphorical road of Life that made us stronger like it always would considering what we'd endured: two miscarriages, three unexpected deaths, a house we would never own and seven anniversaries.

We could've died anywhere we wanted to, but we chose to die here where our love flourished and our life began. Where we'd ripped our hearts out from our chests and handed them to one another, knowing they would care for it as if it were their own.

Although it wouldn't end the way we would've liked, I hope this letter reminds us that in our last moments of living, love always triumphs over death.

IN LAUDAMUS JACK

I'd never written a Halloween story, although it is my favorite time of the year.

I was browsing through the Internet for a good wallpaper for my computer when I came across an image that stayed with me for a long time-well, two months is a long time.

I wanted to express how much Halloween means to us "Halloweenites". I think I'll do a Christmas story next time.

HIS boots clopping along the rough gray asphalt, Chad Hanson wiped a film of sweat from his brow with his left forearm when he saw the bleached-wooden church sign standing along the shoulder of the road. The words WELCOME TO WALPURGIS had been scrawled across the middle in a spangly golden font; the phrase JACK IN LAUDAMUS was scrawled three inches below. He snorted, praying that he wasn't about to venture into the same town from the movie *Footloose,* massaged his chin with his left hand and gave it a dismissive shrug.

He shook his head, jerked the strap of his black North Face daypack further up onto his left shoulder and sighed. He inhaled the pungent aromas of wood smoke and pine sap deep into his lungs and sauntered past the sign. He raked his right hand through his short reddish-brown hair, stuffed his hands deep into his front pockets and strolled away from the sign, his backpack (and the contents inside) shuffling across the middle of his back.

A sharp autumn breeze roused the treetops and sent burnt-orange leaves dancing like drunken cheerleaders; tree shadows inched their way across the road, streaking the pebbly gray shoulder with odd cryptic fingers. The faint-purple sky and the red-orange treetops below looked pleasant and magical to any adolescent eye; it spoke of quiet nights sipping hot chocolate in the company of a crackling fire.

He followed the main road into town, a cookie-cutter stretch of one and two-story stucco and clapboard houses sitting on postage-stamp lawns surrounded by white picket fences laced with orange and black streamers; something out of The Saturday Evening Post. Some houses were brightly decorated with cardboard cutout of ghosts and green-faced witches with crooked boil-covered noses, dark Styrofoam tombstones with gimmicky names (he chuckled at the one aptly named BEN DEAD) and gap-toothed jack o'lanterns with blazing orange eyes. He spotted a few bright colorful inflatables that made their front lawns look like a car dealership; one depicted a witch grinning eerily from behind a bubbly black caldron or a cluster of tombstones surrounded by old-fashioned ghosts in long white gowns with wide haunted faces.

Long paper-white banners were strung above the street proclaiming little greetings like HAPPY HALLOWEEN and other enthusiastic greetings in a dripping black font. He was halfway across the block when he expected the next one to say something else closely resembling that but instead what he saw was DON'T FORGET ABOUT JACK. He gave a confused sigh, shook his head, cupped his right hand around the right strap of his daypack and considered asking someone for a ride but he hadn't seen a single vehicle in sight; not a car or truck anywhere.

He watched the children parade across town dressed as ghosts, witches, ghouls, horror-movie slashers, comic-book heroes and villains and zombies only to stop and compare their loot with the other kids before bursting off toward the next house. Their parents gave chase, dressed in sweaters and jeans and boots, the expressions on their faces shifting from bright-eyed ecstasy to a heavy-lidded exhaustion.

Small snippets of conversation floated around him as he walked by each person.

"...to wait for me." A young girl of about thirteen said to a little bald boy in a bloody doctor's uniform.

"...the ones they give us at school." said a short heavyset kid walking alongside his father in a vampire's costume.

"...and you won't get any. Do you understand?" said the scornful voice of a young brunette kneeling in front of a sniveling little boy dressed as a foot soldier.

Of course, it was Halloween. In all the confusion brought on by his own self-inflicted wounds, there were plenty of reasons for him to forget. The mingled expressions of joy and wonder on the children's faces filled him with a lingering sense of nostalgia.

He knew those days were long gone but he still treasured them. On the other hand, he felt a little sad for these children as well. Sooner or later, the roles would switch then *they'd* be the ones chasing *their* children across town; another recycled fact brought to you by the kind folks who brought you Life.

He caught a few curious glances from other residents who passed out candy from the confines of their front porches and gave them a hospitable smirk followed by a gentle nod. An overweight redhead and a plump dark-haired boy were sitting on the front porch of a brown stucco bungalow passing out candy to a group of children when he saw it. An ancient memory resurfaced from his childhood and just the thought of it filled him with a dominant glee that was too strong for him to ignore.

A fat pumpkin with a jagged toothy grin sat perched on the edge of their fence where it and the main gate met, gazing across the street with round orange eyes. When Chad approached the fence, he swung his right hand in a whistling arc and slapped the left side of the jack o' lantern. It spun, wobbled end over end like a Jell-O mold and toppled face-down onto the sidewalk. It burst apart, spilling its pulpy orange innards across the asphalt; the brightly-lit candle that was placed inside of it died with a quick angry hiss.

He greeted them with a mischievous grin, followed by a mock salute and sauntered away, chuckling under his breath. He didn't hear what the ugly bat or her even uglier son had to say because he'd never cared then and he wouldn't care now. As a child, Chad

had earned his degree in "bullying" and wasn't afraid to show it; nothing was off limits when it came to what he wanted and there were plenty of kids who knew the penalty if he didn't get it. It was the whole reason he'd been kicked out of college in the first place and now he'd get to ply his trade once he got back home.

He reached the end of the block and stopped at the mouth of a four-way street crowded with other residents passing pleasantries with their neighbors before being dragged away by their sugar-induced offspring. He squinted past the crowd, their voices rising and falling amongst the gentle whisper of the breeze when a nearby voice rose from behind his left shoulder.

"...that same ratty black jacket that he wore last year."

He peered over his shoulder and saw two women marching across the street; they looked to be in their mid-twenties or so he hoped. The blonde wore a knee-length black skirt, knee-high brown leather boots and a checkered gray vest over a white blouse. Her friend, a striking brunette, wore a blue cotton sweater with a pair of denim jeans and hiking boots; she was way cuter than her bleached blonde companion.

They looked and acted more like college students than high school seniors. If he were back at college, he would've turned on the charm for sure.

"Excuse me, ladies." He said, raising his right hand. "I seem to be a little lost. I was—"

"You're not lost." The blonde nodded, her cheeks blushing. "You're in the right place at the right time."

"I'm on my way to Cincinnati."

"You've got plenty of time to get there." The brunette said. "Why don't you stick around for the big festival tonight. Everyone's going to be there."

"Stop it, Lacey." The blonde slapped her friend playfully on the shoulder. "We don't even know—"

Before she could finish, he introduced himself. They shook hands one at a time, first the blonde and then the girl named Lacey; the blonde introduced herself as Teagan.

"Are you new in town?"

"No, I'm just passing through."

"Did you go to college?"

"Yeah." He said uncomfortably.

"Why don't you stick around?" Lacey pleaded. "Jack would love to see a fresh face in the crowd tonight."

"Is he the mayor or something?"

They glanced at each other, their faces flushed from restrained excitement, and giggled. The cute maniacal sound of laughter made Chad feel distant and a little uneasy.

"Lacey is playing her flute this year." Teagan stated, her lips drawn up into a supportive grin. "I tried to play my banjo but it didn't go too well."

They took each other's hands, stepped around him and walked toward the west side of town. When he thought he'd never see them again, they stopped beside of the curb, turned and peered over their shoulders. Their pearly white smiles stretched across their faces and the small twinkle in their eyes told him he hadn't been the only victim of their young and suggestive beauty.

"If you decide to come by tonight," Teagan said, then snuck a glance at Lacy. "we'll make you feel really comfortable."

She winked at him and followed her friend down the street until they were consumed by the crowd. He glanced at Lacey's apple-bottom ass jutting out from beneath her skirt and lost the battle with his inner urges. His stomach gave a low guttural growl, reminding him that he hadn't ate anything since back at that truck stop in Haydenville seven hours ago.

He slipped his free hand into the inner pocket of his brown-leather bomber jacket and checked the time on his I-Phone. It was five after seven and the sky was beginning to darken; no stars but he could see the faint impression of a cuticle-white moon floating high above.

He scanned his surroundings and noticed a little Mom and Pop sitting at the same end of the street where Teagan and Lacey had gone. He hadn't seen a McDonalds or any other greasy spoon since he'd left the highway, so his options were slim. He couldn't wait until he got back to Cincinnati, although his parents would be as mad as Republicans, and get a good home-cooked meal.

The street lights gave a low hum, flickered and spread a fresh cone of sodium-purple light onto the crowd. Shadows lengthened across the curbs and sidewalks, each one reminding Chad of the same army of rats that once marched to the hypnotic chorus of The Pied Piper's flute.

He slipped his cell phone back into his pocket and gazed up at a third banner strung high above the end of the street. In the same dripping black font, it said JACK LOVES US ALL.

Who the hell was this guy?

Was he the town founder, alas Christopher Columbus? He hadn't even met the guy and he was tired of hearing about him.

He hadn't been in this town but ten minutes and he was already begging to put it as far behind him as humanly possible. From where he was standing, the only way back out of town was in the same direction that Teagan and Lacey had gone but even that was a risk. He could always grab a bite to eat (Lord knows he could pretend that "chicken-fried steak" was not someone's dead cat for once in his life) hit the highway and thumb another ride.

He scanned the small cluster of two-story stucco houses flanking the curbs, stepped over the curb and weaved his way through the crowd. The sea of faces shuffling past him were nothing more than psychotropic blurs, their expressions varying between delight and annoyance or both. Once he cleared the crowd, he shook his head and breathed a sigh of relief as the sharp October wind slid its cool tranquil fingers gently down the back of his neck.

The street stretched across the front of a low-slung aluminum-sided building before veering around a tall tree-choked hill; WALPURGIS FIRE DEPT. was stenciled in wood-burnt letters across a large wooden sign posted on the far right corner of the lot. Relief washed over him as he glanced toward the horizon and saw the necklace of tiny headlights floating across the interstate lying off in the east. He stopped underneath a pair of street lamps bathing the left curb above a gleaming metal Airstream trailer that'd been fashioned out into a small café, its windows fitted with lighted clocks and friendly greetings; a blue neon sign fixed to the far right side of the building said PETEY'S; IF YOU MENTION JACK, YOU'LL GET A TWENTY PERCENT DISCOUNT ON YOUR NEXT MEAL was drawn across a large slick-white banner hung across the crown of the Airstream about three inches above the front door.

He sighed, shook his head and felt his stomach clench like an angry fist. *I'd rather eat jack shit then hear another word about this guy one more fucking time*, he thought.

He knew better than to have gotten off the highway in the first place; he should have taken the truck driver's offer to take him the rest of the way. He'd rather take Lacey and Teagan up on their offer to "make him feel really comfortable" rather than see Jack do anything. He'd never done a threesome (although most of the co-eds back in college were easy after six beers) but there was a first for everything.

When he reached the front of the firehouse, Chad spotted Teagan and Lacey standing between two middle-aged men in street clothes and thick jackets. The man on Teagan's left had a tall spindly frame, bowl-cut black hair, and a thick porn-star mustache. The man on Lacey's right had a big barrel chest, short blond hair and puppy-dog brown eyes set inside of a stone-chiseled face.

They were huddled together, their shadows eclipsing four plump bright-orange pumpkins sitting evenly across the middle of a long gray Formica table. A tall broad-shouldered man in a crisp khaki sheriff's uniform leaned forward, bracing the tabletop with both hands and gave both men a steely-eyed gaze.

"We've got to remember, Robert." The sheriff said to the dark-haired man. "We've got to set these down just right or this won't work."

"We don't want a repeat of what happened last time." Robert said, then looked over at the blond. "We don't want to go through that shit again now do we, Gary?"

"I can't see another one of my prized cows go down again." Gary said in a somber tone, then added for good measure. "And let's not forget what happened to your wife Audrey last year."

"Don't remind me." Paul said.

Chad ignored the sheriff's comments, looked down at his feet to avoid any uncomfortable stares and ambled past Petey's. He gave a quick glance at the road lying ahead, the same road that would take him back onto the highway and as far away from this place and their self-righteous Jack and back home where–

"Hey, Chad."

The sweet welcoming lilt of two female voices stopped him dead in his tracks. He closed his eyes and cringed, thinking about how he should've just ignored them and kept going or maybe ran as fast as he could until their voices were replaced by the bellow of evening traffic.

He opened his eyes and glanced toward the front of the firehouse. Teagan stepped around the man he remembered as Robert, brushing her hand against his arm and stopped at the thin narrow crack separating the parking lot from the street. Lacey hurried to meet up with them, her blonde hair bobbing around the back of her head like a gunnysack.

"Where are you going?"

"I was just going to head back toward the highway."

"Nonsense, young man," Paul said, sidling up next to Teagan's right shoulder. "Jack would love to see you."

A knife-edged grin spread across his face, bracketing the corners of his mouth with a fresh net of wrinkles. Chad saw a glint in his eyes solely reserved for fathers who bragged about their child's academic achievements.

"I'd love to stick around," Chad said in a jittery voice. "but I've really got somewhere to be right now."

"It won't take too long, son," Gary said, waving him toward the table. "We'd have you out of here in no time."

Chad saw movement from behind Gary's left shoulder and peered at the parking lot in front of the firehouse. Robert placed an old burlap sack onto the edge of the table and slipped his hand inside. Something inside of the bag jostled, making furtive scuttling sounds and loud hissing noises. He chuckled and slid his arm back out, clenching the thick furry neck of an orange tabby cat like it were a can of his favorite beer.

The cat's second growl caught inside of its throat before spewing a strangled cry across the parking lot. It hissed, baring its tiny jagged teeth and whipped its tail across the air. It snapped its head to one side to free itself, but Robert kept his grip and held it up so that its eyes were reflected in the downward glare of a nearby street light.

Chad met the cat's gaze, saw the tiny flecks of sadness flickering in its piercing green eyes, and felt his skin prickle with fear. He gasped, feeling his heart palpitating. The fear pumping through his veins now churned into a tidal wave of adrenaline that freed his feet from the cold dark pavement.

He raced toward the table so fast he couldn't remember ever feeling his feet touch the ground, and ignored the rhythmic sound of his contents shuffling inside of his pack. He stretched his right arm across the table, his fingers raking the air in a whistling arc when his left foot twisted around his right ankle and sent him tumbling back toward the edge of the table. The cat panicked, dug its back feet into Robert's collarbone, scratched tiny frail divots across his right cheek, leaped out of his grasp and hurried off into the trees.

His boots scraping against the pavement for last-minute toehold, Chad cursed under his breath and crashed face-first onto the table. The table split in half and landed with a bone-jarring thud that sent waves of excruciating pain flaring across his hips. His backpack slid forward, jostling the contents inside and struck the back of his head, bouncing the tip of his chin off the table and rattling his teeth.

He sneered, rolled onto his left hip, rubbed the stars out of his eyes and glanced up in time to see a crowd gathering around him. His cheeks flushed, he met their gaze and sighed; beads of sweat coated the back of his neck and his brow and left lucid grilles stamped along the sides of his gray CINNICINATI BEARCATS tee-shirt. He extended his hand toward Robert, hoping he would help him but he didn't.

Teagan, Lacey nor the sheriff even moved.

No one offered to pull him up. Instead, they drowned him in a sea of shadows and disapproving stares. His face twisted with confusion, he felt something soft and squishy under his right hand.

When he raised his arm to see what it was, a middle-aged brunette woman gave a deflated sigh and fainted. No one helped her up either, (which wasn't a surprise to Chad). Strings of bright orange pulp clung to his cuticles and lay like strange lattice across his fingers; tiny white seeds dotted his slick wet palms.

The anger in Gary's eyes pinned Chad down onto the parking lot like fresh roadkill. He glanced down at the shards of broken pumpkin shells sprinkled around his feet and felt his throat constrict with fear. Teagan knelt beside of him, gathered a piece of broken pumpkin from the pavement and cradled it in her arms like a newborn; a lone tear slid down her right cheek.

"Are you out of—"

"Can I get some help." Chad pleaded, lying on the ground like a turtle lying on its shell.

"How could you?"

"Do you have any idea what you've done?"

It was then that he could feel Teagan and Lacey's "offer" sliding through his fingers. Here today, gone today, a phrase he was so familiar with it should be chiseled on his tombstone.

It's just a broken pumpkin, he thought to himself, *not a dead goldfish.*

Behind her, a chorus of whispers rose and fell amongst the townspeople. Some shook their heads in disgust, shedding a few tears of their own.

"I was just trying to save that cat."

"It doesn't matter now," Paul said, kneeling down beside of Teagan. "The damage has already been done."

Teagan muttered under her breath, her lips twisting into a sad lopsided grimace; tears brimmed in her eyes. The shadows of the townspeople lengthened across the street, stretching toward him as if clawing for the fabric of his very soul. The air around him, although sharper and colder than before, grew thick and suffocating.

"You've doomed all of us, you stupid son of a bitch." Lacey hissed between her teeth. "You shouldn't even be here right now."

"What do we do now?" Someone from the crowd replied in a worried tone. "It'll be worse than last year."

"We'll have to do our best," A voice said from behind him. "won't we?"

Chad tried to speak but all he could do was muster a few incoherent words. A blunt object rapped against the back of his head, slamming his chin onto his chest; stars burst across his vision. He hissed through clenched teeth, his skull throbbing with pain and slumped onto a sea of broken pumpkin shells, dark angry faces and the pitiless black void of unconsciousness.

*****

AFTER what seemed like a long time, Chad's eyes opened on sleep-crusted lids. His head slumped, chin resting on his chest, he groaned against the river of pain still flooding his skull. He blinked until his vision cleared but even that was a mistake he wouldn't make again; tears slid down his cheeks.

He took a risk and raised his head. He peered across a large grassy meadow surrounded by an archway of naked oak trees whose gnarled gray branches jutted toward the moonlit sky; frail autumn leaves were strewn about like expired confetti. He saw a large bright-orange bonfire on his right, casting a soft radiant glow across the meadow.

Four unlit pumpkins were sitting a few feet from the fire in a neat box-like pattern. A harsh bitter aftertaste collected in the back of his throat and his thick cottony tongue clung to the roof of his mouth, his lips dry and cracked.

A thick coarse object poked him in the back, spreading a new river of pain across the bottom of his spine and down his legs. He tried to raise his arms to scratch his cheek but they refused to budge, limiting him to a minimal shrug. He stopped tugging and peered over his shoulder to find that his arms had been twisted behind his back and his hands were bound together by thick strands of braided white rope.

Instinct kicked in and he reacted.

He rubbed his hands against the thick twisted knot on the other side of the tree to free himself but the rope dug harshly against his wrists, etching painful trellises across his skin. He scanned the meadow spread out on his left, at the lush dark-green hills rolling toward the dark heavy forest looming in the distance. He moved as fast as he could, his body racked by a mixture of fear for the unknown and for his own safety.

A thin roiling cloud cover inched its way across the sky, eclipsing the bright alabaster moon. The mingled fragrances of wood smoke and pine sap permeated around the forest and stung his nostrils. Dry kindling crackled and popped like an insane mind; tiny orange coals floated and twirled in the breeze.

A series of brittle cracks echoed from somewhere deep inside the forest. Chad gasped and, his heart thudding with timid curiosity, cocked his head toward the trees. Teagan appeared from the dense network of naked tree branches and stood beside the fire, her thin pink lips drawn up into a wide toothy grin; she wore a sleek black dress with a plunging neckline that exposed the sides of her pale sloping breasts whilst her right leg jutted out from a pencil-thin slit scored along the right hem.

The firelight caught the halo of black mascara hugging her eyes and threw it back against the night. When their eyes met, his body ached with a mixture of fear and arousal. His cock twitched, pressing against the jagged gold teeth of his zipper.

A second twig snapped, then another and then another and then soon one resident after the other stepped into view, their shadows stretching across the meadow. The children stood in front of them wearing the same costumes, their bright energetic faces beaming in the firelight. He heard more movement on his left, flinched and tried to peer over his shoulder, his left boot planted into the cold damp grass.

Gary and Robert appeared from the other side of the forest and flanked Teagan's shoulders. Lacey appeared from behind her, wearing a long flowing white dress with a smaller neckline that exposed the tops of her supple white breasts; a thin brown strap was slung across her chest attached to a small hemp-sewn bag resting against her right hip.

Paul sauntered over and placed a firm hand on Chad's left shoulder, his face heavy with remorse. Chad stiffened, eyes wide and braced himself for the man's next move.

"Look son." He said in a gentle grandfatherly voice. "We know you didn't mean to do what you did and if I had my way about it I'd just let you go but this here is a different matter altogether."

Chad exhaled, spewing thin white ghosts around his face. His shirt clung to his back as large pools of perspiration spread under his arms. He would've given anything for them to let it go but there was something about those damn pumpkins that seemed more important to them than the preservation of life.

"This here is a matter you're gonna have to take up with Jack," Paul said, backing away. "Jack didn't take too kindly to you knocking over that pumpkin and he's gonna be pretty angry for sure. Since we can't have old Jacky Boy taking it out on us, we're sure you'll understand why you're tied to this here tree."

Chad jerked on his restraints again, chipping a few shards of bark from the tree and sent them clattering to the ground in a cloud of swirling black dust.

"Traditions are meant to be continued, young man," Paul said, with a wide pleasing grin. "Halloween isn't just a holiday, you know? We wait all year for this day and we want everything to go perfect. The more we celebrate it, the happier he is."

"'Jack in Laudamus'," Teagan said, in a smoky seductive voice.

Chad's mind flashed back to the phrase chiseled on the sign posted outside of town. He'd been so quick to look away from it that he hadn't put much thought into it. *In Jack We Praise*, he thought.

They repeated the phrase one at a time, first Paul and then Gary and then Lacey and then back to Teagan. Lacey reached into her bag, produced a long bamboo-brown flute and began to play, her fingers dancing expertly across the holes. The children grinned at one another and began to walk hand-in-hand toward the edge of the fire before suddenly leaping into a sideways dance that was reminiscent of Ring-Around-The-Rosy; amongst the music and the dancing, he heard a word that one of them had said before.

Chad glanced away from "The Big Dance" and failed to hold back the knot of sadness twisting his chest. He bowed his head, watching the necklace of childish shadows float across the grass, moving in tandem to the sweet melodious music like animatronic stick figures, and stared down at the four pumpkins still sitting on the ground.

The pool of shadows congealed between the four pumpkins, forming a small puddle of black water that glistened in the light. A bright green stem rose up from the surface of the slick obsidian liquid, followed by the large ribbed cranium of a...

—a pumpkin, Chad thought, his voice strangled by fear.

After the head broke through, it gazed across the meadow with bright luminous orange pupils fitted inside of its slanted dark eye sockets. Once the figure fully rose, its thin withered body hovered three inches above the pumpkins and spread its arms out from its sides; its long black fingers were fitted with long curved white talons. It inhaled, puffing its chest like a penguin, and drew a great ball of smoky pine-scented air deep into its lungs as if it were feasting on the aura of the townspeople's undying dedication.

It cocked its head to the side and glared at Chad like a teacher catching a student passing notes during class, its bright orange gaze rooting his feet to the ground and drew back another deep breath. Chad's crying increased from a strangled cry to a gut-wrenching sob broken up by small peals of maniacal laughter; a thread of snot dripped off the end of his nose; hot lucid tears brimmed in his eyes before sliding down his cheeks.

Paul, Gary, Tegan and the rest of the townspeople gazed up with wonder and sent a chorus of ceremonious applause into the night. The children stopped dancing and gazed upward to meet his menacing orange stare as if he were a mall Santa and not a being from another world.

"Hi, Jack." Everyone roared in loud fluctuating voices.

Teagan bowed, then said. "We have a fresh one for you. He killed your kin but we insist that you accept his soul in return for ours."

His presence was their weakness; his words sweet as sugar.

Chad felt his stomach boiling with nausea. A sense of dread tightened around his throat like an invisible noose. He wasn't sure what this thing was but all he knew was that it existed amongst the shadows, protecting everyone from the barber to the pumpkins they grew in their backyards; he was just an interloper who'd put a wrench in their plans and now here he was, trapped inside of a cage he couldn't fight his way out of.

"We mustn't eat on an empty stomach?" Jack said in a throaty guttural voice. "Now should we?"

Jack spun around like a ballerina, his long black smock swirling around him, his eyes glowing with an intense gaze that sliced across Chad's chest like a bad case of indigestion. Chad gave another eccentric laugh as the town's ceremonial god hurtled Himself at him like a comet, its crinkled black dress flapping against the wind and shrouded him in a cocoon of darkness from which he would never shake off.

With the moon breaking through the film of clouds that failed to conceal it, Chad's agonizing screams were eclipsed by the mingled chorus of sweet lyrical music and childish laughter.

BIG BROTHER

This is a story that centers around the connection between big brothers and little sisters and what we'd sacrifice for the other.

Our job is to protect them from the dangers of society and from the monsters they'll meet throughout the rest of their lives, even if the monster is inside of them.

"ARE we there yet?"

"No." I bellowed above the roar of the wind in our ears.

"How long until we get there?"

"We've still got a ways to go."

"I'm hungry, Tyler." Jan whined. "We've been riding this train for a month."

"It's only been three days."

Her face silhouetted by the soft alabaster moonlight, Jan's long black hair fell across the tops of her shoulders framing her cherub-pale face. The only thing we'd come across since we jumped on from Logan was a stinky old bum and miles of wooded farmland backdropped by tree-choked rises and spines of jagged mountains jutting toward the sky. The days faded into nights while time and a lack of resources festered on our minds.

Her long floral-print dress was stained with faint patches of dirt and dotted with crusts of dried blood. The stench of my skin kept her from getting too close to me, pinning her to an arm's length on my right. Our legs dangling over the side, the wind tousled our clothes and hair.

The mixture of old fashioned boxcars and covered hoppers trailed out from behind us like the legs of a drunken caterpillar, shifting this way and that to conform to the tracks. The lights of the city lying along the horizon resembled a string of Christmas lights, distant yet beautiful at the same time.

I mocked the slanted angle of the moon and peered out ahead, past the front of the train to look for a signpost up ahead; anything that would tell me exactly where we'd been going for the past seventy-two hours.

"You're supposed to be nice to me."

"What do you think I've been doing since you were ten."

I used the handle on the sliding door to hoist myself up, slapped the dust off my jeans, blotted my hands on the front of my tee-shirt and sighed.

I walked over to the other side of the cart, leaned my left elbow against the wall and watched the star-studded sky from between the dark-narrow slats. A loud sniveling sound rose behind me but I sighed and rolled my eyes; my sister had done more crying than any man should ever tolerate.

Had all of my efforts been for nothing?

What else did they expect me to do?

Something twitched in the corner of my left eye. A fist-sized rat scurried across the floor, its little nose and skinny pink tail convulsing with fear and gave one painful shriek before Jan's hand closed around its big furry body. It squeaked, struggling to free itself from her grasp before she twisted its head like a bottle cap, tore it free from its broken neck.

She held it above her face and opened her mouth, revealing two rows of jagged pink incisors. She squeezed its head, pouring a stream of warm red blood past her lips and down the front of her dress. Her throat gyrating with each sip, the rat's dark red juices filled her veins with a sweet sugary nectar that subdued the flames in her nerves.

She licked her lips, then pressed its spasming body against her lips and sucked it down like a juice box.

Once she was done, she licked her lips and tossed it into the far-left corner of the train car. I heard that same sniveling sound from before and rolled my eyes; instead of coming from behind me it was coming from beside of me. The bum was slumped over in the far right corner, his face coated with a mixture of sweat, snot and blood; his left arm had been torn off at the elbow, reducing it to a spongy red stub.

The knife he'd pressed under Jan's chin ten minutes ago was still jutting out of his right leg where she'd planted it after she bit a fist-sized hole in his left arm. Tiny dots of blood speckled his face, stained his ragged dirty clothes and pooled across the floor under his legs. I craned my head in her direction, shook my head in disgust and frowned.

"You're eating a rat at a time like this when you've still got fresh meat sitting right over there." I said, jabbing my thumb at him.

"Ple-ple-pleez." He said through quivering lips. "I'm sorry-sorry-please don't kill me—"

"Don't be sorry." Jan whispered, cowering down on all fours. "Just be food."

As much as I've complained about her, she'll always be my little sister.

*****

WHAT is it like to have a vampire for a little sister? I have my good days and I have my bad days.

My parents, Geoff and Marie Matheson, gave birth to my little sister Janice Lee on July fifth two-thousand-five; she weighed in at seven pounds five ounces. On the night of her tenth birthday, a vampire snuck in through her bedroom window and bit her. Neither one of us, including Jan herself, realized what had happened until the next day when she screamed and woke us all out of a dead sleep; when we saw the blood on her bed we knew it was bad.

"She's just having her period, that's all." Mom had said in an unconvincing voice.

When we saw the two puncture holes in the side of her neck, her words fell on deaf ears. A few days of long conversation, we insisted that Jan was still a member of the family and decided to assimilate around her, which caused a lot of frustration at first. My gerbil Larry and three out of four of our neighbors cats were just a few of Jan's first victims; the gerbil's death was worse than the cats because they were farming cats and usually when they're not found after a long period of time their owners had assumed they'd gone off somewhere and died.

To keep her from going on a feeding frenzy, Mom and Dad took her out of public school and kept her home. Luckily for her, Mom worked as a substitute teacher and was able to teach her right there at the house. We had to walk around the house wearing cloves of garlic around our necks to keep her from ripping our throats out; we didn't like it but it wasn't like we had a choice.

It was worse during the night, though. We had to sleep with a net over the top of our beds with crosses and garlic cloves stitched into the fabric to keep her bloodlust at bay. There were a few nights where Mom would sit on the living room couch with half a pint of ice cream and watch home movies chronicling the first nine years of Jan's life before she became some blood-sucking fiend's midnight snack; when Dad would find her lying on the couch in the wee hours of the morning; they'd argue so much it would put a heavy strain on their marriage.

Not that I was keeping track, but there were some things you just couldn't ignore.

My life changed when Mom made me Jan's "handler" whenever she wanted to go around the woods for one of her nightly feedings. Mostly deer or other types of forest animal but household pets and people (we lived alongside Lake Michelle where most of the good fishing spots were located) were prohibited because it would draw too much attention.

My life, in its own funny little way, was as unusual as a ham dinner on Hanukkah. I couldn't even have any of my friends over at my house for dinner because we didn't want to chance it. It costs me half of my life; I couldn't even use her to retaliate against the kids at school who called her names and beat me up.

I was the guardian of a monster, a former shadow of the little sister I'd protected since birth. I knew Mom and Dad weren't going to live forever so someone had to take the reins. There were times where on more days than I could count that Jan felt guilty for being such a burden.

Of course, not everything stayed honky-dory.

There was a pounding on our door one night. Mom and Dad got me out of bed and hurried down stairs, slipping on their robes as fast as they could. I went into Jan's room, my eyes and brain still foggy from sleep, to make sure she stayed in there just in case.

My heart sunk to my feet when I discovered that her makeshift coffin was empty, its neatly-carved lid propped upright to expose the white-satin bedding inside to the carpet of moonlight flooding through her bedroom window. The sound of footsteps paraded around the living room, followed by a loud petrified scream that sent cold shivers trailing down my spine.

"What the hell–" Dad said in a resounding voice.

"I'm sorry, Momma." Jan pleaded, her voice garbled.

I shook off the fear that pinned my feet to the floor outside of her bedroom and ran downstairs as fast as I could. I slid to a stop at the foot of the stairs, sweat trickling down my face and gripped the banister to keep myself from falling. Jan stood beside of the front door, her long black hair falling down around her left cheek; drops of blood peppered her face, clothes and fingernails.

We gazed at her, our eyes and mouths wide with fear. Outside, the sun sank, spreading a bruised-purple light across the sky.

"What the hell did you do?"

"I was getting out of bed to wake up Tyler when I saw these kids outside walking around outside and they were calling us names and one of them threw a rock at Dad's pickup truck and broke the back window and when I told them to leave they laughed and called me a freak so I leaped out of the window and all I wanted to do was scare them but the hunger hit me and I couldn't stop myself. I wanted-wan-bu-I-couldn't–I tri-bu-I-cou–"

Her words were muddled by her own gut-wrenching sobs.

"Did you kill them?"

She nodded. "Only one of them got away."

"Shit." Dad hissed through his teeth, then shifted his angry gaze in my direction. "Why weren't you up with her like you're supposed to be?"

"It's not my fault."

"The hell it isn't." He said behind clenched teeth. "If you'd done your job, none of us would be in this mess."

"Wow!" Jan sighed. "It's nice to know that you think of me as a mess."

"Shut the hell up, Janice."

"Stop it, Geoff." Mom begged, her eyes brimming with tears.

"You had one fuckin' job to do and–"

"It's not his fault." Jan said in a deep guttural voice.

She clenched the crown of his shoulders with both hands, hoisted him three inches off the floor and pinned him against the corner of the room beside of the front door. Her brute inhuman force shook the house, jarred the living room windows inside of their panes and sent the picture frames sweeping back and forth across the walls like tiny pendulums. Dad recoiled, his face sweaty and pale with fear, and raised his loose-knuckled arms up and across his face.

She repeated her testimony in her human voice and then released her grip.

"Do you realize what you've done?"

"Yes, I do." She nodded. "and I'm sorry."

"Sorry isn't going to buy you a new family."

We knew he was angry but he still shouldn't have said it like that. It was a bitter pill to swallow; not that I was keeping track but there are somethings that don't go unnoticed. Mom wandered away and paced back and forth across the living room, hugging herself with both arms whilst gazing down at the floor to shake Dad's hateful insult from her memory.

"We don't need to act like this." She insisted, chopping her at the air with her hand. "We need to put our heads together–"

We heard the slow growl of a car engine climbing over the hilltop, followed by the sound of tires crunching over loose gravel. Mom moved over to the window, tiny creases of confusion etching her face, and gazed through the narrow slit between the curtains. A mix of red, white and blue lights swept across the window, accentuating the worry lines bracketing the corners of her mouth.

Mom hurried away from the window, clamped her left hand across her mouth to quash another sob and joined us beside of the front door. Dad unpinned himself from the wall, kissed her on the forehead, wrapped his arms around her and peered at me from over her right shoulder.

His look said more than his words could. There was an uncomfortable glint in his eyes that told me he knew it would come to this one day but not tonight. No matter what we said or did, the drastic measure we didn't want to take was now our only option.

Something rapped against the living room window with a muffled thud. We flinched at the sound of broken glass and cocked our heads into the living room in time to see a fist-sized rock burst through the curtain and roll across the floor. The curtains parted like specters and weaved amongst the funnel of cool air whistling through the gnarled toothy grin in the window; moonlight glinted off the trail of broken glass strewn across the carpet.

"Get your galdamn ass out here, you fucking freak." A drunken angry voice bellowed, belonging to Mr. Hoffman, the town barber.

"Damn it, Cal." An authoritative voice demanded, belonging to the one and only Sheriff Randy Chambers. "I told you I'd handle it now get the hell back."

"That little bitch killed both of my sons. I want her hung by the galdamn neck until she stops shittin' and kickin'."

Hoffman's words brought a strangled cry from Momma's lips. Dad held on, reassuring her that everything would be okay when we knew better.

"Get out here, you little bitch." A strangled female cry bellowed.

Mrs. Hoffman, local librarian and now distraught mother.

"Everyone just stay back, damn it." Chamber bellowed. "I'm the sheriff and I'll take care of this, Evelyn"

"Tyler." Dad hissed, tugging at my tee-shirt. "Do it now."

"What?" Jan asked, her eyes wide with fear. "What are we doing?"

"We got to go." I whispered.

When I took her left hand, a cold sensation streaked my veins, coiled around my spine and raised the hairs along my arms and the back of my neck. Although I was scared that she would assault me like she'd done to Dad a little bit ago, I wouldn't be surprised that her keen supernatural senses didn't detected it before.

"No." She pleaded, her face chalky and pale with fear. "We can't. I won't."

"Do you want them to come in here and hurt us?"

"I'll kill them." Her temples throbbed with rage.

"Then we'll have a fucking bloodbath." Dad whispered. "And we can't have that kind of attention."

A tall, broad-shouldered shadow rose across our fiberglass front door, stopped and knocked hard enough to rattle the window. Evelyn Hoffman's cries of misery and grief echoed across the driveway, raking at the night like sharp talons; a blanket of harsh-white light draped the living room windowsill, projecting the floor with a weird overlapping shadows.

"Open the door, Geoff." Chambers demanded. "You'd make my job a lot more easy if you bring the little lady out with you."

"I'm coming." Dad said, then turned and whispered to me. "You need to get her out of here right now."

"I'm not leaving without you."

"Goddamn it, Jan." Mom whispered, her eyes wet and red from crying. "Go with your brother right now. I'd rather go to jail knowing that you're safe with your brother rather than see them put you in handcuffs."

Mom gave me a sad, adamant stare that never saw on her face before and nodded. I tugged on Jan's left hand and tried to drag her toward the back door. She yanked her hand away and began to massage Mom's shoulders until she looked up at her.

"Go!" Dad grimaced.

I wrapped my arms around Jan's waist, ignoring the deathly-cold touch of her skin, and carried her away. She squirmed and kicked but I refused to budge because if I set her down she would've ran back to Mom and Dad. I thought she was going to bite me but she didn't.

"Love you, baby." Mom whispered, a fresh set of tears cascading down her cheeks.

"Go around the back." An outside voice bellowed.

As much as we didn't want to, Jan saw the gravity of the current situation and knew there was nothing she could do to change their minds. I set her down and led her toward the back door, a second wave of cold fear bristling across my skin. Two men began to approach the back door, their shadows projected across the floor by the sour gray sunlight sifting through the screen.

She waited until we were close enough and gave a loud guttural cry. Her eyes now bright red cores of swirling red light, she pushed the door open with such tremendous force that it shook the house and rattled the windows; a mist of jagged brown splinters and two hapless bastards flew across the backyard.

I couldn't see who it was because it happened so fast I didn't have the inclination to care. We were halfway across the back yard when we heard the front door burst open and Sheriff Chambers growl under his breath like an angry beast.

"They're getting away!" He bellowed.

I ignored their accusing voices and followed my little sister head first into a dark and impenetrable world that felt much safer than the one outside of it.

*****

WE got off the train outside of a little town called Kayson, a rural stretch of cozy brick and stucco houses slapped between a trailer park and a shopping center whose grandeur was relegated by the damages of time and financial decline. We made our way across town, past the chain of neon-gilded restaurants, nightclubs, gas stations and other establishments. When we neared the end of town, everything was reduced to shotgun shacks and poorly-maintained lawns littered with toys and cars sitting on cinderblocks.

A roiling black cloud slithered across the fat white moon reducing its soft alabaster glare. The cool summer breeze stirred the trees, tousled our clothes and caressed our skin.

"Where are we going?" Jan asked.

"We're heading north."

"Why?"

"Because we a–" I said, then saw the sarcastic grin on her face. "Smart ass."

I nudged her with her elbow and she laughed. It reminded me of the relationship we'd had before she "changed".

To be quite honest, I didn't know where we could go except for Cleveland or maybe Canada and then figure out what to do from there. Wherever we ended up, we'd have to assimilate there as we'd done back home; might even have to cut or dye our hair while I grew some kind of a beard to hide my face.

"How are we going to get there?" She asked, meeting my gaze.

Under the overhead glare from the street lights, my shadow was the only one I saw. I looked away before she noticed it because I didn't want her to feel any worse than she already did

"We're gonna hitchhike." I chuffed. "I can't just jump on you so you can–"

I didn't realize she'd stopped beside of the cream-colored Buick until I was five feet from her. Before I could turn around, a large blunt object struck the back of my head and sent me stumbling face-first onto the pavement. My breath burst from my lips like a deflated balloon; pain sliced across my skull, squeezing hot lucid tears from my eyes.

I rolled onto my back and, grunting from the pain, glared up at my attacker. He looked to be about sixteen but his thick meaty shoulders and sturdy frame made him look much older. His short brown hair sat above a square pudgy face with wide green eyes, a piggish nose and thick lips; his dingy-white shirt, jeans and boots looked like they hadn't been washed since Obama's first term.

His mouth spread into a self-righteous grin, he planted his right foot on my chest, pinning me to the ground and said, "Stay down or I'll put you down."

A skinny dark-haired boy in a white shirt under an open blue FUBU jacket stepped out of the shadows on my left, pressed a crumpled brown paper sack up to his mouth and inhaled until it hurt. He had a gaunt pale face, sunken cheeks and a clean-shaven head; a thin jagged burn mark streaked across his left cheek and stopped at the edge of his jawline.

"You want some, Nicky?" He said, referring to my attacker.

He extended the bag then yanked it out of his reach and chuckled. Nicky ignored him and grinned at my dilemma.

"Do you want some K-Dog?" He asked.

He extended the bag toward his left.

"Not really but I'll take a slice of pie instead."

A young rawboned boy in a red-tee shirt, jeans and sneakers that probably didn't belong to him appeared out from behind the cream-colored Buick, holding Jan out in front of him. His thick-black eyeglasses did nothing for his wide-set blue eyes or his tan skeletal face. He pressed his face against her left cheek and, ignoring the mask of disgust twisting her features, sniffed the angled slope of neck from under her earlobe before stopping at the crown of her shoulder.

"You walked into the wrong yard, motherfucker." K-Dog said in a chauvinistic voice.

"Where the fuck are you going in the first place?"

I opened my mouth to answer him when Nicky prodded my chest to remind me who was allowed to speak and who wasn't.

"Answer him," He hissed. "or I'll plant this boot in your fucking throat."

"We're going north." Jan exclaimed.

She winced and struggled to free herself from his grasp. He jerked back on her right arm, jostling her head a little and gave her a scornful look.

"The more you fight me," He said with a grimace. "the sweeter it'll be."

The three boys glanced at each other, wide satisfied smiles creasing their faces. This was the kind of happiness they craved for because their parents hadn't given them any because they just didn't care. We were no different than the wings of a fly that were about to be plucked away from our bodies like the petals of a flower or an army of ants scampering blindly under the stinging hot glare of a sunlit magnifying glass.

Her cherub-face sagging with terror, Jan's eyes glistened. She bit down on her bottom lip to contain the scream that would've gotten my head stomped into the pavement.

"Doesn't look like you'll be going anywhere tonight, babe." Sam grunted.

"We run this whole town." Nicky said, motioning to them by swirling his finger across the air in a circle. "Everything you see around you belongs to us. No one does anything in this town without telling us about it first."

I believed him like the other kids in school.

Sam took another drag from his bag, chuckled from behind swollen red cheeks and coughed, his body spasming from the toxic contents swirling through his brain. K-Dog opened his mouth, grazed his slick pink tongue across her left cheek, gave a piggish grunt and slid his hand down between Jan's thighs. My heart thudding with rage at what I was forced to watch, I gnashed my teeth together until my jaw hurt.

When his hand drifted toward Jan's naughty place, I sat up and said, "Get your fu–"

Nicky whipped his left hand hard across my right jaw like a drunk father and bounced my head off the pavement. A strobe of white light flooded my vision before dissolving into tiny pinpricks of stars; more pain blossomed across my skull pressing it against my brain. In the time it would've taken me to shake off the pain, Sam planted his left foot onto my left wrist, pressed my knuckles against the pavement and chuckled.

"Shut the fuck up," He said, wagging his bag across my face. "You're not leaving here tonight until we say, got it?"

A faint noxious cloud drifted past my face. I turned my head to the right and held my breath, hoping I hadn't breathed any of it.

"If you want to leave town." He said. "We get to sample a bit of your cargo." K-Dog said in that same pre-pubescent voice.

When he kissed the crown of her left shoulder, Jan freed her arm from his grasp and slid her left hand down the front of his jeans. K-Dog grinned and chuckled with pride when a bone-jarring crunch emitted across the street; the smug look on his face sunk into a hangdog expression that might've been either ecstasy or misery. He gave a loud painful yelp as she jerked her hand back, cupping his torn testicles between long pale fingers fitted with long pale talons soaked in a dark crimson liquid that dripped between stretched fingers and onto the pavement like a ruptured oil pan.

As much as I wanted to save these pathetic assholes, it was already too late. They'd pushed her buttons for as long as she was going to allow them to, just long enough for her to trap them right where she wanted them; the stench was overpowering much stronger and more potent than the fumes in Sam's bag. Her lips drew back from her bright-pink gums, revealing two rows of sharp serrated incisors between two elongated canines stained pink from months of fresh carrion.

K-Dog stumbled back, his ragged bloody crotch spewing a trail of hot urine and fresh blood across the pavement. She sniffed the odor of blood wafting from her left hand and, her eyes bright with demonic red desire, buried her face deep into her slick red hands. K-Dog slumped onto the shoulder of the road, his arms slumped down by his sides as his eyes rolled back inside of their sockets.

She gave the same piggish grunt he'd given her a few minutes ago and gnawed on his slick red shaft. The loud slurping noises coming from her mouth churned my stomach under a mix of nausea and unease.

Nicky and Sam, their faces shifting under mingled expressions of horror and dismay, backed away from me. When they released the pressure from my hands, I scuttled across the street and used the Buick's rear bumper to hoist myself up.

"Wha-wha-wha-" Sam stammered. "What the fuck, man?"

Jan lifted her head up from her dripping red prize and, nostrils flaring, cocked her head at them. They broke into a mad dash toward the end of the street we'd came from, their sneakers slapping rhythmically against the asphalt. She gave a loud guttural protest, drew her lips into a tight angry snarl and raced after them in a faint-white blur.

Nicky peered over his right shoulder, his eyes wide with shock and drove his right elbow hard into Sam's left rib. The blow sent shockwaves of pain and agony coursing through his stomach, knocking him off balance. He ran to the right and disappeared from my sight, his bulky frame was barely visible through the wall of darkness and knee-high grass.

Sam knelt onto the pavement, cradling his stomach in both hands when Jan finally caught up to him. She leaped onto his back, wrapped her legs around his waist and planted him face-down onto the pavement. She jabbed the talons on her left hand deep into the left side of his neck, gripped his jugular inside of her fist and tore it free like a piece of taffy; he gave a loud gurgle, his body twitching as a river of arterial blood oozed onto the pavement.

She pressed her lips onto the gaping red wound and sucked with ravenous haste, filling her throat with each sweet drop. When his body slumped onto the pavement, she grasped his head in both hands and spun until it gave a dry brittle snap. Her lips coated with thick red blood, she raised her head up from Sam's cold blue corpse, sniffed at the cool summer breeze and peered in the direction where Nicky had gone.

She dropped Sam's head, watched it bounce off the pavement like a basketball and sped off after him. I scanned the street for any witnesses and, ignoring the pain flaring across the back of my hands, hurried after them; my chest rose and fell with each ragged breath. A mixture of fear and anxiety churned inside the pit of my stomach, stung the back of my throat and ignited the thunderous rhythm of my heart; sweat beads trickled down my face and brows.

Nicky was running toward a strip of train tracks streaking across a short grassy hill at the back of a nearby modular, his face blanched with horror. She waited for him to approach the halfway point before she stepped in front of him, a hideous hungry figure borne from the shadows of his nightmares. He froze, his body stiff and trembling with fear, and uttered a loud terrifying scream.

She swiped her hand across his face, filling my ears with the soft pliable sound of torn flesh and ushered an inner gorge toward the back of my throat. The mingled stench of expended bowels and blood now rode on the breeze and made me cringe with disgust.

When he lowered her arm, Nicky's head spun to the left, pressing his jawline against the meaty part of his right shoulder rolled away before it was swallowed by the high grass weaving silently in the breeze. His fat headless corpse staggered across the lawn in a drunken stupor, each step pumping a fresh geyser of blood into the air that aroused my sister's uncanny appetite.

Once he kneeled down, she braced his shoulders with both hands and buried her face into the pulpy red stub where his head used to be. She suckled, her mouth siphoning one sweet drop of his sweet red juices after the other, her hair flailing wildly around her face. When she spotted me from the corner of her right eye, her face coated with "thug" blood, she yanked her lips away as if it were a hot surface.

She backed away, her face twisted with horror and fascination, and gazed down at the atrocity she created; Nicky's headless corpse fell back into the grass. Her face cringing with sadness and disbelief, tears protruded from her eyes and slid down her slick bloody cheeks. She knelt down and cried, her body trembling.

"Help me, Tyler." She sobbed, holding her arms out to me. "I'm sorry. I didn't mean to do it. I swe–"

I opened my arms when she mumbled something under her breath I couldn't make out under the soft whispery wind weaving through the grass. Before I could try to decipher what she said, Jan reared her right arm back and punched me hard across the face. She said something else but the pain in my skull was so unbearable that it muffled my ears and lowered my body into the grass that once swallowed my attacker's decapitated corpse.

The last image I saw before darkness creeped in were the streaks of blood splattered across the front of her dress and the grass billowing softly in the breeze.

*****

ALL of that was months ago, I admit.

I remember waking up later that night inside of an old boxcar on a bed of hay with an old blanket draped across my waist. Startled, I went from one end of the train to the other, looking closely into each and every car from one end to the other in a desperate search for my little sister that ended in tears. Two miles later, I was hungry so I checked to see how much money I had and got off at the next town.

I'd found a bright-yellow note amongst the crumpled ball of twenties and fifties inside of my right pocket and read it. Then I read over and over again.

DON'T WORRY ABOUT ME;
I'LL BE FINE.

As much as I wanted to believe her, there was something about that note that said that I shouldn't. I still had a responsibility handed down to me by my parents even if it meant sacrificing both the life and future that I deserved to have. Jan will always be my little sister and there was nothing I wouldn't do for her that any other big brother wouldn't do for their own.

I've been to so many states in so many days I couldn't tell one from the other. Had I decided to hang around, it wouldn't have been for long. I've been cutting newspaper clippings here and there, each one detailing Jan's never-ending path of death and destruction and blood.

She isn't that far away. I don't know that for sure but I can feel it, a thick cloying magnetism that only real brothers and sisters have and it hovers above me like a storm cloud of depression. I have nothing to be depressed about anymore because I know deep in my heart that Jan isn't too far away.

I'm sitting inside of a three-star motel where five-star men bang two-star prostitutes or truck-stop waitresses looking to abandon their humdrum life and writing all of this on a yellow legal pad. The pen in my hand ran out of ink a little while ago but I've got plenty of pens and plenty of paper and a long way to go before I find my little sister.

And I won't stop until I do, no matter how long it takes.

3RD DAY OF THE 3RD WEEK OF EVERY MONTH

My mother loved her music and she wasn't afraid to tell anyone at any given time of the day.

Dolly Parton, The Judds, Heart, Neil Diamond and Bette Midler just to name a few. Her two favorite Tanya Tucker songs were "Soon" and "Delta Dawn".

Five years after she died, I found "Delta" and listened to it for the first time and wrote this story.

BY the time he padded across the concrete circle hugging the tall marble-white water fountain in the middle of the town square, Sheriff Norm Kisor saw the odd-looking shadow eclipsing the front window of Lizzie's Cafe between the cursive red logo scrawled across the glass and gave a deflated sigh.

Oh, shit, he thought. *Not her again.*

He checked the time on his wristwatch, tucked a folded-up copy of *The Madisonville Daily* under his left armpit and jammed his hands deep into his pockets. The uncomfortable stares on the faces of the customers inside of Lizzie's were enough to tell him everything he needed to know; he was a man of the law and could always tell when someone was lying to him or not.

The early morning breeze carried the sweet smells of hay and wildflowers, reminding him that summer was just getting started. The hairs along the back of his neck and his arms stiffened, spreading goosebumps across his skin.

"Good morning, sheriff." A cheery but familiar voice replied.

When he glanced over at his right, Dawn Matthews was sitting on a metallic green park bench with her left leg tucked up underneath her thigh and her right leg drooped over her left foot. She gazed up at him and cocked her head to the left, her heavy-lidded blue eyes blazing in the early morning light. Her long curly-brown hair fell down from a part in the top of her head, framed her round tan face and curled around the nape of her neck; a red rose with a thin green stem was tucked behind her right ear like a pencil.

Her skin always had a unique glow that seem to blossom from somewhere deep inside of her soul. Her brown floral-print dress lay loosely around her slim waist and fluttered softly around her stick-like legs.

He noticed something on the sidewalk behind her, or at least the shadow of it, leaning against the other side of the bench. He didn't want to say anything because it would've been wrong not to give her a little leeway.

"Good morning, Dawn." He grinned, tipping the brim of his hat. "It looks like it's gonna be a beautiful day today, huh?"

"It sure does."

"Well now, look at you." He said, scanning her up and down. "You look like a sight for sore eyes, Mizz Matthews."

"You know better than to call me 'Mizz Matthews'." She said in a bashful tone. "I'm forty-one and my daddy still calls me Baby but you can call me Dawn."

"Where are my manners? Do you mind if I join you?"

"I don't mind." She slid away from the middle of the bench and patted it with her right hand. "I don't mind tall."

He tipped the brim of his hat, set the paper on the bench seat between them and perched his left ankle on his right knee. She slid a little closer to him, her thin pink lips spread into a wide pleasant grin.

He glanced across the street and peered at the sea of inquiring faces staring back at him from inside the café. Lizzie Stufflebeam, in all her buxom brunette beauty, sneaked a glance at Dawn before pouring a fresh cup of coffee for Hugh Rainey, an old man in a red plaid shirt and jeans with tufts of bedhead white hair jutting out from the sides of his trucker cap. He saw the coffee sloshing around inside the carafe in Lizzie's hand and licked his lips at the sight of that dark and caffeinated mistress he longed for.

"Hey, Sheriff."

A nearby voice blared in his right ear, stirring him out of his trance. He peered back at her, flashed an appreciative smile and patted her right thigh in a friendly manner. Dawn glanced at him, her face and brows creased with confusion, eased her hand away from his left shoulder before setting it back onto her left wrist.

"Are you okay?"

"I'm good." He lied. "I was up off and on all night."

"I'm sorry to hear about that." She said, cocking her head to the right. "Did you have a bad dream? Was it about your wife?"

He wasted no time in finding the right words to say. He'd been thinking about Amanda a lot lately–more than he usually did actually–especially the memories they shared during their seventeen-year marriage before the big-C punched her clock.

"You could say that."

"My momma used to tell me that pain was paradise for the weak." She shrugged and then added. "I never knew what she meant by that but it made perfect sense."

"Why is that?"

A few seconds of silence went by before she said, "Because some people enjoy pain to make up the fact that they're not strong enough to get through their own life. Some people pretend they're happy but she also said that the people who are in love do it more because they're afraid to be alone."

He had to give her credit, she'd been right about a lot of things. He let it sink but not for too long.

"Why are you sitting out here in your Momma's dress?" Norm asked in a curious tone. "I know you didn't get all dressed up just to come out here and talk to me."

She cupped her hands together and gazed up at him with a dream-like quality in her eyes. Her face turned a lovely shade of pink that accentuated the vulva-pink rouge spread across her cheeks; there was a sense of wonder and affection on her face that he hadn't seen or felt since Amanda died.

"I'm in love, Sheriff."

"Really?" He said, his voice beaming with elation. "So it wasn't just a bunch of gossip cooked up by all of the blue hairs down at the VFW."

A few seconds went by before he prodded her on the shoulder.

"Are you gonna tell me about the lucky fellow or are you gonna leave me hanging?"

"He's not that lucky."

"The hell he isn't." He said, then shifted around on the bench to face her as she'd done for him. "If I were twenty years younger, I'd dance outside of your bedroom window until you came out to kiss me."

She cooed, her eyes glinting like ice chips. She sat up in her seat, slipped a hand into the front pocket of her dress and brought out a small black and white photo. In the photo, a suave young man with manly features and slick black hair leaned against a railing overlooking what looked to be The River Thames. He wore a shiny gray suit, dark tie and a brown bowler hat above his square-jawed face; a red pocket square jutted out from his right front pocket. The corners of the photo were crinkled and dog-eared from nostalgic nights under a blanket of stars where dreams blossomed like wild flowers.

"He's from London and his name is Reginald Barrington."

His brows arched, he said, "You've roped yourself a prince, huh?"

"He's a prince for now but eventually he'll be king and he's promised to make me his queen." She tucked the photo back into her pocket. "He lives in a tall castle on a hill over–

"Have you seen it?"

"Seen what?"

"His castle."

Her face went pale and motionless, making her look as if he'd caught her off guard. She glanced down at the bright-yellow curb, her ears muffled by the wind. A burnt-orange ladybug scuttled across a flattened Styrofoam coffee cup lying flat along the curb before flying toward the northeast corner where MacDonald's Antiques and L&B's Books lain.

"What else did he say?" He asked.

She blinked, glanced up from the curb and met Norm's prying gaze. The mixed expression of joy and childish curiosity shifted across her face before the glow returned. He peered over her shoulder toward the northwest corner of town and drummed his fingers nervously against his right thigh.

Behind her, tree shadows spilled along the carpets of sunlight spread along the curbs and sidewalks along Hope Street. The old clock tower rose in the distance, its shingled green steeple looking dark and ominous in the clear blue sky.

"He said he loved me with every beat of his heart and that one day." She sighed. "He would take me for his bride. He has twenty servants, fourteen bedrooms with their own bathrooms and a kitchen with the finest chefs from France."

Norm whistled and said, "Damn, girl. I don't think you can get any fancier than that."

"He just wants what's best for me."

As Dawn twirled a loose strand of hair around her finger and glanced up at the early-morning sky, Norm glanced toward the sea of faces still peering out at him from inside the café. Hugh Rainey had taken the stool near the front window, gave Norm a lopsided sneer and spun back around to take a sip of his coffee. Lizzie glided across the window, grasping a coffee carafe in one hand and flashing a strange hand signal with the other.

From where he was sitting, it resembled the "Hook 'Em Horns" symbol he'd seen on television back when he actually cared about college football (he couldn't give half a crap about basketball, college or pro) only she'd flashed it in a sideways gesture. After close inspection, he'd felt so stupid for not knowing what she meant but his mind was a little foggy on account of not having his morning coffee.

"I'd have to invite you over for dinner sometime, Sheriff." She said, thumbing his left shoulder. "I'll take you on a tour of his I mean our mansion and then take you around London in a horse-drawn carriage and show you–"

A bell rang out across the street, cutting her off in mid-sentence. Lizzie, Hugh Rainey and a middle-aged bald man in dirt-stained work clothes stepped out of the café one at a time; Norm knew the bald man was Jacob Crandall, owner of a little general store on the southwest corner of the square called (what else) Crandall's Corner. It wasn't how they were acting that aroused Norm's attention but it was because of where they were looking.

"What time did he say he was coming?"

"He's not coming." She nodded. "He's sent me a bus tic–"

A loud grumbling sound seeped into the town square, cutting her off in mid-sentence. Her face and brows creased in confusion, they glanced in the same direction that Lizzie and the others had done a little while ago.

A lime-green pickup truck appeared from around the corner, its front windshield bathed in tree shadows. It stopped between a red Subaru and a white Honda and screeched to a halt, tainting the air with the stench of burnt rubber. The engine was left idling as thick white clouds of exhaust spewed out from a rusted metal tailpipe and dissipated in thin air. Norm heard a second bell, followed by another and then another until it was all he could hear.

Mike Danson (a tall broad-shouldered man in a plaid shirt and jeans) appeared out of Danson's Motel of course and listened for the driver-side door to open; Lyle Camp stepped out from his barber shop on the corner of Hope Street, the open neckline of his long white coat exposing a V-shaped sliver of a light blue shirt and red tie; Susanne Tripp stepped out of Pratt's Photos in a peach blouse and black slacks, her long blonde hair stirring lazily in the breeze. Other proprietors and their customers stepped onto the town square and stared at them from a safe but respectable distance. A few townspeople, the ones who made the long drive from here to either Memphis or Greeneville to make a decent wage, joined in the noose of quizzical stares flooding the town square; a few of them traded whispers amongst themselves. A group of teenage boys sped past the front of the crowd and skidded to a stop, their tires leaving crescent black marks in the asphalt and looked on with both awe and curiosity on their faces.

Norm slipped his gray ten-gallon off his head and wiped the film of sweat from his brow with his right arm. He heard the distinct sound of hurried footsteps shuffling across the hot gray tarmac and placed his hat back on his head. A figure appeared from his left, its tall brawny build blotting out the bright golden rays of the new-risen sun glinting off Dawn's rings and Norm's badge like a chrome bumper.

"Mornin', sheriff."

"Mornin, Cooter."

He tilted his head to one side and gazed up at a tall middle-aged man wearing jeans, muddy brown boots, and dark-green coveralls. He had thinning dark hair, coarse brown skin, thick broad shoulders; a net of worry lines bracketed the corners of his basset-hound green eyes and bulbous lips. Norm rose up from the bench and stretched until he could hear his joints pop and crackle like bubble wrap and relaxed in time to shake Cooter's hand.

After the two men exchanged a hushed conversation, Dawn said, "What the hell are you doing here, bro?"

Cooter closed his eyes, shook his head and sighed. He opened them and stared down at his sister with a heavy, morose expression on his face. Norm was familiar with that look, as was everybody else in Madisonville; the poor sombitch's father had pulled him out of bed to fetch her and bring her back.

"I'm here to take you home, sis."

"I don't need to go back there." She said. "I'm on my way–

She glanced over her right shoulder, eying the battered brown suitcase leaning against the other side of the bench. The big brass tacks bordering the top and bottom were streaked with tiny scratches; it had more wear and tear on it than their father.

"Daddy's worried sick about you. He wants you to come home so we can eat breakfast together."

"I'm not hungry." She hissed. "I'll wait until Reginald picks me up so that I have real food. The kind of food cooked by–"

"the best chefs from France?"

A line of confusion creased Dawn's forehead as she gawked suspiciously up at him. He patted Norm's shoulder and, with a low painful grunt, knelt down beside of the bench. Cooter was three years older than his little sister, which meant old age was still playing hell with his bones.

"How–" She muttered, her face creasing. "How did you know?"

"I've known for a long time, Dawn. And so have you." He said, his voice brimming with sympathy. "Everything you've told everyone was the same thing he told the other women he scammed. Do you remember when you stole Momma's brooch from her jewelry box Daddy put in the attic and pawned it in Johnson City?"

Her face flushed with shame, a tear protruded from the corner of her right eye and cleaved a lucid trail across the patch of rouge still blooming across her cheek. Her face devoid of any expression, she mumbled through pursed lips before raising her voice so that everyone could hear.

"He said that if I sent him some money he would send me a ticket in the mail and then take me–"

"'to his castle on the hill overlooking London and make you his bride'. You weren't the only he told that story to, sis. He's not real. Reginald Barrington is just a fake name made up by somebody who lied to steal your money. He didn't really love you, Dawn. He lied to you just like he–"

'Lied to everyone else' was what Cooter wanted to say.

Norm had been informed of the situation by Dawn's father, Bo Matthews and did his best to keep it under wraps. Thanks to his secretary Hannah, it didn't take long for everyone in town to know what happened. He never understood the validation people got from spreading gossip but that's what you get when you live in Small Town America; people with nothing better to do than cut people down behind their back.

Dawn leaped up from the bench, her face twisted with mad feral hunger and gave a pained gasp. She lunged at Cooter and began to pound her tiny white-knuckled fists hard against the center of his chest. He stood ramrod still, his body never faltering under the damage she failed to inflict.

Realization led to foolishness, which then led to her being angry at herself for believing *Reginald*'s deceitful fantasy. She'd gone to great lengths such has treating her family like garbage and selling her deceased mother's most prized possession to be with that cold, heartless bastard. If there was one thing a person could always hold onto, the one thing that would always meant the most, it was love; pure and unconditional love.

Norm would've intervened by now but not today. Not on *the third day of the third week of every month* when everyone in the town of Madisonville could set their watch and find this woman sitting right back on that very bench, bragging about and waiting for a man who *never* existed.

The crowd gasped in unison. Norm flashed an authoritative stare at the crowd and raised his hands in a calming gesture.

Her resolve diminishing with each passing second, Dawn's fists slackened into a slow-motion barrage of gentle taps; her arms grew weak from exertion and flopped down against her sides. Her hair lay across her head in light brown tangles as a river of sweat beads and tears slid down her face and distorted her makeup, sending rings of wet black mascara oozing down her cheeks. Her head slumped toward the middle of her back, she drooped over and sat down on the edge of the curb.

Norm heard a chorus of faint whispers rising up from the crowd; he could see that a few of them were crying. Cooter stooped down, cradled his little sister's hips, hoisted her off of the curb and onto her feet. He crouched down to retrieve her suitcase from the sidewalk, his eyes still constricted from lack of sleep, and walked beside of his little sister.

Her head resting against his right shoulder, she wiped her face with her right hand and lowered her arm back down. Norm breathed a sigh of relief, shook his head and drew a long pocket of wildflower air deep into his lungs.

"He said he loved me and that–"

"he'd take you for his bride." He reminded her while snatching her suitcase from the sidewalk "You'll make any man a beautiful bride, sis. It just won't be today."

As Cooter carried her off, her misguided aura parting the crowd like Moses, Norm sauntered into Lizzie's Café with the sad realization that all it took was a few sweet words to whittle the human soul down to nothing more than a broken heart.

A DIFFERENT KIND OF THERAPY

This story is for all of the bullies out there.
We hope you're happy about everything you ever did.

The following conversation was recorded on April 26, 2018 at 10:15 p.m. It was found six hours later by two uniformed officers from The Logan City Police Department at 3:45 p.m.

Thanks for seeing me on such short notice, Doctor Moore.

No problem, sir. I'm sorry I didn't get your last name.

Ryan Hudson. I wouldn't have called if it wasn't important, but I had to see you.

(Door clicks. Shuffling footsteps)

It's a nice day, isn't it? I like it when the sun bounces off the edge of the skyscrapers. It makes them look like knives.

Huh?

Nothing. I was just saying that it's a nice day.

My son is going on a class field trip to the zoo today. He's pretty excited about it.

I bet. I know you have other patients to see so I'll try to be–

It's okay, Mister Hudson. You're the only person I have scheduled today so there's no rush. I'll be closed until Tuesday because I'm going to Cleveland this weekend.

Vacation?

Funeral. My best friend died.

I'm sorry to hear about that.

That's okay. What is it you wanted to see me about?

I can't shake this feeling no matter how hard I try. I need to find out even if it's the last thing I do. Aren't you going to write all of this down?

No, I'm recording it.

Really? That little thing will record everything we say. It doesn't look like a tape recorder. At least not the ones I remember.

Yeah. It looks like a ball point pen but it beats having to write everything down.

(Moore clears his throat)

That's cool.

So, what it is that's–

Sorry (sighs) How can people be so inhumane these days? Is there any kindness left in this world? We've got so much going on around us that we never take the time to embrace every second of our life and treat people as we'd like to be treated. Where I come from, respect is a two-way street; you give it, you'll get it.

To be quite honest, some people have to do so in order to establish dominance.

I'm not saying people can't be social with one another but why can't they just not measure our necks for nooses.

If you disrespect them, don't be surprised if they do it back to you.

(Moore clears his throat)

That's what I thought, too but then I started to think about something that happened to me when I was a teenager and it made me think otherwise.

Tell me about it.

Are you sure?

It's what I'm here for (Moore scoffs) isn't it?

True. Well I wasn't part of the popular cliques, you know. I never went out for any extracurricular activities because my parents were always dragging me from one town to the other because my father couldn't hold a job to save his ass, so it didn't really make much sense for me to make–can I get a glass of water?

Sure.

Thanks.

(Footsteps padding across the room. Faucet hums, then dies. Glass tinkles)

Please continue.

I was thirteen and very shy around most people, but my only friends were the books I liked to read. I read a lot a poetry and horror fiction and I still do. They're the only things that managed to stick around in my life.

Books are a great distraction.

Then I got to realizing very quick that being different didn't mean you were accepted for who you were. It just made me a bigger shit magnet for every swinging dick in that–

(Silence)

What's wrong, Mister Hudson?

I'm sorry I didn't mean to cuss.

It's okay. I've heard much worse coming from my other patients. Please continue.

So, then they drag me to this crappy little town called Logan because my father wanted to be closer to his family although they didn't give one iota of shit about me or my mother. And it wasn't like I could say no because I was thirteen but then I also like to think that Mom just went along with it so he'd shut the hell up about it.

Was he ever abusive toward you and your mother?

He liked to beat us up on days that ended in 'why'

It's a common thing for victims of abuse to give in to their abusers demands in order to make their lives easier for them and their children.

Anyway, I had to go to this school on top of this hill and they had these pansy ass colors, too. Who the hell walks around wearing purple and white? I wouldn't be caught dead in those colors if I–are you okay, Doctor Moore?

I'm fine.

You were biting your lip just a few seconds ago. Are you in any kind of pain?

My knee's been giving me fits, but it's okay. Keep going, please.

I was walking to my locker one day when my books were slapped out of my hand and they spilled out onto the hallway. My Superman comic slid under some kid's shoe and he stepped on it and left a big shoeprint on it. One of the teachers was nice enough to come and help me pick everything off the floor and then write me a note so I wouldn't get wrote up for being tardy.

Did you find who was responsible for slapping your books out of your hands?

A couple of eighth graders named Travis Wilson and Jason Adler.

And did you confront them?

Oh, hell no. I didn't want to make matter worse, so I ignored them in the hope that they would do the same. You know, respect being a two-way street and everything. But then I realized they were the gym teacher's assistants and not only did they pick me last in all of the activities but they told everyone a bunch of rumors about me that weren't true and really hurtful..

I'm sorry to hear about that.

That's okay. But then nothing hurts more than when your parents believed them no matter how many times you told the truth.

Was there anything about that place that you liked?

One thing, maybe.

Okay, good. Now we're getting somewhere. Was it your favorite subject? Did you make friends with a teacher?

Her name was Sandra Mohler.

A girl, huh?

There are girls and there are angels. She was an angel. Five-foot-nine, long dark-brown hair and the most gorgeous green eyes.

Did you ever ask her out?

If I was too shy around other people, what makes you think I was gonna do that?

Even if she turned you down, it would've helped you shake off your shyness. The only thing you should've been afraid of was what she would've said.

I never got the chance to ask her out especially since–

We can stop here if you like.

No, I need to get this off my chest or it'll keep tearing me apart.

If you insist but I need to inform you that I reserve the right to stop the session at any time.

I bought a notebook and started writing all of these poems about her. My private thoughts and feelings were in these poems, too and I only did it because I knew she'd never go for a lump like me but then I thought that I would give them to her one day to let her know how I really felt. I mean, girls like poems, don't they?

It depends.

I was writing two and three poems a day and every one of them was about the dreams I had of her and the life I dreamed of having with her. The way her top lip slid up to show a little gum every time she smiled and the way her eyes glinted in the overhead lights when she stared up at the blackboard during class.

You'd gotten this far. Why didn't you show them to her?

It wasn't like I could hide them forever. I was standing beside of my locker one day and I hung my Red Sox cap on the inside hook when I saw Sandra standing at the other end of the hallway inside of her little clique of friends and laughing about something one of them said. I took my journal out of my bookbag and started writing my next poem when my notebook was snatched right out of my hand and when I turned around that stupid prick Jason was holding it over my head and then his fat ass boyfriend slammed me up against the wall and held me there while he read every line out loud to everyone in the hallway and when he was done he'd tear out the pages and crumple them up and drop them onto the floor. Each word he read was like a knife in my heart and he just kept plunging that blade into my heart and soul deeper and deeper and deeper inside of me, laughing while all of my private thoughts were no longer private but laid out on the table for everyone to see.

Did any of the teachers come out to help you?

Yeah, after everyone else laughed me right out of that place. I ran home screaming and crying and I begged my parents not to make me go back and they–

(Hudson sniffles)

–made me go back there and then everyone called me names and then the principal took me aside and told me that Sandra's parents threatened to sue if I didn't stay away from her so I never said a word to anyone at all for the rest of the time I was there. And the nightmares were something too, Doc. All I could hear was their childish laughter and then snippets of my personal thoughts echoing through the hallways of that cruel and sadistic place. There are times when I dream about being a father but then I realize that they're gonna have to face tough times like that and I say no no no I'm not doing this to them. I'm not going to subject them to that kind of disrespect.

Life is full of challenges, Mister Hudson. It's how we persevere that makes us the person we are.

Why couldn't they just respect my space and leave me alone? Why do people have to be so inhumane to the kid standing in the corner doing nothing to no one? I'd rather bash my toes in with a sledgehammer then go about the rest of my life knowing that I had anything to do with–

I'm sure it wasn't as bad as you thought. I'm actually a proud graduate of–

I know you are. I know more about you than you think.

What makes you–

You have a wife named Penny who works as a secretary at a local accounting firm. Your daughter Erica goes to Logan Middle School and she's captain of the volleyball team.

I think we're–

No, I don't think we're done, Doctor Moore. Or should I call you by your real name, Travis Wilson.

(Silence)

Don't tell my name didn't ring a bell? I mean there was only one Ryan Hudson who attended Logan Middle School.

If I could just go on record and say that I'm–

You're only saying that because you're afraid of what I'm capable of doing. You took your wife's last name because you did–

SHUT UP!

It wasn't very hard to find you especially since they put your picture in the health and medicine section of the local newspaper. It was right next to the caption LOCAL DOCTOR WINS NATIONAL–

You never loved Sandra like I did, you little twerp! I'd been talking to her in gym class for the past two years while you were off writing your sappy-ass sonnets and acting like you were too chickenshit to say anything to her.

Now there's the Travis Wilson I remember from high school. The same sadistic, broke-ass prick who bullied everyone because if his life sucked then so should everyone else's.

(Glass slides across table)

I'm not going to do anything to your family for what you did to me because then that would be wrong. It doesn't make sense for me to go after them for the pain you caused me.

(Silence)

Why so quiet, Doc? Josh wasn't as quiet even after I cut the brake line on his car.

You killed Jason?

I've been pretty busy these past few weeks. I even paid a visit to Sandra, but just in case you're–

How is she?

Sitting poolside with a margarita in one hand and the pool boy's dick in the other. She didn't turn out to be any different than the girls she used to hang around with. Married to some cee-eee-oh by their thirties, drinking Bloody Marys' and cabana boys until three and blah-blah-blah.

You're an asshole, you know that.

You're the asshole, Travis. You and Jason and that fucking school and my parents made me the asshole I am today. By the way, Jason's death is going to be a closed casket deal since that fat fuck didn't have a chance in hell of stopping his car before it hit the tail end of that semi at ninety miles an hour.

What's-what-what–

(A soft gurgle fills the background)

Are you okay? You don't look too good, doc.

I can-I can't-my throat is–

They were right about aconite. It really does work.

Call-call the–

(A loud bubbling sound fills the background)

You sweat profusely, and you have an irregular heartbeat and then you slowly start to ashphyx–

(A soft thud followed by the sound of shattered glass)

Well, I feel so much better now that I've got all of that off my chest. I think I'll take a drink too. No sense in having it all go to waste. Oh, shit. I didn't know we were still recording so I'll just go ahead and take a sip and-mmm that is some good water. Let's just go ahead and shut this—

VOICE RECORDER DIES

<u>A PROPER BURIAL</u>

AS I stated before, writers like to mix things up. Mystery and horror or in this case, a western horror.

As a child, if I had a penny for every time I walked into the living room and saw my father watching a western on television, I'd been one rich little shit. I thought they were boring and the farthest thing from my mind until I watched Big Jake, Tombstone and Unforgiven.

I wrote my first western horror story after watching a scene in "The Horse Soldiers" starring John Wayne and Rock Hudson and it was published in the anthology, "The Book Of Cannibals 2". It isn't featured here but like many others, you will see it in a future collection. This story was inspired by Jack Ketchum's "The Western Dead" and if you haven't read it please do so.

<u>1885</u>

"GRANDPA!" Clay exclaimed, squinting into the gloom.

"Howdy, partner." A familiar voice said in an uneasy tone.

When he stepped out onto the front porch, the cool spring breeze snapped him out of his fatigued state. A skinny old man appeared at the foot of the front porch steps, his rail-thin frame outlined by the waxy-white moon. His wrinkled skin–which had once been white as the moon itself–now had a soot-gray tint and a thin cap of wispy-white hair stuck up from his large liver-spotted head. He wore a dingy and ragged salmon-colored shirt under a pair of blue-jean coveralls; his bushy-white beard hung three inches past the tip of his chin and the matching mustache nearly shrouded his upper lip.

He had a sorrowful look on his face like a dog staring down the barrel of a gun. He braced the sides of his hat with both hands, his craggy gray fingers tapping against the ragged brim.

"What in tarnation are you doin'?"

"Did you gone foregut?"

Clay glanced to his right and saw his big brother Pete leaning against the porch railing, all six-foot-three of him. He wore a pin-striped blue shirt and black pants under a camel-colored frock coat. The big brown Stetson on his wide bullet-shaped head shaded the top half of his face save for the wreath of salt-and-pepper beard hugging his square-jawed face.

He peered up at the moon and sighed when he realized what time it was. It wasn't that he'd forgotten; he just wished that it'd happened in the middle of the day not in the middle of the night.

Why should he worry?

He was more worried about if and when Laura was going to come back anytime soon; he hadn't eaten a good home-cooked meal in weeks and he could sure go for a bowl of her famous beef stew. This time, when she did come back, he'd do whatever she wanted as long as she stayed; anything.

"Why does the house look so damn dark, son?" Grandpa asked curiously. "Why don't you tell that pretty lil–"

Pete gave a fake cough and cut him off in mid-sentence. He jerked his head in Clay's general direction and mouthed the word "no". Grandpa nodded, bowed his head and fixed his gaze back at Clay, his rheumy-gray eyes glistening like ten pennies.

"I'm sore I–"

Clay cut him off with a dismissive wave of his hand and nodded. He couldn't expect his grandfather to be up on current events; he had matters of his own to worry about. Pete craned his head toward the watercolor sky and then back at his brother.

"We best git goin', little bro." He said. "We best get there before sunup."

Clay sighed, motioned for them to wait outside and lumbered back inside. The place had been too dark for his liking but the past always had a way of making you adjust to the future; it would be cold and dark for quite some time. He slipped on a dingy white shirt, brown boots with matching pants and a white down coat; he couldn't remember the last time he used his Colt but since time was of the essence he gave up and strapped on his suspenders.

"Are you comin'?" He asked, casting a sideways glance at his brother.

"Why can't eye?"

"Any other time you bring him here," He said, shutting the door behind him. "you've gon rode away from here like you saw the devil sose I end up doin' it mself."

Clay was walking up to Grandpa when Pete came stomping after him, his big heavy boots clomping against the hard packet desert. He spun around on his heels, his fists raised and ready and fired an icy cold stare that stopped the big man dead in his tracks. The look had scared him plenty of times in the past when they stood a knee high to a grasshopper but it didn't work tonight.

"You got sumthin' to say?" Pete said, inching his face closer to Clay's "Then spit it out?"

"I just think it's a lil strange when you decide to help me tonight seein' is how I've been doin' this on my own for five doggone years."

"I've got my reason. Don' you worry cause after dis you never gone see me 'gain."

Pete flapped one massive manly hand at his little brother and walked back to Grandpa.

That wasn't exactly what Clay had wanted but there was no way to reason with a big stubborn bastard like him. Pete was always "playing the victim" when he didn't get attention for not doing what everyone else around him had been doing. Clay glanced past his brother's shoulder, absorbed the black desert landscape sprawled out before him, drew his breath deep into his lungs and sighed.

In the time it'd taken him to get ready, a full moon sat high in the night sky spreading an alabaster glow that outlined the spines of the mountains that rose along the horizon. The short grass prairie weaved in the breath of the wind; the stream behind his brown stucco abode churned and bubbled around wet dark rocks while glinting in the downward glare of the moon. He felt the hairs along the back of his neck stiffen at the sight of the treacherous black prairie waiting to swallow them as it'd done plenty of other ancestors before them.

When he glanced back at his brother, a muscle twitched in their jaws as if they were fighting off the urge to hit each other. Pete slipped his pistol out of his holster, spun the chamber and watched the moonlight reflect off the edge of the barrel before he holstered it.

Something struck the ground with a heavy thud. They flinched and spun, their scarred black bootheels kicking small clouds of dust across the hard-packed sand. Clay's skin prickled with fear; his heart thudded like thunder.

Grandpa knelt down and plucked his right arm from the ground between his feet. It'd fallen off at the shoulder, revealing a flaky gray stub; the bones jutting out of his fallen arm were reduced to thin pockets of powdery-white dust carried off in the breeze. He flicked his gaze from Clay to Pete and held his arm in the air above his head like a torch.

"It's just my dad blame arm." He said. "Are we gonna get ma ass back into the dirt fore sunup or sit around here nippin' at each other like a bunch of old biddies."

*****

THEY headed north through the mountains, per Clay's instructions.

He'd buried Grandpa in the west as far and as much as he could before moving off to the east until tonight when he realized he couldn't bury him there anymore. North was as good as he was going to get at least for now before he'd have to start combing the South.

He'd gotten a good look at the scenery over yonder and had planted a few grave markers around to help him pick out the proper places. He'd dug out a lot of holes, six-feet-under and six-feet-wide, and left them open to make it easier for him to bury them again. He hoped he could still find them.

Clay gathered a lantern and an old shovel with a scarred wooden handle from the shed and lit the lantern with a box of matches Pete had given him. He kept the wick down just enough to allow them plenty of light to see where they were going and carried the shovel perched on his left shoulder. Pete held his Grandpa's rotting arm and decided to walk in between them to avoid getting hit; he thought that if Clay had the chance to ring his bell with one good swing he'd take it.

"I want you boys to understand somethin'." Grandpa said, wagging a lone finger at them. "Life is somethin' you should never take for granted cause I sore did and look what hapn'."

They followed the two-track dirt road that started from the front of Clay's house and stretched along the crick before connecting onto a straight stretch in the direction they agreed to go. When they entered the mouth of the forest, Clay licked a drop of sweat from his upper lip and felt the hairs on the back of his neck rise again. He felt naked without his pistol but whatever lurked out there in the shadows would go down with one good swing.

"I ad a chance to make my life somethin' special that most young'uns only drep about. I used to deal cards and shoot a bullet like the res' of them but there were a few times when I didn't get so lucky. My goose could've been cooked several times fore' now, let me tell yaw. I gotta hand it to your Grandma Bessie, though. She had the patience of a saint and such a gud heart I'd think to meself that I never deserved her and I still don'." He said, then stopped and gazed over his shoulder at Clay. "Where did you bury your grandma?"

The question made Clay's heartbeat accelerate. The bright orange glow from the lantern splayed across their faces, cloaking it in a mask of half-light and half shadow.

"Thirteen miles south."

"Okie." Grandpa nodded. "Did you burry her right?"

"I buried her the way she always wanted to be." Clay said, shrugging a lone shoulder.

Grandpa mumbled under his breath. He tried to take his hat off with his right arm and scowled when he realized that Pete had been carrying it the whole time. He brought the back of his right hand hard across the meaty part of Clay's right shoulder and drew his lips back in a tight angry snarl.

"You bess not be jerkin' my chain."

"Grandma wanted to be buried with her ass in the air so that anyone who ever disrespect her cool come by and kiss it. I was just doing what I was told."

"I can't believe her."

Clay waited for the look of stunned surprise to fall across his grandfather's face before he cracked into a smile. Pete shook his head, clamped his hand across his mouth and glanced down at his feet to hide the comical look on his face.

"She said you'd do at."

"Do wha?"

"She new you'd get a burr in your ass if she toll me to tell you she was burry like that when she isn't."

Grandpa's forehead puckered with confusion and his mouth shrunk into a tight-lipped snarl. He saw the mischievous grin on his grandsons' faces, gave them an angry scowl and whopped them both across the shoulder with the brim of his hat. They chuckled again, unfazed by the playful slaps and felt the tension between them sliding away.

They continued on and followed the road for another three miles before the forest finally opened; Clay felt a little better about being out of the darkness although he'd never been afraid of it before tonight. The road snaked through a wide open field of high grass on the left and a flat grassy plain on the right. A thick leafy oak tree stood on the right, its spiky-haired shadow rippled across the prairie; the high grass billowed in the breeze that caressed their faces and stirred their coats.

"As eyes saying," Grandpa said, hitching his pants with his left hand. "I wish ever day of my life I hadn't laid eyes on that woman but hell I couldn't help it."

Pete rolled his eyes and mumbled something under his breath. Clay reared his head back, scrunched his face together and stared annoyingly at his brother.

"Me, your papa and your cousin Jed comin' back home from hauling a herd of cattle to Abilene and we were gonna be a day behind because of a storm before I could feel your grandma's body warth again."

They nodded but that was all.

"We's pickin' up some supplies from a general store in Theodore when eyes saw her standin' at the counter. She had the prettiest dark hair that wen pas her shoulders and the prettiest brown eyes I'd ever seen. She wore one of those long dresses with the knots at the bottom and a white shawl with all kinds of beads on it. We changed our mins' after she left and followed her about six miles outside of town. I couldn't get that beeyoutifull smile out of my head no matter how hard I tried and ever time I thought of it I felt a little jingle in my spurs."

The old man's cracked gray lips pulled back in a wide pleasing grin and massaged his crotch with his left hand. The note of erotic satisfaction in Grandpa's voice made Clay's stomach churn with disgust. He swallowed and tried to put himself in another time and another world where he didn't think about his grandparents playing slap and tickle under the covers.

"We's found her living on this patch of land next to a crick bed but she wasn't alone. She had two little Injuns and a couple of elders livin' with her and dey's cookin' outside of their little teepees but the two women livin' with her boot day's weren't as purdy as her. We rode onto their camp and shot every woman and child there cept her and the ol' man she'd been kissin' wasn't just standin' in my way but he was shakin' some kind of dog gone bag in my face and spoutin' all kinds of Injun language. I din't know what he was doin' but if eye'd known then what eyes new now I'd would've just shot them both and rode off with watever they had."

They'd cleared the tree by now and went onto another straight stretch. The night was silent save for the rhythmic call from the cicadas and the wind moaning in the treetops. Pete yawned, licked the roof of his mouth and regarded at the surreal beauty of the great dark frontier.

"We's shot that old man and kicked him into the river that day. We's got off of our horses and–and–." His voice cracked.

His head slumped over and his shoulders sagged. There were a lot of things Clay had enjoyed in thirty-six years but this wasn't one of them. There was something nauseous about watching a man's pride crumble like stale bread; his soul leaked out into the shadows and receded out of sight never to be seen again.

"I member jumpin' on top of her and she fought me the whole way and then I tore her clothes off and then slapped her ded' cross the face and rolled her onto her belly. By then, your Paw and Jed were over there holdin' her arms down and all I could hear was her screams and when I got 'side of her she was tight as a fist but I got her to loos up after a while and pounded her snatch but good til' I forgot all about your grandma's warmth and when I had my fill Jed tied her hands together with rope and then tied it to un of the tent stakes and all I could hear was their belt buckles jinglin' like somethin' fierce and den thay took their turn and when thay's done thay fillid her with lead and left her dere to bleed like a stuck pig but now that I think about it at least the poor girl didn't have to suffa like we do."

A few moments of silence passed before Grandpa said, "And that's wer that dang curse come from. That old Injun was a galdamn medicine man. Slap us with a curse harder than my Pappy's switch was wat he did."

Clay had heard the story more times than he cared to but there was nothing wrong in letting an old man say what was on his mind. A dead old man, in fact. He could've shut him up at any point and time but he couldn't bring himself to deny him that nor could he blame the old man for feeling like he did and for that he'd let him say whatever he wanted as long as it made him feel better.

They didn't forget what happened to Jed and Great Grandpappy, either. Jed's wife found him in the barn with a bottle of rotgut whiskey and a double barrel in his mouth; his top teeth were clamped onto the top of the barrel–at least the ones that hadn't been blown into the wall or managed to stay in place after years of tobacco use. And Grandpappy? Poor bastard was checking the fence around the chicken coop when his horse lost its footing and fell on top of him; by the time anyone found him the coyotes made sure he didn't scream again.

Grandpa rubbed his eyes but kept on trudging. There weren't enough tears in the world to make up for what they'd done to that innocent woman. And in for their dastardly deed, their family was cursed to repeat this process over and over and over again.

Two miles later, he lost his footing and hit the ground sideways. Clay lowered the lantern and found the old man's right leg lying on the ground beside of him, wriggling like a worm on a hook; a carpet of powdery-white dust spilled out. Pete wanted Clay to carry him but when Clay reminded him about the tools perched on his shoulder the odds were not in Pete's favor.

He set the tools and the lantern down long enough to hoist the old man onto Pete's wide fleshy back, retrieved his tools and led the way.

"You bes not bite me," Pete warned Grandpa. "or I'll blow your damn head off."

Clay jerked his head to the side, motioning for them to follow him into the forest. They slapped at a few overhead branches that grappled at their clothes and skin; shafts of bone-white moonbeams sifted through the trees, spreading brittle black tree shadows across the forest. The sound of dry leaves and frail twigs crackling under their feet echoed through the forest and barely muffled the resounding chorus of cricket calls.

Once they found the right trail, Pete asked Grandpa, "What's it like?"

"Wha?"

"The afterlife. What's it like?"

Grandpa glanced up at the sky, his rheumy gray eyes glistening in the firelight. He sighed in Pete's ear, causing the big man to cringe and pull his head away. Pete shook off the noxious smell of wet dirt and rotted breath from his face and fought back every fiber in his body to not curse at his brother for making him carry this old bag of bones.

"I really can't tell ya." He said in a slow riveting voice. "It's kinda hard to describe it you know."

"Damn." Pete winced. "You're breath smells like you died."

Grandpa jabbed him in the ribs with his left boot until Pete winced. Clay led them over the crest of a hill and glanced up just in time to see the marker he planted in front of a pair of thick gray oaks. Clay glanced into the pockets of darkness and moonlight filling the forest and sighed, his eyes roving across the other white-painted grave markers he'd placed throughout; plenty of places to bury the kind of sin that'll never stay grounded whether under the bright-blue heavens or inside the warmth of Hell's fiery catacombs.

The hole was so clean and hollow it made Grandpa whistle with glee. Pete sighed, slid the old man onto the ground next to the edge of the grave and lowered him inside.

Clay approached the grave and held the lantern low enough to see his grandfather's face. Pete and the old man shared an uncomfortable glance, then fixed a somber glance back at Clay. Clay saluted his grandfather; Grandpa gave another cocky grin and returned it using the slowly decomposing arm.

"I'll see you boys later."

They laughed and then set to work filling the grave with dirt. They told him he could talk while they did as long as it had nothing to do with his and Grandma's sexual escapades (or as Pete said it *es-ki-pates*) When the grave was fully covered, the forest became quiet once again save for the crickets still chirping in the darkness.

Pete stomped his boot onto the hard-packed dirt to make sure it would hold. At least for now. Clay held the lantern as high as it would go for him to see when he saw something out of the corner of his eye. A second grave had been dug up on the far right side of the tree; it too had a grave marker like the one he'd placed.

"Tanks for diggin' the other hole." Clay said, then snorted. "It'll save me the trouble of having to do it next year."

Pete leaned the shovel against the side of the tree and stared down at the open grave with a hangdog expression on his face. His six-foot-three frame outlined by the flickering orange glow coming from the lantern, he scratched his beard distractedly.

Thin pockets of dirt clogged their cuticles and stained their rough-hewn hands. A sheen of sweat coated their foreheads, trickled down their cheeks and glued their shirts to their backs.

He pivoted from beside of the tree and gave his brother a somber look. Tears welled up in his eyes, glistening in the light. Clay's cheeks flushed, his features softening with both fear and confusion.

"Not you, too." Clay pleaded.

Pete slipped a hand inside of his coat pocket and produced a thin slip of gray paper, its edges jagged and thin. He stretched his arm out from his side it toward his brother's face and held the slip of paper pinched between his thumb and forefinger.

"It's not mine."

Clay sighed, his breath issuing from his lips in a quick horror-struck wheeze, and stared at his own obituary.

UNCLE BUBBY

I know this isn't a horror story but I had to include this one. My love for crime-noir stories have started since I read Max Allan Collins' "A Matter Of Principle" at the age of twelve and then decided to move onto Jim Thompson's "A Hell Of A Woman". This story was inspired by another noir story called "Attack" by Ed McBain (Writing As Hunt Collins) and this day I still read it every chance I get.

I'd also just become an uncle for the fourth time and as strong as I think I am I'll always think about the obstacles my niece and nephews will have to face in life. I'm sure I share this fear with a lot of other parents and, like all writers, I shed that fear on paper.

Hell hath no fury like a parent scorned, right?

SOMETHING moved along the front of the house sitting across the street. Bright colorful neon flickered from the electronic sign beside of the Mom and Pop I'd been parked at for nearly an hour and glinted off the front bumper of my burnt-orange pickup like broken glass.

A young skinny girl in a short-sleeved pink shirt and frayed blue jeans stormed out the front door and down the front porch stairs toward a blue Oldsmobile Cutlass, mumbling under her breath. She reached in the driver-side window, jerked her arm back out of the car, slapped a pack of cigarettes against her right hand, slipped one between her lips and lit it with a bright-pink Bic. The breeze drifted into my front cab, bringing the mingled aromas of pine sap and wood smoke across my face; the soft purr of Friday night traffic was a lullaby in the night.

I lowered the visor and looked at the dog-eared photo taped onto the inside. In the photo, a rail-thin redhead with pale freckled skin wearing a strapless white dress and brown leather boots with neat-black curlicues stitched along the sides leaned against a thick oak tree; *MAY 99* was scrawled across the lower right-hand corner in bright golden font. I'd only seen her a few times in the past before she wore that dress or knew what a glamour photo was.

It was only a few days ago when I discovered she was gone, a letter scrawled in both desperation and fear. All I knew was that her name was Hailey; beautiful little Hailey.

I raised the visor back into place as a red Volvo pulled into the slot beside of me. I peered down at the passenger floorboard and cupped my hand over my eyes in a half-assed salute as if I were waiting for someone. I glanced back across the road, trickles of cold sweat sliding down my back and hips, and watched the bright-red tip of her cigarette weave in the dark.

I slid my hand inside of my black racer jacket, tapped the six-inch barrel of my S&W 686 until the barrel prodded my right hip and snatched a few quick breaths to prepare myself. I waited for the driver of the Volvo to go inside before I slid out and shut the door behind me. The door coughed, spilling flakes of rust onto pavement; I didn't want to leave my truck here but I couldn't let them see me coming.

An angry December wind tore at my cheeks, teased my hair and grazed the back of my neck. The thought of a beautiful sandy beach and my beautiful woman kept me from getting too cold. A brand-name gas-station-slash-convenience store sat on the corner of the next block, glowing brighter than an albino's bare ass.

The house–like all of the others slapped down beside of it– looked as if they'd been made out of glue and popsicle sticks. Once word got around to what I was doing, it didn't take long for me to fire up the proverbial grapevine to find out where she was. The trail of breadcrumbs and back-alley snitches who would sell their Mothers for a buck had led me here.

The town itself was just another cluster of middle-class housing tucked back from the highway like the classmate everyone liked to fuck with. A local VFW, a library no smaller than an airport bathroom and a post office had been tossed in somewhere along to give the place a false sense of belonging; a trailer park was scattered along the southwest side of town. I don't think it even had a name and if it did I didn't care about it.

Somewhere, an education was being wasted.

As far as I was concerned, this town and I had something in common. We didn't exist.

This was the part of me I tried to hide from everyone; the devil that sat on my shoulder and whispered sweet little lies in my ears, reminding me that the next move was as legit as reaching over for the snooze button on the alarm clock beside of my bed. I've had plenty of days and nights like this, but they were tucked much further away than the houses on this block and stuffed deep into the pockets of my past where I've sworn to keep them forever.

I kept my hand inside the front pocket of my jacket and hooked my fingers around the Wesson's smooth-walnut grip. A gray Ford Escort glided past me, carrying a rowdy caravan of drunk college students that howled along with a techno beat that thrummed against the windows. When I caught the mingled odors of mildew and urine wafting from the front of the house, I bit down on my bottom lip to keep me from getting nauseous.

She wasn't as young as I thought. She looked like she could take care of herself, too. She may have been small-town pretty at one time before all that smack.

I slipped the gun out of my pocket, flipped it in the air, caught it by the barrel and let her hear my footsteps. She turned, her pale cracked lips and heavy-lidded eyes wide with panic. She mumbled an incoherent plea, her cigarette moving along with the rhythm of her lips; a stream of warm piss trickled down her left leg, leaving a large concentric patch on her thigh.

I gritted my teeth and struck her hard across the left temple; her hair flew around her head like waves of amber fire. She spun around on pain-stricken legs, dove face-first into the cold patch of mud beside of the Cutlass and lay there like a broken stick; the cigarette had flown from her hand, spewing bright-orange coals across the lawn and landed into the mud with a low snake-like hiss.

I bent down to check her pulse to make sure she was still breathing and found tiny puncture holes in her arms; the faint imprint of a thin line hugged her left bicep. There was no telling how many pretty faces he'd turned to shit; she was another casualty on his list, a notch on his belt.

I flipped the gun back around, scanned the property and skulked up the front porch stairs. The stairs groaned under my weight. I cleared the last step and crept across the landing when the front door opened with a low groan, spilling a carpet of amber-colored light across the porch.

"I thought you were going–"

A tall heavyset figure appeared in the doorway wearing a gimmicky tee-shirt, blue-jean cutoffs and light brown-wicker sandals. Our eyes met. He then peered over my shoulder, saw the girl lying unconscious beside of the Cutlass and took no time in putting two and two together.

He cursed under his breath, spewing a strand of saliva from the right corner of his lip and slipped a hand into the back waistband of his cut-offs. He had thick brown dreadlocks (a mistake on any white person) narrow blue eyes and a tiny silver ring jammed into his left nostril. He knew I didn't come to talk about The Watchtower or Jesus Christ even at ten-forty-five at night.

"You son of–"

I fired, sending waves of recoil bursting through my arm. The first shot shattered his last two teeth; the second punched through his left nostril and out the back of his skull; chunks of soft red pulp sprayed the wall. He stumbled back inside the house, arms and legs flailing, and landed on a tacky overstuffed brown couch.

His gun, whatever it might've been, flew across the room and out of reach. He slid down the edge of the couch, his eyes wide with horror, and slumped down in front of the coffee table. On the coffee table, a glass ashtray sat on the right packed with half-spent joints; the flat screen in the far corner of the room displayed an early episode of *Dark Shadows*.

The wind flew into the room, sending mixed tendrils of gunpowder, marijuana and spent bowels across my face and stung my nostrils. I shook off the spikes of recoil still vibrating against my rotator cuff and held the gun down against my right thigh.

I padded through the living room and through a door less entry into a wide dirty kitchen with lime-green walls. A round wooden table sat on my left, cluttered with burnt spoons and severed strands of bright yellow tubing; a mountain of dirty dishes sat inside of a stainless-steel sink under a halo of buzzing flies. With each step I took, the dirty linoleum floor popped and crackled under my feet like bubble wrap; a roach skittered across the other side of the kitchen and disappeared inside the tiny space between the fridge and the stove.

A trail of dirty clothes streaked across the hallway toward a scarred white door. Fist-sized holes peppered the walls; there was nothing more destructive than a junkie with no smack. I followed the dirty clothes passed the bathroom and scowled at the noxious stench permeating from inside; too busy going to La-La Land to flush the toilet.

The door at the end of the hall was slightly ajar, allowing a jagged L of light to slice across the floor.

"It's okay, honey." said a soft nasally voice. "Lay back and let it take you to a place you've never been before."

I nudged the door with the barrel of my gun and let him see me. The lamp sitting on the floor in the far-left corner gave the room a gaslight glow; more clothes and recycled syringes were scattered across the shit-colored carpet. A skinny bald man sat on the edge of an old bare mattress stretched across the opposite end of the room.

I peered over his shoulder and saw a pair of skinny pale legs stretching toward the foot of the bed. He glanced over his shoulder at me, slid off the edge of the bed and stood, his hands bunched together by his side. His arms were corded with muscle and shrouded with bright-colorful tattoos; he looked like he'd done his fair share of time in a lot of places that guys like me would consider our home away from home.

She lie naked across the bed, looking less and less like the beautiful little Hailey I'd seen in the photo, exposing a list of things that no man should ever see: dark-brown areolas on flapjack breasts and a patch of bright-red hair tucked between her legs. A hypodermic needle stuck out of her right arm and her bright red hair was fanned out across the mattress like a blood-red pillow.

Her big green eyes were narrow and dark from the shot he'd just given her, sending her on a one-way ticket to Cloud Nine.

"You want a taste, big man?" The pusher said, rousing my attention away from her.

I tightened my grip on my gun. The light glinted off the edge of the second needle cupped inside of his right hand. His brown-black pupils widened; his fingers twitched as streams of high-octane meth pumped through his veins.

"No." I said, holstering the gun. "I just came for the girl."

"No can do." He shook his head. "I don't think I can allow to do that."

"We'll see, shit stain."

He grunted, pivoting on the ball of his right foot and pitched the needle across the room like he was going for the bullseye. I crouched, heard the needle fly over the top of my head in a straight whistling path and ran across the room. The needle struck the wall behind me and wobbled like an old door stopper.

I shifted my weight onto my left hip and snapped a left hook hard across his right jaw. He stumbled back, face scrunched in pain, and hit the wall. He shook it off, growled behind tightly-clenched teeth, and swung a fury of tight-knuckled fists at my face.

I knew I could've taken him out with my gun but I wanted to take my time with him; I wanted him to know that he was out of business–for good. He buried a left uppercut in the pit of my stomach hard enough to knock the air out of my tires and stood back, fists poised and ready. Stars bursting across my vision, I hit the wall and cradled my stomach.

He bounced on the balls of his feet like a boxer, hissed between thin pursed lips and threw a left jab. I snatched a quick breath, my vision wet and blurry, jerked my head to the side and heard his fist strike the wall. The brittle crack of broken bone echoed across the room as he gave a painful yelp and cradled his fist inside of his hand.

I tore the needle out from the wall, in case he tried to go for it, and tossed it on the floor. I wrenched my hands around his neck, lifted him three inches off the floor and pinned him against the wall. When I began to squeeze, he grunted and slapped at my wrists; the backs of his feet struck the wall in a frantic flight-or-die dance.

His eyes bulged out of their sockets as the dark-blue pallor on his face now bloomed to a choke-purple. I ignored the chorus of moans coming from the other side of the room where Hailey was still lying and pressed my fingertips into the sides of his neck. He gave a low dying wheeze and slumped over, spilling his courage down his pant legs and onto the floor in a brownish-yellow liquid.

I dropped him like an unwanted letter, watched him slide down the wall into the puddle of his own excrement and took a second to gather my thoughts. I strode across the room, tore the needle out of her arm and sat her up on the edge of the mattress; her skin felt cold and waxy. I draped my jacket over her shoulders, slid my hands under her knees, raised her off of the mattress and carried her out.

I set her on the porch, resting her head against the front porch railing and hurried back across the street to retrieve my pickup. I parked behind the Cutlass, letting the engine idle and carried her across the front lawn. The girl in the pink shirt was still splayed out across the driveway; she wouldn't come to until later when I was nothing but a taillight in an endless stream of other taillights coasting down the highway.

I opened the passenger door, laid her down on her side, shut the door and drove away.

*****

I was stretched across my hammock inside of my beachside hut, gazing out at the same bright blue ocean that kept me from getting too cold two nights ago when I had to become the person I promised I'd never be again and tried to purge those thoughts from my head. The gentle sigh of the wind and the susurration of the waves lapping at the shore had lulled me to sleep a few hours ago but the dreams of death and dying that I'd collected over the years roused me awake. I sat up, stretched until my bones ached, threw my legs over the side of the hammock, took a sip from the mug of steaming hot coffee sitting on table next to me and listened to the ocean's inner most secrets.

171

A shadow floated across the corner of my right eye. I looked over in time to see my girlfriend Nohea step through the door, carrying a thin stack of mail in her right hand. Her long black hair was tucked around the left side of her head and cascaded across her neck like a sleek dark cape; she wore a peach-colored off the shoulder dress and a big exotic pink flower tucked behind her left ear.

She flashed a smile that made my heart skip a beat, followed it with a wink and tossed a long white envelope onto my chest. I returned the wink and watched her saunter into the kitchen, her curvy brown body sashaying out from behind her.

The letter was addressed to me from Newark, Ohio. A sticker of a giant red O was fastened to the tri-folded lapels on the back. I took another sip of my coffee, set the cup back down, tore it open and set the envelope on the small wicker brown table.

"Hey, Big Bro. I can't thank you enough for what you did by bringing my daughter home safely. Calvin was beginning to doubt you but I knew you'd find a way. I don't expect you two to be the best of friends but I can't only hope that one day you two can set your differences aside for Hailey's sake. I know we didn't talk about a payment but we insisted on giving you something for your troubles."

A check for six thousand dollars was enclosed.

Two spaces below her name, she'd written, "P.S. Hailey is in rehab and they say she's doing great. She can't wait to go to Hawaii and spend time with her Uncle Bubby."

I sat staring at the letter for quite some time when something brushed across my left shoulder. Nohea appeared from my right, greeted me with another one of her patent pearly-whites and straddled my waist. When I slipped my arms around her, she leaned in for a kiss I didn't want to end.

"What did it say?"

"Nothing I haven't heard before."

I slipped both items back inside of the envelope, tore it into tiny pieces and dumped it into a nearby wastebasket. She scrunched her face together and winced but she knew we were financially secure enough not to need my sister's money. We fell back onto the hammock, her sleek cocoa-buttery skin pressing softly against my own, and continued that kiss long after my coffee got cold.

One thing was for sure.

Grudges are forever.

Family always comes first.

ODIO

This is one of those stories I like to apply to the category I like to call "a bully story". I referred to it as a story that once you pay attention to it and then set it aside so you can write it later still manages to keep coming back to remind you it's still there.

I wrote this story back in '09 and submitted it twice before it was finally accepted into an anthology that never saw the light of day. I was sent a sample copy to see if I liked what I saw and I did; I was so happy that I (to coin a popular eighties song) was walking on sunshine. I learned later on that the collection would never be released and the story would never see the light of day which was an utter disappointment.

I thought it was flat and unappealing so I chucked it into my "trunk" folder and didn't touch it again. Two years later, I went back to it, changing this and adding that.

I thought about what people do when they have something that they don't want anymore. After two failed endings, this one pretty much took care of itself.

"HEY, Claire." I said, waving her over. "Come look at this."

It was a six-by-nine hardcover book with a dog-eared leather-gray cover. The title was scrawled across in cryptic white font three inches from the top, said *ODIO*. The bottom right hand corner of the last O had a thin jagged crack that sent an animated river of blood oozing across the cover.

We were standing inside of a large kiosk in the far left corner inside of Minerva's, a flea market that'd been stuffed into an old department store building that closed down before malts and poodle-skirts were replaced by I-Phones and (sadly) man-buns. We'd collected everything that we'd come for–Claire loved her knickknacks as much as I loved books–and this was the last leg of our seemingly endless journey through this gigantic place. When she came over to see what I was talking about, the field of kiosks spread across the place reminded me of open-faced cubicles, each one baring junk of all shapes and sizes; proprietors stood outside of their kiosks with kind optimistic eyes, waiting for the next customer to come strolling along.

They'd sold everything from power tools, video games, paperback and hardcover books, tie-dye shirts, sports memorabilia, hunting gear, children's toys, DVDs and VHS', figurines, shoes, household appliances and whatever other hunk of junk they could salvage from their garage and make some money. In the end, it would all end up in the same place it was before you bought it, someone else's garage where it succumbed to cobwebs and mold before its inevitable demise.

I glanced over at the two svelte-looking women who'd greeted me a few minutes ago from behind a large Formica-topped counter and nodded; they nodded back. A brunette wearing blue-jean cut-offs and a dark-blue tee-shirt leaned against the counter, flipping through a magazine. The woman next to her, a frumpy-looking woman with boyish-cut brown hair wearing a gray NASCAR tee and dark sweat pants, sat on a metal-cushioned stool thumbing through her cell phone.

I caught the lopsided curiosity etched across their faces and brushed it off as I held the book up for Claire to see.

"The cover looks very brooding." She nodded. "But there's no author name."

"I know. I don't know anyone in their right mind who would publish a book and not include their name on the cover."

"Maybe they just forgot." She assumed. "Could you find that out by tracking down the publisher?"

"It wouldn't hurt." I said, shrugging my left shoulder.

I took it off the shelf, gave both the front and back covers a quick glance and set it on top of the other two. As I approached the front counter, Claire leaned over and planted a soft kiss on my right cheek.

"It looks as if it was self-published." I said, taking her right hand. "I'll see what I can find out."

I raised the back of her hand to my lips and pressed them softly against the long white scar below the indentation between her second and third finger. She had it ever since she was ten when her parents left her brother in charge one night and he used her hand for an ashtray.

Her cheeks turning a lovely shade of pink, she gave me a wide porcelain-white smile. In her white floral-print sun dress and white deck shoes, she looked as radiant and pink as ever. Her pale blonde hair sat on her head in an asymmetrical sweep above a heart-shaped face fitted with her blue eyes glinted in under the downward glare of the store's recessed lights.

A Garth Brooks song spewed out from the big-boxy speakers fastened to the wall above each kiosks. I set the books on the counter, dug my hands into my pockets and stepped back; Claire slipped her arm through the crook of my right arm and rested her head on my shoulder. The brunette slipped a piece of cardboard between the open magazine and glanced up at me, her face creased by a wide appreciative grin.

"Can I get you anything else?" The brunette asked, light blazing inside of her heavy-lidded brown eyes.

I shook my head and grinned. When she scanned my findings, her face lit up and her eyes widened. She prodded her left hand against her friend's right knee until she looked up to see what all of the fuss was about.

The brunette slipped a No. 2 pencil from the small ceramic pink coffee cup sitting beside of the cash register and tapped its beet-red eraser against the stack.

"Is that what I think that is, Mary Lee?"

"Yes, it is, Flo." The brunette said.

Flo tucked her cell phone back into her pocket, snatched a quick breath, and rose up from a brown-leather barstool with haste. The mingled expression of confusion and awe on her face was the same one I'd seen on the faces of my students when they didn't have a pop quiz. She sighed, raked a hand through her brown pumpkin-shaped hair and rubbed her palms together.

"Are you talking about the book with no name?" I asked. "Do you know who wrote it?"

"We don't care about that, mister?" Flo stated. "We're glad to get rid of it."

"Is it that bad?"

"No." Mary Lee said matter of factly. "We're just glad someone else can enjoy it."

She tapped the no-name novel with her pencil again. "This one is free."

"Did one of you write it?"

Her face creased with confusion, Mary Lee glanced at her best friend and chuckled. Claire's hand twitched inside of mine and her brows furrowed.

"You think we wrote it?" Flo snorted. "That's a good one."

"Hell no." Mary Lee chuckled.

"Your sign says three dollars."

Mary Lee slipped a pencil from the little wire-mesh cup sitting beside of the register and tapped the eraser against the cover.

"Do you know?"

"Not really." Mary Lee shrugged.

"You mean someone just donated it to you without putting their name on it?"

"I guess."

"Well which is it?" I asked.

"We don't question donations, sir." Flo said, "We just sell the galdang things."

"Do you know anything about it at all?"

The expressions on their faces shifted from elation to anger. Mary Lee pursed her lips together so tight her worry lines bracketed the corners of her mouth and gave me an accusatory stare. Flo shook her head and drummed her cheap Press-On nails against the countertop one at a time in an edgy, rhythmic staccato.

My face grew hot; my skin prickled and the hair along my arms and neck grew stiff. I could either walk away with my dignity intact or give them the finger on my way out.

Mary Lee chucked my purchases into a crinkled plastic grocery bag and slid it across the counter. Claire squeezed my hand again and nodded toward the front of the building, her face etched with worry.

"Thanks for shopping with us, sir." She replied in an arrogant voice.

I kept my composure and collected my bag, my throat cluttering up with a score of swear words I decided not to say. As we walked away, I heard them mumbling under their breath.

"...at it ever again."

"...his problem now."

When we were far enough away from their kiosk, Claire whispered, "Fuck them."

On our way out, we told everyone who was coming in to stay away from their kiosk.

*****

AFTER breakfast Monday morning, I stuffed the book into my satchel along with a stack of papers I'd graded last night and kissed Claire goodbye on my way out. When it came time for lunch, I took it out and carried it and my sack lunch into the teacher's lounge.

My friend Troy Woodson was sitting at the round Formica table in the far left corner of the room, munching on a burrito bigger than his own hand, or at least it'd looked that way from a distance. He was six-foot-two with a skinny muscular frame and a clean-shaven head to accentuate his big boxy face; a thin net of wrinkles surrounded his wide-set green eyes. He wore a tight gray Parker High School tee shirt and tight purple shorts that emphasized his crotch.

When I approached him, he waved me over and wiped his mouth with a fistful of white napkins. He saw the brown paper sack in my hand, shrugged his shoulders and took a sip from a large red straw jutting out of a tall Styrofoam cup. The bright carpet of sunlight streaming through the curtains caught the corner of my book and lured his attention; the windows were slightly ajar to allow the breeze to come in because the school board refused to fix the air conditioning.

Outside, a pack of bright-yellow school buses sat at an angle outside of a squat brick building their bumpers kissed by the harsh-white glare of the mid-afternoon sun. It was mid-April and we were gearing toward Spring Break. We compared our lunches, me with my PB&J on wheat, apple slices and eight potato chips (Claire was a stickler for the nutritional facts on the back of the bag) and his massive burrito and decided that it was best neither one of us said anything.

"It's not every day I get my hands on something Mexican."

"This coming from the same guy who picked up a Latino from that bar two weeks ago and then wondered why he had a flat tire."

"You think you're funny, don't you?" He asked. "What did you want to talk about?"

While he wrestled with his lunch, I told him about the incident on Saturday only I left out the parts that weren't any of his business. After I was finished, he gave me a quizzical look.

"Are you kidding?"

I shook my head and bit off a corner of one of my sandwiches.

"And they still didn't tell you who wrote it?"

The water cooler on the far right corner gave a loud groan and sent a massive bubble rising toward the surface. I finished the apple slice I'd been holding between my fingertips for almost twenty minutes and plucked a potato chip from the bag.

"Does your brother still run that bookstore in Columbus?"

He nodded, drained his cup in one giant swig, crumpled his trash into one crinkled ball, popped open the lid of his cup and stuffed the crumpled wrapper inside.

"Can you ask him about this?"

He ignored me, glanced over my shoulder and winked at something from across the room. When I followed his gaze, the French teacher, Mrs. Thompson–who always sat on the opposite end of the couch facing the far-right corner of the room–returned the wink. She wore a tight red blouse and a white polka-dotted dress that hugged every curve of her trim narrow frame; her bright-red hair was fixed to the back of her head by a thin black stick.

"Are you kidding me?" I said between bites.

"What?"

"Do you realize what'll happen if you fraternize with a fellow teacher? Greene will terminate your ass."

Outside of Troy's warm friendly exterior beat the heart of a proud bachelor who preferred the company of women. No strings attached, of course. He had no qualms about what an inter-office romance could do to his career as long as he got laid.

My stomach clenched. I ignored their playful exchange and continued to eat. I slid the book over to his side of the table and tapped the cover with a half-eaten apple slice just as Flo had done so with the tip of her pencil.

"Huh?" Troy asked, his face creased with confusion. "What did you want?"

"I need your brother to tell me who published this book."

"Oh, okay. I'll let you know what I find."

"Thanks, man."

He tossed the cup across the room, made a swishing sound with his lips and hit the trashcan beside of the water cooler. He picked up the book, patted my right shoulder and went on his merrily little way. Ten minutes later, I left the teachers' lounge and saw him chatting quietly with Mrs. Thompson, the looks on their faces were anything but professional.

Who am I to stop my friend from getting his fill? Is it my job to stop him from getting fired?

The book was tucked under his arm and pressed tightly against his left rib but there was something different about it that made me look back to make sure I wasn't losing my mind.

The puddle of blood that'd been oozing across the middle of the cover was gone.

*****

TWO nights later, I was sitting in the living room recliner reading a Shirley Jackson novel when I looked up from the corner of my eye and saw Claire grimacing over a stack of paperwork spread out across the dining room table. She worked as a real estate agent and had to prepare a ton of paperwork for a house she'd sold a few days ago. We agreed to spend two days a week putting our cell phones on vibrate and turning off the television to clear our heads.

I stopped every so often and glanced at her before she realized it, her thick black glasses winking under the downward glare of an overhead bowl lamp. After the fourth time, she caught me and flashed a playful grin at me. Her sky-blue eyes flaring with a mix of both affection and curiosity, she slid her glasses off her face and set them on the table.

She slid out of her chair, sauntered across the room in a slow seductive stride and sat on my lap. She hadn't done that since our third date, two months after we first began dating back in high school.

I sighed, set my book onto the little coffee table beside of me, wrapped my arms around her and slid my face across the right side of her neck; her vanilla-scented skin made my body prickle. She leaned in for a kiss, her soft-pink lips glowing when my right pocket hummed. She felt the vibration that followed, cooed and flinched her eyebrows; we snickered at its impeccable timing.

"Is that a cell phone in your pocket," She said in a seductive voice. "or are you happy to see me."

"I'm always happy to see you."

After we kissed, she climbed off of my lap and strode back to the table. When I slid the phone from my pocket, a familiar name glowed from the front screen.

"Hey, Troy. What's shaking good buddy?"

It'd been two days since I saw him but I figured he was still hunting for information about the book.

"Good buddy?" He said in a slightly accusing voice. "That's a strange word coming from someone who doesn't have the balls to say how they really feel about their friend."

"Say what?"

Claire saw the confusion on my face and, brows furrowed, looked up from her work. I scooted myself onto the edge of the couch and, my face creased with confusion, perched the arm I used to hold my cell phone on my right knee.

"You've always been like a brother to me and yet you talk about me like that behind my back."

"What are you talking about?"

He gave a pneumatic sigh and followed it with a loud burp that rattled his larynx. I motioned for Claire to stay seated, my free arm extended across the room, and shook my head.

"I always knew you were jealous."

His voice was slurred. I heard the sound of crackling static but I wasn't sure if it was coming from his end or mine.

"Are you drunk?" I scoffed. "Do you realize you have class tomorrow?"

"I'm not stupid, Justin." He murmured. "I read about it inside your goddamn book. You're jealous because I can have any woman in the world and you can't. Hell, I could take that pretty little wife of yours away from you if I wanted to."

His suave egotistical voice broke into a low wheeze. He gave a relaxed sigh, followed by a choking sob.

"I thought I was your best friend."

"You've drinking again, haven't you?" I said, scratching the back of my head. "Sit tight. I'm on my way over."

"Don't you–"

I killed the call and stuffed my cell phone back into my front pocket. Claire rose out of her seat, her face creased with worry and waited for me to answer.

"He sounded like he was drunk."

"When isn't he?"

"I'm gonna go over there and make sure he doesn't hurt himself." I sighed.

She rolled her eyes, lips tightened with anger, and sighed. This wasn't the only time I've had to drop whatever I was doing and run to Troy's aid whenever things got out of hand.

I took a light jacket off the back of one of the dining room chairs and slipped it on. Claire followed me to the front door where I retrieved my car keys from the two-pronged piece of pegboard hanging on the wall. She followed me out to the driveway, gave me a quick kiss on my right cheek and went back inside as I backed out of the driveway.

A bulbous-white moon sat high in the starry black sky, glowing faintly behind a thick roiling cloud cover. I cut my Subaru toward the west side of town and took a right, cutting through a small cookie-cutter subdivision of cozy brick and stucco homes and turned right onto County Road 67.

I followed an old gravelly road through knee-high yellow weeds, heavy thick pines and gnarled gray oaks. My headlights pierced the darkness, throwing odd shadows that weren't supposed to be seen by human eyes. A black snake squirmed across the road, its slick dark form an ominous talisman of impending danger that I knew nothing about.

To be quite honest, I *was* jealous of his carefree lifestyle; it was like trying all thirty-one flavors and then coming back for thirty-one more. I was happily married and nothing or no one in this world could persuade me to fuck it up; nothing.

The other half of what he said was everything I'd told Claire two years ago as we were leaving the rivalry football game between Parker High and Shallow Rock. I knew she hadn't told him because, in her words, she'd "rather smell pig shit from a distance than talk to him".

If he hadn't heard it from us, then where? I hadn't said it to any of the other teachers at school so it couldn't have come from them.

Two minutes later, I pulled my car through the entrance of a massive trailer park backdropped by a wall of dense-green trees like the ones I'd passed on the way here. I turned left at the main road and drove three blocks until I found the right one, a slate-gray aluminum-sided number with a red USC Trojans flag hanging across the front window. I killed my headlights, parked next to his red Chevy, slid out of my car and knocked on his door.

When the door eased open on the third knock, I stepped inside and shut it behind me. The place was silent save for the mingled sounds of a clock ticking from the wall above the living room television and a soft pop song spewing from the opposite end of the house.

I peered down the hallway and saw the bathroom door standing ajar, spreading an L of soft brass light across the hallway; odd shadows bled across the walls and floor. I gave a derisive snort, shook my head and followed the half-lit corridor toward the bathroom. I stepped inside, drowning myself in a blanket of thick stifling heat and steam that fogged the massive sink-top mirror.

No Doubt spewed from the little Bluetooth speaker sitting on the far-left corner of the sink. I killed the speaker and leaned casually against the sink with my arms folded across my chest and waited for him to react. Nothing; nothing but the rhythmic tap of water dripping from the faucet.

"What do you have to say for yourself?"

Silence.

"Okay." I intoned. "We'll just try this."

I took a step toward the toilet when something tapped against my left leg, stopping me in my tracks. I grimaced at the thick coppery smell stinging my nostrils, burning the back of my throat. I glanced down, my brows furrowed, and watched the cloud of steam drifting through the bathroom in lithe surreptitious coils slowly dissipate.

Troy's left arm jutted out through one side of his white-plastic shower curtain and sat perched on the edge of the tub, his fist grasping the ribbed yellow handle of a box-cutter. A long jagged gash was etched across his wrist, exposing the soft pink flesh beneath. Blood slid down the tiny three-inch-blade in dark-red pearls and dripped onto the book lying face down on the floor beside of the tub.

An alarm rang in the back of my head, urging me to *run just fucking run* but I couldn't. Beads of icy cold sweat trickling down my spine, I grasped the shower curtain in both hands and tightened my grip until the plastic gave a loud crinkling sound. I flung it back, jarring the curved metallic hooks together like tuning forks and stared down into the tub with wide panic-stricken eyes.

The thick coppery odor intensified, tingling the back of my throat in waves of acidic fire. My mouth falling open on slack-jawed hinges, I stumbled back into the countertop and gave a loud terrifying gasp. Tendrils of heat seeped past my skin and into my bones, I threw my arms out from my sides, grasped the doorknob with my left hand and the edge of the sink with my right.

Troy was lying waist-deep inside of his tub in a pool of hot soapy water, his brawny athletic body dimpled by beads of sweat, condensation and blood. His head was slumped forward, his chin resting firmly on his chest, his aphrodisiac green eyes were now diluted down to a blank motionless stare. His right arm rested limply against his hip; his cracked pale lips were twisted into a lopsided grin.

Waves of cold fear bristled across my skin and raised the hairs along the back of my neck. I lost my grip on the doorknob and knelt onto the floor, tears brimming in my eyes.

My cheeks flushed with intense anger, a strangled cry issued from somewhere deep in my throat. I bit down on my bottom lip to keep from crying out and felt the taste of my own blood coating my tongue. A ball of confusion and anger swirling in my chest, I clamped my hands together until my knuckles turned white and tiny cuticles were branded deep into my palms.

I knew it was too late to save him but there was also a part of me that if I had I'd have punched him in the mouth for pulling something like this. I wiped my eyes with the backs of my hands and crawled toward the tub on my knees, my vision growing more blurry and weak by the second. I stretched my arm across the foot of the tub, killed the faucet, leaned over the side and buried my face in my hands.

My lips and eyes wet with tears, I held his face in both hands, and spewed an incoherent string of cuss words at him until my voice died down to a low, painful wheeze. His rugged tan skin had faded to a sickly-white pallor, its somber cold touch sending waves of electric dread tingling through my skin. I patted the sides of his face as quick as I could, hoping to stir him awake (because even I knew slapping him wouldn't help his cause) and saw something stirring from the corner of my left eye.

My body rigid with fear, I peered over my left shoulder. A cloud of blood rose up to the surface like a mushroom cloud and stained the island of soap bubbles floating above his stomach in a pastel-pink shade.

Not that; not the one thing I couldn't avoid when he stood up from his chair.

He hadn't exactly cut it off but he sure tried. A crooked incision was etched across his shaft from one side to the other as if he'd started it from one side and then once the first try didn't work decided to start from the other end. Now, it hung down from between his legs in an L; bits of skin and flesh floated under the surface of the water in tiny flakes like fish food.

I slapped my hand across my mouth, backed away from the tub and fell back against the cupboards under the sink. My body trembled while my mind continued to grasp the concept of what I'd just seen. I could understand him having sliced his wrists but.. this was just–

Although my mind was too foggy and distorted, there was only one word that I could use to associate with what I was seeing: lunacy. Pure and total. All I knew was that I had to leave before things got too bad for my liking.

(I read about it inside of your goddamn book)

I didn't know what he meant by that but I wasn't going to stick around and play twenty questions figuring out why. I saw the book still lying face down on the carpet only there was something different about it.

The river of blood dripping onto the book's spine was now streaking across the cover in the same fashion as it was when I first bought it. What did it all mean?

I sat up, wiped the sweat from my brow and took two deep breaths to shake off the fear-induced paralysis seeping into my bones. There was a side of me that wanted to leave it here and let someone else worry about it but I had my reasons.

How could my words come off harsh enough to drive him to...to...this?

How did my words get onto the page in the first place?

I retrieved the book, used the edge of the countertop to hoist myself up from the floor and stuck it in my back pocket. I wiped my fingerprints off the edge of the sink amongst anything else I'd touched and hurried back out to my car.

The cool spring breeze seeped through my half-open window bringing with it the smells of fresh carrion and pine sap; it caressed my forehead with soft, chilly fingers. Moonlight filtered through the encroaching forest high above, spreading alien shadows across my front windshield.

Nausea churned deep inside the pit of my stomach and rose toward the back of my throat like lava. I reduced my speed and, my tires crunching over loose gravel, eased my car onto the shoulder of the road. I flung my door open, lurched over the rocker panel and, blocking my face from any oncoming traffic, heaved until it hurt.

After I had nothing left, I pulled up to an all-night convenience store and bought a bottle of orange juice from a frumpy old woman in a blue shirt and tight jeans. When I pulled into the driveway, I drank the bottle straight down, heaved a collective sigh and unfurled my stiff-white fingers from the top of the steering wheel. I slid out from behind the wheel, my eyes still wet and blurry from all of the crying and the vomiting I'd done a few minutes ago, and locked my car on my way inside.

The house was dark save for the light fixture above the oven and the pools of mute-gray moonlight streaming through the curtains; shadows were splayed across my house like cryptic ink-blots. I hung my jacket on the back of a nearby chair, kicked my shoes off across the living room and over beside of my recliner and crept into the bathroom.

I turned on the shower, stripped down to my bare ass and pulled the curtain back. Steamy hot water poured down my back, slipped across and down my shoulders and pounded the stress out of my muscles before it dissolved in the torrents of water sliding toward the drain. I scrubbed myself down as hard as I could but I knew nothing would cleanse that image of my best friend's corpse out of my memory no matter how hard I tried.

When I reached the bedroom a few minutes later, Claire was sleeping peacefully on her side; moonlight poured through the blinds, grasping at the covers and highlighting her pale blonde hair. I eased the covers back, slid in beside of her and threw the covers back across me. I laid there for some time, tracing the curlicues stenciled across the ceiling until sleep finally took over.

I had a dream that I was lying in a bathtub filled with hot soapy water and castrated sex organs while Troy stood outside the tub, leaning casually against the sink with his arms laced across his chest, bellowing a loud maniacal laugh.

*****

WHEN we woke up the next morning, we were greeted with the news of Troy's death from a text I'd received on my cell phone from one of the other teachers; they told me that Mrs. Thompson had indeed gone over to Troy's place and found him lying in the bathtub. I did my best to look surprised when I was told about it.

"What happened over there last night?"

"I just made him a cup of tea and made him take some aspirin." I shrugged. "He'd drank a little more than what he usually does on a regular basis. All he did was throw up half of the time I was there but he seemed okay when I left."

I couldn't bring myself to tell her the truth because not only had I not shaken it off yet but I also knew she wouldn't believe a word of it. She offered to cook breakfast but I gently brushed her off and settled for cereal instead. As we were getting ready for work, she asked me if I was okay and I told I was.

I kissed her as she hurried out of the house and then pretended to have forgotten my phone. I waited for her car to pull away when I slipped my phone from my satchel and called the school to tell them I wasn't coming in today. Principal Greene was sympathetic to my plight, as he always was with everyone, and hoped that I would feel better by Monday.

Troy was my best friend and this book killed him. I wanted to know why and there was only one way for me to find the answers I was looking for.

I locked the front door on my way out, grabbed a cup of coffee from one of those Star Bucks rip-offs you see on every corner and headed out of town. The sun was a blind-white beacon in the clear blue sky and there was a slight chill to an otherwise cool spring breeze. I'd left the book back home because I couldn't bring myself to look at it without going back to that terrible night when my best friend became the poster child for abstinence.

When I pulled up to Minerva's around ten thirty, I got a text from Claire: U CALED IN SICK? R U OK? I told her no but I wasn't feeling up to going to work because of what happened with Troy. She came back with a sympathetic greeting of her own and told me to relax.

I gave myself a pat on the back for coming up with that on such short notice; now I know how exciting it felt for my students when they lied to me about their homework. The bad news was that I only had so much time to do everything I needed to do and then get back home before she did.

When I arrived at Minerva's, there were probably fifteen people floating around the place. I took a right, just as we'd done two days ago, and made my way passed a makeshift diner that sold greasy food on even greasier plates. As a show of respect, I browsed all of the kiosks along the way until I reached the right one.

When I found it, it'd been closed off by an aging blue plastic tarp that'd been strung up across the doorway by thick bands of white rope. I approached the tarp, eased the left flap aside and peered in to see if they'd either closed down for lunch or hadn't opened yet.

The only evidence that they were ever here were the odd horse-shoe shaped trail of small round imprints from the rubber-topped table legs streaking across the dusty linoleum floor like animal tracks in the snow. Here today, gone tomorrow. Thin pockets of cobwebs had gathered in the corners of the ceiling above the kiosk and fluttered lazily in the soft cool torrent of air spewing from a nearby window fan.

"They left a long time ago." A new voice said.

I spun around and peered into the kiosk on my right. An arthritic old man stood, leaning over the top of a waist-high glass-topped counter packed with cheap gold watches and handmade jewelry; the three sided shelf behind him held an array of vintage porcelain knickknacks and stuffed animals. His wispy white hair lay in a neat combover across his liver-spotted head; his narrow blue eyes, thin pink lips and broad nose was accentuated by a net of wrinkles brought on by years of wisdom and whiskey. He wore blue jeans, cracked brown-leather boots and a red pocket tee with an old company logo stitched across the left front pocket.

"I see that."

He squinted his eyes and gave me a suspicious glance. "Weren't you here last week?"

"My wife and I were."

"Now I remember you." He said, then added. "Your wife bought a few ceramics from me that day. A cute blonde with a scar on her hand, right?"

I nodded, a thin lipless smile spreading across my face. He waggled his finger and shook his head at the notion of this being a small world. Instead of Garth Brooks, a Lady Gaga song spewed from the speakers.

"Do you know where they might've went?" I asked, jabbing my left thumb over my shoulder.

"I wish I could." He said, jostling his head to one side. "They didn't even say goodbye when they."

"They left? Do you remember what time?"

"It was about an hour and a half after you and your lady friend left." He said, emphasizing with his hands. "After you two left they started packing everything up as fast as they could. It was like they were on fire and they had to get it all together or burn up. They kept talking to me about how they were glad to have gotten rid of that damn thing."

"What did you think they meant?"

"Some damn book." He mumbled. "I thought they were losing their cotton-picking minds if you ask me. The brunette was going on about how they had to get rid of it to keep it from killing them, too."

"Really?"

He nodded, a smile dancing on the corner of his lips.

"Those potato-brained twits even tried to sell it to me but I don't read that twisted shit."

I shook my head and sighed when something prodded my left shoulder. I glanced back at him, meeting his gaze. He held up a ceramic knickknack of two conjoined geese wearing blue and red bonnets; the anxious smile etched across his face accentuated the pleading glaze in his eyes.

I bought the knickknack and a small stuffed teddy bear in a bright red tee-shirt I thought would look nice on my desk. Once I bought a second knickknack, he gave me their full names.

*****

NOW it made sense.

After I sat in the car and Googled their names, I found out the old man had been right. Although it'd gone to great lengths to kill my best friend, I had to know what else this book was capable of doing. According to the information I gathered, it'd left an indelible mark on those women's lives that nothing could erase.

In the summer of two-thousand-seventeen, Mary Lee's husband Larry had read the book and decided to step out into his garage to swallow the rest of the anti-freeze he kept under his worktable; she told the authorities that the book made him think that she never loved him anymore. Flora's husband Clyde had read the book the following summer and dove head first into a wood chipper; she claimed that her husband read that she'd been making funny of his "erectile difficulties" to her friends.

And two years later, it made Troy Woodson believe that I was jealous of his carefree lifestyle.

The title was enough to send a warning out to anyone who wouldn't have turned a blind eye to it like I had. It was Latin for "*hate*".

How could I have written what I was thinking if I hadn't even read the damn thing yet? Had it put me under some supernatural spell, forcing me to rewrite the pages without my knowing? The pages of a journal were meant to be filled with our daily thoughts and feelings and then kept out of the prying hands and eyes of the people around us; this one had sucked every hateful thing I'd ever said about people behind their back, whether it was out of anger or not, and then mentally scribbled them across the pages without me having to know about it.

The long drive back home had given me plenty of time to piece it all together. Or at least some of it. I couldn't blame them for wanting to get rid of it but I wished they'd done it the right way so none of this had ever happened.

When I got back to my house, Claire's white Toyota was sitting on the right side of the driveway facing the front porch. If I'd done all of that research on my laptop at home instead of doing it on my phone, I would've been here when she got home. I checked the time and date on my cell phone, slapped myself playfully across the forehead and gave a foolish sigh.

Every Thursday, Claire and her best friend-slash-coworker Joanie left work an hour early to head out to Kingston Mall and browse the stores. If I'd gotten back here in time, I would've just ordered pizza, stretched out on the couch and watched a movie.

I climbed out of my car, hurried to the end of the driveway to pick up the mail, tucked it under my arms and carried everything inside. I hung my keys on the hook, kicked my shoes off into the cubbyhole beside of the door and strolled into the living room. I set the mail on the dining room table, wandered toward the bedroom and paused outside of the doorway.

Claire's bright yellow jacket (the one with the gold COOPER REALTY badge stitched onto the left front side) sat in a crumpled heap at the foot of our bed. Her briefcase was open, lying face down on a square of papers and file folders that'd spilled out across the bed. My senses tingled because her jacket was always draped over the back of her dining room chair and her briefcase had always sat beside of the front door.

I hurried out of the bedroom and out to the living room when that same thick coppery odor I smelled at Troy's hit me like a pie in the face. I grimaced and, face scrunched together in disgust, followed it into the kitchen. I pushed through the white bat-wing door, slid the front of my tee-shirt up and over my nose to ward off the smell and paused next to the refrigerator.

Claire stood in front of the sink, gazing silently through the thin butter-colored curtains draped across the kitchen window. Her shoulders bowed, her pale blonde hair glinted in the patch of mid-afternoon sunlight flooding the countertop. She'd slipped out of her work clothes and into her ribbed cotton-white wedding dress she wore five (six next April) years ago.

"Hey, baby." I said. "I know you told me to take it–"

"Do you love me?"

"Of course I do."

I sauntered over, grasped her shoulders in both hands and spun her around to face me. When I gazed down at the front of her dress, a chill trickled down my spine; a jolt of surprise struck the base of my brain. My flesh prickled as a wave of nausea churned inside the pit of my stomach.

I stumbled back, a mixture of sadness and shock tearing through my chest, and struck the fridge hard enough to jar the contents inside. My fingers trembling, I bit down on my bottom lip to suppress the acidic gorge rising toward the back of my throat.

She glanced at me with sunken heavy-lidded eyes, her skin glowing like creamy porcelain. Her lips twitched into a half smile as beads of sweat broke out across her forehead and slid past her temples. A strand of bleached-blonde hair clung to the crown of her forehead above her left eye like a hook that snared the very fabric of my soul with the intent of tearing it apart.

Sporadic drops of blood coated the front of her dress, the largest one staining the V-shaped tip of her neckline. I peered over the top of her left shoulder and saw chunks of bright red flesh clinging to the stainless-steel basin. A second onslaught of fear raked at my heart and pinned my feet to the kitchen floor; my eyes widened and my hand slid away from my mouth.

"How could you say those cruel things about my hand?"

"Wha-wha-what are you talkin–"

"Don't bullshit me, Justin." She hissed, her left hand cinched into a fist. "I read what you wrote in your precious goddamn book. I deserve to hear the truth from you. Tell me right now."

"What did the book say?"

"I didn't ask for it but I guess I'm too busy using it as a way to get sympathy, huh?"

I snatched a quick breath and sighed, uttering a tiny childish wheeze; tears brimmed in my eyes. I couldn't convince her that the only time I said those words were to myself in anger some time ago when she told me that a customer friend of hers had referred her to a plastic surgeon. This was one scar I'd caused myself; a scar that would never go away.

"Do you think I need sympathy now?" She said through a twitchy sarcastic grin.

A rhythmic tapping sound echoed from somewhere inside the kitchen. The last time I'd heard that sound was last night while I was crying over my best friend's body.

The thought escaped me as soon as I stared at the pool of blood spreading across the floor beneath her feet. She slid her left arm out from behind her back and raised a flat pulpy-red stub that used to be her right hand; bits of manicured bone jutted up from the middle of the stub like star-shaped sprinkles on a child's cupcake. Jagged rivers of bright red blood slid down her forearm and dripped off the end of her elbow.

She peered over at her handiwork, her eyes wide with sinister approval, and gave a wild maniacal laugh that rattled her voice. The sound of it seemed to plant my feet harder onto the floor and soak my bones in a fear-induced paralysis.

"Do you think I'm pretty now?" She pleaded, her legs wobbling. "Am I, Justin? Tell me honey am I pretty enough for you now? Tell me I'm pretty tell me tell me tell me–"

Her eyes fell shut like an opera curtain and her body went limp; her arms slumped down from her sides and her right hand curled into tiny pale fists. My body racing with both adrenaline and fear, I pushed myself away from the fridge. I threw my arms out to catch her but it was too late.

The back of her head slumped to the left and rapped hard against the edge of the countertop with such force that it rattled the windows. Her head snapped to the right, emitting the loud brittle snap of bone; the sound alone clawed a painful divot across my chest and tore through my soul like frayed fabric. Her body jolted forward from the impact and struck the floor face-first, bouncing her head off the linoleum.

Waves of fear and panic pulsating through my body, I knelt down beside of her and cradled her in my arms. Tears burst from my eyes, a salty white concoction I thought I'd shed enough of last night and blurred my view of her dead lifeless corpse. I screamed her name over and over again until it echoed inside the dark chasms of her unconsciousness.

*****

IT'D been a week since Claire died and I haven't slept or eaten in days. Not even since the funeral which coincidentally occurred one week after Troy's. I pretended to appreciate the endless caravan of apologies and notes of encouragement from mine and Claire's co-workers but after a few weeks The Sympathy Train had done left the station.

I've scanned every inch of this book from front to back and I still don't understand how it does what it does, how it dug so deep into two people's minds that it drove them to commit violent acts to themselves.

I didn't even see any words on any of the pages. Each one of them were blank; all two-hundred and sixty two pages. I'd spent the night counting them, flinching every time the pipes creaked or a car came passing by.

I haven't been to work in days and everyone who comes to the door to see what I'm up to always end up walking away, feeling both confused and disappointed. The second I realized Claire was dead I made a promise to rid the world of this vile disgusting thing as quickly as I could. Every attempt to destroy I'd made were just prime examples of pure stupidity.

I tore out page after page, tearing it free from the adhesive that held them together. When I came back, the book was still laying on the floor in the same condition it was when I bought it. The next day, I set it inside of the charcoal grill–it'd been the first time since last summer–and soaked it with gasoline and dropped a lit match on top of it; my eyes burned with the same wild desire as the flames that consumed it.

After a few minutes, the flames didn't have a chance. They died, leaving the book in the same condition I'd bought it in. That night, I carried the book back inside, tossed it across the room, knelt down and cried.

If I couldn't burn it, then there was only one other way to cast this cruel object out of my life forever. I wasn't proud of myself but there wasn't any other way around this. Sure, I could wrap it in some kind of binder's twine and stick it in a box in the attic and pray that no one–not even my future children and grandchildren no matter how imaginary they are–will ever discover its true intentions.

I collected a few of Claire's things into a cardboard box and drove out to the second-hand store on the west side town next to that community outreach center. I waited until it was dark before I'd done it because I didn't want anyone to see me; even wore a dark-blue baseball cap pulled down just far enough to hide my face from the surveillance cameras they warned me about. I popped the trunk, stuck the book inside of the box, dropped it into the giant gray plastic trash bin marked DONATIONS and drove away.

I was a good distance away from the store before I uttered the same maniacal laugh I'd heard coming from Claire the day she died. The more distance I'd put between myself and that book, I began to feel that same sense of elation and freedom Mary Lee and Flo felt that day.

I know what I did was wrong. I know what dangers await the book's next owners and I hope they can forgive me for what I've done just as I'd forgiven the two women who sold it to me and to the people who sold it to them and so on and so forth.

Oh God, I hope.

DARK AVENUES

I woke up one morning and wrote three writing topics on a small notepad and examined each one of them. Out of the three of them, only one caught my interest: write something from your childhood. I'd gone to summer camp when I was eight and one of the things we did was go to a local cemetery and do headstone rubbings.

I vaguely remember the names and dates chiseled on all the tombstones and marveled at the time they'd spent here. I felt like I was carrying the memory of their existence around with me. Whether it be a picture or a family heirloom, we'll always be reminded of the mark they left behind.

This story is for those who still carry them around; who know that when they've entered the room and for those who never give up the hope of seeing them again. It was published on Amazon as a Kindle book in July of 2012.

1

"HAVE a good weekend, Kevin."

"Thanks, Angel. I'll see you on Monday."

Kevin Perkins hurried out the back door of Angel's Pizza, the sharp tangy smells of herbs and sauce trailing out behind him, and into the cool July air. He peered over his shoulder and shook his head at the row of employees' vehicles occupying the customer parking lot at the rear of the building because he knew Angel would blow a gasket when she found out they were parking there.

He considered going back to help but he knew Angel wouldn't have any of that. To those that knew Kevin Perkins, they knew better than to pull him back inside after five o'clock on a Friday night.

He looped the strap of his black nylon canvas bag up and over his head, slid it across his chest and strode across the street toward a spacious parking lot at the rear of a two-story brick apartment building. He knew he wasn't the only one who disliked having to park over here and then walk all the way across, but they didn't have a choice.

He greeted some of his other co-workers along the way (trading a few handshakes and nods with the men and a few gentle hugs with the women) and walked over to the driver side of his car. A trio of female college students in scantily-clad clothes paraded out the back door of the apartment building, giggled about something one of them said and climbed into a bright yellow Mini Cooper. They sped off in the direction toward town, spewing a loud chorus of laughter from the Cooper's open windows.

As he opened the back door on the driver side, something rose up from the corner of his eye and screamed, "Hey, Kevin!"

Startled, he flinched and slapped his chest. Erin Deeds leaned against the passenger door, her long red hair spilling down the sides of her broad pale face from a part in the top of her head. Her horn-rimmed glasses glinting in the waning sunlight, her floral-print dress hugged the contours of her pear-shaped body. He thought he could've avoided her just this once, but he didn't think it was possible.

"Hey, Erin."

"Where are you going?"

"I'm going home for the weekend."

"Will you be busy tonight?" She asked with a lisp.

"Yes."

"What cha doing?" She asked.

"I'm going to the cemetery."

"I just thought you'd like to go to the movies some time."

"I'd like to," He nodded. "but now is not a good time."

"Do you want some company?"

"Maybe next time."

"You want to have dinner at my house." She pleaded. "My Mom makes this delicious tuna-noodle casserole."

To say that Erin Deeds hadn't become infatuated with him since she began working here six months ago was like saying that water *wasn't* wet. Although he wanted nothing more than to be her friend and co-worker, she'd always eat lunch with him and never take her eyes off of him.

At this rate, she'd ask him if he wanted to count the cracks in the parking lot together if it got a "yes" out of him. It was cute that she'd found him comfortable to be around, but it was inhumane to watch someone beg.

"I'll take a raincheck." He said and opened the driver-side door. "How about next weekend?"

Her face and eyes beaming with joy, she said, "That'd be great. Thanks, Kevin."

"Take care, Erica."

She waved and strode across the parking lot toward the restaurant with a spring in her step that was hard not to miss. He opened the back passenger door, tossed his canvas bag casually onto the back seat and shut it. He turned and peered through the copse of trees rooted along the back of the real estate company, saw the parade of vehicles pulling up out front and fought the urge not to rush back inside.

Angel's Pizza sat on the corner of Greene Street inside of a red brick building with a flat-tiled roof and three large storefront windows; the sign stood on the far right corner of the parking lot, displaying a neon image of a skinny woman in a flowing white gown with a pair of angel wings holding a pizza box in her left hand. The words ANGEL'S PIZZA were scrawled below her bare white feet in cursive white calligraphy; a comic-book dialogue balloon above the angel's head proclaimed it was "heavenly good since 1956".

He'd only eaten the food here once when Angel offered him a slice during his interview and even then it wasn't "heavenly good", but he understood the rigors of advertising. He climbed into his dark-blue Toyota Corolla, backed out of his slot and sped off in the same direction that the Mini Cooper had gone.

He turned left and followed Greene Street through a cluster of more brick apartment buildings, one and two story clapboard houses, two-story Greek-style houses with Greek letters stamped above their front doors and a string of local businesses he'd heard of but was never inclined to try out. He coasted onto Kisor Avenue, a rising slope of bars and nightclubs throbbing with techno music and brightly-lit neon windows that beamed across the pavement. The throng of people parading past him, dressed in their own selective attire, reminded him of moths hypnotized by the warm ambient glow of a porch light.

He stopped off at an all-night convenience store to pick up a bottle of orange juice and thanked the chunky brunette woman in the blue tee-shirt on his way out. He followed the main drag toward the overpass above I-33, took a sharp left onto another residential street and drove on for three miles. He took a right onto another street and steered his car through a tall black-iron gate fixed onto the heads of two white-stone pillars; the words HAMILL CEMETERY were stamped across a scarred bronze plaque fixed to the front of the left-side pillar.

Light and dark marble and granite tombstones scattered the hillside, jutting up from the ground like half-dug fossils of no substance; each one decked out with wilted or freshly-blooming flowers or wreaths. It was backdropped by a wall of leafy oaks and gnarled poplar trees that bowed softly in the breeze. He parked his car along the shoulder of the road and, the sound of gravel crunching softly underneath his tires, sighed; the clock on his digital radio said five-fifteen.

He twisted around in his seat, retrieved his bag from the back seat and climbed out. He thumbed the button on his key fob to engage the locks and slid the strap of his bag back over his head and across his chest.

On his right, a middle-aged woman in a cream-colored gypsy skirt and red blouse was kneeling before a white marble tombstone with a small American flag rooted in front of it. She was flanked by two teenage girls, one brunette and one blonde; the brunette wore a pink shirt and a denim skirt while her sister donned an ankle-low white dress and a light blue blouse. When the blonde met his gaze, he greeted her with a curt nod, waited for her to return it and sauntered away without saying a word.

The scene itself filled him with a nostalgic sense of pain and grief. He'd sat many days and night pressing his fingers against the words and numbers chiseled across Terri's tombstone until he could draw them in his sleep. His cheeks flared like red-hot pokers; no matter how many times he'd come here to get away from her it was as if his mind never strayed too far away from her in the first place and he was fine with that.

He was halfway across the hillside when a sharp iciness streaked down the middle of his back. His skin prickling, he pivoted around, shaking the contents inside of his bag.

Nothing.

The three women had departed from the white tombstone and made the long trek back across the cemetery to their vehicle. Now that they were gone, the eerie stillness inside the cemetery seeped into his bones and left him feeling a little odd. He sighed, swiped his left hand across the film of sweat coating his forehead and blotted his palms on his left thigh.

There were plenty of tombstones for him to choose from, but there had to be something unique about them that drew his attention. The others that sat off in the distance resembled gray-black smudges on a lush-green canvas.

He stopped beside of a black granite tombstone and felt the cool evening breeze stroking the back of his neck. He wrapped his left hand around the strap of his bag and scanned the cemetery. Tree shadows bracketed the right side of the property, concealing a few headstones from the soft warm rays of the evening sun.

He snatched a short breath and said to himself. "You can do this. You know you can."

It didn't feel the same without her and it never would. She wasn't trotting ahead of him, talking about her day while he carried their canvas bag (the one he was using now) and holding her hand. It was like sliding a glove on the wrong hand–it didn't feel right.

He approached a knee-high marble-gray tombstone sitting thirty yards away from the edge of the forest, read the name chiseled across the front and exhaled. It said:

MARILYN GRAHAM
JULY 12, 2002-MARCH 7, 2019
RIP MY BEAUTIFUL ANGEL

Almost three months ago, he thought to himself.

He sighed, slid his bag free from his side, eased it onto the ground between his feet and knelt in front of it. He didn't know the young lady personally but there was something about her that caught his attention. It broke his heart to see someone die at such an early age; it always reminded him that Life should never be taken for granted because we never know what'll happen from one day to the next.

He unzipped the bag and removed each item one at a time, setting them carefully on the top of the bag. A roll of tape, a packet of paper and a flat plastic tray with an array of colored chalk; the colors ranged from light to dark, from periwinkle blue to tombstone gray. He tore four strips of tape from the roll using his teeth and fixed the first sheet of paper onto the tombstone by applying all four strips of tape to all four corners of the page.

"Alright, Marilyn Graham." He said jokingly. "It's your turn to go on The Perkins Wall Of Fame."

He gave a good-natured sniffle, selected a piece of dark-blue chalk from the tray and rubbed it sideways across the page. After a few minutes, he lowered his hand and blew off the excess dust to check his results.

A sense of puzzlement overcame him. The headstone said MARILYN GRAHAM but the name on the paper said MCCORD.

2

WHEN he stared at the name on the page again, Kevin's brows furrowed with confusion. He set the page labeled MCCORD on top of his bag, slipped out a fresh one and fixed it onto the tombstone. Thick smudges of gray dust coating his fingertips, he repeated the process.

Instead, the name POLK surfaced across the page. He held the chalk loosely between his fingers and peeled back the left side of the paper to check the name on the tombstone again. The salutation chiseled across the sneaky ribbon located between her name and time line hadn't shown up either.

He removed the second piece of paper, placed it on top of the first and replaced it with a third. He shrugged, selected a piece of worn-down black chalk from the tray and repeated the process again. Once he was finished, he dropped the chalk back onto the tray and saw the name ROBERTS spread across the paper.

He turned his head away from the tombstone in time to see a cream-colored Buick gliding past him toward the front gate, its hubcaps and grillwork glinting like mechanized teeth. He blinked, knowing it'd belonged to the three women who were standing at the white marble headstone and greeted them with a two-finger salute; the car gave a respectable honk and coasted out of sight.

He sighed, forced a smile from the corner of his mouth and turned his attention back to Marilyn Graham's headstone. He glanced down at the half-shaded grass weaving in the breeze in a failed attempt to grasp the concept of why the girl's name hadn't appeared on all of the pages. He braced his hips with both hands and tilted his head to one side when an idea struck him.

He slid closer to the front of the headstone, slipped a fresh slip of paper out of the packet and held it up to the light. He shielded his eyes from the sun, peered down at the company name stamped across the lower left-hand corner, (KOONTZ PAPER CO., it said) set it down and placed on a fourth.

After blowing off the excess dust again, the name TAYLOR bloomed across the page. He bowed his head, resting his chin on his chest and sighed. A bird cried out from somewhere inside of the trees as if it were laughing at him from afar, but he brushed it off and glanced back at the tombstone.

He raised the chalk toward the paper when the cold sensation returned. His skin prickling, the hairs along the back of his neck grew stiff and his mouth shrank. The tree shadows grew thicker now, eclipsing the patch of sunlight bathing the tombstone.

Tiny beads of sweat cascading down his face, he caught something in the corner of his left eye and glanced over to see what it was. A tall shadow of thick sloping shoulders and a heart-shaped head hovered behind him in a curious child-like manner.

Thin strands of hair weaved around the back of her head, whipping at the air and clawing for the tops of her shoulders.

He thought it might've been the caretaker, a gaunt thin-faced man with thinning brown hair named Saul, but even he knew Kevin had come by occasionally. He always came over to check on him but mainly it was to shoot the breeze while he collected all the dead flowers and picked up trash.

"If you don't cause any trouble," Saul had said to him and Terri that day. "I don't care how many of these things you do."

After Terri's sudden departure, Saul had kept his promise.

"Hey, Saul." He smiled, lumbering to his feet. "Is Eileen giving you more—"

He used the top of the tombstone to hoist himself up and pivoted around to greet Saul, his face creased by a wide friendly smile. No Saul; just the same tombstones he'd seen every Friday night for the past six years.

If it wasn't Saul, then who else could it be?

A sense of uneasiness came flooding back at him, seeping into his bones and prickling his skin. As much as he didn't want to admit it, Erica's dinner invitation was starting to sound very enticing.

He knelt down in front of the tombstone, rolled all four pages into a separate funnel, fitted each of them with a rubber band and set them inside the left compartment of his bag. He slid the tray along with the roll of tape and the half-open packet of paper back into the other compartment and zipped it shut. He rose to his feet and slung the strap of his bag up and over his head and across his chest.

"Sorry, Mary." He nodded to the headstone. "I'll see you again later."

He walked back to his car, tossed the canvas bag onto the back seat and drove away. He was glad to have had the weekend off so he could clear his head and make room for tomorrow; there were plenty of things to be done around the house so maybe he wouldn't gloat about it. Angel knew what it was like to lose a loved one, to have a piece of your life stripped away from you so unexpectedly.

All he wanted to now was go home and put this crazy day as far behind him as humanly possible.

He took a shortcut into town to avoid the jungle of Friday night traffic and stopped off to pick up his dinner at Dragon Express. On his way out, the two women sitting at a corner table beside the display window looked up from their plates and greeted him with a flirtatious smile and a real-time wave. He replied with a kindly smirk and a short nod that left them staring dumbly at each other and went back to eating their food like nothing happened.

With the smells of pork-fried rice and sweet-and-sour chicken wafting through the front seat, he drove three miles out of the city and turned left onto a cul-de-sac sitting on the crown of a tall grassy hill. The neighborhood was strangely quiet for it being a Friday night, but then he wasn't the only one who was having an off day. He drove down to the end of the block and parked his car up on a slanted concrete drive beside of a brown-stucco bungalow, killed the engine and gathered his things.

He unclipped his seat belt, climbed out, followed the cobblestone path running across his front lawn and clambered up the front porch steps. The sky had a watercolor haze. He glanced over the left side of the porch and gazed down the hill toward the city sprawled out below like a toy model and felt relieved that he and Terri had moved away from there years ago.

There were a few windows lit up inside the houses strewn along the block. This neighborhood was mostly occupied by low-income families and golden-age retirees looking to hide from the humdrum of the city and—hopefully—live in peace before they're slapped into a rest home or until their number was called. He had to admit, now that he'd moved out of the city, he was content with the isolation and silence that came with living here, although there were days where he wouldn't mind some company.

He unlocked the front door, stepped inside and flipped the switch on the wall, flooding his house with brass-colored light. He gave a relaxed sigh, hung his keys on the pegboard above the light switch and tapped the door shut with the side of his right foot. He set the bags on the couch and engaged the locks (although most of the crime occurred in the city, it still didn't hurt to be safe).

The light revealed a spacious blue-carpeted living room complete with elegant oak furniture and two beautiful touch-lamps with floral-print bowl shades sitting on sleek wooden coffee tables; framed photos dotted the living room's bright beige walls. A small dining room sat on the far left under a brass three-headed chandelier; a small kitchen sat toward the end of the house with a white marble counter and a stainless-steel sink bathed in the alabaster glow of a lone fluorescent bulb. A small corridor stretched toward the three remaining rooms of the house, its walls also plastered with more gilded picture frames.

He kicked off his shoes, set his dinner on the dining room table and sat down. He ate what he could—both egg-rolls, half of the rice and chicken—and then stuck the rest in the fridge. He took a shower, dried himself off and slipped into a pair of blue plaid pajama pants and a tight red tee-shirt.

In the reflection of the bathroom mirror, he sighed at the net of worry lines bracketing the corners of his deep-set blue eyes and then raked a hand through the short mop of black hair above his tan oval face. He sauntered back into the living room, retrieved his canvas bag from the couch and carried it into the room between the master bedroom and bathroom.

He'd go days without stepping into this room, but today's little venture through Hamill Cemetery had been long overdue; there was something even more unique about this room than he could ever find in any other cemetery. He exhaled a plume of cold realization from his bones and padded across the room, his bare feet pressing into the plush blue carpet. The two windows on the far left and upper right-hand corner of the room were bathed in shafts of radiant twilight.

A small worktable with two orange-cushioned stools sat on the far-left corner of the room stacked with wood and gold-plated picture frames of various sizes. The aforementioned picture frames speckled across the bright-peach walls displaying other headstone rubbings that spoke of an earlier time when his life had been much different and more enjoyable. Although it'd taken years to collect them, at least he could say that he hadn't done it alone.

The names that leaped out at him weren't just reminders of the past, but pebbles tossed into the ponds of time that spread large ripples through the past and beyond. Jimi Hendrix, Janis Joplin, Paul Newman (whose death had torn him apart), Lena Horne, Frank Sinatra and other celebrities; there were also other names of other people would had made a profound impact in the lives of others such as a fry cook from Japan, a Scandinavian swimmer and a regular who'd been coming into Angel's Pizza since the restaurant's first conception. Somewhere amongst these frames, beyond these artistic smudges of chalk, were the names of an academic scholar, a painter, an athlete, a dancer or an aspiring film maker; another leaf on the branch on another family tree.

He and Terri had traveled far and wide to obtain these names and the memories they shared in between would not be forgotten. He stared across the room and glanced at the frame sitting under the window on the upper right corner. In a ribbed golden frame, in a light charcoal dusting, the name inside said: TERRI L. PERKINS; her favorite color was gray.

A GUIDING LIGHT AND A LOVING WOMAN had been chiseled across the front of the tombstone below Terri's timeline (APRIL 9, 1982-MAY 12, 2019). She was more than to a lot of other people who'd been graced with her presence, but none of them held a candle to the love and light she'd given him over the past seven years.

The light pouring through the window glinted off the far right corner of the frame, shrouding it in a mask of half-light and half-shadow. Although he'd known it word for word, he reread the passage etched across the front of the rubbing under her name because there were times where he'd gotten it wrong; it wasn't easy picking the right words for your wife's tombstone. He didn't preserve her name to seek sympathy from others or for artistic reasons but only because his love for her was stronger than he could ever define.

There was nothing he could do for her now, but he thought this was a good start. He would've given anything to trade places with her, but he knew she'd never want him to think like that no matter how sad or depressed he felt. He'd despised the loneliness that was derived from her death, but there was nothing he could do about it now; the tumblers were set in place and the chain wrapped around his heart was locked up good and tight.

He unzipped the bag, set the four rolled-up posters onto the worktable and zipped the bag shut before placing it across the two stools. He would've gone to work on them any other time but with everything that happened he added it to the mental list of other chores that needed to be done. He killed the light on his way out, snatched a bottle of water from the crisper in the bottom of the fridge and strolled into the living room.

He watched ten minutes of an Alfred Hitchcock movie on cable when a Kid Rock song blared from his cell phone. He kept his eyes on the television and tapped the green ACCEPT button on his cell phone without looking at it.

"Hello."

Everyone at work referred to him as "the maestro of toppings" but Kevin knew him as Jacob Rogers. Mingled waves of loud conversation and rock music floated amongst the background, making it hard for them to hear each other.

"What cha doing?"

"I'm home watching television."

"I thought you'd want to come out tonight." Jacob replied.

"I would've." He lied. "If I didn't have a ton of stuff to do around the house tomorrow."

"I didn't hear you. Hold on a sec."

He waited. The music in the background had died down to a low roar. He repeated his excuse and heard Jacob sigh on the other end of the phone.

"I know." Kevin nodded.

"Are you sure you don't want to come out? We can wait for you to get here."

"That's okay."

"I can always get you later on."

"Sure, you will." He said, then chuckled. "Are you sure?"

"Yeah I'm sure."

"I'll hold you to it."

"Take it easy, man." He said, grinning. "If you need a ride later on tonight, let me know."

"Okay, man."

"Tell Ariel I said 'hello'."

"I will."

Kevin killed the call, set his cell phone onto the coffee table and rolled his thumb and forefinger against the bottom of the third finger on his left hand. It hadn't been the only time he'd done that when he knew better; he was glad that he hadn't done it at work because then he'd have felt more foolish than he did now.

He exhaled, glanced down at the thin white line hugging the third finger on his left hand and bit down on his bottom lip. It'd become a routine reflex for him to reach down and spin the phantom wedding band around his finger because it made perfect sense. Now it was just a reminder of the many things he'd lost along the way.

He'd been making a lot of promises to his friends lately but he'd been taking a few of them back for personal reasons; broken promises were irreplaceable. He knew at some point he'd have to break off the chains of his self-inflicted isolation and take the time to smell the roses. He could do that whenever he wanted but not in the same way his friends had; he preferred pizza and a movie to ingesting large amounts of alcohol and grinding your pelvis against a complete stranger under the sounds of incoherent music (or at least that's what they're even calling music these days) spewing from a coin-operated jukebox. He'd chosen a sheltered life because without Terri didn't think he had a life at all.

He drained his water bottle and thought long and hard about the promises he made, he leaned back on the couch and watched television.

3

THE next morning, Kevin opened his eyes and glanced at the dust motes dancing amongst the shafts of sunlight pouring through his bedroom curtains. He rolled over, glanced at his alarm clock and felt neither surprised nor confused about having woke up at eight-fifteen. There was something, however, he wished he could have back even if it were for just one day.

For the past seven years Terri had always greeted him by massaging his chest with her hand or by planting a soft kiss on his cheek, followed by her patent pearly-white smile. Mornings like that were just a thing of the past, tiny sleep-induced sensations that dissipated like soap bubbles seconds before he opened his eyes and long after the tears poured down his cheeks. As much as he expected to feel those same sensations, his internal alarm had kicked in minutes long before his bedside clock had.

No matter how much he wished for it, there was only one way he'd ever feel her touch again. He knew that day would eventually come (sooner rather than later, he thought) but until then he'd have to keep going.

He threw off the covers and slid out of bed. When his feet pressed down upon the cold hardwood floor, his skin prickled from head to toe; his brain snapped into overdrive.

He padded out of the bedroom, followed the sunlit hall around the corner and into the kitchen. He poured himself a cup of coffee, made a bowl of cereal and carried both items to the dining room table. He chased the cereal down with the coffee and a small glass of orange juice and went off into the bathroom to brush his teeth.

On his way back into the bedroom, he glanced at the door leading into the art room and said, "Good Morning, baby."

In the summer of two-thousand-ten, Kevin and Terri met three years after he began working at Angel's Pizza. She was a history professor at the local community college and although she'd made enough money for him to quit his job he chose not to live a life of laziness and luxury; he believed that if two people lived together then they were responsible for everything, including the finances. They dated for six months before he finally took her up on her offer to move in; three years later they were married.

The first three years of their marriage had gone by in a never-ending blur of mid-afternoon kisses, post-midnight sex and headstone rubbings; he was afraid it would all go so fast he would never get a chance to treasure them forever. Their moods varied with the seasons, always shifting between taking the opportunity to enjoy the weekends during the summer to hibernating in the winter with plenty of things to do to help time go by. They'd always attend The Oak River Parade once a year, but other than that she was at work before nine and ready for bed by ten unless she had to grade papers.

Two years later, one elegant summer evening, he'd surprised her at work and talked her into going out to dinner. It would've been the first time in three weeks because they'd hosted two dinner parties with three of her other colleagues, whom Kevin had nothing in common with. They'd walked across the parking lot together when a stranger wearing street clothes and a gray pullover with a collegiate logo on the front pulled a pistol from the waistband of his jeans, told her "I loved you" and shot her point blank three times in the chest. His body racked with a mixture of shock and disgust, tears blurring his vision, he'd knelt onto the pavement and cradled her in his arms until the ambulance arrived.

Although he'd never left her side, not even for a minute, she was declared as a DOA; dead on arrival. When no leads came forth, her killer was never found. She was subjected to a long line of unsolved murders that would be chucked it into a box and added it to the growing pile of others sitting on a shelf in the basement until the file itself was dog-eared and dusted.

Her absence had taken a heavy toll on him. Save for the ghostly presence of a missing wedding band, he'd call out for her every once in a while, knowing that she would never reply back.

He sat on the edge of the bed to change his clothes when he spotted the ribbed golden picture frame sitting on his bedside table beside of his frosted glass touch lamp. In the photo, Terri was lounged out across an overstuffed bench seat next to a double-sided window, her thin pale hands resting firmly across her lap.

She wasn't pretty by any standards, but she was beautiful enough for him, and the man who murdered her obviously. She didn't go to great lengths to be the prettiest woman on earth because there was much more to her than that.

Her pixie-cut black hair sat evenly above her elongated face, leaving a small asymmetrical sweep high above her forehead. Her beige skin had an internal glow that was magnified by even the slightest yet normal emotions: a smile here and a wink there; it had a fire he never knew existed but only felt the heat of it when he slipped her into his arms at night or long before sunrise. Her prominent whiskey-colored eyes sat below thin dark brows, bracketed by smooth patches of skin pocked with faint wrinkles that could only be seen from up close; her small pink lips sat below a sleek upturned nose.

She had a grace that no one could duplicate. Her kisses lingered along after she left the room; her touch always left his skin tingling for hours. She was *more* than perfect.

He kissed the three fingers on his right hand, his eyes blurry with tears, and pressed them against the picture frame. His cheeks flushed and, holding back the ball of sadness dying to burst through him, held back the urge to cry. He exhaled, wiped the tears from his eyes with the back of his left hand and set the picture back in its rightful place.

"One day down." He smiled. "A hundred more to go, baby."

He slipped into a pair of tattered jeans, dingy work boots and a gray tee-shirt pocked with crusts of white paint. He grabbed the two packets of seeds from the shelf above the kitchen sink, filled a pitcher with water and stepped out onto the front porch. The cool summer breeze caressed his skin and teased his hair like a desperate lover.

Under a bright blue sky streaked with faint white clouds, the cul-de-sac was alive; to his left, the Peterson children were riding their bikes up and down the street while making lame attempts at laser sounds and barking about who was dead and who wasn't. To his right, Mrs. Langton sat on the front porch of her one-story brown stucco shoebox next door squinting at the tiny black font on a folded-up copy of the morning paper. Dogs trotted along fenced-in yards, barking at the people strolling past but more at the kids frolicking in the street; birds soared above the same leafy oaks and tulip trees who spread their spiky-black shadows that shaded the curbs and sidewalks.

He tucked the packets into his right pocket, fled down the front porch stairs and sauntered across the front lawn. He walked around the left side of the house, opened the front door of the small aluminum-sided tool shed and collected the shovel and hoe and two bags of potting soil. He set them outside, closed the shed door and carried them out to the tiny flower bed running along the left side of the house. Behind him, the city glinted like broken glass.

His neck warmed by the harsh-yellow sun, Kevin crawled down across the flower bed and tore out handfuls of dead weeds. When he was finished, his hands were dirty and thin pockets of dirt caked his fingernails; lucid snakes of heat wriggled off the dry dirt, pressing against his cheeks. Beads of sweat cascaded down his forehead, dampened the back of his neck and pressed lucid grins across the sides of his tee-shirt.

He'd considered moving the flower bed to the front of the porch but thought better of it after he remembered that it made sense for him to keep it here because the sunlight was more attracted to this side of the house. At least he wouldn't have to go outside and water them when all he had to do was open his bedroom window and do it from there.

He opened the bag of potting soil, sprinkled it evenly across the empty flower bed and used a hoe to mix it with the dry dirt. He opened the seed packets, knelt down on all fours and planted each seed in the same neat order as he and Terri had always done the year after they first moved in.

Sunflowers on the left and marigolds on the right but not too far to the right. He'd saved that particular spot underneath his bedroom window for Terri's yearly favorite: an Easter Lily. He rose up on his feet and pressed the head of the hoe into the soil when he saw something in the corner of his right eye.

He slightly cocked his head over to see what it could've been and, his brows furrowed, peered over his right shoulder. Instead of a head and shoulders silhouette, it was that of a pair of slender legs with full calves and slim ankles. As elongated as they were, they might've been five feet away from him; a thin cloth–he assumed was a dress or maybe a skirt–rippled carelessly above the top of her calves like a ceaseless pool of dark water.

A cold chill traced the contours of his spine, freezing him in place. His grip on the hoe's splintery wooden handle tensed until his knuckles turned white and his muscles stiffened; his nails pressed tiny half-moon impressions into his palms. He wasn't sure if the sun was playing tricks on him or not but pure logic would suggest that it was, that this had all been a figment of his sunburnt imagination.

The breeze grew steadily fast now, tousling his clothes and hair and stroking its cool deft fingers across his skin; the hackles along the back of his neck went stiff. A soft whispery voice spewed into his right ear, sending a second river of goosebumps trickling down his arms and legs.

"Kevin. Kevin."

It began as a low whisper before rising into a loud–

"Kevin! Kevin! KEVIN!"

octave that pierced his ear drums and burrowed into his brain like a power drill. The intensity of the voice sent another cold chill swirling down his spine. He bowed his head and, shoulders drawn tightly together, winced through tightly clenched teeth.

The whisper and the wind both died at the same. Another voice called out to him now, both familiar and distant.

"Shut up!" He bellowed. "Shut up! Shu–"

"Hey, Kevin. Are you okay?"

"Of course." He said, nodding. "What can I do for you?"

"Can I talk to you for a minute?"

Mrs. Langston stood on her front porch, craned her head over the left-side railing and waved him over. His cheeks flushed, he sighed and placed the hoe carefully on the ground. He stacked his hands above his head to shield his eyes from the sun and followed the steep grassy slope of front lawn toward the fence separating the far right corner of their properties.

She had a short wispy-white hair, a friendly smile, almond-shaped brown eyes and thin pink lips to accentuate her warm and caring demeanor. She'd been living in that same house long before he and Terri moved there; he could remember plenty of times when she and Terri would lean against the fence and chat until sundown.

Behind her, a middle-aged brunette and a young ginger-haired girl stood in front of a one-story house, tossing a red ball to an energetic golden retriever with a white collar.

"Hello, Mrs. Langston."

"What the hell are you screaming for?"

"Oh, nothing." He lied. "I just...it was a damn bee flying around my ear."

It was all he could come up with on such short notice.

"Don't you just hate those fucking things?"

Kevin snorted, taken aback by her spit-fire honesty. He'd never heard her talk like that before, but he liked it because he was on the good side of it.

"What can I do for you, Mrs. Langston?"

"I told you before." She reminded him. "Call me Edie. Mrs. Langston makes me feel like I'm old?"

"What can I do for you, Edie?"

"Can you to mow my front yard?" She asked, rubbing her hands together. "I'd really appreciate it, Kev. I can't pay you—"

"If you give me one of your homemade apple pies," He said, gently tugging her hand. "we'll call it even."

She patted his hand, bowed her head, and glanced back up at him. Her lips pursed, her eyes looked glazed.

"I remember how much Terri loved your apple pies."

"I know." She replied in a somber voice. "I miss those days when she would come by just to chat or ask if I needed anything from the store."

He nodded and, his cheeks flushing, bit down on his bottom lip to keep the ball of sadness from bursting out of his chest. She cupped his face in both hands, kissed both of his cheeks and strolled back inside. As gentle as her hands felt, they neither cooled his cheeks nor pacified his lingering sadness.

He returned to his house, placed the hoe and the bag of potting soil back into the shed and gathered his lawn mower. When he wheeled it over to Mrs. Langston's yard, the brunette woman and her daughter coerced the dog back inside of their house and shut the front door behind them. Everyone he'd talked to after Terri's death had suggested that getting a dog would help fill the loneliness she left behind.

Mrs. Langston's square-shaped lawn started from the right edge of her front walk before snaking around to the back and to the left. A pair of thick oak trees spread spiky shadows across the far left corner of the front lawn and along the first two steps leading up to the front porch; a pair of metallic wind chimes tinkled, mingling with the sharp whine from the chains on her porch swing. LANGSTON stenciled across each side of her bright-yellow mailbox in bold black font, glowing in the harsh downward stare of the early morning sun.

He parked the lawn mower along the edge of the fence, fired it up after two tries and pushed it along the fence, spewing thick tails of grass in its wake. When he reached the back yard, he gazed over the hill at the city sprawling out below; Lake Michelle was a thin dark-blue film against the bright blue sky. He whistled a familiar tune under the mower's rumbling engine and spun it back around to start the next section.

His back and forehead dripping with sweat, Kevin finished the back yard in a matter of minutes. He guided the mower back to the front of the house and cut a fresh path across the edge of the walkway. He was halfway through when he noticed a pair of bony-white feet perched on the side of Mrs. Langston's walkway, leaving her toes poised two inches above the grass.

He craned his head up from the front of the lawn mower, his body nearly jostling with surprise, and glanced up at a young heavyset girl; she looked to be sixteen maybe seventeen. The top two buttons of her short-sleeved white blouse were unfastened, exposing the network of bright blue veins streaking across the middle of her chest and down across the tops of her breasts like those on a road atlas. Her red plaid skirt fluttering around her thick pale legs, her gaze never wavered from Kevin.

Her canary-yellow hair spilled down across the crown of her shoulders from a part running across the top of her head, framing her round pale face before curling under her earlobes. She had a wide nose with flaring nostrils, a crinkled chin and full chalky-pink lips. Thick rings of wet black mascara circled the bags below of her heavy-lidded blue eyes and sent thin obsidian tears streaking down her cheeks.

He extended his right hand, fingers spaced apart, and motioned for her to stay. Her eyes glinting under the sun, she ignored his request and stepped down onto the cool green grass, her toes nearly inches away from the loudly whirring blade. He opened his mouth to protest her next move when he glanced down at the tiny flecks of blood splashed across the front of her blouse and paused beside of the walkway.

He hoped that he hadn't ran over her toes. Maybe she'd walked into the blade, explaining the drops of blood on the front of her blouse.

He squinted at something he hadn't noticed until now. There was a thin red line etched across the middle of her throat from one side to the other. Maybe it was a tattoo or some new-age fad everyone was trying out these days like "man-buns" or something else that would eventually fade away like all of the others.

She tried to speak, but her lips sunk and twitched like those of a comatose patient. He thought she might've been Mrs. Langston's granddaughter (God knows she was young enough) but she hadn't identified herself yet. She rested her right jaw against the crown of her right shoulder, spilling a curtain of hair across her face.

She peered at him with her left eye, its sharp haunting gaze bearing down on him, and mumbled something under her breath.

His brows furrowed, he leaned in a little closer and perked his ear to the wind in an attempt to hear what she was saying over the roar of the mower. He wasn't very good at reading lips but what he seemed to make out seemed to make no sense.

Ehmur, ehmur, he thought.

When he raised his hand to wave her onto Mrs. Langston's front porch, she jerked her head up from her shoulder and cocked it back in a forty-five degree angle. Her eyes wide and flashing with revulsion, the thin red line stretched across her throat opened like a set of amphibious gills gasping for air. A thin river of blood brimmed along the open wound, slid down her throat and pumped at the air between them; it spilled across the front of her blouse and splashed onto the pavement.

His eyes wide, Kevin's face sunk with petrified terror; his brows drew tight again and his mouth twisted into a lopsided grin. Fear hit him like a bucket of ice water, prickling his skin and chilling his blood; his muscles went stiff. A river of arterial blood spurted from the right side of her neck and slapped across his left cheek.

He flung himself away from her, released his grip on the lawn mower, and gave a loud grunt that rattled his chest. Nausea churned in the pit of his stomach and sent a ball of bile rocketing toward the back of his throat; his legs wobbled like an old door stopper. He hit the ground on all fours, planting his hands and knees hard onto the hot vapid earth, and retched until his throat burned.

He felt something splash across the back of his neck, warming his skin. A thick coppery odor stung his nostrils, escalating his nausea. As the fingers on his left hand stiffened and curled, he gripped a chunk of grass in his right fist and gave a loud gagging sound.

"Kevin."

He blinked, plunging himself back into reality. He sat up and, his knees still rooted into the ground, peered aimlessly around Mrs. Langston's yard. He heard his name again, this time it was coming from the front porch.

He gazed down at the sidewalk where all of that blood had landed and found none. He slid his left hand across his cheek and swung it back around his face; nothing but the same dirty hands he'd seen a few minutes ago. He followed the sound of his name and saw Mrs. Langston standing on the edge of her porch, gawking intently at him.

"Are you okay? You look like you've seen a ghost?"

"A ghost." He snorted. "I was just thinking about something that happened a long time ago."

"If you're tired you can take—"

"I'm fine." He insisted. "Really I am."

She gave him a once over and clasped her hands together. "If you ever need someone to talk, I'll always be here."

"Thanks." He nodded. "I'm good."

She nodded and sauntered back inside. He swiped the film of perspiration from his forehead with the back of his hand and fired up the lawn mower again. After he finished, Misses Langston kissed him lightly on both cheeks and set a bright blue grocery bag onto his left hand.

He thanked her, pushed the mower back into the shed and locked the door on his way out. He carried the pie inside and, shutting the front door behind him, into the kitchen. He set it on the corner of the countertop, swiped his forearm across his brow and turned on the kitchen faucet to wash his hands.

He shook the excess water from his fingers, opened the cupboard below the sink and plucked a dishtowel from the big ceramic bowl inside. He closed the cupboard, pivoted on his heels and leaned against the sink to dry his hands.

He thought back to the girl with the severed throat and shook his head in dismay. Was she just another figment of his stressed-out imagination like the floating shadow he saw at the cemetery and the other one he'd seen awhile ago? Was it normal to see people bleeding all over the frigging place, too?

It might've been the sun playing tricks on him, but as much as he wanted to believe that he knew he couldn't. There was another reason, however, that he was feeling like this—the anniversary of Terri's death was just a month away but luckily he was already prepared for that.

After a nice lunch, including a guilt-free slice of Mrs. Langston's apple pie, he carried a bottle of water into the living room and stretched out on the couch. Gusts of cool air drifted through the house, enveloping him like a blanket and soothing his sunburnt skin; dust motes danced in the shafts of sunlight streaming through the dining room windows. When fatigue started to overwhelm him, he gave a slight twitch and sat up.

He checked the time on the cable box, slid both hands down his face, swung his legs over the side and rose. There was still a little bit of daylight left so why should he spend it cooped up inside.

A thought crossed his mind.

After a few minutes of self-deliberation, it didn't seem like a bad idea at all.

5

AFTER he washed up and stepped into a fresh set of clothes, Kevin snatched his canvas bag from the art room and locked the front door on his way out. He grabbed a bottle of Coke from a mini-mart and cut across town via the college district, passing a lively throng of college students whose cheery smiles hid the pain of their academic burdens like masks at a Halloween party.

He parked his car in the same spot as yesterday, slid his canvas bag off the back seat and shut the back door on his way across the street. When he stepped past Marilyn's headstone, the cool summer breeze was like a false promise, dry and mediocre; every breadth of the wind felt just as thick and sweltering as the one before it.

As he stepped past Marilyn's tombstone, the air didn't grow cold and consume him with fear. There were no phantom shadows looming over him like a schoolyard bully seeking unjust compensation.

He approached the tombstone on his far left, knelt down in front of it and opened his bag. It was the *kerbed* type of tombstone (he'd remembered it from the ones he'd seen when he was buying Terri's), a four-inch thick chunk of marble-gray granite; it was polished to a mirrored shine and the thin metal funnel placed before it was ringed by an array of thin colorful friendship bracelets and packed with dead flowers.

The words chiseled across the face of the headstone in gold Garamond font said:

BURT DANIELS
OCTOBER 5, 1955-JUNE 13, 2008
THE BEST DADDY IN THE WORLD

He fixed a fresh piece of paper across the face of the tombstone, plucked a sliver of stone-gray chalk from the flimsy plastic tray and exhaled. He rubbed it across the paper in slow measured strokes, blew the excess dust away and saw the word UND blooming across the page.

He traded the old piece of chalk for a fresh one of the same color and repeated the process. When the word ERTH bloomed across the page, he tossed the piece of chalk back onto the tray and sighed. What the hell am I doing wrong?, he wondered.

He'd accomplished a lot in the past couple of hours, working on the garden, mowing Mrs. Langston's lawn and his encounter with the strange girl all of it was bound to catch up with him. He'd been married to a lively carefree woman who always grabbed life by the horns and held on for as long as she could so it was nothing for him to do the same. However, today was not one of those days.

He bowed his head and, his shoulders slumped, buried his face in his hands. He closed his eyes and took a few deep breaths to fight off the wave of shame washing over him. None of this made any sense, but that was easier said than done.

Had he pushed himself too far? Possibly.

It was turning out to be one of those days where he should've stayed home and taken that nap after all. The rubbings were more of an everyday ritual he'd continued in order to honor Terri's memory, something he used to fill the empty void between night and day when he so desperately missed her. He slid his right hand down his face, cradled it loosely in his palm and let out a harsh breath.

He finished the drawing, set the piece of chalk back inside of the tray and swiped his hands together to shake the dust from his fingers. When he glanced up at the words on the page again, he gave a deflated sigh, leaned in a little closer and blew away the excess dust.

The phrase UNDER THE TWO GLASS DOVES appeared on the page. He caught his breath, sucking mingled plumes of honeysuckle and pine sap deep into his lungs, and repeated the phrase over and over again in his head. His eyes wide, he clamped his hand across his mouth and sighed.

He took his hand away from his mouth, peeled the right side of the paper back from the headstone and glanced at the words that were supposed to be there but weren't.

"What the fuck?" He scoffed.

His doubts confirmed, he slid his hand away and glanced down at his feet. There was only one conclusion he could come to at this point that would make any rational fucking sense: fatigue.

He peeled off the page, set it on the tray and stuffed both items back into his bag along with all of the others. He zipped it shut, apologized to Burt Daniels' grave and lifted the strap of his bag over his head and laid it across his chest. He took two steps away from the headstone, the contents of his bag jostling against his right hip when he glanced up at a middle-aged couple standing in front of Marilyn Graham's grave.

They had the same heavy grief-stricken looks on their faces that he'd seen on plenty of other faces, including his own. Her toffee-brown hair sat in a bob above a round tan face with wide hazel eyes, a broad nose and pointed lips; she wore a flaring sapphire-blue dress over her short willowy frame, brown-leather open-toed sandals and a silver necklace with an oval silver locket. He was a tall beefy man with broad shoulders and a head full of dark hair that sat above a square chiseled face with heavy-lidded brown eyes, a strong nose and thick lips; he wore a button down blue shirt, jeans and gray sneakers with white stripes running down the right side.

He'd slung his left arm across the top of her back below the base of her neck and gently massaged the crown of her left shoulder, his right hand jammed into his front pocket. Her eyes blurry with tears, she opened her mouth to say something when a gut-wrenching sob burst from her lips and cut her off in mid-sentence. She turned and buried her face against his right shoulder and balled her right fist together until her knuckles turned white.

Kevin glanced down to avoid any embarrassment on his part, clenched the strap of his bag in his right fist and sauntered away. Tiny stalks of grass weaved in the breeze as the treetops whispered sweet nothings in everybody's ears. He'd spent plenty of days kneeling over Terri's grave, shedding enough tears to go around for everyone.

He approached his car, opened the back door and tossed his bag onto the seat when something clutched the back of his shirt. He was spun around with such force that his arms flew out from his sides and he was slammed up against the rear driver-side door. Shockwaves of pain burst through his body, spread across the base of his spine and down the backs of his legs and squeezed the air from his lungs.

The impact sent his head jostling to the left before coming back around. He doubled over, wiped the tears from his eyes and gazed at his attacker.

One minute, the man was consoling his sobbing wife and now he was ready to pound Kevin's brains into the street for no apparent reason. A loud insistent voice emerged from behind the brute, echoing across the cemetery. Kevin peered over the man's shoulder and saw the grief-stricken woman sprinting toward them, her sandals slapped against the pavement like wet feet on asphalt.

"What the hell are you doing here?"

"Take your fucking hands—"

"What the hell were you doing around my daughter's grave?"

"Who are you?" Kevin asked, his face creased with confusion.

When she caught up with them, she panted, "Stop it, Harry. He didn't do anything."

"You hurt my little girl didn't you, you son of a bitch."

"I don't know what the hell you're talking about."

Harry reached out with his left hand and clutched the front of Kevin's shirt. Kevin slapped it away, fired an angry look at him and bunched his fists together.

"Stop Harry. Just stop it."

"Shut up, Lacey." Harry said through tightly clenched teeth at her, then said to Kevin. "I saw you here yesterday doodling all over my daughter's headstone. What the hell were you doing here anyway."

"I don't know what he's trying to insinuate," Kevin said to Lacey in a calm reassuring tone. "I didn't do—"

Harry shifted on the balls of his feet, peered over his shoulder and sighed. Kevin glanced at the woman who Harry referred to as Lacey and opened his mouth to speak when he noticed a look of wide-eyed horror forming across her face.

"Please don—"

Before Kevin could follow her gaze to see what she was seeing, it was already too late.

6

WHEN he came to, his body heavy and stiff with pain, Kevin peered up at the ceiling through stuffy-white eyes. He slid his dry tongue slowly across the film of sleep paste clinging to the roof of his mouth and grimaced at the taste. An undulating chorus of soft voices, even softer footsteps and quick sporadic beeping sounds resonated in his ears; waves of lemon-scented antiseptic drifted around the room and stung his nostrils.

He slowly raised his left arm, rubbed the whites from his eyes with the knuckles of his hand and blinked a few times until his vision became clear. A dull ache throbbed across his forehead, pinching his temples hard enough to make him squeeze his eyes shut to avoid the light. He sighed and sat up on his elbows when his left arm buckled and slid out from underneath, slamming him back onto the bed.

The back of his skull bounced off the pillow, whipping his neck to the right and sending a second wave of pain coursing down his spine. A nearby voice yelled for a doctor but he wasn't about to try that again to find out who'd said it. He bit down on his bottom lip to push through the pain, gripped the metal bed railing in his left hand and rolled onto his side, facing a tall beige curtain that separated his room from the next.

A parade of soft footsteps scrambled across the ER. He heard the quick clang of metal tapping metal as the curtain was flung open, bathing him in a second wave of cool air. He squeezed his eyes shut once more to avoid the overhead glare of the florescent light on the wall behind his bed.

"I need you to stay calm, Mister Perkins." A rough authoritative voice said. "I'll explain everything just stay calm."

He winced and rolled over on his back. A tall middle-aged man dressed in a crisp black policeman's uniform approached him from the left. He had a clean-shaven head, a strong chiseled face with a hawkish nose and thin pink lips; the big silver badge fixed to his left front pocket glistened in the light. The doctor was a young dark-haired man in a creased white lab coat underneath a blue pin-striped shirt and a red tie; his oval pale face was acne-free and his demeanor was more than cordial.

Now that he knew who the man was, he was glad he hadn't said what he wanted to say before. A heavyset blonde in bright-pink scrubs and white hi-tops sauntered past the nurses station holding an old brown clipboard in her left hand.

"I'm Officer Ned White." The policeman said, lacing his arms across his chest. "I'm with The Shallow Rock Police Department. I'd like to ask you some questions?"

"Officer." The doctor pressed. "I don't think that right now is a good time–"

"Hey, Doc." White said in an insistent voice. "You do your job and I'll do mine."

The doctor shook his head and sighed.

"Would you like to tell me what happened, Mister Perkins?"

"Sure."

With the doctor's assistance, Kevin was propped up in bed with a couple of pillows and slowly reiterated the entire scene from beginning to end; he left out the part where he'd discovered the strange phrase from Burt Daniels' headstone. White scribbled everything down as quickly as he could on a small notebook and read it back to him for clarification.

"What did you say to Mister Kline to make him strike you?"

"Nothing." Kevin said, then raised his left hand. "Mister Kline? I thought he was Marilyn Graham's father. Are her parents divorced or something?"

"I'm not sure about that. However, they wanted to talk to you as soon as you woke up."

The doctor came in a few minutes later to check on Kevin whilst firing angry scornful looks at Officer White from the corner of his eye. He diagnosed Kevin with a mild concussion and prohibited him from any and all activities for the next twenty-four hours. Kevin sighed and rolled his eyes at the "good news" especially when the doctor emphasized that he wasn't allowed to drive himself back home.

"Get a ride from someone, Mister Perkins." The doctor said, patting Kevin's shoulder on his way out.

Kevin thanked him, signed his discharge papers and rose slowly out of bed. He leaned against the bed railing and waited for the lingering effects of vertigo to fade away before moving another muscle.

He stuffed his papers into his right front pocket and followed Officer White down an open marble-gray corridor that stretched past the nurses' station. Men and women in sharply creased medical scrubs either hurried off to other rooms or huddled around each other, carrying large electronic tablets inside the crooks of their arms in the same manner they used to carry their books back in high school.

They exited the ER through a metal door with a tall rectangular glass window with a thin wire-black screen and stepped into a large waiting room with gilded picture frames speckled across its rough white walls and small cushioned chairs sitting on soft gray carpet. Stacks of month-old magazines were scattered across knee-high wooden tables; an array of puzzles, coloring books and kid's toys were clustered along the far-left corner of the room. Two flat-screen televisions were fixed to the left and right corners of the ceiling by large L-shaped brackets screwed into the wall; one was showing a news report about a missing boy and the other was playing a rerun of Spongebob SquarePants.

An old couple in hand-me down clothes occupied the three chairs on the left, mumbling to each other and shaking their heads about the missing boy. White waved to a trio of teenage boys sitting on the far-right corner; two of them chuckled as if one of them said something funny to the other.

The tallest of the three boys sat in a chair underneath the television, thumbing through a slim-black cell phone gripped loosely in his right hand. He wore a white muscle-tee, black sweat pants with the high school's logo (SHALLOW ROCK STALLIONS) in bold yellow font streaking down his right leg and gray sneakers. He had short spiky-black hair above a strong boyish face and steel-blue eyes that must've sent the girls at school into a hypnotic daze.

The tall heavyset kid sitting to his right had a saggy pale face with slanted dark eyes and a thick mouth; he wore a tie-dye shirt with the number 44 plastered across the front in bleach white letters, gray sweat pants and black leather sandals with thick Velcro straps that pressed into his fat doughy feet. The skinnier one of the group wore a slate yellow jersey with black shorts and different colored sneakers; his Utah Utes ball cap perched on his head shaded his tan square face and spread a thin black visor across his deep-set green eyes.

The woman Harry Kline had referred to as Lacey observed them from across the room and rose out of her chair. Harry snatched her wrist out of the air, whispered something in her ear and nodded; his face looked heavy and apologetic.

When he was done, he held her hand and walked alongside of her. She tossed a ball of spent tissue into a nearby wastebasket and smoothed out the wrinkles in her dress; her eyes and cheeks were red from crying. Under the recessed lights, tiny creases of sadness hugged the corners of her mouth and eyes, making her face look more heavier than it seemed.

As they approached each other, they shook hands.

"I just want to apologize for what I did." Harry said in a slow remorseful voice. "It was immature and uncalled. I know it doesn't make up for it but things haven't been going good as of late."

"I'm sorry about your daughter."

"I'm actually Marilyn's uncle." He said. "Ever since her father killed himself, I've treated her like she was."

"Marilyn's been dead for quite some time and it hasn't been easy, Mr. Perkins. " Lacey explained. "I assume you don't know what that's like."

Kevin raised his left hand and, without saying a word, tapped his thumb against the faint white halo hugging his third finger. An uncomfortable silence permeated around the waiting room as Harry sighed and bowed his head to hide the shame on his face.

Lacey shook her head, her face crumbling under the weight of a shared burden.

"My mistake." She said solemnly.

A fresh set of tears shone in her eyes and slid down her cheeks. She bowed her head, took another ball of tissue from her purse and dabbed it against her eyes.

"It won't happen overnight but things will get better as the days go by." Kevin said in a reassuring voice.

He took Lacey's left hand, twined her two middle fingers with his forefinger and patted it gently across her knuckles. Lacey pondered over what he said and nodded, her eyes glistening. Harry nodded, pursed his lips and shrugged. When Kevin waived his chance to press charges, they traded more pleasantries and left.

White wished him a speedy recovery and walked over to join the three teenage boys still waiting for him in the corner of the room. The more Kevin thought about what he'd said to Lacey Graham, the more tangible it sounded. He knew deep down inside it would only get worse, but he wasn't going to tell her that no matter how angry he still was at Harry for hitting him.

On his way out, Kevin caught a suspicious glance from the boy with the cell phone. The other two greeted Officer White with praise and complicated handshakes, but this one didn't. His gaze never wavered from Kevin even when Officer White stepped past the other boys to greet him.

Kevin heard White say something to the boy (something about a friend) but the roar of a nearby television drowned him out. He exited the hospital through a pair of automatic sliding doors and followed a wide concrete sidewalk toward the parking lot. The cool evening breeze ruffled his tee-shirt, stroked the back of his neck and tousled his hair; tree shadows pooled across the curbs, connecting with the others that were there before them.

He was halfway across the parking lot when he swore he could feel the boy's gaze still bearing down on him. He rubbed the back of his neck and peered over his shoulder to see if his curiosity had killed the cat or saved it. For now, the pussy was spared.

He found his car sitting in the parking lot at the end of the second row, peered through the rear passenger door window and breathed a sigh of relief. He was certain that he'd tossed his bag on the back seat before Harry attacked him but everything had happened so fast he wasn't sure. He opened the driver-side door, found his keys sitting inside the cup holder in the middle console and sat down.

He climbed in, leaned back in his seat and closed his eyes. He drew back a sharp intake of air, filling his lungs with the old-car smell and sighed. He tried to wrap his mind around the situation at hand–the rubbings, the girl with the severed throat and now this–only for it to slip away.

It was too much for him to bare. With the anniversary of Terri's death looming right around the corner, he wasn't sure if he could keep it together. He had to though, if not for him then for her; he could become a failure in the eyes of everyone around him but not her because she was his rock.

He sighed, slipped his cell phone out of his pocket and Googled the number for a local towing company. Within ten minutes, a bright red pickup truck with a ribbed-metal flatbed and flashing amber-colored roof lights arrived. A tall heavyset man with a head of thick dark hair and a matching dark beard wearing a dark blue mechanic's uniform and big heavy boots stepped out and greeted Kevin with a kind friendly handshake; the name RANDY was stitched across his nametag in cursive red stitching.

After the driver loaded Kevin's car onto the flatbed, they climbed in together and drove away. They didn't talk much save for how their day was and what happened at the cemetery. Randy cut his white behemoth through the heart of the city, its heavy engine fluctuating from a high to a low growl whenever he changed gears; the roof lights swiped a halo of amber-colored light across the street. The mingled smells of food from the local establishments they'd passed along the way wafted into the front cab and made Kevin's mouth water.

When they arrived at Kevin's house, the watercolor sky flared brightly over the city. After Randy unloaded his car, they shook hands and went their separate ways. Kevin waited for the truck's taillights to disappear before hiking up along the edge of the driveway and opening the rear door to collect his bag from the back seat.

He sighed, shut the door behind him and strode across the front yard toward his house. He unlocked the front door, stepped inside, locked it again and kicked his shoes over beside the coffee table. He didn't bother with the lights because his eyes were still a little sensitive to any kind of light.

He followed the makeshift pools of sour gray light across the house, down the hallway into the art room and placed his bag back onto the worktable where he'd taken it from. He retreated to his bedroom, stripped out of his street clothes and into a pair of blue plaid pajamas and a plain gray-tee. He padded into the bathroom, opened the medicine cabinet, popped the lid on a bottle of pain relievers and chased them down with half a glass of water.

He closed the cabinet door and, in the shaft of sour light pouring through the bathroom window, saw the knot protruding from his forehead. He hadn't been hit this hard since back in the eighth grade when Dominic Forrester punched him after he found out Kevin had escorted Gail Bowers to her third-period math class. It wasn't as big of a knot as the doctor had told him but it was there just the same.

He strolled out of the bathroom and into the kitchen where he made himself of a PB and J and poured himself a glass of milk. His mind focused on both sleep and hunger, he sauntered past the living room oblivious to the tall blonde girl with the severed throat sitting on the edge of the living room couch with her hands placed softly across her lap and a silently curious look on her ghostly pale face beaming under the sickly-white glow of a newly-risen moon.

7

SHE sat spread eagled on a jagged strip of grass bordering a wide gravelly road with her left knee bent and her right leg extended. She could hear the car's engine idling but the harsh-white glow of the headlights obstructed her view of the car that sat idling some five maybe six feet away. She winced at the pain jarring against the middle of her back as hot lucid tears distorted her vision.

She tried to lift her hands to shield her eyes from the glare of the headlights but her arms failed to move. Her eyes drifted over to her right hand, then her left and her breath shuddered. Her arms had been stretched out from her sides and secured to the middle plank of a rickety wooden fence with Plasti-cuffs.

Her thin-silver necklace, which dangled loosely across her chest, glinted in the halogen-white glare of the headlights. She tugged fiercely at her restraints but her attempts to free herself were weak and futile. She hissed through tightly-clenched teeth as the knots nudged against her wrists, etching lattice-shaped dimples into her skin.

A car door creaked open on corroded hinges, spilling a patch of brass-colored light and an Iggy Pop song out into the night. The door neighed, then coughed as it shut, muffling both the light and the music.

She flinched at the sound of footsteps crunching gradually over loose gravel and combed the darkness beyond with wide petrified eyes. There was something sinister about that sound, but she was too scared to think straight.

Rock music continued to blare out from one of the open doors. A tall shadowy figure materialized from her left, stepped into the glare of the headlights and walked toward her in a slow teasing pace; a lone moth beat its wings against the right-side headlight long enough to sense what was going on and fluttered away.

A second figure followed the first while a third stepped out from somewhere and leaned against the right front tire. The first figure knelt down beside of her on one knee and gave a disappointed sigh. The second figure stopped in his tracks, tucked his hands deep into his pockets and tapped his left foot repeatedly against the ground.

"If you tell us where it is," the figure said in a thick syrupy voice. "We promise not to hurt you."

"I don't know what you're talking about." She sniffled. "I don't know what you're looking for. Please don't hurt me."

The figure on her left threw an arm around his back and plucked something from the waistband of his jeans. His left fist grasped the thick wooden handle of a large combat knife with tiny metal teeth running down the opposite side. Her lower lip trembled with fear as he turned the knife over and over, examining it in the headlights.

"I'm trying to be really nice about this, Mary." The second figure replied. "If you don't tell us where it is, then we're gonna to get really nasty."

"I'm telling you the truth." She pleaded. "I don't know-"

Before she could finish, the figure on her left cursed under his breath and swung the knife in a whistling arc across her–

Kevin's eyes shot open as he drew back a long breath and sat straight up in bed. He grasped the bedspread tightly in both hands and, his spine rigid with fear, scanned the room with wide revolted eyes. A fresh sheen of sweat coated his brows, soaked the back of his head and shone off the back of his neck.

Moonlight poured through the curtains, throwing long grasping bars across the foot of the bed. He sighed, released his grip on the blankets, flexed and unflexed his hands until the stiffness dissipated from his fingers and the color bled back onto his knuckles. He bowed his head, swiped his left arm across his sweat-glazed forehead and glanced out of his bedroom window.

Full moon. No stars.

The perfect night for a bad dream.

He tossed the covers aside, threw his legs over and sat up on the edge of the bed. He rubbed the whites from his eyes with the backs of his hands until his vision cleared. He perched his right elbow on his right thigh, cupped his chin in his right hand and focused on the patch of moonlight spilling over the windowsill and down the wall.

This was the first nightmare he'd had in years since after Terri's death. Two days after her funeral, his dreams had become nothing more than a repetitive replay of that fateful night from her last words to the sound of the gunshot and back again. When Terri's sister Stephanie had stayed the night so she could help him go through her things, she'd heard him screaming her name across the house and hurried to his bedside to calm him until he was safe.

For anyone to be forced to relive the most tragic part of their past was more sinister than anything borne from the *dark avenues* of their mind where nothing existed but a black pitiless void that not even the sharpest of eyes could find solace in; where screams of horror and misery echo all around and the lingering sense of fear made the strongest of men and women weep and cower to their knees. He figured that everyone had a dark avenue of their own and that it was just as dark and sinister as his.

He reached over for the small glass of water he kept on the right-side of his bedside table, scythed in moonlight. The bright-green numbers on his digital clock sitting on the opposite end of the table next to his lamp cast odd shadows across the tabletop; it said three fifteen. He drained the glass in one swig, sighed with pleasure at the river of icy coolness soothing his bone-dry throat and set the glass back onto the stand.

He rose up, pressed his bare feet onto the cold hardwood floor and felt his skin prickle; his eyelids snapped open like No-Sale signs in an old cash register. He trudged out of the bedroom, his face still groggy from fatigue and sauntered across the hall into the bathroom. He was standing between the shower stall and the sink when he realized he'd flipped the light switch on the wall beside of the doorway.

A cone of amber-colored light burst from the overhead fixture and hit him like a shot of mace. He hissed through clenched teeth, squinted his eyes against the glare and bowed his head toward the sink to avoid it. He turned on the faucet, inched his head closer to the sink and splashed a few handfuls of cold water across his face.

When he raised his head up from the sink, tiny lucid beads of water dripping off his face, something shone in the corner of Kevin's left eye. He glimpsed up in time to see a strobe of harsh halogen light bursting through the bathroom window. At first, he thought—as is always the case—it was a passing motorist making an illegal U-turn to get back into the city.

Then he heard the chain-smoking cough of unoiled car door hinges, followed an explosion of loud rock music. His mind kicked into overdrive and cleared the veil of sleepiness from his brain. *They were the same sounds I'd heard com–*

Before he could fathom their origin, a pair of shadowy figures slinked into the streams of light and crept toward the window. One of them wiggled what looked to be a large knife in their hand while a chorus of soft whispers echoed off the light-blue tiled walls.

"Tell us where it is. Tell us where it is, tell us where it is, tell us where it is, tell us where–"

The voice surged into a loud echoing demand.

"Tell us where it is, TELL us where it is. TELL US WHERE IT IS! TELL US WHE–"

His body surging with adrenaline, Kevin released his grip on the sink and pivoted on his heels; his bare sweaty feet squeaked across the white linoleum floor. His heart thundered as he drew back a sharp intake of air, his eyes wide with horrid fascination.

His hands curled into white-knuckled fists, skin prickling with fear, he paused and gazed out through the bathroom window.

Nothing but darkness.

No headlights.

No voices.

No loud music.

Nothing but the clear night sky and cones of monochrome light bleeding across the cul-de-sac from the street lights. He lowered his hands, his fists slowly unfurling and took two deep breaths to calm his nerves. He shook his head, hoping that one of his neighbors weren't passing by in time to see him acting like this.

Fear subsided as he looked away from the window. He snatched a hand towel from the bottom shelf of the rack fixed to the wall above the toilet and dabbed it carefully across his face. His thumb tapped the knot on his forehead and spread a river of pain down his face.

He made a mental note not to do it again and tossed the towel into the wicker brown clothes hamper standing against the wall across from the toilet. He sighed, stared at his reflection in the mirror and leaned over, bracing the sink with both hands.

"What the fuck am I doing?" He asked himself.

It was one of those questions that no one would have the answer for but him.

All he wanted to do was continue a long-standing tradition that he and Terri enjoyed together; to carry that other half of her around with him in his pocket as a reminder that she'd never strayed too far from his thoughts. He'd never had this much trouble in the past, so why now?

Why was such a harmless hobby playing tricks on him, pulling and tugging on his psyche like a department store brat with a sweet tooth? He was sure no one else's hobbies of this type had taken such a chaotic turn like this. Would a stamp collector find a hidden message inside of a stamp? Or maybe even a coin collector?

Maybe he could move onto one of those after all of this was over; whenever that would be.

He killed the bathroom light on his way out and glanced over his right shoulder at the mixed carpet of moonlight and shadows flooding his house. He padded back into his bedroom, peeled off his tee-shirt and used it to wipe the film of sweat from the back of his neck.

He shook his head in disbelief, sighed and tossed his sweaty tee shirt onto the floor below his bedroom window. He slid the top drawer of his bedside table open, retrieved the bottle of sleeping pills and examined the bottle in the light. Stephanie had left them here over a year ago after her last visit just in case the dreams came flooding back again.

He chewed the pill, closed the window and sent the curtain slumping against the wall. He slid back under the covers and watched the odd moonlit shadows stretch and oscillate across the ceiling until sleep finally took over.

8

"HEY, Kevin." Erica said, her face beaming. "How was your weekend?"

"It was okay." He nodded, filling the massive steel sink with hot water. "How was yours?"

"Mom and I went to Davidson Park and walked The Lincoln Trail." The gleeful tone in her voice made it sound like they'd gone to Disney. "And then we did some swimming and had a picnic. We were so tired from all the fun we had we crashed as soon as we got home."

"I'll bet."

Angel, Erin and Jacob handled the customers in the lobby whilst Kevin scrubbed every pizza pan and cutter in between him wiping the tables and checking the trash cans. Fred, Angel's most reliable delivery man, had even pitched in with the customers when he wasn't running around town in a dark-blue Ford Escort with a white plastic ANGEL'S PIZZA sign attached to the roof. It was twelve-thirty and the lunch rush was starting to—as Angel had stated twice today—turn into a more of a "lunch riot".

The mingled smells of tomato sauce, cooked meat and fresh vegetables were pushed out through the kitchen by the large coils of heat wafting from the tall brick-style pizza oven sitting along the left-side wall. The brown-tiled floor stretched past a large refrigerated countertop that sat along the right-side under a spine of florescent light fixtures with eight inside compartments stocked with freshly-made toppings; it then spread out in front of a white marble counter stacked with touch-screen cash registers.

The dining room consisted of round Formica-topped tables sitting on a marble-green floor with gilded picture frames dotting across coarse white walls; recessed light fixtures spilled soft cones of whiskey-colored light across the room. A local radio station spewed through the recessed speakers reminding everyone that they played nothing but "the classic hits of today and yesterday."

As he wiped down the tables, Kevin could hear Angel in the back barking orders to the others to make sure they were getting done on time; those same employees had probably wished they were washing tables instead of working inside of a hot, muggy kitchen with a five-foot-six brunette who could flip her "bitch-switch" (as Jacob liked to call it) at any given time. Once the customers received their orders and left, three or four more would take their place and so forth. The rush seemed to go on forever; Jacob slid one pizza into the oven after the other and sighed with contempt for every customer who pulled up into the parking lot.

Busy days are good days, he reminded himself.

When the lunch rush receded to a steady pace, Kevin hurried out of the kitchen to wipe down the table next to the trash receptacle on the far-right corner of the lobby. He glanced out the side door and beyond the parking lot at the activity going on at the park across the street. A middle-aged woman wearing brown leather sandals with matching braided straps, a pair of purple-cotton shorts and a white tee-shirt tossed a bright red ball at an eager Dalmatian puppy with a bright blue collar; a pair of college students in hippie clothing sat under a tree playing guitar and a bongo drum in front of a small crowd who grinned and nodded their heads to the music; children played and people laughed.

A family of four glided across the bike path stretched across the rear of the park on a black and gold tandem bike. The ecstatic stares on their faces reminded Kevin of an old chewing gum commercial he'd seen back in the eighties but that one had featured two twin girls in white shorts and a red tee-shirt. Patches of sunlight and shadows spread evenly along the curbs and sidewalks;

birds flew overhead, their swift origami shadows floating above the park.

From the recessed speakers inside the restaurant, Mazzy Star sang "Fade Into You".

Two little children–a chubby blonde girl in a pink-tee and bright blue shorts and a skinny dark-haired boy in a red-tee and denim coveralls–occupied a nearby booth bickering at one another while their mother scrawled through her cell phone and pretended to care. A liver-spotted old man in dark slacks and a thin-striped white shirt occupied the table nearest the entrance leading into the kitchen, picking the pepperonis from his slice as if they were contagious. There were a few college students in summer attire—shorts, sandals, sneakers with socks and loose-fitting shirts—laughing at something one of them said while a few of them gaped at their cell phones.

There weren't many customers around and when there were they didn't stick around for long. This had been the usual sort of traffic that flowed in any time after the lunch rush had ended; it would only be a few hours before he clocked out and headed back home.

After a red pickup truck rumbled past, something emerged out of the corner of his left eye. He peered through the same glass door and saw a strange figure standing on the far-left corner of the lot under the shadowy canopy of a leafy oak tree deeply-rooted between the restaurant and an optometrist's office. He glanced at the customers filling the row of tables facing the front of the restaurant and wondered why no one could see her.

Upon further inspection, it was *her* but she looked much different than before.

She glanced back at him, her arms still slumped down by her sides; the thick pockets of damp black mascara dripping down her face had gnawed away the skin below her eye sockets, exposing thumb-sized crescents of slick red flesh. Her sleek blonde hair fluttered in the breeze with reckless abandon, caressing her face like a quivering pillow of golden feathers. Her red plaid skirt wavered around her hips, dividing her curvy black shadow stretching across the asphalt; larger pockets of rotting flesh spread down her thighs, calves and legs to reveal more highways of flesh, muscle and sinew.

He took two deep breaths to quell his anxiety. His fist tightened around the dripping wet dishtowel, sending thin rivers of frothy-white suds cascading down his fingers. A mix of fear and curiosity rooted his feet to the floor, closing tightly around his throat and denying him a voice.

Beads of sweat trickled down his forehead, streaked the back of his neck and pressed his work shirt to his ribs. Their gazes locked onto one another, strong and hypnotic like star-crossed lovers. His heart stammering, he failed to gather any saliva to coat his bone-dry mouth.

She extended her right arm out from her side, curled her fingers into a half-fist and waved, beckoning for him to come closer. He dropped the towel inside the bucket, inched his way toward the door and gripped the U-shaped metallic handle in his slick foam-covered hand. He pushed the door open, stepped out of the restaurant and onto the parking lot; lucid snakes of heat wriggled off the pavement, sending a fresh torrent of sweat sliding down his body.

She took a gentle step back, her shadow lengthening across the yellow lines stretching across the road and mumbled. He stepped past a white minivan with a company logo (ABBY'S DRYWALL) plastered across the driver-side in dark blue font and heard a soft-spoken whisper in his ears.

"They murdered me." She sighed. "They murdered me. They murdered me."

She tipped her head back in the same forty-five degree angle, brought her left hand around and pinched both sides of her throat with her thumb and forefinger. The red line still etched across her throat opened, spraying a stream of dark blood across the air onto the pavement, its thick coppery smell wafting in the breeze.

When he reached the strip of asphalt separating the parking lot from the street, Kevin watched in horror as the blood oozed across the searing hot asphalt. He stopped in his tracks and, the wind rushing him from all sides, watched the pool of blood coagulate to form a coherent phrase.

THEY MURDERED ME, it'd said.

The mingled odors of hot copper, heat and rotting flesh stung his nostrils and churned the pit of his stomach. He tried to say something, anything that could decipher the distance between sanity and *in*sanity when something tugged on the back of his work shirt and cinched his collar tightly around his throat. Some unseen force wrapped around his stomach, lifting him off of his feet and jerking him back with such force that it trapped the air inside of his lungs.

Kevin fell backward, nearly jerking his head back between his shoulder blades and collided with the pavement. Air exploded from his lungs as tiny phosphenes burst across his vision; his teeth clacked together, spreading a bone-jarring pain across his face. His right hand skated across the sidewalk in front of the building, leaving a bright red abrasion across his palm.

He hissed between tightly-clenched teeth and, writhing like a child in a supermarket, slapped frantically at the thick muscular arm hugging his stomach. A cool breeze swept across the parking lot, tousling his hair and pulling him back into reality.

"Calm down, killer." A familiar voice pleaded.

He stopped and peered over his shoulder at a familiar face. Behind him, the customers had rose from their seats and watched with wild-eyed interest; a bleached blonde college student–to no surprise to anyone–held her cell phone up to the glass and said something to one of her friends. He rolled over and pushed himself up onto his feet, his hands warm and red from the hot black pavement.

"What the hell was all of that about?" Fred scoffed.

"I'm sorry."

"Are you okay?"

"I'm good." Kevin said, giving him a dismissive brush of his hand. "I had a bad weekend and I saw her standing—"

"If I wasn't serving Misses Bowers," He shook his head in surprise. "you'd be a slab of fucking roadkill right now."

When he peered over his shoulder and gazed at the middle of the street, Kevin felt his heart sink. The girl was gone, along with the pool of blood and the message that'd been scrawled across the pavement.

"Who did you see?"

"I'm sorry." He said and looked away. "I thought I saw someone standing in the middle of the street."

Angel burst through the front door on the opposite end of the restaurant and jogged toward them, her dark brown bun bobbing against the back of her head. His cheeks flushed with both shame and guilt, Kevin leaned against the front of the building and saw a mix of terror and relief etch itself across her face.

"What the hell?" She had a motherly inflection in her voice. "Are you trying to give me a fucking stroke?"

"It's alright, Angel." Fred brushed his hand at her. "He's not feeling good."

Bracing her hands against her hips, she asked, "How many sick days do you have?"

"I don't know." He said. "And I don't really care to know."

"It's not up to you, Kevin."

He hadn't used any of his sick days since Terri was shot.

"I want to see you after you're done." She said sternly. "And I don't want to hear another word about it."

After they followed her inside, Kevin gathered up the trays while Fred offered to take out the trash from both cans in the lobby. With Angel's "insistence", he agreed to a week vacation.

"I hope that helps." She told him.

As Angel gave him a hug, Kevin apologized again and clocked out. He thanked Fred, consoled a wildly sobbing Erin Deeds and reassured Jacob. Walking out the back door, he chided himself for being so blind to what the girl was trying to tell him.

As far as he was concerned, they weren't even delusions.

He didn't know what they were but there was only one way he was going to find out.

9

WHEN he eased his car onto his driveway, Kevin glanced out of his driver-side window and Mrs. Langston sitting on her front porch, reading the morning paper. He snatched his cell phone from the middle console, killed the engine, climbed out and shut the door behind him. It felt a little odd for him not to be at work right now but then maybe Angel had been right for once; he *had* been so overwhelmed that he hadn't made enough time for himself.

"Kevin." She bellowed, squinting at him through her glasses. "Is that you, Kevin? What are you doing home so early?"

"We weren't that busy today."

It was the only lie he could come up with on such short notice. He'd garnered a knack for that lately and thought maybe he should write a book about them; call it On Such Short Notice. He'd make killing off that for sure.

"Well, if you get bored today." She bellowed. "I'd appreciate it if you could–"

"I'll be very busy today, Mrs. Langston." He replied. "I'll be available tomorrow."

"Oh ok."

He waved at her before heading into the house. He kicked the door shut with the tip of his boot, hung his keys on the rack beside the door and carried his to-go container into the kitchen. He didn't have much of an appetite right now, but he knew later on that he would.

He ran into the bedroom and headed for the closet. He eased the massive mirrored doors aside, slid some clothes to the side and found it exactly where he'd left it. A dented cardboard box marked TERRI'S OFFICE in quick black scrawl sat on the far-left corner of the floor; a dark blue sticker of a VW Beetle was stuck to the top of the lid amongst a scrim of dust from years of neglect and ignorance, the words HMMM BUG blooming across the bottom of the car in a bubble-gum pink font.

The sticker struck a chord deep inside of him, brought him back to a place he didn't want to go. With everything that'd gone on for the past two days, this wasn't the best time for him to think about her now. No matter how hard he tried to push it away, it was still there like a hard lump inside of his throat.

She'd bought the sticker from a little machine beside the exit doors of a nearby restaurant where they'd gone to celebrate her acquisition of what else but a bright-pink VW Beetle. He implied that she should put it on the back bumper of her car and kissed her as they'd made their way out to the parking lot. The week after her death, he'd found the sticker in the top drawer of her desk while he was gathering her things together and stuck it on the top of the box.

It only seemed fitting that he'd put it there considering how much the car and the sticker had meant to her. He swallowed the ball of sadness swelling in his chest, swiped the tear away from the corner of his eye and set the box on the bed. He flung the lid aside and dug through the contents until he found her laptop sitting in the bottom amongst an old stapler and an unopened box of Number-Two pencils.

He set the laptop aside, closed the box back up and slid it back into its original place in the bottom of the closet. He carried it out to the table, fired up her laptop and put on a fresh pot of coffee. Once the coffee maker was finished, he filled a cup and returned to the table.

When he sat down, an array of colorful icons were scattered around the festive backdrop of a winding country road strewn with bright red-orange leaves and flanked by an encroaching forest. He guided the little arrow across the screen and accessed his web browser. A few seconds and a slight blink later, the screen came alive, exposing Terri's favorite search engine.

Shafts of mid-afternoon sunlight seeped through the curtains, swarming with teeny dust motes. He typed in the name MARILYN GRAHAM and waited. A small hourglass appeared on the screen, spinning one direction and then the next and then back again.

After the screen blinked again, a list of possible websites appeared on the monitor. Two pages later, he found a website for the city's local paper—*The Shallow Rock Gazette*—and clicked it. The web page offered such features as allowing viewers to watch the city council meetings (*yawn*, Kevin thought) via web cam, a local movie critic's article on the latest comic-book movie (which didn't sound good when he saw the headline), agricultural tips, sports news, obituaries and local happenings.

He clicked on the Obituaries tab, took a sip of coffee and waited for the screen to load. Once the page loaded, the first local death he'd seen was of an old man who escaped from a nursing home only to be clipped by a drunk driver. He shook his head, his chest clenching with sadness, and tapped the arrow on the right side of the screen to access the next page.

He reached over for his coffee mug when a familiar face bloomed across the screen; the same face who'd strummed the strings of his sanity day and night until her song could be heard, one whose lyrics spoke of pain and desperation, of sadness and loss. The name MARILYN ROSE GRAHAM was located on the left side of the article in bold red font. On the opposite end of the name was a five-by-seven photo of a heavyset blonde girl smiling brightly for the camera; she wore tight black pants and a button down white blouse with a black tie.

She'd been valedictorian in her class, received Honor Roll three times and even became a member of The National Honors Society. She never went out for a spot on the cheerleading team nor did she try to become part of the in-crowd like everyone else; the time that she'd spent tutoring most of a handful of ninth and tenth-grade students had put her onto the path to becoming a teacher. At first glance, she could've been a follower, but she'd taken the role of leader and wanted nothing more than to make a difference in this world; had he and Terri became parents, he was certain Marilyn would've ended up their child's teacher.

Her father, Gerald Graham, worked as a steel-mill operator for fourteen years before he was laid off due to the rash of financial failures that still grip the country today. Three months after, when jobs had begun to become scarce, he'd hung himself in the basement of their house in Trinity Estates. Sadly, little Marilyn had been the one who found her father dangling above the floor like a cheap Halloween decoration.

He liked to think that she'd excelled in both academics and in life so that her father would've been happy about how she'd turned out. In a way, it'd driven her to be who she was long before she'd left this world at such a young age.

He read the obituary two more times, took another sip of his coffee and set it back down.

"'Her body was identified by her parents after it'd been found shackled to an old wooden fence along Taylor Run Road two weeks ago'." He read aloud.

He clamped his right hand across his forehead, gave a deflated sigh and pondered his next move.

Where had he heard that name before? As a kid, he'd heard plenty of stories back in high school about what people did up there and quickly brushed the thought from his head. He closed his eyes and shook his head, his head reeling with a mixture of worry and confusion.

Realization hit him like a ball of steam, snapping his senses alert. He raised his head up from his hand, craned his head over to his left shoulder and peered down the hallway. He leapt out of his chair, stormed down the hall in two quick strides and pushed the door open that led into the art room.

He padded across the room, his bare feet pressing softly against the carpet and gathered the four rubbings. He carried them out to the dining room, set them on the table and unrolled them one at a time until he found the right one. He spread them out across the tabletop, gathered a few heavy knickknacks from the shelf in the far-right corner and set them onto all four corners of the page to hold them down.

He unzipped the canvas bag, retrieved his chalk tray and set it on top. He scanned the array of light and dark colors, selected the right one and gently rubbed it across the page below the word TAYLOR. As the chalk gave a comforting shush against the paper, he stopped every so often to blow off the excess and took a tentative step back from the table to survey the results.

When he saw the words RUN ROAD appear on the page, Kevin drew back a long breath and clamped his hand across his mouth. His body rigid with terror, he spun away from the table and sighed. His hand tensed around the piece of chalk until his fingers and knuckles turned white; his heart thudded with fear.

Everything he'd gone through these past few days had finally become clear. He'd never felt more like a fool until now.

She was a desperate plea for help, a cry that would go ignored for years to come long after it was buried under a statute of limitations. She'd unlocked a deeply profound part of himself that he never knew existed and pulled back the cloth that separated the realm between the living and the dead he knew had always existed.

She wanted to bring her killers to justice, but she couldn't do it herself. She needed someone who could act as her eyes and her ears; someone who would understand her message and act as professionally as possible. Since Terri's death, the only thing he'd done to help the dead was to preserve their name and timeline inside of cheap gilded picture frames and plaster them across the walls of his hobby room.

He hurried back to the table, took a sip from his mug to swallow the bitter taste in the back of his throat, slid back into his chair, clicked on the ARCHIVES tab located along the top right-hand corner and waited. After a few seconds, a chronological order of back issues starting with the paper's first printing (December

1942) bloomed across the screen in a bright green font. He clicked on the one marked MARCH Two-Thousand-Nineteen, rubbed his hands together and watched the tiny hourglass swirl in the middle of the screen.

The headline proclaimed in black type face: BODY OF HONOR STUDENT FOUND. A grainy colorful photo depicting a rickety wooden fence surrounding a wide grassy meadow backed by a tall screen of thick oaks and pines was located on the lower right-hand corner.

According to the report, a local fisherman was leaving Lake Michelle when he saw something lying against the bottom of the fence at approximately ten-forty-five. He'd parked his pickup and checked her pulse; when he found none he hopped back into his truck and called the police at a bait shop half a mile away. An hour later, the police and the media had flooded the scene like paparazzi.

He passed up a series of articles, one about an event that a group of college students were holding to benefit the cancer wing at a local hospital, a second article concerning a former presidential candidate who was coming to Portsmouth to speak to the students at a local middle school about global warming proceeded to Page Three. In a second photo, Harry Weaver held his sister tightly against him with one arm while using the other to block the camera flash from hitting her in the face, burying her tear-streaked face into the front of his shirt. The mask of concern and anger etched across his face said it was more out of respect to her than out of disrespect for them.

In the background of the photo, a black plastic body bag lying across a gurney was being loaded into the back of the Coroner's vehicle. More photos were provided, showing small groups of police officers in crisp black uniforms rooting around the scene in search of evidence.

The pictures sent vivid images parading through his mind.

Sadness tore through his chest, driving a jagged spike into his heart. His cheeks flushed as he blinked back the river of hot tears welling in his eyes and gazed away from the laptop as if the pictures were too contagious. He felt himself slowly crawl down those dark avenues again, back into that dark corner of his subconscious where pain and misery are neighbors waiting to slap his pride on the tabletop between them and gnaw at the very fiber of his soul until there were nothing left but a pile of bones so they could lick the gristle off their fingers and laugh like the sick gluttonous bastards they were.

It was a sight he'd known all too well. The tears, the questions, the deep realization knowing that your loved one was separated from this world by the cruel twist of fate.

He remembered every second of that terrible night when he sat on the curb, sobbing uncontrollably into his blood-soaked hands while the crowd peered over crime scene tape and other shoulders to gawk at him as if he were a zoo exhibit (*come one, come all, see The Sobbing Man in all his broken-hearted despair*). The only difference between him and Lacey Graham were that she and Harry were spared a photo that showed the pain etched across their faces. On the night of Terri's death, he resembled a dark cardboard cutout people perch on their front porches to scare off intruders.

Nothing can repair the damage that follows the death of a loved one. Not even a brand-new I-Phone.

He wiped the tears from his eyes with the back of his left hand and continued reading the article. It mentioned that Mary had recently earned a scholarship to Stanford University to pursue her Bachelor's degree in teaching. It also stated that her boyfriend, and starting quarterback for the high school football team, could not be reached for comment.

Kevin scrolled up to the top of the site, clicked on the tab marked LINKS and waited. When the next page opened, he scanned an entire list of web pages posted in bright yellow font on a gray marble background, took another sip and double-clicked on the high school's official website.

The screen flickered over to an animatronic photo of a giant wolf's head with piercing yellow eyes; the side flaps of its aging gray snout flared in anger along with its nostrils, exposing two rows of jagged white teeth. After he clicked on the wolf's head, he was taken to a large photo of a stout bald man in a white shirt and red tie standing with his arms laced proudly across his chest next to a painted mural of the same angry wolf's head plastered across a cream-colored brick wall. The words SHALLOW ROCK HIGH SCHOOL were spread above the photo in a massive golden arch that looked as if it'd been done on a version of Print Shop that didn't exist anymore; the motto "turning little cubs into fierce wolves since nineteen forty-five" was strewn across the bottom of the photo in a bright red font.

He moved the arrow over to the tab marked ATHLETICS and clicked the left mouse button. There, he found a team photo of the coaching staff sitting below a long list of this year's top athletes; he slid the arrow across their faces and saw their names pop up inside of a tiny black box. He scrolled down the screen and saw the caption PLAYERS NOT FEATURED IN PHOTOGRAPH located on the bottom right-hand corner.

The names were Dylan Polk, James McCord and Greg Roberts. He tapped his finger repeatedly against the tip of his chin and tried to remember the last time he'd seen those names. The first names didn't register but the last names rang a bell.

He perched his elbows on the edge of the table and reached over for his mug when a sudden realization hit him again. He leapt out of his chair again and back around to the headstone rubbings still spread out across the tabletop. He reached across the table and snatched the pinky-thin piece of gray chalk from the table behind the laptop when something burst across his dining room window.

10

HIS body prickling with shock, Kevin clutched the back of the chair with both hands ready to gaze into the face of his dead counterpart, and felt his skin bristling with fear. He peered up from the table, his thumb and forefinger still grasping the sliver of chalk and felt the hairs along the nape of his neck grow stiff. Sweat broke out along his forehead in tiny lucid rivulets, pasting the back of his tee-shirt to his spine.

A blue jay was perched on the window, its head jostling this way and that. It tiptoed along the window, its beady black eyes glinting in the sunlight and burst away from the window in a bluish-white blur. He took a few deep breaths and waited for the momentary sense of shock to dissipate from his nerves before getting back to work.

He bent over the table, rubbed the piece of chalk across the page marked MCCORD and blew the excess dust away. When the name JAMES appeared, he backed away from the table and felt a phantom coldness tracing the contours of his spine. The chalk fell from his hand, struck the edge of the table, landed on the seat of the chair in front of him (where Terri had once sat) and swayed back and forth.

He clamped his left hand across his mouth and gazed down at the page, his scalp tingling with shock. He backed up against the doorway beside the hallway and felt his legs weaken. He slid down the wall, sat on the floor, drew his knees toward his chest and buried his face in his hands.

Why me?, he thought, *Why did it have to be me?* His brain was buzzing with so much activity he failed to answer his own questions. He hadn't the foggiest idea how to solve a murder than he knew how to tie a sheep shank or repair a car.

He rose up from the floor and, his body pumping with energy, retrieved the piece of chalk from the seat of the chair. He rubbed it across the page marked ROBERTS, blew off the excess, took a sip from his coffee mug and glanced down; the name GREG bloomed across the page. He moved onto the page marked POLK, rubbed the piece of chalk across it too and blew off the excess dust only—

This is impossible, he thought, eyeing the blank spot on the left side of the page. He tossed the spent sliver of chalk onto the tray, selected a new fresh stick of black chalk and repeated the process. Adrenaline racing through his veins at breakneck speed, he moved the chalk back and forth across the page as fast as he could until his hand glided across his face in quick blurry movements.

He stopped, blew the dust away and cursed under his breath. He tried it again, his fingertips pressing tightly against the sides of the chalk stick until his knuckles bled white.

The first names of each of the two absent-minded athletes were as visible as the laptop on the table except for this one. His brows creased with confusion, he set the mug down again, rubbed the chalk across the page again and blew off the excess. He closed his eyes, drew a long breath deep into his lungs and slowly rubbed the pads of his fingertips against his temples.

"What the fuck am I doing wrong?" He asked himself. "What the fuck am I even doing?"

He tossed the splinter of chalk between the three wide-open pages and balanced his hands on his hips. He carried his half-empty coffee mug off the table into the kitchen, pour it out into the sink and left it sitting on the countertop. He tossed the sliver of chalk into the trashcan and came back into the dining room to glance at the rubbings again.

Why weren't they featured in the photo if they were a part of the team? What could've been more important than that?

He could just imagine how angry the coach must've been when they arrived a few minutes after the picture had already been taken; they might've even gotten there while the picture had been taken and decided not to bother with it. He was sure their parents would've had a lot to say as well.

He walked back to the table and sat back down when something stirred inside of his right pocket. He flinched, jerking his right leg in a spasmodic twitch and reached his hand inside. He gazed down at the number flashing across the screen, thumbed the green ACCEPT button and caught it on the fourth ring.

"Hello."

"I'm trying to reach Kevin Perkins."

"This is he. Who may I ask is calling?"

He expected to hear a cheap sales pitch from someone promising him a grand vacation or a recording reminding him that his health insurance wasn't as good. Instead, all he could hear was the sound of heavy breathing.

"This is Lacey Graham."

When he realized who it was, Kevin snatched a quick breath and sighed. He had enough surprises for one day.

"How are you doing today, Misses Graham?"

"Please call me Lacey."

He shrugged. "Okay, Lacey. How did you get my phone number?"

"Uhhh." She said, her voice trailing off. "Officer White gave it to me. Yeah, Officer White that's who it was."

"Okay."

He wasn't entirely sure that he felt comfortable with Officer White giving out that sort of information and made a mental note to confront him about it. He wasn't even sure about the odd timbre in her voice that made it sound rehearsed and a little robotic.

"Harry and I still feel bad about what happened." She said, her voice pinched. "We'd like to invite you over for dinner."

"That's okay, Mrs. Graham. There's no need to–"

"I insist. It's the least we can do."

"Okay. What time would you like me to be there?"

"Can you come over right away?" She asked in a soft pleading tone. "I know you're probably busy but—"

"It's okay. Just give me your address."

He retrieved a pen and pad from the kitchen and scribbled down The Grahams' address. He thanked her, killed the call and stuffed the cell phone back into his right pocket. He stuffed the note with The Grahams' address into his left pocket, shut the laptop down, drew the curtains shut and left the pages scattered across the tabletop.

He could use a home-cooked meal for once. He wasn't getting any younger by eating all of the fast food he'd consumed the past forty-eight hours.

He snatched his keys off the hook beside the front door and locked the front door on his way out. The mid-afternoon breeze stirred the treetops and grazed his skin with feathery-cold fingers; the sun beamed like a lighthouse beacon. He climbed into his Toyota, his sweaty calloused hands gripping the steering wheel, and backed out of the drive.

Mrs. Langston was standing next to a tall svelte looking woman in a white blouse and brown slacks with sharp-edged creases. The woman's black hair was molded into a thick dark bee-hive that rose three inches off the top of her head and she wore too much red lipstick; the frames of her horn-rimmed glasses glinted in the sunlight when they spotted him. Kevin watched Mrs. Langston whisper something to her friend and then glance suspiciously at the back of his car.

He hadn't thought about how he was going to tell Lacey Graham about his newfound evidence because the last thing he wanted was to make her feel uncomfortable. He took the side streets to avoid the infuriating rush of afternoon traffic and followed a hulking red Hummer with a ribbed tailgate almost six blocks before it turned right onto a side street.

He cruised through large sections of modest-looking stucco and clapboard homes that sat on knee-high neatly-trimmed lawns adorned with comical yard ornaments and black-iron numbers fixed to the front doors. Tree shadows rippled across the bright-yellow curbs, pooled along the streets and sidewalks; the wind sighed through the treetops, spilling its most erotic secrets to anyone willing to listen.

He followed the main road out of town and drove past a small white brick building with a lopsided tiled roof and boarded up windows sitting on a patch of knee-high weeds, looking as dark and ominous as a child's nightmare. A few miles later, he drove past a gas station/mini-mart with a large white banner strung above its front door announcing DEALS OF THE DAY in large black font.

Two miles later, he spotted a giant white sign squeezed into a U-shaped cup of burnt red brick sitting on the opposite end of the road. TRINITY ESTATES was scrawled across the front in bright blue cursive font below a small neatly-painted strip of tiny homes glowing under a large yellow light; there was a sappy inspirational quote scrawled along the bottom of the sign he couldn't see too good. He drummed his fingers against the steering wheel, waited for a blue SUV to pass him in the opposite lane and turned left onto a wide concrete drive.

The road rose upward, cleaving a wide trail through a wide grassy meadow backdropped by a tall screen of leafy oak trees. He stopped at the top of the hill, checked his directions again and drove through a wide expanse of elegant brick and clapboard houses sitting on picture-perfect lawns that probably cost more than he made in six months. A high concrete wall bordered the massive housing community like the wall of a maximum-security prison in an old John Carpenter movie.

The mingled sounds of dogs barking at imaginary things, childish laughter and chirping birds echoed against the clear blue sky. He enjoyed the sweet scent of barbecued food wafting up his nose and tried his best not to salivate too much.

He obeyed the fifteen-mile-an-hour speed limit posted on the signs along the curbs and followed the main road toward the far-right corner of the housing development. He parked behind a green Ford Taurus sitting along the curb in front of a one-story brown stucco house with a green shingled roof and a large wooden deck in the back. He killed the engine, tucked the note with the directions into his left pocket and checked the time on his radio.

He took a few deep breaths, climbed out of his car and followed a bluestone path lined with thick evergreen bushes toward the front porch. An old park bench sat under the roof on the right side of the porch soaked in a yin-yang of sunlight and shadow, flakes of rusted-green paint scattered below. The flowerbed running along the left side of the porch was nothing more than an open casket of cracked dirt and a tangle of wilted-brown weeds.

Sighing, he approached the front door, his sneakers making tiny whispers across the dusty concrete porch and pressed the tiny pearl-colored doorbell. He tapped his fingers against his thighs, keeping with the familiar tune playing inside of his head and waited. He scanned the rest of the cozy-looking houses sitting back from the curb and waited for Lacey Graham to wave him inside with a sincere smile on her face and a barbecue grill roaring in the back yard.

He heard the front door give a knuckle-crackling click and felt a wave of relief wash over him. In a breezy floral print dress, Lacey Graham peered at him through the half-open door; her short blonde hair, light beige skin and sea-blue eyes gave off an elegant glow. He waited for her to welcome him in but her hand froze around the cold brass doorknob, her right foot was planted across the threshold as if to block him from going any further.

"Hello, Misses Graham." He smiled.

"Do I know you?"

The hesitant tone in her voice puzzled him.

"You called me and told me to come over and—"

"Oh, I did." She blinked twice. "I'm sorry. It hasn't been a good day for me."

"I'm kind of glad you called because I have something to—

He heard a shuffling noise from behind him and watched something like fear tug against the worry lines on across Lacey Graham's face. His body froze under a mixture of fear and surprise, pinning his feet to the porch and raised the hairs on the backs of his arms; his heart thumped as his lung spasmed.

He saw movement in the corner of his left eye and caught a thin lanky shadow emerging from behind him, nearly eclipsing the patch of bright afternoon sunlight flooding the front porch. He caught his breath and spun around to confront the stranger when something hard struck him across the face. His head whirled back around before it could make a complete turn, wrenching his neck; arcs of white light snapped across his vision like a slave trader's whip.

His left temple pressing against his skull, he tried to shake it off with no luck. Waves of pain flooded through his brain, burst across his upper body, coiled around his spine and sent him kneeling onto the porch. Hot lucid tears flooded his vision as his eyelids drooped shut, dropping him into a deep bottomless void whose obsidian black folds hugged him with wide open arms.

11

WHEN he regained consciousness, Kevin viewed the world through narrow, heavy-lidded eyes. He could barely make out the trio of shadows rising through the blanket of fog obscuring his vision and winced at the light surrounding them. He felt so dizzy his neck began to roll back and forth as if it were too weak to support his head.

A chorus of muffled voices muttered from behind the shadows, each one sounding just as incoherent as the other. He wasn't surprised that he couldn't hear them because he could barely remember bits and pieces of what happened before he was blindsided. He gathered the courage to raise his left hand and rubbed the cobwebs from his eyes until his vision became clear; elation washed over him as his senses returned to normalcy.

"...get this done..."

"...not fuck around then..."

"came for and leave..."

He found himself inside of a spacious living room with soft blue carpet and lime-green walls pimpled with gilded picture frames that dated back to an era where bloodlines were born and legacies were created. A large flat screen television sat atop of a wide polished oak credenza flanked by a DVD player and a large cable box similar to the one he had back home. He peered at his reflection in the television screen and caught another reflection beside of his own.

He snatched a quick breath, peered over his right shoulder and found Harry Kline and Lacey Graham were huddled together in front of an overstuffed white couch. She leaned her head against the front of his short-sleeved tee shirt, tears glistening in her eyes. A small bib of blood had caked the right side of Harry's mouth and made a bee-line toward the tip of his chin.

He peered past the top of Lacey's head and beyond, scanning the right side of the house for where the voices were coming from. Instead, he found a stuffed deer's head hanging on the wall above a stone-hearth fireplace with a white-marble mantel; two straight-back wooden chairs sat at an oblique angle in front of the fireplace like set on an episode of *Masterpiece Theatre*.

Kevin pressed his hands against the floor and gradually sat up. He leaned back against the couch, sighed and shielded the sunlight from his eyes with the back of his hand. When he peered back at them, Lacey was the first to see him, then Harry; she wiped the tears from her eyes and nodded.

"Are you okay?"

"I'll live." Kevin sighed. "You?"

"The big one got a shot at me." Harry said.

"I see that."

Lacey tried to say something when a herd of footsteps paraded into the room and stopped. They strode into the room one at a time with the same smug and confident demeanor they had back at the waiting room in the ER two days ago.

The bald one, whom Kevin remembered burying his face in his cell phone, wore a gray tee shirt, jeans and black sneakers. The spiky-haired boy wore jeans, a pair of brown hiking boots and a light-blue Abercrombie and Fitch tee-shirt. The heavyset kid wore the same tie-dye shirt, gray sweat pants and black leather sandals he'd worn back at the hospital.

They stopped and stood in front of the television and stared down at them like disappointed parents. The only sounds they could hear were their labored breathing and birds still chirping outside.

"It looks like somebody's awake." The heavyset kid said in a daunting voice.

"We can see that, Greg." The bald teen shook his head.

"What the hell are you doing here?" Kevin asked.

"We're the ones in charge, asshole." The spiky-haired teen said and kicked Kevin's right foot. "We'll be the ones asking all of the questions."

Although his brain still felt light-headed, Kevin didn't take too long to decipher who was who. If Greg was the heavyset hippie, then Dylan was the spiky-haired boy and James was the bald one.

"What the hell are *you* doing here?" The spiky-haired teen inquired, kicking Kevin's left foot.

"Lacey called me and told me to come over." Kevin said through loosely-clenched teeth. "She said she had–"

"I didn't call you."

He glanced at her with a confused expression on his face.

"Did you call him?" She asked Harry.

"I was in the kitchen when these goofballs showed up."

A cloud of unease filled the house like invisible electric. It raised the hairs on the back of Kevin's neck and arms; Harry and Lacey glanced back at the three boys and Kevin followed suite.

"Hey, old man." Dylan roared, his arms spread out from his sides. "Don't talk about us like we're not in the fucking room."

"That's not important, Dylan." James said to him, then said to Kevin. "What does any of this have to do with you? I know you're not a member of the family because I've met all of them before so why don't you enlighten us."

"You wouldn't believe me if I told you." Kevin sighed. "Why should it even matter?"

James opened his mouth to say something when Dylan dismissed him with the wave of his right hand. Greg ambled toward the fireplace, shook his head and leaned his enormous bulk against the back of one of the chairs sitting in front of the fireplace. Kevin drew his knees up to his chest to keep James from kicking him again and massaged his temples with the first two fingers on each hand to soothe the pain pounding against his skull.

"It was just a misunderstanding between us and Kevin." Lacey replied. "It's nothing for you or anyone else to be concerned about."

"If that's the truth, then fine." James said to her, then at Kevin. "We'll just stick around here until get what we came for."

"Bullshit." Harry grimaced.

"Do you even know what it is?" Greg snickered. "Do you have any idea what we're here for?"

"I could give a shit." Harry said. "I want you out of my sister's house right fucking now."

Dylan cupped his chin inside of his hand, flashed Greg a narrow sideways glance and peered casually up at the ceiling. Greg snickered, pushed himself away from the back of the chair and stormed across the living room with the gait of a colossal giant invading a small medieval village. Each footstep sent the picture frames sashaying across the walls, vibrated the floor beneath them and drove spikes of fear deep into the marrow of their bones.

Harry released his grip on Lacey's hips, set his mouth into a hard line and squared his shoulders like he were ready for a fight. Greg pivoted on his right hip, grunted behind tightly clenched teeth and drove his right foot hard into Harry's face. Lacey coiled herself into a tight ball, drew her knees high and tight against her chest and shielded her face with both arms; Kevin reared his head back, scrunched his face together and peered over his left shoulder at a small overstuffed sofa sitting against the wall.

The impact whipped Harry's head back between his shoulders, squeezing a painful grunt from deep inside of him; a stream of blood and two broken teeth flew across the room and splattered against the carpet. Harry's head slumped back down and, his mouth twisted into a lopsided grin, propped his chin onto his chest. James snickered and clapped, his cheeks beaming beneath the wide pleasing grin on his face.

His chest heaving with exertion, Greg wheezed, "Shut the fuck up, old man or I'll bury you right next to that little bitch."

Greg wiped the sweat from his forehead with the back of his left arm, flared his nostrils in anger and stalked back to the left side of the room. Lacey reached over her shoulder, plucked a few Kleenex from the dispenser sitting on the end table beside of the couch and dabbed them gently against Harry's bloody mouth. He took them from her, nodded at the three boys and gave her a reassuring pat on the meaty part of her left shoulder.

Dylan stepped forward and glanced down at Kevin. "You still didn't my question, Kevin?"

"How do you know my name?"

"After we went home from the hospital that night, I snuck Ned's notebook out of his pants pocket while he was asleep and took a picture of the page with your name written on it. I thought about paying you a visit but it didn't really make sense because you didn't have what I've been looking for. When we came here to get back what was ours, you came knocking on the door and everything just fell into place." Dylan said.

"How do you know my girlfriend?" James asked.

"I don't."

"Stop lying, asshole." Greg cautioned.

"Like I said before you wouldn't believe me if I told you."

Dylan shuffled closer and knelt down in front of them. He gave an exhausted sigh, made a steeple with his fingers, reached his right arm around and groped at the back waistband of his jeans. When he flung his arm back around, he gripped a nickel-plated 9mm tightly in his right fist.

Everyone except for Dylan and Greg flinched in terror. James turned his head away and clenched his fists together; Lacey slapped her left hand across her mouth, her eyes wide with surprise and buried her face into her brother's tee-shirt to muffle the scream bursting from her lips. Kevin went stiff for a moment, braced the carpet with his fingertips until they turned white and sighed; Harry held his sister's face tightly against his chest, tears brimming in his eyes and whispered softly in her ear.

The sight of the gun brought a bad nostalgic aftertaste to the back of Kevin's throat and conjured his most darkest memory. Although Terri had been shot with a Smith and Wesson .38, a gun was still a gun.

"You better start talking." Dylan said, sweeping the gun across their faces. "or I'm gonna splatter your brains all over that fucking couch."

Kevin sighed and glanced over at his fellow hostages. Lacey raised her head up from Harry's chest and met Kevin's gaze, her brows separated by a thin faint line.

"I don't know how to say this any other way but I know it's going to sound crazy." He said in a generous voice. "All I can tell you is that you've got to believe me."

He held nothing back, starting with the afternoon it all began, added the melee at the cemetery and ended with their present situation. When he was finished, Greg glanced sardonically at Harry and back to Kevin.

"How hard did he actually hit you?"

"I ought to shoot you for wasting my fucking time." Dylan suggested.

"Hey, asshole." Greg chuckled. "Did your supposed rubbings tell you how all of this is going to end?"

"I want what I–"

James crept away from the living room window and tugged on the back of Dylan's left sleeve. Dylan hissed through his teeth, craned his head around and rose up from the floor.

"Is that really necessary?"

"What?"

James gazed hesitantly down at the pistol in Dylan's hand. Beads of sweat glinted off his acne-scarred forehead, glistened off of his brows and slid down his cheeks. The uneasy look on his face told Kevin that James had thought about whether or not he should mention having it around.

"The gun?" Dylan inquired. "Did you forget why we're here? Did you actually think we were going to let them walk away after we got what we came for? We're in this situation because you and your cock-tease couldn't keep it together. I'll use whatever means necessary to save my ass and my football career whether you like it or not."

He raised his left hand in the air, shook his head in anger, flicked James across the tip of his nose and flashed him a wide obnoxious grin. He sighed, turned his attention back to the three hostages and leveled the gun in Lacey's face.

"Hand it over right now."

"I don't know what you're talking about." Her lips wet and quivering.

"We know you have it." Greg grimaced. "Tell us where–"

"Mary never confided in me all of the time. If she has something that belongs to you, it's the first I've heard about it."

"She's lying."

"No I'm not." She pleaded, then glared at James. "I didn't know about Mary ever dating him until three months after they made it official at school."

When Dylan eased closer to her, Lacey curled up into a ball and raised her arms over her face again. Her face eclipsed by the shadows of her arms, she let off a loud agonizing sob that brought a smile to Greg's fleshy white face.

"There's no need for this." Harry pleaded.

"Shut up, asshole." Greg advised.

"Why don't you shut–"

The sound of fingers snapping cut them off in mid-sentence. They stopped and traced the sound back to Kevin.

"The two glass doves." Kevin said, brandishing a peace sign.

Her face sagging with disbelief, Lacey flashed Kevin a perplexed look. James buried his face in his hands, sighed and shook his head.

"How did you know about the doves?" She mumbled, her eye still red from crying.

"I didn't."

"Then how did–"

"How else would I have known?" His voice was gravelly and sympathetic. "I wasn't lying when I said Marilyn was talking to me through my rubbings."

"We don't care to hear about your sex life." Greg snickered. "We just want what we came for."

"Where are the two glass doves?"

"They're in her bedroom on her–"

Before she could finish, Dylan lowered the pistol and snatched her by the crook of her right arm. She yelped in protest as he jerked her up from the floor and onto her feet like a child throwing a tantrum in a crowded supermarket. When he pressed the barrel of the gun against her right temple, her knees buckled with fear.

"Since she knows where they're at." He said to Greg. "Follow her into the little whore's bedroom and see if this whacko is telling the truth."

He grunted and pushed her away. She stumbled across the room in a drunken pirouette, her short brown hair swirling around her face, and collided with Greg. Greg trapped her in a tight hug, buried his face in her hair and slid his tongue slowly across her right cheek.

When he saw the repulsive look on her face, Harry grunted and tried to push himself up from the floor. Kevin threw his left arm across Harry's chest to keep him from making anymore sudden moves.

"If you try anything," Dylan said, then shrugged at Kevin and Harry. "I'll kill them and then I'll come find you. Now go."

Greg clutched the crook of Lacey's left arm in his fat pale hand, led her out of the room and down the hallway; Harry peered over at Kevin and nodded. Silence enveloped the house save for the intermittent sounds of hurried footsteps and shuffled objects. They caught the familiar sound of wood sliding against wood, followed by a guttural incoherent threat and then a second wave of footsteps parading back down the hall.

Lacey returned first, Greg not too far behind. Her head bowed, a fresh set of tears streaming down her face, she slumped back down onto the floor in front of the couch and curled up next to Harry. Kevin had never seen two people come together from a tragedy like Harry and Lacey partly because he'd never had such a strong kinship with his own brother and sister.

For them, it was a time for clean slates and good memories that made up for all of the bad ones. Death broke their hearts; courage helped glue them back together.

His face creased by a wide satisfying grin, Greg handed a small plastic CD case over to Dylan, shook his head and glanced over at them before glaring back at him.

"I knew that little cunt was lying to us the whole time." He said through clenched teeth.

"Is it the right one?" James asked, staring incredulously.

"It looks like it."

"Then let me see it."

"Hell no." Dylan chuffed. "The last time I let you hold it we ended up in this godawful mess."

James nibbled on the corner of his bottom lip, gazed solemnly down at the floor between his feet and braced his hips with both hands. It wasn't the only time he was reminded of it and in a way he knew it made Dylan feel good; it gave a sense of power that fed his insatiable ego.

"The only way we're going to know is if we watch it." Greg suggested. "We don't want to do all of this for nothing."

Dylan and James glanced awkwardly at him.

"What about them?" James asked, prodding his shoulder at the three hostages.

"We can't show it to them."

"Is it gonna matter?"

They shared a long pause that made Kevin feel uneasy; the air inside of the room became thick and suffocating. As much as he didn't want to admit it, whether or not it was what they were looking for, all three of them were going to die.

With Lacey's assistance, they turned on the television and set up the DVD player. After Dylan and James found the small skinny black remote sitting under the television, Greg slid the DVD onto the tray, pushed a button the upper left hand corner of the machine and waited for the disc to load.

12

The footage began in the corner of a large room.

The camera zoomed back, revealing a wall lined with floor-to-ceiling mirrors on one side; neatly painted characters and a few lines of inspiring remarks were painted along the top. Treadmills, stair climbers and weight benches sat on a slick marble-gray floor, shafts of sunlight streaming through the wire-mesh windows; thick leafy tree shadows bled across the corners of the windows like cryptic burn marks.

Three inches away from the camera, Dylan sat on the edge of a weight bench, wearing a plain-white tee shirt, sneakers with ankle-low socks and gray sweat pants. His clean-shaven head was slick with sweat; it bonded his tee-shirt to his xylophone-like ribs.

"Watch that fucking thing." Dylan rustled, flinging his right arm out in front of him.

The camera jostled, filling the screen with a momentary series of sporadic blurs. When it realigned itself, the camera panned back to Dylan who was now pacing back and forth between a stair climber with black-rubber praying-mantis like arms and a slanted weight bench stacked with five gunmetal-gray plates.

"Be careful, asshole." James said from behind the camera. "If you break this, my dad will kill me."

"Whatever."

"What time did he say he'd be here?"

James stretched his hand across the front of the camera, exposing a thin bony wrist fitted with a giant gray digital wristwatch. It didn't stay around long enough to show the time.

"Do I look like his mother?"

"With a little makeup you could."

"Bite me." Dylan scoffed. "What time do you got?"

"Five minutes after four."

"He better get his ass here, fucking pronto. We've got a game in five hours."

When James chuckled at Dylan's response, the camera shimmied and filled the screen with white and dark blurs. His laughter subsiding, he aimed the camera back toward his best friend.

The massive wooden door on the far left corner of the room burst open and clapped shut. Dylan pivoted on his heels and gave a sigh of relief when he saw Greg striding toward him. Greg glanced conspiratorially around the weight room, his arms pressed tightly against his sides.

"Did you get it?"

"Who's the fucking man now?" Greg grinned, opening his left hand.

The camera zoomed in on a pair of two long hypodermic needles sitting in the middle of his fat pasty hand. The wide pleasing grin on his face was full of more shit than his father's.

Dylan hissed. "This better be the right shit, Wide Load."

"The guy said this is the maximum dosage. That fucking quarterback won't have a chance to shit or wind his watch by the time we get to him."

"Hold this fucking thing."

The camera shifted, filling the screen with another series of dizzying blurs. When it was righted again, James stepped out from behind the camera and sat down on the edge of the weight bench beside of Dylan; he wore a slate-gray tee shirt and purple shorts that molded nicely against his thick muscular legs and thighs. They removed a long strand of bright-yellow rubber tubing from their front pockets and ordered Greg to fasten the tubing around their biceps.

Dylan killed the DVD, slid the tray open, retrieved the disc and slid it back into the case. James stacked his arms across his chest and stared down at the floor to hide the perturbed expression on his face. Greg grinned with satisfaction, pumped his fists in the air and stood next to Dylan who held the disc between the thumb and forefinger of his left hand, his face split by a wide lipless grin.

The sunlight filtering through the windows caught the tiny diamond ring on Lacey Graham's left hand clamped tightly across her mouth; a fresh tear streamed down her cheek. Harry gazed up at them, his face disfigured by a mix of fear and surprise. Kevin gazed down at the tip of James' left boot, his brain clouded with seething hatred.

Marilyn Graham had been killed for discovering her boyfriend had used illegal PEDs to win his way to a state championship and possibly make him a five-star recruit that all the big colleges would've killed for. And no one would be the wiser.

"We're all adults here." Dylan chuffed, then said. "I think we know what happened after that."

"I wonder what your stepfather would say if he were here right now?" Kevin declared.

"I doubt he'd even care."

Kevin shook his head, watching the glow of triumph dissipate from their faces. He thought he saw something moving along the wall behind Greg's left shoulder, but he wasn't sure; the pain pressing against his skull made it hard for him to want to turn around. He glanced up at Dylan, his mouth set in a hard line.

"He was pretty concerned with why you didn't say hello to them." He wiggled his finger at Lacey and Harry. "You didn't want to say anything to them because then you would've asked them about the disc and they wouldn't been able to tell you because they didn't know about it until I'd mentioned it earlier. Hell, I didn't even know about the disc until Marilyn–"

"What the hell are you talking about?"

"It isn't going to matter anymore." Greg said to Dylan. "We ought to kill them and get the hell out of here."

"You killed Marilyn the night before you were supposed to get your picture taken with the team. You were late getting back to the school because you didn't want people to notice that Marilyn was missing and that you were nowhere to be found so not everyone would put two and two together." Kevin said, pushing himself up onto the edge of the couch.

"Shut up."

"You realized the disc was missing the next day after your argument and you were afraid she was going to find out what you did and get back at you by telling everyone. When she refused to give it up," Kevin continued. "you took her out to Taylor Run Road, tied her to the fence and cut her throat and waited until you could come back and retrieve the disc."

"Wait a minute." Harry winced. "Are you telling me that you murdered my niece because you wanted to win a fucking football game?"

James shifted on his left foot, gnashed his teeth together in a furious grin and whipped the back of his right hand hard across Lacey's left jaw. The sound echoed across the house like thunder and sent her flying back into her brother's arms, throwing a small curtain of hair across her right cheek.

"She died because she stuck her nose where it didn't belong." Dylan said, pressing the barrel of the gun against Lacey's head.

"Fuck you." Harry fizzled, clutching onto his sister.

When Lacey brushed a strand of hair from her cheek, swiping at the tiny bib of blood on her chin, Dylan raised the pistol and shot Harry Kline above the right eye. The report cracked across the house, echoed off the walls and resonated against the windows. Kevin threw his head to one side and squeezed his face together to brace himself against the loud buzzing sound resounding in his right ear.

Harry's eyes went wide for a moment as his head snapped back between his shoulders again. Soft red pulp, vulva-pink brain matter and tiny skull fragments sprayed out the back of his head and stained the couch. His head slumped forward, exposing a large entrance wound three inches above the base of his neck.

Lacey screamed, rose up to her knees and cradled her brother's head in her spindly brown arms; hot tears streamed down her face. Greg crouched down behind her and clamped his thick pale hand across her mouth to muffle her screams but she elbowed him and threw herself back across her brother's corpse. He staggered back but not too far, his jagged yellow teeth set in a thin tight grimace.

"No!" She screamed, her face warped with shock. "Oh, God no. No, no."

Kevin took a few deep breaths to fight the wave of nausea and fear churning inside of his gut. A sense of guilt suddenly overcame him as if this had all been his fault. If he'd gone to Erica's house instead, none of this would've happened. He considered pulling her away from Harry's corpse but he didn't see how that would make things better or spare him from a bullet.

"You son of a bitch." Lacey bellowed.

She leaped off the floor, lost her footing and toppled face-first onto the floor; her dress fluttered as a burst of air exploded from her lungs. Dylan pressed the barrel against the back of her head and pulled the trigger.

The gun barked, sending a second blast across the house that shook the picture frames on the wall, rattled the windows and aggravated the pain still pressing against at Kevin's skull. A geyser of blood exploded into the air and came back down as the bullet struck the back of her head; her body twitched as a puddle of brownish-yellow liquid poured out from under her dress and spilled across the floor. The stench of gunpowder and sweat permeated through the house like the bad stench it'd become a few minutes ago.

Kevin loosened his grip from the floor and, his body surging with a mixture of fear and anger, clenched his hands together until his knuckles turned white. Greg glanced at him from the corner of his eye, drew the scent of Kevin's slow rising anger deep into his lungs, crouched down into a half squat and waved his hands back and forth as if motioning for Kevin to take his first and final swing.

Something quivered in the corner of his right eye, making rapid-fire tapping noises against the wall on the other side of the room. The giant deer head hanging on the wall above the fireplace swayed like a pendulum, its beady black eyes glinting like wet marbles.

"WHAT THE FUCK!" James roared.

The deer head flew off the wall and sailed across the room, its beady black eyes glinting with something other than light. Before he could turn to realize what was happening, Greg grunted as the trophy's furry brown skull struck him in the back, knocking the wind and his legs out from underneath him. He gave an exhausted wheeze, doubled over and face-planted onto the floor; his arms and legs spread out from his sides as he gave a loud wheezing cough.

James ducked and hit the floor in a push-up position and Dylan dove onto the left side of the couch; the disc fell from his hand and slid under the couch.

The flying deer head bumped the edge of the television, spreading a branch of spider-legged cracks across the screen and struck the wall behind the living room window punching out a wide hollow impression in the plaster and slid down to the floor.

Dylan scanned the room, his eyes wide and blazing with fear, rolled off the couch and onto the floor. He scrambled to his feet and crawled across the room toward the kitchen like a mirage.

Kevin snatched a quick breath, rose up on his knees and grappled for Dylan's right foot when something struck him from behind. He grunted, his bones jolting with fresh bolts of pain, and landed in a heap next to Lacey Graham's cold motionless corpse. He rolled onto his back, sighing through clenched teeth and tried to wriggle himself free from his attacker's grasp.

He stared up in time to see James rising up on his knees. He felt the boy's right hand clutching the meaty part of his left shoulder, pinning him to the floor and reared his left fist back. He crossed his arms, linking his wrists together and raised them up and across his face.

The boy's fist struck the back of his left arm. Kevin curled up into a ball, pressed his feet against James' chest and pushed him across the room; James' teetered back, his eyes wide with fear as his arms and legs flailed wildly out from his sides.

Kevin heard a grunting sound from behind him and peered over his shoulder, heart thudding inside of his throat. Greg was hunched over, pushing himself from the floor one side at a time. His body still bristling with anger and agony, he rose up on his feet and kicked the big boy hard across the face sending him back onto the floor like a bug blindsided by a windshield.

His arms slumped against his side, he scanned the room, eyes wide with horror. The mingled cloud of gunpowder and expended bowels wafting into his lungs without permission, something moved in the corner of his left eye. He leaped back, fists poised and ready and peered into the left corner of the room.

James was lying across the deer head in an awkward recline, his arms and legs spread out from his body like a stick person. A pair of gnarled light brown antlers jutted out from his chest, poking through the front of his tee-shirt. Blood pumped the air, spreading a large dark-red bib across the front of his shirt and dripped onto the carpet.

He scanned the room in a desperate search for Dylan and found nothing but a faint carpet of sunlight smeared across the back door off from the kitchen. His heart sank into the pit of his stomach; a bitter aftertaste stung the back of his throat. A mixture of guilt and sadness washed over him; hot tears shimmered in his eyes, blurring his vision and cascaded down his cheeks.

I'm sorry, Mary. You trusted me to do this and I failed.

His ribs flooding with pain, Kevin heaved himself up from the floor, dragged himself out onto the front porch and listened to the distant whine of police sirens inching toward the house. He wiped the tears from his eyes with the back of his hand and made a solemn promise to live his life to the fullest; no more wishing he was dead and resting peacefully in Heaven with Terri.

There was plenty of time for that. Plenty.

Besides, he had a lot of promises to keep to a whole lot of friends.

13

One Week Later

THE Lazy-Eyes Motel was a two-story slab of shit-brown stucco slapped along the outskirts of downtown Columbus that catered to a mishmash of junkies, prostitutes and other denizens of the criminal world. Its soft blue neon sign stood tall and proud beyond the carpet of lights that made up most of the city's beautiful grandeur and spread its phosphorescent glare along the windowsills; the broad-shouldered vending machine sat on the end of the open sidewalk hummed with the rhythm of the crickets chirping in the darkness. The bright blue glow of a television seeped along the edges of the chintzy-pink curtains draped across the windows of Room 7 whose dented white door shared the same pockmarked fashion as all the others.

"The best channels ever, my ass." Dylan Polk hissed, pressing his thumb hard into the television remote.

He sat across the edge of the bed, his legs stretched out in front of him. Dirt stains smudged the front of his tee-shirt, mingling with the finger marks of grease he'd gotten from the pizza he ordered yesterday. He wasn't sure how much funds he'd had left but he assumed it wasn't much; it wasn't like he could take money out of his mother's checking account without her or the cops knowing about it.

He'd been here for over a week now and had no plans of sticking around anytime soon. It was more fun to commit the crime than to hide from it; there were amenities when it'd came to be an escaped criminal. No more assigned bed times, no more getting up early for school; he was his own man now and he could do whatever he wanted.

He was about to flip over to the next channel when a familiar face flashed across the screen: his own. It was a sketch artist's rendition of his face and the sloppiness that'd gone into it made him laugh. He set the remote on the bed and watched the news report with the same wide-eyed interest of a football fan waiting for their favorite team's next move.

He wished they'd have used his senior class photo instead.

As the photo bloomed across the screen, the sleek brown-haired anchorwoman said, "It has been a week since authorities have been able to locate one of the remaining three boys responsible for the murder of Lacey Graham and her seventeen-year old daughter Marilyn and the victim's uncle Harry Kline. He fled the scene last week before police arrived at The Graham residence to discover the two elders' bodies lying dead in the living room along with the body of a second conspirator, an eighteen-year old boy named James McCord and seventeen-year old Greg Roberts. Roberts was arrested and taken to Southeastern Regional Jail where he committed suicide. If you have any information on Dylan Polk, please notify the—"

As the anchorwoman's face flashed across the screen, he grinned from ear to ear and killed the television. The very thought that they were going to catch him seemed far-fetched at this point; if he stayed on the back roads like he'd been doing for the past few days they'd never find him. He sighed, laced his hands behind his head and leaned back against the headboard, his eyes gleaming with admiration.

"It's not Acapulco or anyplace tropical but it'll have to do."

He chuckled again when the television flickered back on, repeating a phrase from the previous news report. He sat up and watched the sketch artist's rendition of his face bloom repeatedly across the screen as if someone had looped the footage and left it running.

"For the murder of Lacey Graham and her daughter Marilyn."

He thumbed the red square button on the top left corner of the remote again and killed the television. The footage disappeared. Once he set the remote back down, the television sprang to life once again.

"...and her uncle Harry Kline...for the murder of Lacey Graham and her seventeen-year-old daughter Marilyn..." The anchorwoman repeated as the photo bloomed repeatedly across the screen.

"Piece of shit television." He grimaced, climbing out of bed.

He marched across the space between both beds (they only had a room with a double bed available) and over to the waist-high oak bureau sitting under the two rectangular mirrors fixed to the wall behind the television. He slid the television three inches to the left, stretched himself over the top and reached down behind the bureau. He grabbed the plug, yanked it out of the wall and draped it across the top of the bureau like a scarf he didn't wear anymore.

When he raised his head, he stared into the right-side mirror and gave a terrified gasp. His eyes widened with fear as his lips quivered; the ecstasy once etched across his face sagged into a soft mask of complete and total terror. He spun around on the balls of his feet, his right hand clamped across the front of his chin; his legs carried him toward the floor, no longer able to hold the weight of his fear.

Her sleek blonde hair spilled across her shoulders in a ghostly-white cape, framing her heart-shaped face while hooking the undercarriage of her earlobes; the rings of wet dark mascara hugging her steel blue eyes slid down her cheeks, exposing tiny gnarled cracks slowly etching across her skin. The cold blue tint of her skin glowed in the harsh carpet of light glowing from the wall lamp above the nightstand sitting behind her as the matching blue veins creeping across her breasts twitched like worms rising from wet grass. Her cracked pink lips spread into a wide pleasing grin, sending more tiny cracks down the edge of her jawline and along the nape of her neck; her red plaid skirt fluttered around her pasty-white legs.

This wasn't possible, he told himself. *You're just tired, that's all. You just need to get some sleep, and everything will be fine in the morning.*

No matter how much he wanted to tell himself that he was just imagining this, the fear still brooding inside of him said differently. She was here to finish the rest of what that guy had started and seek revenge for what he'd done to her–and her entire family.

She tipped her head back, spraying a geyser of blood down the front of her blouse. He slipped his hand away from his mouth and gripped the edge of the bureau to keep himself steady.

When he leapt away from the dresser and hurried across the room to retrieve the gun, something struck his left hip and flung him across the room like a rag doll. He struck the headboard above the other bed, landed on the mattress and rolled onto the floor; his chest undulating, his lungs ragged and deflated. A river of pain flooded his chest, streaked down across his hip and bubbled deep inside the pit of his stomach.

The mirrors quivered inside of their frames, catching parcels of light along their gilded edges and then burst outward. A mist of jagged glass exploded across the room, bouncing off Marilyn's motionless form, and struck the wall behind the beds before landing softly onto the cheap-blue bedspread. He tried to gather the courage to leap off the floor and run but his body refused to break free from the shackles of his own fear and all he could manage was another terrified gasp; a bone-deep paralysis pinned him to the floor in front of the second bed.

As he opened his mouth to speak, Marilyn knelt beside of him, her cold calculating stare found him, glinting with a fire hotter than love and deeper than revenge. She pinched his lips together and leaned her face against his. His skin grew cold.

When she snapped her fingers, he could hear both the scarred gold chain and the deadbolt snap into place; the curtains drew shut, obscuring the glare of the motel's neon blue sign.

"It's not Acapulco or anyplace tropical but it'll have to do." She said in a mocking voice, a wide malevolent grin on her face.

ME AND MY GANG

Since my parents attended a George Romero double-feature at a local drive-in the night before I was born, I've been an avid fan of the zombie genre.

Every Halloween night, once the beggars have succumbed to bed, I slide a pre-ordered pizza from the oven and drop in my DVD copy of the B&W version Night Of The Living Dead. I've done it every year for the past ten years and I've kept it going since. Now that I've collected the original Day Of The Dead and Dawn Of The Dead, I watch them in reverse that it coincides with the sky.

This story was wrote at the same time I was working a part-time job at a local eatery and thought it'd be a good concept. Who wouldn't want to be locked inside of the same place with the same people they saw on a weekly basis?

"I bet you can't shoot her from here."

"Do you remember what happened last time you say something like that, Rick?" Matt cautioned him, gazing out across the rear parking lot.

"Remember what happened last time you lost a bet?"

"There's no way I'll lose again."

Matt raised the bolt-action rifle, trapped the dead woman in the crosshairs of his scope and concentrated. She was a meager-looking blonde with a scrawny face, rotting-gray skin and delicate cheekbones; her left arm hung loosely down by her side, hugged by the spaghetti-thin strap of her bright-pink dress. He drew back a deep breath, exhaled and pulled the trigger; the report echoed through the back lot as the stock slammed into his shoulder.

When he raised his head, she was still stumbling between the grease trap and the metal-green dumpster sitting fifty yards away on the far-left side of the parking lot, her milky-white eyes gazing downward; a chunk of concrete had been punched out from the wall of the building behind her.

"I told you." He snickered.

"I wasn't focused."

"Bullshit."

"Okay, okay." Matt said, waving him off. "What do I have to do this time?"

"I want you to—"

"I'm not cooking dinner in Tara's underwear again."

"Do you mind if I continue?"

"Go ahead."

A second of silence passed between them.

"I'm not walking across the power line above the parking lot." Matt forewarned.

"You have to hook up with Kyra."

"That's not a dare." He snorted. "Besides, the only guy who had a shot at her—"

"Is part of the walking dead in case you forgot." Rick reminded him. "I overheard her and Tara talking about you yesterday. I think she's got a crush on you."

"Remember what happened last time you told me that? I made a complete fucking fool of myself."

Wagging his finger, Rick said, "I didn't tell you to walk up to that woman and ask her out. All I said was that she was checking you out."

"It's the same damn thing."

Matt leaned against the wall of the supply room, sighed and shook his head. Everything had happened so fast; one day he was picking up his paycheck and then the next he was stuck inside of his own workplace in the back of the supply room shooting zombies like rubber ducks at a carnival kiosk.

"Are you two done back here?" A sarcastic female voice shouted amongst the sound of footsteps.

"I was just starting to pull up my pants." Rick said with a sardonic smile.

"Don't slap his ass like you always do when we're done."

Matt's sister Jessica appeared out from behind a stack of cardboard boxes sitting on one of many tall perforated metal shelves beside the back door. Although they'd worked there for many years, they didn't think it was necessary to wear their uniforms.

"Too much information." Matt cringed. "What you two do in the privacy of your room isn't any of my business."

"Whatever."

The bickering had come with the benefits of being brother and sister. Some believed that they were twins but they were really born three years apart.

They had their mother's jet-black hair—hers was long, his was always cut short to the nape of his neck—their father's well-built frame and their grandmother's brown eyes. Rick took Jessica in his arms and kissed her on the cheek. Although they'd been dating months before the virus first hit, they were the oddest-looking couple Matt had ever seen; he wasn't about to complain because Jessica's happiness was (and always will be) his number one concern.

After she returned the kiss, Rick asked, "What did you want?"

"Dinner's done."

Matt glanced down at his wristwatch; it said 8:45. The moon beamed across the thick black sky; it soaked the treetops and spread great black shadows across the curbs. The wind stirred the treetops, blew fallen leaves and pine needles across the asphalt in thin sporadic patterns.

A fat furry-brown spider scuttled across the macadam before a bald fat corpse scooped it up and mashed it between his rotting black teeth like it were a piece of homemade jerky. Chewing, the zombie staggered across the parking lot, oblivious to the river of brown liquid sliding down his chin.

They didn't leap across great distances; they trotted with the apathy of a drunk the morning after, their mouths wide and black like a turkeys in a rainstorm. Some had been fresh from the grave or still in the midst of decomposition, their soft-gray skin drawn tightly around their bones. They were someone's family members, best friends, golfing buddies, co-workers; someone they truly cared about.

"Should I even ask what we're having?"

"Another-All-You-Can-Eat."

"I don't know how many of those I can take."

"It's better than nothing." Matt said matter-of-factly.

Shrugging their shoulders, they followed Jessica out of the supply room.

*****

WHEN they reached the lobby, everyone had been sitting around the family-sized booth on the far-left side of the lobby, their eyes giddy and warm. Brock and Tara were sitting on the bench seat stretched across the massive white Formica-topped table; Jessica and Rick sat across from them and Kyra sat beside them, looking across the table at no one. Matt slipped the strap of his rifle up and over his shoulder, leaned it against the doorway between the supply room and the lobby and slipped into the bench seat across from Kyra; the morose frown on her pale angular face shifted into a wide pencil-thin smirk.

The lobby was a twenty-five by forty-two sized room with white tiled floors occupied by spotless white tables and metal cushioned chairs that reminded customers of most nostalgic fifties drive-ins. The massive front windows (soaked in crimson neon from the signs proclaiming COME BACK on the left and AND BRING YOUR FRIENDS on the right) were covered with thick wooden slats that barred any contact from the walking dead. According to the large framed photos speckled on the oak-paneled walls, Mary's Burger Town was once a popular carhop from the days of yesteryear before it was purchased and remodeled; since then it'd been the sponsors for a number of little-league teams and catered to many college faculty members, three mayoral candidates (although only one of them won) and a few regulars.

273

Munching on a chicken strip and deep-fried mushrooms, Matt glanced across the table at Kyra, lacking the urge to look away. She nibbled on a cheese stick, her long pineapple blonde hair falling across the crowns of her shoulders and framing her soft-white cheekbones. Her doe brown eyes, surrounded by thick rings of jet black mascara, winked in the downward glare of the florescent panels; she wore blue jeans, a silky velvet top with a lacy border and thin spaghetti straps.

He noticed she was about to stare back at him and snapped his glance back down at the food placed before him. She smelled like cotton candy but she had a mouth like an angry Southern.

"Did you hit anything today?" Her voice was like that of a child begging for another bedtime story.

"I only hit five." He said. "Not my usual number."

"Don't forget the one you missed a few minutes ago." Rick said between bites.

"You missed."

"I had the perfect shot but she wouldn't stand still."

"Don't beat yourself up about it." Jessica arched her brows.

"I won't."

"You'll get back in the hang of it." Kyra nodded.

"You'll get back in the hang of it." Tara mocked Kyra, inciting a chorus of laughter from everyone including her.

"These things happen."

"They call it 'the shaky gun hand'." Brock said, peering over Tara's shoulder. "It's like when a gunfighter knows he's getting too old because his hand starts to shake and he can't shoot right. I read about it in a book my cousin gave me."

Matt nodded.

They were halfway through dinner when Brock slipped a tiny remote from his front pocket, ignoring the curious glances from his other co-workers. The CD player from inside the kitchen kicked on; The Who filled the restaurant with "I Can't Explain." When the crowd reacted to the sound of the music, Brock gave a coy snicker.

Jabbing her fist playfully into his thigh, Tara said, "How did you get that thing to work?"

"Remember when we got the guns from the pawn shop down the road?" He asked. "I grabbed a bunch of batteries from the supply room while they were gathering up things."

"And when were you going to tell us?"

"When the time was right."

"Maybe we could look for an active radio station."

"Jesus, Tara." Brock said through tightly-clenched teeth. "When are you going to realize that we're all that's left?"

"How do you know for sure?"

"If we weren't," He said. "then The National Guard would've been here by now."

Sighing, Tara dropped her hot dog into the checkered paper boat, flung his hand away from her chest, slid out of the booth and stalked across the lobby into the kitchen. Silence was now at the head of the table, save for the quick furtive glances passed between the others; the current situation halted everyone's appetites.

Brock gave an apologetic hiss, slid out of the booth and followed her. Tara was leaning against the sandwich counter, head and shoulders slumped over in defeat with her face buried in her hands. They'd done this every few weeks but not to where the others were tempted to throw them outside if they didn't get along.

For as long as Matt could remember, Tara and Brock had been dating long before Jessica and Rick first met. He was tall and rawboned with sandy brown hair, a wide nose, green eyes and a thin handsome smile. She was five-nine, three inches shorter than Brock with pale skin, thin red lips, hazel eyes and long black hair.

Although they weren't married, they fought like they were.

"They'll make up in a minute or two." Jessica said glumly.

"They always do."

"It's not her fault."

The others waited for Matt to explain.

"She's tired of being here, eating the same thing day after fucking day."

"She goes out to the roof sometimes."

"Sometimes that's not enough." Matt said. "Paranoia starts to set in after a while. The walls start closing in around you and you think that if you don't get out soon enough you'll go stark raving mad and that's the last thing anybody needs."

"Is everything okay?" Rick bellowed across the lobby.

"We're fine, man."

"I wonder what they're talking about." Kyra asked, nibbling on her second cheese stick.

"Whatever it is I just hope she doesn't—"

Something crashed from inside the supply room. Wasting no time, Matt and Rick leapt from their seats, grabbed their rifles from the floor and headed back the way they'd come. Kyra and Jessica backed away from the table, their faces twisted with terror.

"I'm taking out the first mother fucker I see." Rick said.

"Just don't shoot me, blockhead."

The door jostled forward as if it were being pushed from the other side. The door gave a low whistling groan as the hinges grinded against the door emitting the shriek of wood against metal; small splinters spilled onto the floor like dandruff.

"You may want to get in here, Brock." Rick said, glancing at them from the corner of his eye.

"What the hell is going on?"

"What does it look like?"

The door swung open with such force that it rammed the doorknob into the wall beside the doorway. When they stepped into the small foyer between the bathrooms, Matt glanced over their shoulders and saw the back door standing wide open; it was clear how they'd gotten in. He was so sure that he'd locked it yesterday after they came back from getting supplies, but so much had happened that day and he'd just simply forgot.

The zombie staring back at Matt wore ratty blue jeans and a red plaid shirt torn along the lower left side to reveal an exposed rib cage; the left side of his face had been peeled away along with his lips, revealing blackened teeth and rotting gums. The fiend on Rick's side was a squat heavyset woman with thick pale arms, a three-layer chin and big black eyes; she wore a flowing floral-print muumuu and a giant strand of pearls around her thick puffy neck. Behind them, Kyra clenched Jessica's hand and cowered back toward the trash receptacle on the far-right corner; they knew the drill if they were ever outnumbered.

Throw the bolt thrown across the nearest door, hop into the Explorer and run for your life. They had no problem agreeing to all of the other rules, but that was the only one they had trouble with.

Rick jammed the barrel of his rifle against the woman's head and pulled the trigger; the bullet had punched through her skull, spraying streams of soft red pulp across the wall. Before the skinny one could react, Matt spun the rifle back around and shot her three times, ignoring the rifle's thunderous recoil pounding against his shoulder, ringing in his ears. As Brock and Tara hurried into the room, he cursed under his breath, spun the rifle back around in a two-handed grip and began to clubbing her across the head.

"Hey, killer." Brock said, throwing his arms across Matt's chest. "She's dead, man. She's dead."

"Of course she's dead, Brock." Rick said, his face warped with distaste. "Her brains are all over the fucking wall."

Matt took a few steps back, strolled into the lobby and glanced down at the floor to avoid Jessica's prying gaze. Lumps of soft red flesh clung to the stock of the rifle, turning its once sleek walnut finish to a cherry red.

"Are you alright?" He asked her and Kyra.

"We're good." Jessica nodded.

"We need to drag this bitch outside." Rick said, waving his hand in front of his face to ward off the smell.

Not only were they old-fashioned "staggers" (as their boss liked to coin them before he left them high and dry), they stunk more after they were killed the second time.

"You just need—"

"I need to go see how the back door got open."

"I'm sure it's nothing."

"Keep telling yourself that when they finally get in here and have us for fucking brunch."

They stepped over the dead guy and into the supply room. Once Jessica got on a roll, nothing could shut her up. He closed the back door, turned the lock into place and slid the four-inch wooden slat into the U-shaped brackets fixed onto the wall on both sides of the door and slammed it in place until it felt secure.

The wind whipped at his clothes and tousled his hair. If he set the slat back into place across the door like he should've, none of this would've happened.

""I know that look on your face." She said, tugging his left sleeve. "Something's bothering you, isn't it?"

"Did you ever think that Tara isn't the only one who feels like the walls are closing in?"

"No. And it's not just you and Tara. It's everybody." She reminded him.

He saw the pained expression on her face and felt the weight of his guilt grow heavier by the second. He looked away, grabbed the two-step footstool out from the bottom of the nearest shelf beside the back door and used it to pull the retractable wooden ladder down from the ceiling. She braced her hips with both hands and watched him sling the strap of his rifle back over his shoulder before gazing down at her feet.

"Where are—"

"I'm going to get some fresh air."

He climbed up and onto the roof, glanced morosely down at his little sister and shut the trap door.

*****

A thin-black cloud drifted across the round alabaster moon, reducing to a sickly-white glow. The town of Hudson, Ohio was a barren black wasteland of silence, imbued by the lingering smell of death. More zombies continued to stumble around, groaning as if giving off a mating call that only they could understand.

Matt sat quietly on the roof, his rifle lying across his lap and thought about his family. He'd missed them terribly, although Jessica was still alive, but the memories they shared before the local cemetery opened up for business would always be up for questioning.

How would things have turned out if they'd survived?

They wouldn't be here, that was sure.

The memories came flooding back to him, one at a time. He and his mother Agnes would spend the day browsing thrift stores and going out to lunch (his treat, of course). He'd sit down with his father Steve on the weekends and watch football, go fishing and scope out the entries in this year's car show that the city had put out every year; like all families there were bad times in between the good ones.

They'd meant everything to him and he'd do whatever it took to have them back today. He was wiping the tears from his eyes with the back of his right hand when he heard a sound from behind him. He wiped the tears from his eyes with the back of his hand and did his best to straighten himself as quickly as he could.

"Are you okay?" Kyra asked, sitting down beside of him.

"I'm fine."

He hoped she didn't notice his eyes were red from crying.

"You went a little—"

"I know." He said. "I'm not used to the walking dead thing."

"I don't think we'll ever get used to it." She said in a grave voice. "It doesn't hurt to have someone else take up the slack."

"I've been taking these things out since they first showed up. I'm twenty-seven years old." He stated. "I've got plenty of years ahead of me before I have anyone looking out for me."

"And how are you going to feel twenty-seven years later?"

"A lonely old man."

"Maybe not." She said, sliding her hand inside of his.

They inched closer to each other, the magnetic gleam of their eyes pulling them together, and kissed. He ran his fingers through her long blonde hair as her cool pale hands slid softly across his right wrist; their tongues coiled inside of their mouths like dueling snakes. He slid the rifle off of his lap and onto the roof as she straddled his waist, pressing her teacup-bosom against his flat muscular chest.

They fell back onto the roof, their hands sliding under their tee-shirts and pawing their bodies with shaky apprehensive hands. When they broke the kiss, Kyra rolled onto her back and eased her zipper down, revealing a soft V of silky blue underwear. He unfastened his belt, slid between her legs, slid down his zipper and slipped inside her soft pliable warmth.

When she felt him slide inside of her, she arched her back and gave a long breathless moan; the air grazed its smooth and electric fingers across their skin. After they were finished, they collected themselves and gazed up at the star-studded sky.

It was then that he understood, even in this doomed universe, there was always light at the end of the tunnel. Kyra was more than just a light; she was everything to him.

With friends like these, he thought maybe life wouldn't be so bad after all.

<u>BIG DADDY</u>

There's just something about fishing I can't shy away from. I still go fishing in the summer before and after football season (Go Buckeyes!) or writing on the weekends to help clear my head from the work week.

The first literary novel I've ever read was Hemingway's "The Old Man And The Sea" because of the old man's undying determination; my other two favorite man-versus-monster stories are Robert McCammon's "The Deep End" and the classic "Lizardman". The one thing I loved about all three of those stories is its central theme: the determination and the thrill of the hunt. Two rewrites later, it was picked up by David Wilson for Deadlights Magazine, Vol. 1.

ROBERSON slid his green Chevy pickup into the third slot beside the boathouse, his headlights sweeping across the black uncanny forest for a split second, and killed the engine. He climbed out, grunted at the ache in his joints and heard the wind sighing in the treetops. He shut the door behind him, heard its rusted hinges give a painful screech followed by the rattling fall of rust falling off the rocker panels and stretched until it hurt.

He walked around to the back of his truck, collected his dark-green nylon gym bag, slid the strap up and over his head and across his chest and padded across the parking lot. He descended the small flight of concrete steps streaked with thin jagged cracks (the city would never pay to have those goddamn things repaired) and stepped down onto the long wooden dock. The pontoon boats that were still docked here floated gently under the downward glare of the milky white moon.

He gazed at the mirrored-black surface of the lake, his shoulders tight with tension, and drew its sweet brackish scent deep into his lungs. He could feel Big Daddy's presence pressing down on the back of his neck between the wind sighing in the treetops and the waves slapping against the dock. Tonight was the last night; no more sleepless nights knowing *He* was still lurking through the murky black waters of The Buckeye State, peering invisibly amongst their surface in search of His next victim.

He'd always admired the silence that lingered around the lake at this time of the night, but this wasn't just a casual fishing trip like all the others before it. A scene like this could give a man time to reflect on the decisions he'd made earlier in his life and wished he'd done the opposite. He sighed.

After he passed the first four boats on the left side, he found his (the word CHAD painted across the bow on both sides in blood-red paint) and heaved a pleasing sigh like he couldn't have been more happier to see it. He stepped over the metal railing onto the boat, tossed the bag onto the bench seat and zipped it open. Inside, he found a fireman's axe, two halogen flashlights, a machete with a short black-rubber grip and a Colt .45 with four fully-loaded clips; big bore bullets he'd purchased through an old Army buddy.

He lifted the bench seat to make sure he'd brought plenty of provisions–life preservers, charts and a few snacks in case he ran out of fuel–and closed it. He left the bag lying open on the floor next to the bench seat, pulled-up anchor, jerked the rope from the dock and let the water's slow-moving current take him only so far before he started the engine.

He spun the wheel to the right, aimed the bow toward the thick unforgiving darkness and headed northeast, cleaving a small trail of frothy white waves in his wake. The wind rushed him from all sides, ruffling his clothes and teasing his clean-shaven head. He wiped the beads of sweat from his bushy salt-and-pepper beard.

At six-foot-two, he had the tall muscular build of a farm hand from the days before selfies and social media became so addictive. His deep-set green eyes sat inside of a wide craggy face scarred by a mix of harsh sunlight and years of hard labor. Before he left home, his thoughts shifting back to his devastated wife Bonnie, he slapped on a sleeveless cotton-tee under an unbuttoned blue shirt, denim jeans and a pair of Gore-Tex hiking boots.

He checked his charts, counted to ten and then cut the engine. Once the boat came to a complete stop, he dropped anchor, and chucked it into the water loud enough to make his presence known. Thick dark forests rose along the horizon of the lake like the backdrop from a movie lot, their thick shaggy heads jutting toward the heavens in an attempt to peer inside of them.

Maybe that was where the thing had come from to begin with, he thought, *maybe someone had wished for it and just forgot to put it back on its leash before it got out of hand.*

Whatever the hell it was, it didn't matter.

It was going down come Hell or High Water.

A loud splashing sound kicked up somewhere on his far left. He drew back a sharp breath, snatched the Maglite from the gym bag, thumbed the button and swept the cone of light across the lake's murky brown surface. He sighed and mumbled under his breath when he saw a smallmouth bass kicking up a racket amongst a tangle of tall brownish-green weeds.

He was surprised to have seen any fish still around since he heard that Big had chased all of the good fish—and the fishermen— away. As a young'un, he and Billy Olson would sneak down here after sundown on the weekends and do some night fishing maybe catch a few croppies or a bass that they could brag about until one of them usurped the other; but as with most friendships, those days were out of reach.

The mayor had thought Big Daddy was just a figment of every fisherman's alcohol-fueled imagination until he'd got a visit from The Big Man himself one day. According to the local grapevine, he was hunting alongside Lake Michelle with his good Mossberg when he came across an eight-point buck lying along the river's edge and assumed that it'd tripped over his own feet. Upon close inspection, he'd watched the deer struggle as Big had pulled the downed animal into the lake's murky brown surface; the whole incident had sucked all the joy out of hunting altogether.

The town grapevine (and what a long goddamn grapevine it was) had said that the mayor and the sheriff had put their every red cent together to post a reward for anyone who could capture it but neither one of them would back it up. Now that Roberson thought about it, he had his reasons for being out here but they were personal and not financial.

Before he decided to hunt the big bastard, Roberson had done more research about it than he cared to. If you wanted to kill a beast such as this, it was better to have both your wits and your intellect in your pocket. If not, he might as well have walked into third-period Math class and pulled his own pants down around his ankles.

According to the articles he'd read, the ravenous fucker had cleaved a path from one corner of The Red, White And Blue long before tonight when Greek coliseums were drenched in the blood of other dead Greeks and witchcraft was just a paranoid thought that made you accountable for murder. The first current sighting was in Oregon in two-thousand-ten when He wandered through a golf course and snatched some rich lady's Shi Tzu before she could reach for her next martini; he cut a path of mayhem and violence across the west, straight into Texas and up through Tennessee whilst wiping His big hungry mouth with The American Flag that guys like him had fought to protect in Nam.

From where he stood, the town of Megan's Grove winked in the distance like tiny trinkets on black velvet. With his right hand on the wheel, he yawned and rubbed his eyes with the edge of his left palm. His days and nights were slowly catching with him and, although he wasn't old by any standards, they added more wear and tear.

Now all he had to do was wait.

Don't worry, Big Daddy.

The moon is full and the night is young and I'll wait here for as long as it takes.

He killed the flashlight, sank down onto the bench seat and laced his arms together when he felt something inside of his shirt pocket prodding at his right wrist. He reached inside, his fingers groping for several prolonged seconds and slipped out half a pack of rainbow-colored Life Savers.

A deep ache struck him square in the chest and his cheeks grew hot and red. He held the pack of candy between the thumb and forefinger of his right hand, bit down on his bottom lip to hold back the sadness solidifying inside of his chest. He slumped forward in his seat and wiped a river of tears from his eyes with the back of his hand.

How could he have forgotten about the last time he'd worn this shirt? The very question had plagued him as much as the nightmares he'd had over those grueling months when he felt like he was only half a man, the kind of nightmares that would make most men shed enough tears to fill a claw-foot tub or see things that weren't there.

He saw the smile beaming across Chad's face as he slid a red Life Saver from the pack and tuck it past his lips; Chad's cheeks beamed with love as a wide satisfying grin spread across his face. He looked away from his grandson in time to see his neon-orange bobber disappear under the water. He hurried across the shore, energized by his grandson's eager mantra of "you got something Grandpa you got something" and snatched his pole out of the ground but when he looked back at Chad to get another reaction from the boy all he saw was a mask of stark-white terror folding across the boy's face. He glanced over in time to see the long black tentacle slip out from between the weeds and wrap around the boy's stomach like a lifeline. Cold fear churning in his stomach, he dropped his fishing pole and ran toward him as fast as he could before losing his balance and falling to the ground, begging for him to run just run to me *as he lost his balance and stumbled just long enough for him to regain his balance and leap across the bank with one outstretched arm; his fingertips grazed across the scaly black tentacle as it jerked his helpless grandson out of sight and through the thin pocket of high weeds, replacing the boy's gut-wrenching cries with a chorus of incoherent gurgling. Through the tears he shed and the screams he bellowed, he pounded his fists against the ground as Chad's dark-blue Cleveland Indians' ball cap floated across the surface of the lake, spreading great concentric ripples across the water.*

A week after Chad's death, Roberson's wife Bonnie had crumbled under the weight of grief and refused to speak anyone–especially him. When the news of Chad's death spread through the town like influenza, everyone called him a drunk, said it was just a figment of his own imagination and that he'd made up the creature just to cover up the fact that he'd killed his grandson. No one believed him; not even his family.

He knew he couldn't tell her the truth because she wouldn't believe him, either. He'd kept this from Bonnie because he knew she'd try to talk him out of it; call him a "crazy old coot" while she hid inside of their bedroom so she could cry herself to sleep at all hours of the day and night.

Something drummed against the bottom of the boat, knocking him out of his sad reverie. Startled, he tucked the pack of candy back into its rightful place, leaped out of his seat and ran across the boat. He leaned over the port side, stared down at the glossy black water and eased over to the starboard side when the boat wobbled to the left.

He seized the railing in both hands and bent his knees to keep from losing his balance, his mind humming with vertigo. In the veins of moonlight glowing across the surface, an odd-looking shadow slithered out from under the boat, floated north in the direction of Wilson Dam, spun around and came back.

"Okay, you big sombitch." He babbled, his thick-knuckled hands grasping the railing. "Let's dance."

He released his grip, ran toward the open gym bag and reached for the Colt when something struck the lake like a fat kid doing a cannonball. A large geyser of water erupted from beside of the boat, splashed along the starboard side and back down. After wiping the sweat beads from his face with the back of his hand, he swept the flashlight across the boat, drew a large gulp of air into his lungs and saw a large black tentacle grasping the second rung of the railing.

He gasped, snatched the fire axe from the duffel bag and swung it in a whistling arc. The blade gave a hacking cough as it sliced the tentacle in half and released its grip from the railing. It leaped across the boat in a wild spasmodic dance, spraying giant drops of thick black blood across the legs of his jeans before sliding off the edge of the boat and into the water.

He hissed between his teeth, ran back to the railing and watched with parental anger as the shadow glided across the water in front of him. He pulled the Colt from the gym bag, ran to the other side and squeezed the trigger in four rapid-fire successions. The recoil rocked against his shoulder as each shot kicked smaller plumes of water into the air only for them to rain back down.

He felt the boat bow toward the water for a split second before righting itself, spreading a radar map of ripples across the surface. His heart stammering, he swung the flashlight toward the port side and snatched a quick breath, his arms prickling with fear. Two thick reptilian palms gripped the sleek metallic railing and pulled down on the edge of the boat like a jock doing a pull up; its curved black talons glinting under the film of water sliding away from its thick scaly hide.

He drew back a breath, aimed and fired, tearing a small chunk from its left hand. A loud inhuman roar rumbled across the lake, sending a fresh carpet of gooseflesh crawling across his arms and a second wind whipping through the trees.

The hands reared back from the railing and slid out of sight. A loud splashed kicked up alongside the boat. Grunting, he ran back to the railing, swept the Maglite's harsh halogen light across the surface of the water hoping to get another shot.

The boat jostled, kicking up a third radar map of ripples and spun around in the opposite direction. He teetered back, his right leg and left arm flailing, and plopped down onto the bench seat. The boat jerked forward a few times before it kicked off across the water like a rocket, spewing a small contrail of frothy white waves onto the front of the boat.

His eyes lit with mad regard, a wide sardonic smile spread across Roberson's face.

"You found the anchor, huh?" He bellowed maniacally. "Now you're working with Phonics, motherfucker."

He leapt up from his seat, scurried across the boat and, his heart racing, grabbed the steering wheel. He yanked the throttle backward and spun the wheel to a sharp left to try to shake him off but to no avail. Instead the boat began to pick up speed, kicking up a larger torrent of waves that slapped against the side and doused him from head to toe.

He broke away from the wheel, raised the Colt in a two-fisted grip and gnashed his teeth together in a fit of rage when he caught movement from the corner of his eye. The creature's alien shadow slid out from beneath the boat, swam toward a bank of trees standing along the shore and gathered itself into a giant dark ball. He saw the boathouse coming toward him at a rapid pace, then saw the front grille of his pickup truck glinting in the overhead glare of a street light before he realized where he was heading.

His stomach churning with fear, he ran back to the steering wheel and gripped it in both hands until his knuckles turned white. The boat hit the shore like a battering ram, the shriek of metal against metal scraping harshly over the rocks and tumbled over. He snatched a quick breath, tumbled over the railing and slammed face first onto the sand.

The impact squeezed the air out of his lungs and sent him into a loud and repetitive coughing fit. A thick gritty aftertaste filled his mouth; he felt something wriggling across his tongue and held back the sudden urge to vomit. He slapped his hand frantically across his face, brushing a large clump of wet brown sand from his cheeks when a loud trickling sound rose up on his left.

Something emerged in the corner of his right eye, drawing his full attention back toward the lake. He didn't want to believe what he was seeing but the pain tracing the contours of his ribs and the wet brown sand spread out beneath him told him differently.

A large black tentacle rose up out of the water, curled in on itself like a scorpion's tail, cleaved through the air and struck the middle of the boat with an inhuman force that would've shattered all the great arenas in Rome. Roberson rolled onto his left hip, shielded his face with both hands, curled himself into a ball to avoid the mist of sharp debris flying across the shore and it rained down around him. The clatter of fallen debris rattled against the night as a thick brown fog spun in the breeze like some downward spiral dying to consume him.

Once the dust settled, he opened his eyes and sat up. A hulking gray form rose out of the water, baring down on him with bright yellow eyes that would've made the strongest of men weak with horror. His face frozen with shock, he pressed his hands into the cool brown sand until it seeped between his fingers and poured out over his knuckles.

Big Daddy stood eleven feet tall, covered with a dark scaly hide. He marched up the shore on two stubby alligator-like feet, his jaws bulging out from his round bony head. His left lip curled upward, exposing two misshapen rows of sharp pinkish-white teeth set inside rotten black gums. Long black tentacles expanded from his sides, rose three feet above his head and wriggled in the air like heat waves on a desert highway.

Like most local legends, he was the blur in the background of every photo taken by every small-town American during summer vacation. He didn't sell tee-shirts, travel mugs or any other cheap touristy items like Loch Ness or Big Foot.

Roberson shook off the heat from the creature's penetrating gaze, spun around on his stomach and scuttled across the shore. He was halfway to the cluster of rocks strewn below the parking lot when something whipped across the back of his knees; pain flared across his ankles and streaked up his calves. His legs slipping out from underneath him, he fell face first onto the sand and grunted at the ripples of pain bursting across his body.

He peered over his right shoulder and gasped at the tentacle wrapped around his right foot; a second looped around his left foot and jerked him away from the rocks. He rolled onto his back and slid across the sand toward the water, lashing at the air with wild frantic hands. His shirt slid up and over his ribs as his back cleaved a half-inch trail across the shore.

Wincing in pain, he saw something in the corner of his right eye–a black rubber grip jutting out of the sand. He gritted his teeth, muscles tightening with rage, and jerked his left foot from Big Daddy's painful grasp. He rose up on his knees, ignoring the monster's guttural protest, yanked the machete free, leaped across the sand and drove the rusty blade between the monster's breasts.

The creature arched its back, aiming its muscular dark chest at the clear moonlit sky, and gave a deep guttural growl. Its bright yellow eyes dilated as geysers of thick black blood pumped in the air and splattered across the tips of his boots. His muscles now guided by anger and revenge, he wrenched his right hand around the handle and pushed with all his might, forcing the blade deeper and deeper until the hilt touched the creature's soft scaly flesh.

Hot tears blurred his vision and a mocking scream burst from his lips. A cold sensation caressed his left shoulder; the mad look of triumph on his face slumped into a mask of sad panic.

The gaze in Big Daddy's eyes spread a river of fire across Roberson's chest as the tentacle whipped at the air and wrapped around his neck. He tried to pull the blade free, the muscles in his arms straining, but it failed to budge. Sirens howled from a distance, slicing at the once eerie but silent night.

The numb sensation of dying washed over him; his eyelids grew weak and heavy. He tugged on the machete again, his breath pluming from his lips in a soft wheezing moan. His legs trembling, he sunk toward the sand.

He stared up at the smug cuticle-white grin spreading across Big's face and felt a sudden surge of energy rising up inside of him, speeding through his veins like a meth-fueled locomotive. Its suction-cup grips pressed down against his throat, sending small beads of water sliding down his right arm.

If it was meant to be, then so be it.

He shifted his weight, rose up from the sand, draped his left arm around the creature's neck and propelled them forward. The creature's eyes widened with horror as their bodies floated above the water for a split second before diving head first into the churning black water. A mixed cloud of bubbles and thick black blood rose swirled around them, shrouding the frozen mask of horror on the creature's face.

As the tentacle slipped away, Roberson's lungs filled with water and snatched his breath; his skin faded to a funeral-like pallor. He twisted the blade one final time as they sunk toward the briny bottomless depths of the lake, their bodies curled into the yin and yang of good versus evil.

I got you, you bastard. After all this time, I finally got you.
No, Grandpa. We got him.

STIFF BREEZE

There's nothing better than to end a collection with an end-of-the-world story. This was one of those stories that came out of nowhere and those kind of stories are the good ones.

I was walking back from the little Mom and Pop on the corner of my block when someone mentioned that the breeze felt a stiff today. An old man, who couldn't decide between a box of Honey Buns or Cosmic Brownies, said something about how there were so many pathogens in the wind. I ignored him, finished my purchases and went back home and wrote this story.

My good friend Becca Besser featured it in her Halloween Blitz blog in October of this year. I didn't add any pathogens though; I like to leave it up to you, Dear Reader.

As for the old man, I hope he decided on the Cosmic Brownies.

MY Uncle Jay and I were inside of his house when everyone went stiff.

It was a bright sunny day in July when my mother Nina and my father Calvin and I headed out to Uncle Jay and Aunt Linda's place for a cookout we always had before I was dragged back to school for my freshman year. We never invited any of our other family members because we had to deal with their snotty stuck-up asses at the family reunion every once a year which was always a stretch. Although Dad and Uncle Jay never got along, it didn't stop us from going.

Jay and Linda lived in one of those stucco bungalows with a red clay-tiled roof and a big backyard that was bigger than the front, crammed inside of a close-knit cluster of other houses just like it. Dogs barked and pools splashed from a distance I was comfortable with.

Uncle Jay was standing on the patio in front of his massive propane grill, flipping three different kinds of meat (not counting Aunt Linda's veggie burgers, bleh) and flashing narrow-eyed glances at Dad every time he finished a beer and plucked a fresh one from the case sitting under the picnic table between his feet. Mom and I were tossing a bright-yellow Frisbee around the front yard for a while until Aunt Linda finished cutting the trimmings for burgers and then took Mom's place. "Sunshine Of Your Love" by Cream spewed from the little boombox Mom bought Uncle Jay last Christmas.

When he slid the last hamburger onto the platter sitting next to the grill, Jay peered over Mom's shoulder and said, "Hey, Mattie. Could you run in and get the condiments out of the fridge."

"Sure." I said, my voice strained from exhaustion.

Before I reached the porch, I glanced next door and saw a young middle-aged couple leading a little six-year old boy with blonde hair toward their back door. The boy carried a stack of action figure in his arms and sobbed as if he were about to carry them to the electric chair; dirt caked his fingernails, clung to his kneecaps and streaked the front of his bright blue tee-shirt.

I ignored them, tossed the frisbee onto the front porch and entered the house through a pair of sliding glass doors. I bobbed my head to the music spewing from Jay's boombox loud enough to vibrate the kitchen windows and opened the fridge. I heard the patio doors slide open again, spewing a split second stream of music into the house and then slide shut again.

I caught a shadow out of the corner of my right eye and grew tense, my scalp and skin prickling with cold fear. I thought this had been Dad's opening to sneak in behind Mom's back and grope me as he'd done three months ago after my thirteenth birthday. I know I should've said something by now but we both knew who Mom was going to believe and it wasn't her daughter; she would've ignored anything I said because Daddy's money made her more submissive and unaware than I would ever become.

"Hey, honey." A familiar but chaffing voice replied.

I slumped against the fridge, breathing a sigh of relief when the mixed stench of flop sweat and stale beer were replaced by the pleasing scent of Stetson that only Uncle Jay wore. I shook off the uneasiness and smiled at him while all six-foot-four of him moseyed over to the other side of the kitchen with a perturbed grin on his big doughy face.

"Your aunt sent me in here for her fucking multi-grain bread." He mumbled, then snorted. "She'd eat poison ivy if they made a loaf of bread with it."

I chuckled and knelt in front of the open fridge to resume my search when the breeze picked up and swept over the house. It muffled the music spewing from Jay's boombox, shook the treetops like newborns and reminded me of the whispers my friends shared behind my back before homeroom. When the breeze dissipated, a low wheeze filled the kitchen, merging into a loud startling gasp.

I rose to my feet and cocked my head to where the sound was coming from. Jay leaned across the sink, his thick-fingered hands gripping the edge of the countertop until his knuckles turned white; the loaf of bread had flown from his hands and rolled across the kitchen floor. He glanced out the window, his eyes and mouth wide from shock as the color began to drain from his face; I hadn't seen him this scared since back in 2016 when Aunt Linda had her first of two miscarriages.

"What the–"

The panicked wheeze in his voice lured me over to the window, my body racing with curiosity. I massaged my hands and peered through the white crop-top curtains draped across the kitchen window. I couldn't believe what I saw but it was as plain as the nose on my face.

Nina and Calvin and the hummingbird fluttering in front of the bird feeder above Dad's head and Aunt Linda were frozen in place. Stiff and motionless, they looked like nothing more than wax figures in a museum: Mom was caught hovering above the bench seat across from Dad, her hands hugging the back of her dress and tucking it underneath her thighs as if she were about to sit down; Dad was crumpling an empty beer can in his hand and letting off an old fashioned burp through a lopsided grin in a non-comical display of manliness; Aunt Linda was caught balancing herself on one foot with her head cocked toward the front of the house and both hands cupped around her mouth.

The grill kept going and so did Uncle Jay's radio which switched from "Sunshine" to "Just An Old Fashioned Love Song" by Three Dog Night. Something glinted in the corner of my eye but the procession of footsteps parading across the kitchen drew my attention instead. I spun around in time to see Uncle Jay tearing ass toward the living room, mumbling Linda's name over and over again.

He bounced his right leg off the corner of the coffee table, hissed through half-clenched teeth and lost his balance. He teetered back and, arms pinwheeling out from his sides, slammed his massive bulk onto the living room couch. In the soft blue glow of the television, he stared up at me with a mingled expression of surprise and shock on his face.

"Jeez, Mattie." He sighed. "Don't just stand there and wait for me to bust my head open before you decide to help me. I need to get out there and see what the fuck happened."

I shrugged and hurried over, my heart racing with panic. The light coming from the television shifted from a soft blue glow to plumbeous tint that made Uncle Jay sit up immediately. He brushed me off with a dismissive wave of his hand, snatched the cable remote from the coffee table and thumbed up the volume.

"In case you've just joined us," A middle-aged brunette in a bright-yellow blouse stated in a soft informative voice. "we've been following a breaking news story. There have been reports that a vast number of American citizens have suddenly frozen in place. There have been numerous reports that the breeze had started from the northwest corner of The United States before sweeping down across the rest of the country but we don't have any real information to confirm it. We have live footage from all over the country and those of you watching at home parental discretion is advised."

The first footage showed a cul-de-sac in Eugene, Oregon; the wind had swept through during a big block party leaving the streets dotted with wind-blown litter and rotund metal barbecue grills spewing tails of thick white smoke that dissipated in the breeze. The second piece of footage came from a monolithic water park in southern Texas; the stairways leading toward tall colorful water slides were streaked by stiff-legged swimmers while others floated lazily in the wave pool like a child's ill-forgotten bath toy. The other pieces of footage took place in an amalgam of highways clogged with broken chains of mid-afternoon traffic, shopping malls with neon-gilded signs declaring false promises and residential parks crowded with stiffs that reminded me of store-front mannequins.

"We will do what we can to bring you all of the informa–"

Uncle Jay muted the television, slid the remote back onto the coffee table and inched up to the edge of the couch. He raked his hands across his clean-shaven head, slid them down his face, clamped them across his mouth and sighed. I thought back to the footage at the block party and thought about the golden retriever wandering through the motionless crowd, wagging its tail as it sniffed at their feet to get their attention.

I replayed that heart-wrenching image in my head until I felt my chest constrict and my cheeks flush. A river of hot tears brimmed in my eyes and slid down my cheeks but before I could wipe them away Uncle Jay had leaped up from the couch and hugged me. He buried my face in the front of his tee-shirt and patted my back in a series of slow concentric circles that made me think of those late-nights when Daddy came up stairs to grope me before the whiskey put him down.

"It's okay, honey." He whispered. "Everything's going to be okay."

As much as I wanted to believe him, everyone was a skeptic, including me. If I were to shed tears for anyone outside of this house, it should've been Aunt Linda and the lost dog. My drunk horny father and my submissive mother on the other hand would receive as much sympathy as he would've had he gone to prison.

I broke the hug and hurried across the house toward the bathroom. I slumped over the sink, clamped my hands over my tear-soaked lips and sobbed until it hurt. I snatched a hand towel from the shelf beside of the sink, tucked a strand of pineapple blonde hair behind my left ear and swiped the rag gently across my face.

The cold touch from the rag cooled my flaming red cheeks but failed to ease my fears. I was very familiar with the whole "end of times" spiel especially on the news during New Years' Eve or in the midst of twenty-twelve, but I took it all with a grain of salt. I always thought that the apocalypse could happen due to anything between an airborne disease and a great massive flood.

"No!" A familiar voice bellowed from inside the kitchen. "Oh, God no!"

I flinched, my body rigid with fear. I bolted out of the bathroom and stopped halfway to the living room. A lone tear slid down my right cheek.

His face sagging under a mix of panic and terror, he leaned against the sink and gazed out the kitchen windows once more. He mumbled something under his breath because it might've been something I wasn't allowed to hear. I followed his gaze and felt my eyes widen with fear. Mom's left arm jerked, giving a loud brittle snap that was obviously drowned out by the roar of Rush singing "Fly By Night" coming from Jay's boombox. It slid out from underneath her chest, dragging her thin-fingered hand toward the edge of the tabletop and slid off at the shoulder.

We watched in horror as Mom's arm slid down her left hip, bounced off the edge of the bench and plopped onto the ground like a fish out of water. Blood pumped at the air, soaking the grass and sliding down her left hip. She toppled back, her right arm jutting out from her hip and struck the front of the house; the same bone-jarring thud that shook the windows also rattled my bones.

I pivoted, pressed my hand against my chest and sat down in the middle of the kitchen floor. I clamped my right hand across my mouth and hunched over to keep my body from shuddering; nausea churned the pit of my stomach and stung the back of my throat.

"No, no." Jay pleaded, lips trembling. "No, no oh dear God no Linda not her he–"

The panic-stricken tone to his voice coiled around my spine, rooted me to the floor and prickled my skin. His gaze never wavered from the front lawn as streaks of sunlight underscored the big red splotches flaring across his cheeks; his lips trembled.

I glanced up at him and, opening my mouth to mutter the first incoherent word from my lips, when something flashed in the corner of my left eye. I cocked my head around, scooted across the kitchen floor and peered through the triple-paned patio doors. I gazed across the driveway passed Uncle Jay's Chevy and Mom's Honda, at the rear of a two-story white clapboard house next door.

It had a wheelchair ramp that led up to the back door and a strand of white clothesline strung between two oak trees rooted diagonally along the far right side of the yard. I scanned the house and caught it on the third try. A flickering orb of bright orange light whipped across the second story window on the far-left corner, snatching at the shadows filling the house.

"Look, Uncle Jay." I gasped, rising to my feet. "Who lives there?"

"A young couple." He stammered. "Why does it matter?"

When he joined me by the window, he perched his left hand on my right shoulder. He cupped his hands around his eyes, pressed his face to the glass and scanned the property as if he were looking for Waldo.

"We need to help them. That little boy could be hurt."

"No, we don't. What we need to do is keep our asses inside of this house until The National Guard comes."

"Those people could be hurt." I pleaded. "They could use some medical attention or maybe some food."

"And if they need it." He pointed toward the floor. "They'll call for it, but for right now I think we need to stay in here until we get all of the information we need."

"It looks like they're trying to signal for help."

"I know you want to help them," He said, bracing my shoulders. "and that's very brave of you, but we just can't risk it. What we are we going to do if we go out there and the next current comes through?"

I cursed under my breath, slapped his hands away and spun toward the patio doors. I wasn't mad at Uncle Jay because he wouldn't help, but I was angry at the fact that everyone who I still cared about were dead. My world was shattered and yet here I was about to help a group of complete strangers with or without his help.

Before I could wrap my hand around the knob, the pleasing scent of Stetson hit me square in the face. Uncle Jay wrenched his hand around my wrist, clutched the back of my shirt with the other and flung me back like a rag doll. I spun around on drunken wobbly legs and grasped the edge of the stove to keep myself from hitting the edge of the countertop.

Jay flipped the lock into place, leaned against the door and laced his arms across his chest. His mouth shrunk into a tight angry grin.

"We're not leaving this house." He declared. "In the past ten minutes I've lost my wife and my little sister. I'm not going to lose you, too."

Something shattered from inside the house. We froze and perked our ears to hear where it might've came from. Two seconds later, a loud squawking sound burst across the house, but we didn't know exactly where.

"It's in the goddamn basement." Jay said through tightly clenched teeth.

We made a mad dash across the house, our feet pounding quick but softly across the floor, matching the rhythm of our heartbeats. We ran across Uncle Jay's office (which once served as a carport after the house was built) ignored the stacks of paper cluttering his desktop and ran toward a flat wooden door on the far right corner of the room. Jay grasped the curved metal handle jutting up from the wooden door, his sweaty panic-stricken face scrunched together, and yanked it with all his might.

When he flung the door open, my skin prickled. I stepped back, my hands curled into tiny white-knuckled fists, and peered down a flight of solid stone steps. Shafts of sunlight spread abnormal shadows across the rough concrete floor and grasped at the scarred brick walls; the diverse smells of mildew and paint wafted upward, spun around my head and made me wince.

I glanced down for a second to see what might've caused the noise. A dead bird, maybe a sparrow or a robin, was lying spread eagled in the center of the floor next to Uncle Jay's work table. Its beady black eyes glistened like wet stones; its fat brown-feathery head was twisted too far to one side; two jagged shards of glass were strewn across the floor beside of it, glinting amongst a second bed of broken glass.

Before I could investigate any more, Uncle Jay screamed, "Fuck, fuck."

He leaped back from the open door just as the wind sighed through the treetops and whistled through the crack in the window.

He cradled his left hand in his right fist, sat down hard enough to jostle his teeth and scowled in pain. His face and eyes flaring from a mix of panic and shock, he pressed his fists tightly against his chest and bit down on his bottom lip.

"Shut the door, Mattie." He said through trembling lips. "Shut the goddamn door."

I stretched myself across the open doorway to avoid the gust of wind spewing through the broken window, pressed my fingertips against the edge of the door and pulled it toward me. The door's rusted metal hinges shrieked as it struck the floor like a judge's gavel before an unjust sentence. I took a few deep breaths to calm the fire in my nerves and, my chest rising and falling, hurried over to Uncle Jay.

"Don't touch it, honey." He sighed, waving me off. "I don't even want you to see it."

He rolled over, pressing his injured arm against his chest and used his other hand to hoist himself up. I inched over, braced his hips in both hands and walked him back into the living room. He stretched out onto the couch, tore the brown and orange braided Afghan blanket draped across the back and wrapped it around his hand so I wouldn't see it; through the blanket's honey-cob pattern I saw tiny gray dots spread across the back of his palm like a case of tombstone freckles, but I knew that if I said anything he would be angry.

I sat down beside of him and held his good hand while we both cried. Outside, the wind died down; the treetops bowed. We wiped our tears away and tried to gather our thoughts–whatever the hell they might be.

A gauzy gray cloud floated across the sun, drenching the house in a soft somber glow that edged the living room curtains. He cried himself to sleep five minutes later and although I wanted to wake him I just couldn't bring myself to do it. I got hungry instead.

I thought about bundling myself up in a ton of jackets and ski gear and see if I could go outside to get the food that Uncle Jay had cooked earlier, but I didn't want him to wake up and lose his shit when he couldn't find me. Instead, I took advantage of the fact that we still had electricity and made a pan of macaroni and cheese. I locked the doors then the curtains and drew the blinds shut when I saw that Dad's right leg had come off at the knee; his head disappeared two seconds later.

I turned on the television in time to see more reports coming in about everyone's limbs falling off and chuckled at their timing. All across America, everyone was losing something and soon Uncle Jay would lose his hand if not his mind by the end of the week.

It's true what they say.

There's no news like bad news.

<u>ACKNOWLEDGMENTS</u>

I would like to thank the people who have published my stories over the years and have given me the opportunity to do what I intend to do for years to come: entertain the world.

I also want to give an extra ounce of thanks to my girlfriend and all of my surrounding family who have given me all of the time and their patience for me to complete this project.

Thank you, everyone.

ABOUT THE AUTHOR

Brian J. Smith has been featured in numerous anthologies, e-zines and magazines in both the mystery and horror genres. His books, *The Tuckers*, and *Three O'Clock* are still available on Amazon for Kindle. He lives in southeastern Ohio and eats more than enough spicy food that no human being should ever consume, already has too many books and buys more, doesn't drink enough coffee to suite his palate and cheers on The Ohio State Buckeyes.

For a look into Brian's bibliography, you can find his Amazon author page at: amazon.com/author/brianjsmith. He can be found on Facebook under Brian Smith, on Instagram on horrorwriter9 and on Twitter under BJoseph913